Katie Matt

M.A.J.I.C.

and the Oracle at Delphi

Katie Mattie

Cover Artwork by Barrie Rupp
www.pixelogia.com

Photography by Rick Avery
www.rickaveryphotography.com

Paperback ISBN 978-1481960830

Hard Cover ISBN 978-0-9888193-0-6

For more information visit
www.majicbooks.com

ACKNOWLEDGMENTS

M.A.J.I.C. wouldn't exist without the help of an army of friends and family. Thank you to my incredible editing team of Faltos, Ariel Etienne, Cassie Gettinger, Ali Granado, Monica Lopez, Leo Mironovich, Michael Nokes, Michael Prough, Pat Revord, Steph Wachs and Savannah Wunderlich. Special thanks to Celeste Norris and Christina Rogers for going above and beyond the call of duty to edit the entire manuscript.

Thank you to Professor Gary Sieber for help on the O.A. newscast. Andy Wieging, for translating Cronus and Zeus' incantations into ancient Greek. Carli Pacheco for sparking my interest in Greek mythology in seventh grade. Gary Fenker for introducing me to the tales of King Arthur at Estabrook. Ryan Burdick for your constant creative support, and Brianna Jackson for always being my first reader and editor.

Special thanks to my agent, Robert Thixton, for taking a chance on me and *M.A.J.I.C,* and for helping to bring my story to life. To Barrie Rupp, for creating the amazing cover art. It's better than I ever imagined.

Thank you to both my grandpas, Ignatius Mattie and Walter Keeler, for their love and inspiration, as well as the entire Mattie-Keeler family for their unconditional support. Uncle Phil, your visits to Notre Dame mean the world to me.

To all my friends from Ypsi and Notre Dame, you guys inspire me everyday to live my dreams. Thank you for the friendships and adventures of a lifetime.

Finally, thanks to Louie, the embodiment of happiness, and to Irish, for being my guardian before *M.A.J.I.C.* took over.

For David, Mom and Dad

David, thank you for being the best friend I could ever ask for, and for always challenging me to live my dreams.

Mom, thank you for your unconditional love, and for believing in every big idea I've come up with.

Dad, thanks for stepping in the ring with me and fighting to make my dreams come true every step of the way.

"The brick walls are there for a reason. They're not there to keep us out. The brick walls are there to give us a chance to show how badly we want something."

- Randy Pausch

CONTENTS

Prologue

"The Oracle of Delphi is dead."

"I know that. You don't have to remind me every five minutes."

Three tall, slender beings strolled down the hallway of an administration building. Their long, brown hair flowed behind them, matched in radiance by their olive-toned skin. Each wore a silk tunic: one jade, one peach and one turquoise.

The woman in the turquoise tunic shook her head. "Then remind me again why we're here," she said, her voice bitter.

The woman in the jade tunic sighed. "We are here because of the letter."

"A letter that came from the Oracle, who has been dead for eleven years."

"Urania, you did not have to come. I gave you the option to help, to which you freely agreed. So please, help us or leave us. Clio and I can take care of this with Erato and Thalia."

1

"Calliope, I said I would help, and that is what I will do. I just cannot understand why you feel obligated to carry out the requests of a letter you received eleven years ago. Muses inspire works of art. They do not perform secret operations."

Calliope's face was hard. "When the Oracle of Delphi gives you a task, you complete it. I will not disobey someone who can see into the future."

The woman in the peach tunic spoke up. "But why would the Oracle, on her deathbed, go to great lengths to ensure that five thirteen-year-old mortals get admitted into a high school?"

"Clio, she said that if they get accepted into the academy, it may ultimately save one of their lives," Calliope explained.

"She foresaw one of their deaths?" asked Clio.

"I assume so."

"She did not tell you?" Urania asked, stunned.

"The letter only said that in eleven years, we must make sure that these five girls gain admittance into Odyssey Academy. One of their lives may depend on it," said Calliope.

"Humans pass into the afterlife every day. Why does the Oracle care if this specific child lives or dies? Better yet, why do you care, Calliope?" asked Urania.

Calliope was silent.

"You know something you're not telling us!" Urania exclaimed.

"Didn't the Oracle send you two letters?" asked Clio.

"Yes, but the second one is not for us. I have to deliver it in four more years," said Calliope.

"But you read it," said Urania. "What did the letter say about this child?"

"Do not test me," Calliope growled. "If you have reservations about completing the task, leave."

Urania backed down.

"Who are the five girls?" asked Clio. "My charge is Colleen Benton, but who are the other four?"

"Izzy Itello, Melanie Taylor, Jenn Andrews and Alice Payton," said Calliope.

"Izzy's a funny name," said Urania.

"Humans make odd decisions," said Clio.

They reached a wooden door at the end of the hallway.

"This is the room," said Calliope.

The muses stepped inside. Before them, three men and a woman sat in black leather chairs around a polished conference table. All were dressed in business attire, an enormous stack of papers in front of each person. The admissions counselors sorted through the stacks, quietly glancing over each individual sheet.

"Aw, look at them," Clio smirked. "They think they control what is about to happen."

"Take your places," Calliope ordered.

Each of the muses positioned themselves next to a human.

"You are sure they cannot see us?" Urania asked.

"When have humans ever been able to see us?" Clio questioned.

"Three thousand years ago, that's *when,"* Urania snapped.

"Ladies, do not worry," said Calliope. *"You will be able to manipulate the mortals through speech, but they will not be able to see you. Be careful, though. If you touch them, they will feel it."*

"I'm testing it." Urania whispered into the ear of a stout man with a black mustache. *"Hello, Michael Rogers."*

The man looked to his left. After a moment he blinked and refocused on the stack of papers.

"See, we are fine," said Calliope.

"So when do we start?" asked Clio.

"As soon as Erato arrives."

"Where is she? We do not have all day!" said Urania.

"On her way with the director of admissions." As Calliope spoke, the door to the conference room opened. The men and woman looked up. In walked an older gentleman in a pinstriped suit, carrying another colossal stack of papers. A muse dressed in a crimson tunic followed him closely.

"It's about time!" Urania barked.

Erato ignored her, looking straight at Calliope. *"Mr. Kenneth is ready to begin."*

"Did you get him to place your charge's application on top of the pile?" asked Calliope.

"Of course."

The older gentleman set his stack at the head of the table and addressed the assembly. "Morning, everyone!"

The group responded in unison. "Good morning, Mr. Kenneth."

"It is exhilarating to start the admissions process once again!" exclaimed Mr. Kenneth. "The goal is to choose the most brilliantly gifted young adults in the nation and create the leaders of tomorrow. Over the next few hours, keep our notable alumni in mind. People like Peter Elish, the youngest astronaut to date, C.J. Wilson, point guard of the Detroit Pistons, and Beverly Nguyen, the youngest journalist to report on all seven continents. We are looking for students with the same electric spark as their predecessors.

"In the first round of admissions we will evaluate each applicant based on their score on the S.A.E., the Student Aptitude Exam, and their greatest achievement so far in life. We want intellectually gifted students, but more importantly, students who dare to dream. And remember, there are seven thousand applicants fighting for one thousand spots. Choose wisely."

Urania frowned. "Isn't that a little intense? They're judging the applicants based on their greatest achievement by thirteen? They're just kids! Their greatest achievement should be the number of times they've skipped school!"

"Humans are puzzling," said Clio.

"Stupid names and ridiculous expectations," *Urania muttered.*

5

Mr. Kenneth took a seat. "Let us begin. Michael, if you'd do the honors and start?"

The man with the mustache nodded. "Of course."

"Ready, Urania?" asked Calliope.

"Dumb question."

Michael grabbed the top sheet from his pile. "The first applicant is Jennifer Andrews, from Pittsburgh, Pennsylvania. On the S.A.E., she scored a ninety-nine, only missing one question."

The counselors listened intently.

"Her greatest achievement is placing first at the National Middle School Science Fair for creating a home security system using household appliances. She used a PlayStation as the control center."

Mr. Kenneth spoke with excitement. "This is the type of student we are looking for, someone with a natural brilliance! This young lady would not reach her full potential at a normal high school."

Urania spoke into Michael's ear. "Confirm her admittance."

Michael's face lit up. "Sir, I know that we did not plan to officially admit students yet, but I feel that this is a no-brainer. We would be foolish to reject or even think about re-evaluating her application. I believe we should confirm her admittance."

Mr. Kenneth grinned. "I agree! There is no doubt that we would admit her in the next round, so we may as well do it now. Does anyone object?"

No one protested.

"Very well!" said Mr. Kenneth. "Jennifer

Andrews, welcome to Odyssey Academy." Thrilled, he turned to the woman seated next to Michael. "Caitlyn, your first applicant, please."

"I am here to present Ms. Alice Payton of Tipton, Indiana," said Caitlyn. "Alice scored a ninety on the Student Aptitude Exam. Her greatest achievement was starting and running a catering business from her home. She works with her father, and has catered several events, including her grandparents' fiftieth wedding anniversary and her cousin's graduation party."

Mr. Kenneth addressed the group. "How do you feel about this candidate?"

A redheaded man in a blue suit coat spoke first. "She sounds qualified. However, though it's interesting that she started a catering business, it sounds as though it is funded by her family and wouldn't exist without them. Also, although a ninety is a good score on the S.A.E., it's not entirely impressive. I say we wait to see who the other candidates are, and if she tops them, then we admit her."

Calliope whispered fiercely into Caitlyn's ear.

"Paul, are you serious? Not *entirely impressive?*" Caitlyn said, outraged. "A ninety on the S.A.E. is outstanding! Sure, it doesn't look that impressive when compared to a ninety-nine. But if we had read Alice's application before Jennifer's, she would undoubtedly have been accepted. This is a diligent child! She found a creative way to utilize her passion and talent. We would be doing Alice a great injustice not to accept her immediately into the school!"

7

Paul looked taken aback. "Well, if you feel that strongly about her..."

"That was a bit of an overreaction, Calliope," said Erato.

"Oh, like you didn't lay it on thick?" Urania snapped.

"All of these humans are thick beyond measure," said Clio. "The entire premise of this school is outrageous."

"Ladies, focus on the task," Calliope commanded.

"Of course," said Erato. She whispered into Mr. Kenneth's ear.

"I agree with Caitlyn," said Mr. Kenneth. "We shall confirm her acceptance now."

There was a knock at the door.

"Come in!" bellowed Mr. Kenneth.

A young man in track shorts and a t-shirt opened the door. "Hey. I'm not interrupting anything, am I?"

"Not at all, Andrew!" said Mr. Kenneth. "Please, come in."

Andrew stepped into the conference room. Standing close behind him was another tan-skinned woman in a violet tunic.

"Perfect timing, Thalia," said Calliope.

"Did you expect anything less?" Thalia asked.

Andrew handed Mr. Kenneth a green folder. "I just wanted to get this recruit approved for Coach Toren."

Mr. Kenneth opened the folder. "Melanie Taylor of Albany, New York. S.A.E. score of eighty-three."

Paul spoke up. "Now, eighty-three, *that's* not very

impressive."

Thalia looked at Andrew. "Olympics," she said sweetly into his ear.

"Who cares about standardized test scores?" Andrew said, incredulous. "She's the seventh fastest runner in the nation for her age group. This kid has the potential to qualify for the Olympics by at least her sophomore year of college!"

Mr. Kenneth laughed, signing the bottom of the page. "She will do exceptionally well on the track and in school, I am sure. We will confirm her acceptance."

"Thanks, boss!" Andrew cheered. "Good luck with this mess." As he walked out of the room, Thalia followed.

Calliope called out as her sister left. "Thank you!"

Paul focused on Mr. Kenneth. "Sir, I think for the next few applicants we should refrain from immediately admitting them into the academy. We have thousands of candidates, but only a limited number of spots."

"I agree," said Caitlyn.

"Of course," said Mr. Kenneth. He turned to a burly man in a brown suit. "Go ahead, LeShane."

Suddenly, a cloud of black smoke appeared at the back of the room. Calliope, Urania, Clio and Erato turned immediately, their eyes fixed on the cloud. From the smoke, a male figure dressed in a long black robe emerged.

Urania's eyes turned vicious. "What are you doing here?" she growled.

Calliope held still, her eyes glued to the figure.

"Performing my duties," the silhouette said coldly.

9

"No one died, Thanatos," said Urania. "The god of death has no reason to be here."

Thanatos spoke in a rigid tone. "It is my duty to assist one of these souls to the underworld."

"But none of them are dead!" Urania barked. "You are only responsible for souls who have died!"

"I was given strict orders to eliminate one of these humans at this moment in time."

Calliope remained still, her eyes wide.

"Eliminate?" Clio questioned, horrified. "You were ordered to kill one of them?"

"Yes," answered Thanatos.

"That violates Zeus' pact against killing humans. A pact that was made three thousand years ago!" Clio exclaimed.

"Zeus is not here, and given the circumstances, Themis ordered that this human be eliminated at once," said Thanatos.

"Do you realize that this would be the first human a god has killed since the pact was formed?" Erato asked, outraged.

"I am aware of the gravity of the situation," said Thanatos. "Themis would not have ordered this unless there was a special reason."

"What reason could be important enough to violate one of the most sacred pacts in the history of the universe?" Urania asked bitterly.

"If Gregory Kenneth does not die at this moment, the events that are about to unfold will change the fate of the universe forever," Thanatos explained. "I think we all

10

recall what happened last time fate was tampered with. It is not an event that I wish to repeat."

A black sphere of gas appeared in Thanatos' palm. Calliope's stomach dropped.

The sphere spun wildly in Thanatos' hand. Slowly, the god of death pulled back his arm, aiming at the human. In a quick snap, he threw the black orb at Gregory Kenneth.

"NO!" Calliope yelled.

As the sphere shot at Mr. Kenneth, Calliope waved her hand at the ceiling. Immediately, a miniature tornado warped out of the air. Calliope aimed the tornado at the orb, knocking it away from Mr. Kenneth. As the forces collided, the stacks of applications fluttered to the floor. The tornado and sphere extinguished as they hit the wall.

Mr. Kenneth looked up, glancing at the scattered papers. "A gust of wind came out of nowhere," he said, shocked.

The counselors were oblivious to Thanatos and the muses. They recollected the applications and resumed the admissions process.

Thanatos glared at Calliope. "What are you doing?!"

"Do not let him kill the human!" Calliope ordered the muses, running toward Mr. Kenneth. "I cannot use my power because the wind will scatter the papers. We must get the last two girls into the school. That's the event Thanatos is trying to stop! That's the event that will change the fate of the universe!"

11

"How dare you!" Thanatos yelled. He created another black sphere, throwing it at Calliope.

Erato raised her hand, shooting a red stream of energy at the sphere. The stream smashed the black orb into the wall.

Simultaneously, Urania and Clio directed their palms at Thanatos. Urania launched a white orb as Clio threw a silver wave. Thanatos created a shield of gas that covered his body, blocking both attacks.

"You're tampering with fate!" Thanatos bellowed.

Calliope whispered frantically into Mr. Kenneth's ear.

The humans sat at the conference table, unaware of the battle that surrounded them.

As Calliope spoke, Mr. Kenneth became alert. He stood up fervently. "Ladies and gentlemen, there are two students who I feel we should evaluate immediately!"

The counselors looked up in shock.

"Mr. Kenneth, this is a bit unconventional," said Caitlyn.

"We must admit Colleen Benton," said Mr. Kenneth.

"She was actually the next candidate we were going to evaluate," said LeShane, holding up the application.

Urania directed two white clouds of gas at Thanatos. As the clouds reached the god of death, they morphed into chains, binding his hands and feet.

"I present Colleen Benton from Atlanta, Georgia," said LeShane.

Urania approached Thanatos. As she reached to grab his arm, the white chains dissolved in a cloud of black smoke. Thanatos grabbed the muse by the throat and threw her into the wall. Urania's eyes closed.

"Colleen scored a ninety-five on the S.A.E., and her greatest achievement occurred at the White House."

Clio crouched low, propelling a silver wave at Thanatos' legs. Instantly, his knees buckled beneath him. As he collapsed, Thanatos shot a black stream of energy at the muse. The stream tightened around Clio's neck. She gasped for air, struggling to tear the power from her throat.

"After performing at the White House with her school band to promote musicianship in young adults, Colleen took it upon herself to interview the President about how the government planned to enhance education in the arts throughout the country."

Calliope spoke to Mr. Kenneth.

"She's in! She's in!" Mr. Kenneth exclaimed. "She's highly qualified and did something that no applicant has ever done. She saw opportunity at the White House and took it. She's a go-getter!"

"I thought we were going to hold off on admitting people into the academy. We've never accepted so many students right off the bat," said Michael.

"Other than that, do any of you see a reason to object?" Mr. Kenneth asked.

The counselors looked at each other confusedly, shaking their heads.

"Great! She's admitted! Now, Izzy Itello!"

13

Erato shot a bolt of electricity at Thanatos.
Thanatos dodged it, disappearing in a cloud of black
smoke. A second later he reappeared behind Erato. As the
god grabbed the muse's head, her eyes turned black and
she collapsed.

Thanatos focused on Mr. Kenneth, directing his
palms to the floor. Black smoke seeped up from the
ground, creeping its way toward Mr. Kenneth and
Calliope.

"I'm sorry, Calliope," Thanatos said darkly. He
twisted his hands, wrapping the smoke around Mr.
Kenneth.

BOOM!

A burst of purple light crashed into Thanatos,
throwing him into the wall. Instantly, the smoke
surrounding Mr. Kenneth disappeared. Thanatos
scrambled to his feet, searching for the source of the light.
Thalia stood in the doorway, her palms raised.

"Thank you!" Calliope gasped.

"Finish the task!" Thalia ordered.

Calliope turned to Mr. Kenneth.

"We have to accept Izzy Itello!" Mr. Kenneth
declared.

Thanatos fired two orbs at Thalia and Mr. Kenneth
simultaneously. Thalia somersaulted, dodging the orb.

"Sir, we haven't even evaluated her application,"
said Caitlyn.

Rolling out of her somersault, Thalia launched a
purple stream at the remaining sphere, striking it just
before it hit the human.

14

"What's there to evaluate? She's a brilliant young lady who deserves to be admitted to this school," said Mr. Kenneth.

Thanatos stepped toward Mr. Kenneth.

"What's her S.A.E.?"

Thalia jumped on the center of the conference table, standing in between Thanatos and Mr. Kenneth. With force, she shot another stream at the god of death.

"Seventy-eight."

Thanatos countered with a massive stream of black gas.

"Sir, that's quite low," said Paul. "We've never admitted anyone below an eighty before. It is not recommended that anyone below an eighty be subjected to the rigorous material for fear that they will not excel in such a strenuous academic environment."

The two forces collided. Both Thalia and Thanatos held onto their powers, pushing with all of their might. The counselors were unaware that a torrent of purple and black energy hung above their heads.

"If we have never admitted a student below an eighty, then how can we possibly know how she will deal with the course material?" Mr. Kenneth questioned. "Besides, consider her greatest achievement. She collected one hundred dollars worth of cans and donated it to the Humane Society."

Paul's brow furrowed. "One hundred dollars isn't all that impressive," he countered.

"Calliope, hurry up!" Thalia yelled, wincing as she held onto the purple stream.

"Paul, if you were to die today and the last decision you ever got to make was between giving a person a better future or taking away infinite opportunities, which would you choose? Could you die with it on your conscience that you cheated them out of the experience of a lifetime?"

Thanatos and Thalia cringed as they directed their powers. Bursts of purple streams and black gas exploded over the room.

"Sir, I hardly think this is that dire of a situation," said Paul. "I'm sure Izzy will be fine if we do not accept her."

"Really?" Mr. Kenneth challenged. "Or is that just an excuse for you, someone who has gotten everything they've ever wanted in life, to take away a young woman's dream? How can we know how Izzy will perform if we don't give her a chance?"

"I…I…don't…" Paul stuttered.

The counselors were at a loss for words, alarmed by Mr. Kenneth's attitude.

"Calliope!" Thalia screamed.

"We're accepting her!" Mr. Kenneth bellowed at the top of his lungs, slamming his fist on the table.

Stunned, all four counselors agreed.

Thanatos froze, letting go of the stream of gas.

Thalia released her grip on the purple stream. She stood on the table, her chest heaving. In the corner of the room, the black stream choking Clio disappeared. The muse gasped for air.

"It is done," Thanatos said, his voice hollow.

Calliope watched him closely. "You are not going

16

to kill the human?"

"There is no point," said Thanatos. "The fate of the universe has been altered."

"You cannot reverse the outcome?" asked Thalia.

"I could, but the consequences of the reversal would be too detrimental to the destiny of mankind," said Thanatos. "In order to reverse the alteration, I would have to kill all of the humans in this room, because they know that the young mortals were accepted into the school. Doing so would change the destiny of humanity far too greatly. They are not meant to die today."

Thanatos grimaced as he gazed at Mr. Kenneth and Calliope. Calliope stared at him intently, holding her ground.

"There is nothing left for me here," said Thanatos. A black cloud began to envelop his body. "Let it be known, Calliope, that your actions come with strict consequences."

The black cloud covered Thanatos' entire body. A moment later the cloud vanished, along with the god of death.

Thalia jumped down from the table, rushing to Erato. Erato was conscious, and her eyes had regained their color. Clio kneeled in the opposite corner, taking in deep breaths.

Calliope approached Urania, who lay on the floor, and gently touched her shoulder. "Urania! Urania, get up!"

Urania's eyes fluttered. As she focused on Calliope, she gasped. "Did he kill the human?"

"No. We were successful," answered Calliope.

"I told you I would help," said Urania.

"Yes. You did a wonderful job," said Calliope, extending her hand to her sister. "Let me help you."

At the conference table, the counselors watched Mr. Kenneth closely. The old man cheerfully gazed back at them.

"Michael, if you would present the next applicant," Mr. Kenneth said with a smile.

Somewhat hesitant, Michael picked up the next application. "Mr....uh...Phillip Kurtz of Parker, Arizona."

"Our task is complete," said Calliope.

The muses headed for the door.

Thalia touched Calliope's shoulder. "Was it worth it to come here?" she questioned.

Calliope shook her head. "I don't know."

As the muses left the room, Calliope took one last glance at Mr. Kenneth. Turning away, she was satisfied that she had carried out the Oracle's request, but something didn't seem quite right. Calliope wondered whether the fate of the universe had been changed for better or for worse.

CHAPTER ONE

The Dream

"Izzy! Hurry up! They're gaining on us!" yelled Melanie.

"You think I don't know that?!"

"Just come on!"

Shooting through the field, Alice held tight as two shadowed figures chased directly behind her. The hovercraft was climbing to its maximum speed but was going too slow for the danger that trailed at its rear. Jenn, the vehicle's driver, powered the titanium machine to its full potential, maneuvering around rocks and trees that fell in her way.

"Hold on tight!" shouted Jenn.

Colleen and Alice held onto the hovercraft for dear life, watching as the human-shaped shadows drew toward them. Melanie ran to the right of the flying vehicle with Izzy soaring just above her. The two were dodging fireballs that whizzed past their heads, crashing into the ground.

"Alice!" yelled Colleen. "Do you think you can set off a force field?"

"I don't know…I can give it a shot though!" Alice turned around in her seat and lifted her trembling hands.

Pushing toward the figures, Alice blasted a large, glowing silver ball. The ball sped toward the shadows, aiming for their chests.

SMASH!

A direct hit. The collision stalled the shadow's movement, but only for a moment. With a flick of their wrists the shadows threw back the shimmering orb, returning it as if it were a boomerang.

"Izzy! Look!" Melanie roared.

They watched as the orb rushed toward their friends.

"Come on!"

Izzy and Melanie raced toward the hovercraft. Aiming for Colleen, Melanie took a powerful leap. In one fluid motion she caught hold of her target, hugged Colleen to her side and fell to the ground, landing with ease. Izzy zoomed toward the soaring vehicle. She was only strong enough to carry one person, but there were two damsels who needed saving.

Alice or Jenn?

Izzy watched the force field, her mind racing. The orb was at the tail end of the craft, ready to explode. Without further hesitation, Izzy lunged forward and grabbed her target.

"Jenn, JUMP!"

Clutching Alice's wrist, Izzy swooped away from

the vehicle. She flew toward the ground and landed next to Colleen and Melanie. Helplessly, all watched as Jenn continued to drive the hovercraft, the silver orb in hot pursuit.

"JUMP, JENN!" Colleen shrieked.

Jenn turned around as the orb reached for the vehicle. Seconds before impact, she pulled herself free from the driver's seat and jumped out of the hovercraft.

BOOM!

The force field hit its target. The vehicle exploded.

Shards of the hovercraft plunged toward the earth, moving faster than Jenn as she fell. Melanie rushed toward the falling girl, her legs speeding like a racecar. As she drew toward Jenn, Melanie jumped upward, her arms open wide for the catch.

"Gotcha!" Melanie grabbed Jenn and fell to the ground. She took off in a sprint, holding her friend close.

Despite Melanie's life-saving catch, the girls were in critical danger. The shadows were unyielding. They redirected their attention, turning to the five prey on the ground.

"You can run but you cannot hide!" bellowed the shadows. "What a shame…for a while you seemed like a challenge!"

The shadows approached their targets, flaming orbs resting in their palms.

Unwavering, Melanie carried Jenn, running toward Alice, Izzy and Colleen, who were all panic stricken and unable to move.

"Don't just stand there! Alice, start up a new shield!" barked Jenn.

As Jenn spoke, the fireballs were released, raining down upon them. Alice attempted to create a force field but the flames were too swift, ramming into Melanie and Jenn before the shield was produced. The fireballs funneled toward Alice, sweeping up Colleen and Izzy along the way. A split second later the blaze spun toward its final victim.

"NO!"

"NO!" Alice screamed, horrified. Her eyes shot open; her mind was racing and her heart pounding. Beads of sweat dripped off of her face.

Terrified, Alice shook. Something hot covered her body, engulfing her from her chest down. Fearfully, she glanced at her stomach and gasped. There, nestled calmly, was her comforter. Alice was in her bed, out of harm's way. Relieved, she fluttered her eyes and fell back onto her pillow.

"Safe."

After catching her breath and realizing that she had only had a nightmare, Alice rolled out of bed and walked toward the door. With a nervous glance at the mirror, she was comforted to see a pair of worried, sage eyes gazing back at her. Her golden curly hair was intact and her fair skin wasn't burned.

"I'm okay," she sighed.

Alice took a deep breath. She opened the door and

stepped into the lounge. The lounge was one of three rooms in her dorm suite. It was a cross between a den and a kitchen that extended into two bedrooms.

To Alice's relief, two of her friends were safely within sight. A teenage girl with long, dark wavy hair sat at the kitchen table, shoving spoonfuls of Wheaties into her mouth, and a young woman with caramel tinted skin was seated on the couch, a newspaper clutched in her hands.

"Mel!" Alice exclaimed, approaching the kitchen table.

"What's the matter with you? You look like you've seen a ghost," Melanie asked as she crammed in a bite of cereal.

Alice cringed. "I guess you could say that. I just had the most terrifying dream! The five of us were killed by a giant ball of fire after being chased by these two dark figures. Izzy could fly, Colleen, Jenn and I were in Jenn's hovercraft, and you ran as fast as the hovercraft!"

"Well that's definitely the last time *you* eat pizza the night before an important day!" giggled Melanie.

Alice rolled her eyes. "Seriously!"

"It's just a dream you had because you're anxious about the cook-off," said Colleen, flipping through the newspaper.

"I don't know. That *dream* seemed too real. I mean, I felt like I was there."

BANG!

The door leading to Jenn and Izzy's bedroom flew open. A tall brunette and a small blonde came out arguing.

23

"Izzy, I know you have it, so give it back!" demanded Jenn.

"I swear I don't have it!" Izzy grinned.

"Yes you do! I know you do! You're always hiding my things. Why else would you be smiling?"

"Because I'm always happy."

"What are you two fussing over?" asked Colleen.

"The science fair is in two hours and I can't find the key to my invention. Izzy took it, and now she's playing keep away!" huffed Jenn.

"I'm telling you, I didn't take it!" said Izzy.

"Silver key with a little bit of green on the top? It's in the drawer next to the microwave, rolled in the blue socks," said Melanie, her tone nonchalant.

Uncertain, Jenn approached the kitchen drawer and pulled it open. Inside she found Melanie's pair of navy socks. She unraveled the clothing and sure enough, found the missing key.

"Thanks for keeping it in such an obvious place," sighed Jenn.

"Any time," Melanie winked.

"Speaking of disappearing things," said Izzy, "yours truly will be assisting Mario the Magnificent in a magic show today. He'll cut me in half and make me disappear!"

"Make sure he puts you back together before you leave," said Melanie, "but we might *all* disappear if Alice's dream comes true."

Jenn glanced at Alice. "What dream?"

"Last night I dreamt that there were these figures

24

chasing all of us. Izzy could fly, Melanie was running as fast as the hovercraft, and you, Colleen and I were in the hovercraft. I tried to stop the figures with some type of shield, but we ended up getting killed in the end. Do you think it means anything?"

"Psh! Don't sweat it! I have crazy dreams all the time and they don't mean a thing," said Izzy.

"They just prove how nuts you are, that's all," retorted Melanie.

"Actually, Izzy's right," said Jenn. "You're probably just nervous about the big cook-off."

"That's exactly what I told her," said Colleen.

"All right, but don't say I didn't warn you in case something happens," Alice cautioned.

"Anyways," said Jenn, " I better get going. Scott's waiting for me at the science center. It's a big project this year!"

"So early? It's only seven; I thought that you weren't setting up until eight?" asked Melanie.

"We are; it's eight right now. Daylights savings was last night. You know, push the clocks an hour ahead."

Melanie froze. Her eyes bulged as she gazed at the clock.

"Shoot! Gotta go! Coach wanted all athletes down at the track by seven-forty-five, no later!"

Melanie sprang from the chair and dashed into her bedroom. A moment later she was out of the dorm, running to meet up with the rest of her team.

"You know, after living on her own for three years, you'd think Mel would be used to the time changes," said Jenn.

"After three years of living with Mel, I'm surprised you didn't predict this," said Colleen.

"Fair enough," said Jenn. She glanced at her watch. "I really gotta go. I'll see you later!"

"Good luck!" Izzy cheered.

"Thanks!" Jenn left the room.

"What about you, Colleen? Got any plans today?" asked Alice.

"As a matter of fact yes! I have to go to the football stadium with the marching band. We're debuting a new halftime show in honor of the big game against the Trojans."

"Yeah! Go Phoenix!" cheered Izzy.

"We'll see how it goes. I have a bet with Lewis that we'll win fourteen nothin, but he thinks it'll be closer," said Colleen.

"We'll see about that," said Alice.

The conversation continued for a few more moments as the girls prepared for their busy days. However, they were unaware of just how busy a day it would turn out to be.

CHAPTER TWO

Escape from Tartarus

"Will it hurt?"

"The judgment?"

"Yes."

"Heavens no!" chuckled Hermes. "The hard part is over. Although *your* hard part wasn't all that difficult. Going peacefully in your sleep, that's the best way to go."

Hermes sped through the openness of outer space, whizzing past stars and comets as he moved. To his side, the silhouette of a young woman wrapped her arms around his torso, her eyes heavy and wide.

"I didn't know it was my time," the woman sighed.

Hermes shook his head. "Few do, few do. Are you scared?"

"Petrified."

"Not to worry. I sense a good aura from you. You bear a powerful soul."

The woman cracked a sheepish smile.

"But will Hades feel the same way?" she questioned, her voice shaking.

"This is not for Hades to decide, my friend. He is but a guard, and I am his messenger. Your destiny rests in the hands of the Fates. But please, do try and relax. For every soul cast to Tartarus there are millions sent to Elysium. You, I am sure, shall join the millions."

The woman glanced at Hermes, her eyes screaming with fear. Hermes sensed her anxiety. With his free hand he raised her chin, holding it gently in his fingers.

"Your spirit is too kind for hell. When we reach Limbo, I will not let the Fates send you into exile. This I promise," he assured.

The woman gazed at Hermes, her fear subsiding.

"You need not fret much longer. Your judgment draws close," said the god.

A black planet came into view, growing larger as the two sped toward it.

"Oh, God!" the woman groaned.

Hermes squeezed her hand in support.

"I promised."

Soon, they entered the planet's atmosphere, and they plummeted to its surface.

Hermes tugged the woman forward. "Shall we continue?"

The woman nodded.

The world was barren and dark, stretching endlessly outwards. Up ahead, the woman could distinguish a cloaked figure standing on the deck of a ferry. The figure was covered except for a bony hand, which poked from its sleeve.

Hermes gestured to the ferry. "Step on."

28

As the woman stepped aboard, the boat began to move, slipping away from its frozen port. Swiftly it floated down the river.

"Almost there," said Hermes.

From the distance, a glow of silver and gold light came into view. As the ferry stopped at the bank, Hermes helped the woman onto the ground.

"Welcome to Limbo," he said.

They were standing on an open stone platform, the dome of the universe hanging overhead. To the left, two shimmering arches glowed majestically, one silver, the other gold. To the right, a large black hole warped into a twister, spinning its way through the stone floor.

"Is this hell?" the woman gulped.

Hermes let out a slight laugh. "Not exactly, though it is a realm of the underworld. Limbo is the place where the Fates will determine where you spend the afterlife. Let's call it your afterlife trial."

"What places can they send me to?"

"You have two options. Do you see the silver portal over there?" asked Hermes.

"Yes."

"You will either walk into the silver portal of Elysium, the equivalent of heaven, or you will be cast into the black hole which will send you to Tartarus, the equivalent of hell," said Hermes, pointing to the black twister.

"Where does the golden archway lead to?"

"Mount Olympus, home of the gods."

"Any chance I can go there?"

"That is not a question I can answer. You will have to ask Hades," said Hermes, scouring the platform. *Where is Hades?* he thought.

Hades was nowhere in sight. Immediately, Hermes was alarmed. Hades always awaited his arrival, greeting him the moment he stepped into Limbo. Confused, Hermes turned toward the woman, his eyes alert.

"Stay here," he commanded.

Hermes scurried toward the black hole, a golden staff gripped in his hand. Gracefully, he leapt into the twister, disappearing from Limbo. In a rushing gust of wind, he descended to Tartarus. Hermes stood in the middle of a deep, dark cavern. Countless tunnels branched in different directions. Fire circled the edge of the cave.

When Hermes landed, he froze.

Something is wrong, he thought.

The realm of Tartarus was empty.

Suddenly, a thundering noise echoed from one of the tunnels. Distressed, Hermes rushed through the corridor. With his heart pounding, he reached the end of the tunnel and gasped. Standing before him was an enormous door, its entrance slightly ajar and chains hanging limp to the ground. The tunnel was silent except for the echoes of Hermes' heaving breath. Usually, the corridor was patrolled by Cerberus, but the three-headed canine was nowhere to be found.

It can't be... thought Hermes.

A loud explosion rang out behind the door. Startled, Hermes crouched low and peeked past the entrance. Inside the room, Cerberus lay beaten on the floor, his eyes vacant. Hermes looked beyond Cerberus and gasped. Hades was pinned to the wall by an old rigid hand.

"Take us to the dungeons, Hades!" bellowed a voice.

"Take yourself," Hades growled.

A burst of red flames formed from the unknown assailant's palm. In a quick snap, the flames erupted into Hades' face. The god howled in pain.

"Your stupidity will be the death of you. You call it nobility, but it will cast you to your own doom! Now, rethink your actions. Take us to the dungeons," hissed the voice.

The assailant threw Hades onto the ground. Having grown tired, Hades lay still.

"Cronus! Nothing will come from this! Kill Hades now, and we will find another way to free them."

A third figure stood in the dungeon, its body hidden by the shadows of the chamber.

"One final chance, almighty one," mocked Cronus. "Take us now or it will be your demise!"

Hades glared into Cronus' black, menacing eyes. "I welcome death with open arms," he snarled.

"Kill him!"

Cronus towered over Hades' body. At the same time, Hermes bolted from the entrance, raising his staff into the air. Hades watched as Hermes charged at Cronus, the tip of the staff pointed out. A low snicker ripped from his throat.

As he prepared to strike Hades with a killing blow, Cronus made what he thought was a final remark.

"Let this be a lesson, Hades. Foolishness will bring death and the everlasting torment of hell!"

Cronus raised his hand. A massive fireball ignited within his palm.

Hermes drew closer. With vicious grace, he lunged at Cronus and stabbed the golden staff into his arm. Cronus howled as the fireball shot from his hand. Hades rolled to the left, dodging the fireball as it smashed onto the floor.

From the shadows of the dungeon, the hidden figure created a mass of icicles in his hand. He threw the shards at Hades and Hermes. Hades deflected the ice with a blue force field generated from his palm. The shards bounced backwards, nearly striking their creator.

"Hades, run!" demanded Hermes.

The two gods fled from the dungeon, racing through the tunnel. They rushed to the black hole and paused beneath it.

"Open!" bellowed Hades.

The black hole spun faster and faster. It swallowed Hades and Hermes, launching them onto the platform of Limbo. Cronus and the unknown figure chased after them. They clambered through the vortex and emerged onto the platform.

"Hermes!" shrieked the woman's soul. "What's happening?"

Hermes grabbed her arm.

"Hold on!"

He headed for the silver portal.

"This will lead you to Elysium. You will be safe there!" said Hermes, leading her forward.

"Watch out!" she screamed.

A flame whizzed toward Hermes, an icicle chasing at its tail. Suddenly, a blue orb crashed into both the flame and the icicle, forcing them into the ground.

"There's no time to waste! Hermes, we must go *now!*" shouted Hades, his palms raised.

Without a moment to spare, Hermes pushed the woman into the silver portal, sealing it closed with the wave of his staff. He ran into the golden archway, followed by Hades. Cronus shot a fireball at the golden portal.

"Hades, seal the entry!" demanded Hermes.

With a wave of his hand, Hades closed the archway, creating a shield. Cronus' fireball smashed into the barrier. On contact the flames dispersed into the air.

"Cronus, no!" shrieked the unknown figure. "We let them reach Zeus!"

"Relax, Uranus," said Cronus. "We're out of the dungeon aren't we? We can finish this even with Zeus in our way. Now we should go find the spirits who have fled. I'm sure they will assist us."

Cronus and Uranus left the underworld, soaring into the galaxy.

After passing through the golden archway, Hades and Hermes journeyed to Mount Olympus. Through a stream of white and gray swirls, the portal carried them as quickly as it could.

Hermes stared at Hades, his chest puffing heavily. With a deep breath he sputtered the first question that he could think to ask. "Hades, what has happened?"

"It started out as any other day until I heard a bloodcurdling roar from Tartarus," said Hades. "I hurried down to see what the commotion was and as soon as I opened the black hole, the souls of hell came rushing out, stampeding past me. Stunned, I ran down to see what had happened and was shocked to find Cerberus battling Uranus. How could this be? Uranus has been dead for three thousand years, or so I thought.

"Cerberus and Uranus fought, crashing into the dungeon of Cronus. I went toward the chamber to join the fight but was thrown into the wall. Cerberus was dead and as I looked up I found Cronus running toward me. I threw him back, but I was defenseless against both him and Uranus." Hades lifted his hands. His calloused palms were blistered and slashed. "Cronus burned me. My powers are weak." Hades lowered his voice, his chest welling with anger. "Hermes, the Titans have returned."

"How could this happen?" Hermes asked, outraged. "How could this happen when we had banished them into Tartarus for years, locked them into darkness for all eternity? Our strongest magic and chains have kept them at bay for so long, and now here we stand, fighting to survive once more!" Hermes paused, hesitant to continue. He spoke very deliberately. "Tell me, though; what dungeons did they seek?"

Hades growled. "The dungeons containing the rest of the Titans."

Hermes clenched his fists. "May Zeus have the power to prevent such a disaster."

Finally, the swirling colors of gray and white came to a halt, and another golden entrance came into view. Hermes and Hades had arrived at Mount Olympus. Landing in front of its great gates, they entered the kingdom.

Marble castles lined the sandstone streets. Gold smothered the city, draping everything within sight, and white clouds hung overhead, gracefully framing the sky.

Hades and Hermes passed through the kingdom, venturing to the tallest fortress in all of Mount Olympus. When they reached their destination, Hades pounded on the door. Inside, he could hear a quick shuffling of feet. A beady eye peered through the peephole, staring back at him. A moment later, the door creaked open.

In the entrance stood a small, human-like creature. The creature's golden hair trailed down his neck like a mane. He wore a gray tunic that stretched to his knees.

The creature bowed to the gods.

"Lord Hades, Sir Hermes, what has brought such powerful gods to the castle of Zeus?" asked the creature.

"Rigon, we need to speak with Zeus immediately," said Hermes.

"I am afraid King Zeus is unavailable," said Rigon.

"Like hell!" shouted Hades. "King Zeus will see us now!"

From within the castle a young goddess appeared at the top of the staircase. Dark hair flowed down her back, and a silver tunic clung to her frame. Surprised yet confused, the goddess tiptoed down the steps.

"Hermes! Hades!" she exclaimed. "How exciting to see you both! Now Rigon, why must you keep these gods in the entrance?"

"Your fool of a servant denies us the presence of Zeus," barked Hades.

"Athena," said Hermes, "it is important."

Athena sensed his fear.

"You shall see Zeus at once. Come, I will take you," she gestured them to follow as she retreated up the steps.

Athena led the gods to a wooden door, a lightning bolt emblazoned on its frame. As soon as she knocked, a massive god with a thick white beard answered.

"Hello, Zeus," said Athena.

"Why, Hades and Hermes!" Zeus exclaimed. "Welcome! Please, come and take a seat." He held out his hand and four chairs magically appeared. All four gods sat down. "How have my brother and son been? It is astounding to have the two of you here at once."

"Zeus," said Hades thickly, "we have no time to waste. Hermes and I bear terrible news."

Zeus' face hardened.

"Down in Tartarus, an intruder has entered and a prisoner escaped," said Hades. "Uranus has returned and he has released Cronus!"

"Uranus and Cronus!" bellowed Zeus, standing up. "Uranus is dead!"

"Yes, father, that is what I thought. It's what we all

thought. But I swear to you I saw him with my own eyes!" Hermes pleaded.

All four gods were raised from their seats.

"The Dungeon of Cronus is open and Cerberus lay lifeless within it. His blood was shed while fighting the Titans, and all of hell's prisoners were released," said Hades, tightening his fists. "The underworld is now bare and empty. The fire consumes no one, and the only souls left are the Titans locked in their dungeons, hidden from Cronus and his father."

"How has Uranus returned? Cronus killed him centuries ago, and now he's rescuing his killer?" yelled Zeus incredulously.

"My guess is that he never actually died," said Athena, her voice soft but strong. "Cronus said he had killed him, but did anyone witness his father's death? Years have passed, and there have been no signs of Uranus. Could it be that he has been in hiding since his proclaimed death?"

"Athena is likely right," said Hermes.

"But that is not the pressing issue!" shouted Hades. "Who cares how Uranus is back? How ever he survived he was well enough to help Cronus escape. With both of them free, it is only a matter of time until all of the Titans are released." Hades approached Zeus and gripped his shoulders. "If we do not act now, we will find ourselves locked in the dungeons of hell, *forever.*"

Zeus shot a piercing glance at the gods before him, his voice thick. "Hermes…gather the Olympians! Today, we fight!"

CHAPTER THREE

Show Time

Melanie

Melanie made her way to the track, hoping that her coach wouldn't notice she was late. She slipped through the stadium gates and jogged over to a mob of blue and gray hoodies. Luckily, Coach Toren was occupied with a pre-meet pep talk.

"So today, at the sound of the gun, give everything you've got. We are here not by pure chance or sheer luck, but by our talents and determination, our dedication and sweat, and most importantly, because we deserve to be here. In twenty-seven years of coaching, I have never had a more dedicated group of individuals. You've had an incredible season, and this is your reward. Take this opportunity as a challenge to conquer. And remember: running is taking the chance to do something that most people are too intimidated to do. Stand tall, be confident and do what you were born to accomplish."

Melanie smiled. She was in the clear. Toren hadn't

noticed her tardiness.

"And Melanie Taylor, I'd like to have a word with you."

Dang it.

As the team began to disband, Melanie approached her coach.

"What's up?" she asked, her voice light.

"Nice of you to show up," Toren frowned.

"Coach, I'm really sorry. I forgot to-"

"I don't want an explanation," Toren interrupted. "Arriving late to the state track meet is inexcusable! A chance to go to Nationals is on the line, and I can't have my athletes arriving late. Does this title mean anything to you?"

Melanie gaped in shock. "Of course!"

"Then prove it. I want your heart and soul out on that track today. If you show anything less than one-hundred percent, we're sure to go home empty-handed."

Melanie nodded, her eyes lowered. Toren sensed her remorse.

"You've got a big race ahead of you. Go warm up with your teammates."

Melanie jogged toward the locker room. Instantly, she caught sight of two familiar faces, both glaring at her.

"Well, well, well. Looks like *someone's* trying to arrive *fashionably late!*" mocked Mika, her light brown hand on her hip. "I oughtta punch you for freakin us out like that!"

"Hey, give her a break, short stuff. She's still gotta run the four-by-four. But *after* that we can jump her!" teased Kira. Her dark chocolate eyes matched her skin.

"Well, if *somebody* had reminded me about daylight savings time, I would have been here before both of you!" Melanie grinned.

"I doubt it!" giggled Mika. "So, you two ready for the big race?"

"Bring it. I've never been more prepared," said Kira.

"Same here, but we can't do it with only three runners. Where's L.B.?" asked Melanie.

"Locker room, throwin up, as usual."

As if on cue, a young woman with brown sugar-toned skin emerged from the locker room. She had a dazed look on her face as she wobbled forward.

"You all right there?" asked Kira.

"Oh yeah. Just give me a minute," said L.B., bending at her waist.

"You know, you might want to get a hold of those nerves. Don't start hacking on the starting line," said Mika.

L.B. laughed. "I'll take that into consideration."

As L.B.'s stomach began to settle, the girls started warming up, stretching and running on the infield of the track. When they finished, they retreated to the locker room to put on their spikes. Toren approached them, a clipboard in hand.

"All right, ladies; I've got the line-up."

The girls were silent.

"First leg, L.B.; second leg, Kira. Third leg is Mika, and anchoring for us today is Melanie. We got word that South Bend has placed Felicia Turner as their fourth runner. I want Mel to race her."

All four athletes nodded in unison.

"Check-in for the sixteen-hundred-meter relay is soon. You better get going," said Toren. He knocked fists with each of the girls for luck. "Show 'em what you've got! One lap each, and you're done!"

Anxiously, the four-by-four squad made their way to the check-in official. Mika glanced at Melanie, a broad grin stretched across her face.

"You're up against Felicia Turner! Let's get ready to rumble!"

"This'll be a race to remember," said Melanie.

"Do you think she'll be able to handle this?" asked L.B.

"Who, Felicia?"

"Yeah."

"You never know how things will turn out. It could be a really close race."

"Aw, she's just being modest," said Mika. "You've got this in the bag!"

"Just don't try to downplay yourself, Mel," said Kira. "You know you're a talented runner; we all know it. Just get out there and do your thing. We'll be waiting at the finish line."

Melanie smiled faintly, attempting to hide her true feelings. Felicia Turner had been Melanie's athletic rival ever since her freshman year. They attended neighboring schools and fought ruthlessly for the title of fastest runner in their conference. Last year during their final race as sophomores, a photograph showed that they had crossed the finish line at the exact same time. Not this year, however. Melanie promised herself that only one person would win the race, no matter what.

Soon enough, the girls were signed in for the relay. L.B. led her teammates onto the track, baton in hand. Suddenly, a team decked in scarlet uniforms stepped onto the track. Four athletes stood next to each other, but only one caught Melanie's attention. The fourth runner, a lean girl with bright auburn hair looked exactly as she had the previous spring. Felicia Turner had arrived.

Butterflies fluttered wildly within Melanie's stomach. One year had passed since her last race against Turner and here they were as juniors: stronger, faster and more skilled. This was her chance to prove how far she had come, and she couldn't let herself down. If Felicia wanted to win, she would have to run the race of her life, because Melanie was more focused than she had ever been.

As the teams stood in line, the front two runners were called down to the start. Melanie stood next to Mika, enthralled and restless. This was it.

Alice

Alice arrived at the academy's dining hall. Inside she found a small group of food tasters and judges sitting at one of the lunch tables. Usually the cafeteria was lined with wooden tables stretching from wall to wall, filled with hungry teenagers rushing to eat. Today, though, only two tables were set, making the room feel hollow.

Alice ventured to the kitchen and pushed through its swinging doors. She was relieved to find her cooking partners, Niroo Lee and Nikki Williams, awaiting their head chef.

"Hey, guys!" said Alice. "Any word from the judges yet?"

"Nope," said Nikki. "They're still waiting for Ryan Rivera and his team."

"Maybe if we're lucky he moved to Alaska yesterday!" said Niroo.

Alice grinned. "Oh, don't get my hopes up!"

SMACK!

As Alice spoke, the doors of the kitchen crashed open. In strolled a tall young man with gelled brown hair. Two assistants followed at his heels.

"Speak of the devil," said Nikki.

"Oh, Nikki," sighed Ryan, "that's no way to talk about yourself. But I guess with hair like yours and that utterly disgusting face, it's quite the compliment."

Ryan's eyes were dark. A smug leer drew upon his face.

Nikki glared at Ryan and bit her tongue. She was dying to make a comeback but fought to hold it in.

Ryan walked toward Alice and brushed her cheek with his hand. "And I must say, Ms. Payton. I am quite surprised you showed up. Come to watch your cooking career be flushed down the toilet, have you?"

Alice glared at Ryan. "Actually, no. I came to prove that not only am I the best chef in our class, but that I can beat low-life, egomaniacal scum like you."

"Ah, temper, temper. Bitter because you can't accept who the better chef is; I understand. But perhaps if your brain was larger than a pea, you'd be able to win something for a change."

"Yo mama!" hollered Niroo.

Ryan rolled his eyes. "I've had my fill of insolence for today. Leslie and Chris, follow me."

Ryan and his assistants strode to their cooking station.

Outside of the kitchen, the head coordinator of the cook-off had just arrived. Martha Weddingsworth, a sixty-two year old woman from Jackson, Mississippi, was a food expert. After becoming a world-renowned chef in the eighties, Martha created an annual competition, going around the country to different high schools and colleges in search of the next big chef. This year, she had chosen to host the contest at the special talents school, Odyssey Academy, in Delphi, Indiana, after hearing rave reviews about two of its finest culinary students, juniors Alice Payton and Ryan Rivera.

The academy's news station, O.A. News, accompanied Martha, ready to capture every second of the competition.

Alice, Niroo and Nikki waited in the kitchen along with Ryan and his assistants, all preparing themselves for what lay ahead. Nikki helped Alice tie her uniform as Alice placed her chef's hat on top of her head. Seconds later, Martha Weddingsworth's assistant, Molly Hibber, entered the kitchen. Molly's thick glasses nearly swallowed her face.

"Um…Mrs. Weddingsworth would like to speak with you all in the dining hall," said Molly, her voice meek.

The student chefs filed into the lunchroom. Martha stood before them with a big smile.

"Good morning, good morning!" she cheered.

Alice and her crew responded with a polite hello while Ryan and his team stood unresponsive.

"First and foremost, I would like to congratulate Mr. Rivera and Ms. Payton for qualifying for this prestigious competition," said Martha. "For fifteen years I have sponsored the Weddingsworth Cook-Off Challenge. We seek out the nation's top student chefs, searching for the best of the best. This year, after a thorough examination of all applicants, the Weddingsworth Corporation has chosen these two stupendous individuals to display their talents and battle for a cash prize.

"Today's grand prize will be a twenty-five thousand dollar scholarship for the college of your choice to pursue a degree in the culinary arts. The winner will pose for the cover of my very own magazine, Martha Monthly, and will travel to Paris and spend the summer cooking with one of the world's finest chefs, Leonardo Dumont."

As Martha spoke, Alice's face lit up. She was amazed at the thought of flying to Paris and cooking with Leonardo Dumont. Leonardo was the author of seven bestselling cookbooks and owned his own thriving restaurant. Alice's dream was to open a restaurant herself, and the publicity that would come from being on Martha's magazine would get her talents recognized. The twenty-five thousand dollar scholarship was also a necessity because the income from her summer waitressing job wasn't enough to pay for her schooling. The only thing left standing in Alice's way was Ryan Rivera, who stood unimpressed at Martha's revelation.

"Now, I'm sure you are both very eager to hear what you will be preparing for us today," said Martha. "Let me introduce Mr. Patrick Pear, our head judge for the day."

"Thank you Martha," said Mr. Pear. "Mr. Rivera and Ms. Payton, today you will prepare a four course Italian dinner. We expect an appetizer, your choice of soup or salad, the entrée and finally a dessert. You will be judged in three important categories: taste, quality and originality. A judge will stand in the kitchen to keep an eye out for any cheating. If either contestant engages in foul play, he or she will be removed from the competition and disqualified. Good luck to both of you, and congratulations once again for making it this far."

"And with that, we shall begin the cook-off!" said Martha. "In the kitchen you will find all of the necessary equipment. We have set up a variety of ingredients that you will pick from. No outside ingredients are allowed, and only use the utensils provided. Molly will guide you to your stations and set the timer for two and a half hours. Good luck to you both!"

Molly led Alice and Ryan to the kitchen. Inside, she pointed to the island counter, which lay covered with pots, pans and ingredients.

When the students were out of the microphone's earshot, Ryan whispered into Alice's ear.

"Although you don't have a snowball's chance in hell of winning this, good luck," he hissed.

Alice glared at Ryan, restraining herself from responding. Irritated, she approached Nikki and Niroo.

"Guys, let's do this!"

Alice approached the island counter with Nikki and Niroo in tow. Ryan and his assistants advanced from the opposite side. Molly held up a timer and cranked it to two hours and thirty minutes. The two contestants shook hands as the timer buzzed and the cook-off began.

Jenn

At the academy's science hall, Jenn Andrews hurried through two big oak doors. She entered a large circular room that was overflowing with the campus' scientists. As she walked, Jenn scanned the room for her own invention. In the center she caught sight of a friendly smile. There stood Scott Meyers, her boyfriend and lab partner for three consecutive years, his silver hair spiked skyward.

Jenn walked to her lab station, her face apologetic. "Sorry I'm late, hun."

"Not a problem," said Scott, handing her a white lab coat. "I got a couple of guys to help me wheel in the experiment."

She put on the coat. "How's it look?"

"See for yourself."

Scott pulled back a large black tarp that covered the invention.

Jenn was satisfied with what she saw. Sitting motionless on a platform was a freshly constructed hovercraft, the size of a small car. The hovercraft was shaped like a jet but lacked wings and doors. It had three seats, one in the front and two in the back. The steering wheel was smooth and maneuverable, placed to the left of a series of switches and gages.

The exterior of the craft was silver titanium. The sides were painted lime green and had a yellow logo, M.A., for Meyers-Andrews.

"It's perfect!" said Jenn.

"Just about," said Scott. "We need to make sure it's working properly."

"Right. I'll start it up and you check for any glitches."

Excited, Jenn hopped into the driver's seat. She took the key from her pocket and stuck it into the ignition. With a light flick of her hand, the hovercraft began to whir. Scott circled around the machine, searching for any loose wires, scratches, dents or anything else that could detract from the score they were about to receive.

"So far so good," said Scott.

"Yes!" cheered Jenn. "And I think that the

48

environmental aspect of our invention will score some bonus points."

The hovercraft was indeed environmentally safe. Instead of running on gasoline, Scott and Jenn had concocted a new solution of high-grade alcohol that powered the machine.

Content with the invention, Jenn turned off the vehicle and jumped from her seat. For a moment she gazed at the hovercraft. As she studied it, her face slowly dropped.

"I know that face. What's wrong?" asked Scott.

"The hovercraft's fantastic, but I'm bummed that the Transporter wasn't ready in time for the fair. If I had gotten it to work, there's no way we could lose," said Jenn.

"It's a huge project, Jenn. I think you're forgetting how complex it is. No one has ever made a teleportation device before. If you complete it, you'll be the first."

"*When* I complete it. Not if."

Scott smiled. "I meant to say that."

"It doesn't matter, though," said Jenn. "We finished the hovercraft. We've got a good chance!"

At the front of the hall, a woman stood at a wooden podium placed onstage. She spoke into a microphone.

"Ladies and gentlemen, may I have your attention, please? Thank you all for coming to Odyssey Academy's twelfth annual science fair. It is a pleasure to have you, and on behalf of all the judges, we are very excited to see what you have created. It gives us the chance to see what incredible ideas are stirring in your minds and what is in

49

store for the future of science. With that being said, we will begin the judging process."

Jenn grabbed a pair of aviator goggles. She leaned toward Scott and kissed him on the cheek.

"First place, here we come!"

Izzy

"Ms. Izzy Itello!" a voice bellowed enthusiastically.

Izzy spun around, searching for the person who had called her name. She found him standing in the doorway of the auditorium.

"Hey, Mario!"

The young Italian man walked up to her and grabbed her hand. "Ciao, Ms. Izzy! I am so happy to have you here! The show will go very well with such beautiful assistants!"

Izzy blushed. "Assistants? It's not just me?"

"I have two lovely assistants! Ms. Natalie Swift is waiting for you downstairs in the dressing room. Come, Ms. Izzy! I will show you to your room."

Mario and Izzy descended to the basement and entered a pastel-colored dressing room.

"Ms. Izzy, please make yourself at home. Your costume is on the rack. And thank you once again! I'm sure the audience will love our show!" Mario exclaimed.

"No problem! This'll be fun," said Izzy.

"Oh, and if you have any questions I'm just upstairs." Mario exited the room.

Left alone, Izzy looked at the dressing room, amazed. A giant mirror swallowed the north wall. Unable to resist herself, she began posing like a super model, placing her hand on her hip and flipping her hair.

"So, you like the big mirror too," someone laughed.

Izzy looked to her right and saw a teenage girl leaving the bathroom.

"I need one of these in my dorm," Izzy giggled, embarrassed. "How have you been, Natalie?"

"Can't complain. Getting a few gigs here and there, so I won't be in debt to this school forever."

"I know what you mean! I doubt I'll ever pay it off!"

Izzy examined Natalie's outfit, hypnotized by her attire. She wore a stunning red dress that rose a few inches above her knee.

"All right, I'm gonna go and help Mario set up. You have the golden dress over on the rack. I think you're going to like it!" said Natalie, her voice fading as she exited the room.

Izzy hurried to the rack and picked up the dress. Just like Natalie's, it was cut just above the knee and shimmered with sequins. Below the rack sat a pair of matching gold stilettos intended to make Izzy appear to be average height. Izzy rushed into the bathroom and slipped on her dress and shoes. Once finished, she fluffed her blonde, bouncy hair and swung the door open.

Playfully, Izzy jumped in front of the oversized mirror, striking another pose in her new costume. In the middle of her stance, she looked up into the glass, surprised to see a young man's reflection standing at the door.

"Jayden!" Izzy squealed.

Izzy spun around, sprinted to her boyfriend and leapt into his arms. Jayden dropped a bouquet of flowers he was holding, and hugged Izzy to his chest. Izzy pulled her head back to kiss him on the lips.

"Hi there!" said Jayden, breathless.

"Hi!" said Izzy.

Jayden picked up the flowers. "These are for you."

Izzy stuck her nose into the carnations and breathed.

"They're gorgeous."

"Not as gorgeous as you."

"You think you're so cute!" Izzy giggled.

"I try," Jayden grinned.

Izzy ran her hand through his ruffled brown hair.

"So, are you staying to watch the magic show?" she asked.

"I wish, but we're shooting the news a little earlier today. They need their weatherman on time."

"Hmm, that's all right. If the show goes well we might perform it again anyways. But tell me, Mr. Mother Nature, what's today's forecast?" Izzy questioned teasingly.

"Well, this afternoon we'll see dark clouds and heavy precipitation, and tonight it's gonna be you and me at Arcadia Café," said Jayden, his eyes bright.

"The new restaurant just off of campus?"

"Yes ma'am!"

"All right! Well then, you better hurry along and go predict the weather. The sooner we're done the sooner we're together!" Izzy smiled.

"I'll get right on it. Have fun in the magic show!" said Jayden. "You'll be spectacular."

Jayden bent down to hug Izzy and kissed her softly on the forehead. Reluctantly, he walked out of the room and climbed up the spiral staircase, heading to the school news station in the center of campus.

Izzy took her flowers and set them on a couch. A few moments later she heard Natalie's voice calling from the top of the stairs.

"Izzy...hey, Izzy!" Natalie yelled.

"Yeah?"

"You ready? The audience will be here any minute. Come on up."

"Oh, okay!"

Izzy walked out of the dressing room and climbed the towering staircase to see Natalie and Mario waiting at the top.

"Showtime!"

Colleen

Colleen Benton was at her high school's football stadium, home of the Indiana Phoenix. The school's ultimate rival, the Iliad Trojans, came from a large high school in northern Ohio. Today's game continued an annual exhibition match between the two teams.

Passing through the home team tunnel was senior Lewis Quinn. With a container of cheesy nachos in one hand and two sodas in the other, he juggled the football feast and approached the marching band. Clumsily, he pushed his way through his fellow band mates into the trumpet section. Colleen grabbed one of the sodas so Lewis could keep his balance.

"Did I miss anything?" asked Lewis, his skin the same caramel tone as Colleen's.

"Not *really*. Mike Patton intercepted the ball at the fifty, but there was a flag on the play," said Colleen.

"Is it still twenty-one to twenty?"

"Yeah, Trojans' lead."

"What about Reynolds? How's he throwing?"

"Not too shabby. He threw a touchdown pass just a few seconds ago, but we fumbled the ball."

"Man…why can't they hold onto the ball?" Lewis asked, taking a bite of his nachos. "It's basic football."

"Football? *Football?* What could *you* possibly know about football?" a voice chuckled.

Colleen and Lewis spun around, searching for the face that belonged to the voice.

"Chandler Comet!" said Lewis. "Come on over!"

A young man with bright orange hair and as many freckles as there were people in the stadium, pushed his way toward Colleen and Lewis, plopping himself in-between the two.

"I said, what could you know about football, hmm?" Chandler repeated with a smirk.

"Why, about as much as you know about that

54

trombone of yours and probably more," grinned Colleen.

"Well, then you must know little to nothing about the game, because I hardly know anything about this hunk of metal. I just copy what the section leader does, and that seems to be working perfectly," said Chandler, waving his trombone in the air.

"So perfectly that it got you last chair," Lewis teased.

"Yes sir! The best worst player you'll ever find!" said Chandler. As he placed his arms around Lewis and Colleen's shoulders he burst out laughing. "You've got cheese in your baby goatee!"

Lewis wiped his chin. "It's a beard, not a goatee."

"You only have four hairs," said Chandler.

"Twenty-two."

Colleen giggled. "So, what could *you* possibly know about football?"

"Much more than that instrument! Watch, I'll predict this next play," said Chandler. "You see number fifteen, Reynolds, the quarterback. He'll fake a handoff to the halfback and throw a touchdown pass to number eighty-two, Austin Hamilton."

"Right, and I'm Usher," said Lewis. As he got the words out of his mouth, the ball was snapped. Colleen and Lewis stood dumbfounded as Reynolds' pass to Hamilton was completed for a touchdown, just as Chandler predicted.

Chandler and Colleen cheered wildly. Lewis stood, stunned as the extra point sailed through the uprights.

Chandler glanced at Lewis with a look that said *"I told you so"*. Lewis laughed and gave him a high five.

"Good call!"

"Thank you, thank you," said Chandler. "Now, check out the Trojan's wide receiver, Trey Pairs. Number eighty-eight, he's a freshman from Troy, Indiana. This kid is going places, mark my words. In his first varsity game he scored six touchdowns! If we lose, it will be because of him."

"You think we'll lose?" asked Lewis.

"Of course not! We've got Reynolds on our side! I said *if* we lose."

As the clock counted down to zero, the drum major blew his whistle. It was the band's cue to prepare to march onto the field.

"Oh man, looks like it's about time for the halftime show," said Colleen.

"Well then. I best be gettin back to my section. Can't perform without your last chair trombonist!" said Chandler. He patted Lewis on the back, turned around and headed toward the line of trombones.

"Come back after the halftime show!" called Lewis.

Chandler waved his hand in agreement. The drum major gave another toot of his whistle and the marching band formed into four perfect rows as the clock struck zero.

CHAPTER FOUR

Three Broken Dungeons

Cronus and Uranus soared through the galaxy in search of the souls who had escaped Tartarus. While passing through space, Cronus peered at Uranus venomously. His short, peppered hair was disheveled, matching his crooked face.

"Well done, Uranus! I am out of that wretched dungeon, and here you stand before me, full of life. I must say, breaking through the underworld with a star was brilliant! Tell me, how did you find my dungeon?"

"I could sense you calling me, a desire as strong as that of a man dying of thirst searching for water. It drew me to your chamber. From outside of Tartarus I could feel your pain. An invisible dagger pierced my heart, and the shrieks you cast filled my ears. Mere seconds of unbearable torture…I can only imagine what you have been through," said Uranus, his old eyes lowered.

"Torture is an understatement. For too long I was hidden in the dark, only to be graced with light's presence when my eyes were shut, imagining such a privilege. The chained door never opened and the floor never softened in its centuries of existence. I am forever done with such a lifestyle, if one can call it that. Today is a new day," said Cronus.

"And forever more shall you reign! Shall we *both* reign in a kingdom so powerful. Gods will fall to their knees when they see us, praising our breathtaking power. Goddesses will plead for our company and worship our greatness. People, though they cannot see us, will feel our presence and witness our wrath. Such a future nearly exists. We are just within reach!"

"Today marks the first day of our regime," said Cronus.

As Cronus spoke the planet Saturn came into view. Black clouds swallowed the planet and a collection of rings circled its perimeter. Cronus and Uranus entered into the dark world. The land was covered with craters. Cliffs could be seen in the distance, towering jaggedly into the sky.

Cronus scoured the world, searching past the fog. As expected, the souls were roaming freely. At first sight of the Titans, the spirits panicked and began to run.

Cronus lifted his hands.

"Halt!"

The souls froze in place, terrified to move.

"Lifeless beings, hear my words!" shouted Cronus. "I understand your pain, I sympathize with your fear and I share your desire!"

The souls lifted their heads, confused. The being

whose wrath they dreaded spoke to them as equals.

"We share a common fate," continued Cronus. "Since your demise on Earth, each and every one of you has spent the afterlife imprisoned in the pit of hell. By sheer luck and by taking a risk, you have released yourselves from exile and now search for a new purpose. I too have run away and now seek a purpose of my own. This has been my objective since the day I was sentenced to Tartarus. I seek revenge on the beings who cast me into hell. I promise my desire will be fulfilled.

"You, however, lack a way to gain your own reprisal. The same beings who cast me into hell have cast you beside me, subjecting you to a destiny of eternal torment. Here I stand before you, bearing an opportunity. I offer you a chance to gain vengeance on those who have sent you to Tartarus. Together we shall send the *saintly* gods that have kept you from Elysium, straight to hell themselves!"

The souls were hypnotized.

"Complete vengeance and total control, you say?" asked one of the spirits.

"Yes, and much more!" said Cronus. "Do you not wish to see your tormentors burn in hell? To watch them beg for forgiveness as you laugh at their terror? It is a fate worse than death and a punishment that they deserve! Their payment is overdue and I say it's time we take what we've earned!"

"How do *we* gain such revenge?" asked another soul.

"Help us to help you!" said Uranus. "Lead us to the dungeons of the Titans, and break down the doors. Together we shall release the gods and depart for Earth. There, we cannot be seen by its living spirits and will remain safe from the gods and goddesses that rule on Mount Olympus. Once we have secured our rule on Earth, we will overthrow Mount Olympus and claim it as our own. Tartarus will soon be crowded with Olympians begging for mercy."

"So what say you? Do we have an agreement?" asked Cronus.

The souls stood motionless, waiting for someone to reply. Finally, a spirit thrust his fist into the air.

"To the dungeons!"

Like a tidal wave, the rest of the souls raised their hands, shouting in approval.

"Come now!" yelled Cronus. "Help us release the Titans!"

A group of souls eagerly approached Cronus and Uranus. They jumped upward, floating toward the atmosphere of Saturn. All of the spirits followed as they passed into outer space.

The frenzied mob rushed to the underworld. They boarded the ferry, which magnified in size at the sight of all of its passengers. Once the ferry landed, Cronus, Uranus and the souls entered into Limbo. Without hesitation, Cronus approached the black hole. He was the first through the vortex, landing in Tartarus.

Once everyone passed through the vortex, Cronus peered at the souls.

"Where might we find the Titans?" he asked.

"There is a set of dungeons tucked at the back of Tartarus. I believe you will find your brethren there," answered one of the spirits.

"Take us to it."

The soul led Cronus, Uranus and the spirits through a dark corridor in record time. Three mammoth-sized entryways stood at the back of the tunnel, bolted shut with chains and shackles.

Cronus studied the doors, his heart pounding.

"Where's the key?" asked a spirit.

"Key? *Key?* There is no key!" snorted another soul. "If it were truly *that* simple, the Titans would have escaped millennia ago! The chains are sealed with great magic and power. The only way we're getting past that door is if we break it!"

"We could bring in a star," said Uranus.

"No. It'll explode throughout Tartarus completely. We cannot risk injuring or killing a Titan," Cronus objected.

"Well, sir," said another soul, "how were you freed?"

"Uranus and I broke through from the inside out. We blew the door off its hinges using our powers."

"Then why not do the same to these dungeons? Obviously you cannot push the door open, so why not pull?" asked the soul.

"Gods are strong, but not *that* strong. Unless you're Hercules, I see no way we can pull the door open. Pushing from the inside out is by far more easily done.

Now, unless any of you are supernaturally strong, start thinking of realistic ways to get inside these prisons," snapped Uranus.

"But sir, there is a way to pull the door open," countered the soul. "One of the tunnels leads to a giant who can match the strength of Hercules…or at least come close to it."

"How do you know of this giant?" asked Cronus, intrigued.

"What else does a condemned man have left to do when he is banished to hell? I've explored every section of this purgatory in search of a way out. I came across this monster on one of my journeys."

"And he is not chained or confined?"

"No. He merely sits on the floor. Boredom fills his days."

"Bring him at once," ordered Cronus.

"Yes, sir." The soul exited the corridor.

Moments passed as Cronus and Uranus waited by the dungeons. Suddenly, a thunderous noise could be heard, echoing throughout the tunnels. As the giant came into view, the souls made a pathway. He trampled into the center of the room.

"Well done!" cheered Cronus. "He is considerable in size and appears as though he can accomplish the task." Cronus stepped away from the chambers. "Giant, open the doors that hang before you."

The giant approached the first door. He placed both hands on the wooden structure and yanked.

BOOM!

With one tug the door flung open. Cronus watched, elated. The giant moved to the second chamber. With a forceful jerk he tore the entrance from its molding, dust erupting into the air. He gripped the third door, easily throwing it to the ground.

Cronus was frozen in disbelief. From the shadowy dungeons, humanlike figures emerged into the corridor.

"Amazing," Cronus breathed.

Dressed in battered tunics, the Titans walked slowly, their faces stiff and pale.

"Cronus! Uranus! What has happened?" a god cried out.

"Brethren! Say farewell to these despicable dungeons and welcome your new life!" Cronus shouted. He approached the god who had spoken, gripping his thick shoulders. "We are back, Hyperion. We are all back! Zeus and his Olympians sit at Mount Olympus, knowing I have escaped and that I have planned to release you! The great Titanomachy is not over. It has only just begun!"

"But Uranus is alive! How can this be?" asked Mnemosyne, her black hair blending with the tunnel.

"Uranus, whom you thought I had killed, never died. During the Titanomachy, Uranus and I faked his death. At the time, I could sense that the Olympians would win the war. By no means was I ready to give-in, unwilling to accept an eternity of punishment. So for a shred of hope, for a chance to escape Tartarus, Uranus exiled himself to Saturn. There, he hid out of the Olympians' sight, waiting to rescue us!"

"How did you break down the doors?" asked Oceanus, a coarse gray beard draped to his chest. "We have tried to escape countless times by using our powers. It is impossible to do such a thing!"

"You cannot break through with only your powers," said Cronus. "As I have learned, magic seals the dungeons and can withstand any of our magical capacities. However, strength was not any of our main abilities and when the chambers were made, the foolish Olympians neglected the idea that extreme power could collapse the hinges. The chamber I was concealed in was only strong enough to hold myself. My fireballs alone could not penetrate the wood. When Uranus broke into my cell, the door was not strong enough to resist both of our powers.

"Your chambers were designed so that three gods, even combining their abilities, could not break through the door. However, this giant had enough strength to break the entryways and release you all."

"So you're saying that if we had just been strong enough to push the door open, we would have escaped?" asked Crius, his dark hands beginning to shake.

"Exactly! You would have had to be supernaturally strong to break the chains, but that's precisely the point! Contain your rage, though. Channel it to the Olympians, those who sent you to the chambers!"

"Why did you wait so long to rescue us, Uranus?" Phoebe asked harshly.

"Finding Cronus' chamber was not an easy task," said Uranus. "It took centuries of searching and scouring the underworld from outside its walls to sense his presence. Once I had found Cronus I could not break into his chamber. I had no way to break into Tartarus alone from outer space, for Hades would surely have stopped me. I had to break directly into Cronus' dungeon to assure the plan was a success.

"Finally, after many years, I entered Cronus' chamber. I burst through the underworld by striking a collection of stars with ice. Instantaneously, the stars exploded, ripping into the dungeon. The walls of the underworld rebuilt as soon as I entered the chamber, magically sealing themselves. Cronus and I then escaped by blowing past the door."

"But Atlas! What became of Atlas? His power is strength. He could have helped! Why isn't he here?" asked Tethys.

"Don't you remember? Atlas was punished another way. He was not destined for the dungeons. Instead, he upholds the planet Earth," said Mnemosyne.

"Those Olympians, they think they're so clever!" cried Thea.

"Oh, but they are!" said Coeus. "It was *us* who spent years locked in Tartarus, and *they* who have ruled the universe so freely. Had we been the smarter gods, it would have been the other way around."

"And now we get our chance!" said Cronus. "*We* have the chance to be the smarter, wiser, and stronger gods. *We* have what they do not. What was supposed to be an eternal punishment was cut drastically short. It has given us an overwhelming desire and made our spirits much, much colder. Here we are, bitter, tired and craving vengeance!"

"I say we flood Mount Olympus! Drown every god who rests on sacred grounds!" shouted Oceanus.

"To battle at once!" yelled Iapetus, his red eyes fierce. "It had never crossed my mind that this day would come. Now that it has, I can wait no longer!"

"Ah, but you must wait, at least for now. We cannot attack at this moment, for the Olympians will expect war. Before we plan our strike, we must attend to an issue on Earth. There, we are safe," said Cronus. "I say we leave for Earth and prepare a strategy to overthrow the Olympians."

The Titans raised their fists in agreement.

"Then come, brothers and sisters! Together we shall venture to Earth, the land of our hope, land of our future, land of our retribution!"

The Titans roared in anger. Energized, Cronus turned around and passed through the corridor. Uranus and the Titans followed behind, along with the souls. The giant remained by the dungeons, poking its head through the newly opened chambers.

Cronus led the Titans and souls into Limbo. At the center of the platform he addressed his brethren.

"Today is a day to be remembered!" he yelled. "Let it be known as the day the mighty Titans escaped!"

The fugitives swept through the underworld, leaving its barren realm. They soared through the universe and soon found themselves hovering over planet Earth. Before moving any further, Cronus added one more god to

66

the malicious crowd. Atlas, the biggest of all the Titans, released Earth from his shoulders.

Once all of the Titans were present, Cronus floated toward the surface of the planet.

"Cronus, where do we go?" asked Hyperion.

"Greece!"

Cronus launched through Earth's atmosphere like a torpedo. The souls and Titans mimicked his maneuver, shooting head-first into the world. As quick as a bullet, they crashed into the land of Greece. A violent tremor shot through the ground.

Once the earth settled, Cronus peered at all of the Titans, his face maniacal. The Titans were out of the Olympians' bounds, untouchable and secure. After thousands of years, they were finally free.

CHAPTER FIVE

Gods of the Round Table

Inside the castle of Zeus, the Olympian gods sat at a large round table. All were impatient and furious, waiting for their king and the message that they had been so urgently called to hear. Hermes sat fidgeting, unwilling to break the news to his fellow deities. Athena remained calm, quietly pacing back and forth.

Finally, Zeus and Hades entered the room. As they appeared, each of the gods stood and bowed to their king. Zeus barreled to his throne at the head of the table. The Olympians took their seats and waited for him to speak. They watched him keenly, searching for any sign of relief.

Zeus peered at his brethren, his eyes heavy. "Great Olympians, I am honored that you have come to my palace in such a time of need. I bear terrible news and implore your assistance."

The Olympians sat alert.

"It has been brought to my attention that an intruder has broken into Tartarus. The Titan Uranus has entered its realm and the Dungeon of Cronus has been opened. Cronus has escaped."

The Olympians gasped.

"This is an outrage!" yelled Ares, slamming his fists on the table.

"Silence!" barked Hades. "Your king has not finished!"

Zeus glanced at Ares. "Cronus and Uranus have complete access to the underworld. As far as we know, the rest of the Titans remain imprisoned. However, we believe that they too will be released. Hades has also informed me that the souls of the underworld have escaped and are presently on the loose. They, however, are not a threat to us, but a minor problem in this tangled web."

"How has Uranus returned? He was proclaimed dead!" roared Ares.

"We assume that he never died. Cronus must have lied about Uranus' death. However, we do not know where Uranus has been for the last few millennia, and we don't know how he managed to come back, " said Athena calmly.

"How can we be sure it was Uranus? Is there a possibility it was another god?" asked Hestia.

"It was definitely Uranus," said Hermes. "Hades and I saw him and Cronus."

"Then why didn't you stop them? Cronus has been locked away for years and is probably as weak as one could physically be. He should be an easy target!" yelled Poseidon, his trident raised in the air.

Hades stood up, his freshly bandaged palms gripped to the table.

"Fire and ice powers against a speedy little man and a god who can deflect things?! It would have been suicide no matter how many years he spent in Tartarus! Ah, but if *mighty* Poseidon had been there, everything would have been fine and nothing would have happened!"

"Things would have been much better off. Cronus certainly wouldn't be galloping around the universe!" growled Poseidon.

"Then why weren't you there, oh powerful one? I remember! Because when the universe was divided into three sections, you won the seas and oceans while I got stiffed with the underworld! And why didn't Prometheus get a premonition of this happening, eh?" Hades asked bitterly, diverting the attention away from himself.

Prometheus lowered his head. "You know as well as I do that I cannot control when or how I get a premonition. They come at random and find me. I do not call to them."

"Stop!" barked Hera, her old eyes stern. "We cannot point fingers at a time like this. Last I checked, we were well above pettiness."

Hades and Poseidon sat down quietly.

"Zeus, what do you suggest we do?" asked Aphrodite.

"That is the very reason why I have called this meeting," said Zeus. "We need a plan...a very skillful and powerful plan that will defeat Cronus and Uranus before we find ourselves locked in Tartarus. The Titanomachy had seemingly ended, but I am afraid that it was only a prologue. The real battle is on the horizon and we must meet it head on."

"What do you think Cronus and Uranus plan to do? If the Titans are released, where will they go, and what do they want?" asked Apollo, gripping his bow.

"The Titans want what they tried to attain in the Titanomachy," said Artemis. "Cronus is addicted to power and becoming king of the universe is the only thing that will satisfy him. He could stay in the underworld, but he could also take his crew somewhere safer. Wherever the Titans go, it will be a sanctuary."

"Ah!" squealed Athena, jumping from her seat. "I know where they will go! Although the Titans would be secure in the underworld, there is only one place where they would be completely protected from us." She paused, taking a moment of silence.

Hermes raised his head.

"Earth," he whispered.

"Yes," said Athena. "Think about it! We cannot cross into Earth's atmosphere because of the curse, and humans cannot see gods. Zeus' lightning bolts wouldn't affect the Titans from so high up, so we would have no way to physically attack them. If the Titans step onto Earth, they will be untouchable."

"We must stop them at once!" said Hephaestus. "If we can reach Cronus and Uranus before they depart for Earth, then we can stop them from doing anything else."

The Olympians agreed.

A pounding knock sounded at the door. The gods waited in silence as Hermes answered it. Rigon stood in the entrance, his face panic-stricken.

"Master Zeus, I beg your forgiveness, but I have an urgent message from Lady Gaia," Rigon's voice trembled.

Zeus held his breath.

"Lady Gaia found it necessary to inform you that her husband Uranus and son Cronus have returned to planet Earth. They were accompanied by the Titans and an army of souls."

Zeus lowered his head.

"Now what do we do? The Titans are hidden and safe! They could find a path to Mount Olympus. Zeus, I refuse to go down without a fight!" bellowed Ares.

"And a fight we shall have!" said Zeus, lifting his head. "The Titans are on Earth, and now we know it. Our job is to keep Mount Olympus protected." He turned toward Rigon. "Fetch the map of Earth at once."

Rigon bowed and scurried out of the room.

"First," began Zeus, "we need to find where the Titans are located. The map will show us a glimpse of what they're doing. Secondly, Prometheus, please attempt to get a premonition."

Prometheus closed his eyes, placing his fingers on either side of his forehead. After a moment, he lowered his hands and opened his eyes, his lips curved into a grimace.

"Zeus, I cannot."

"It is all right, Prometheus. It is not your fault," said Zeus.

Rigon reentered the room, a large paper cylinder

72

clutched to his side. Zeus took the cylinder and rolled it onto the table, revealing a map of the planet Earth. The Olympians gathered around it.

"How does it show the Titans' location?" asked Hestia.

"It is not your ordinary map," said Athena.

She waved her hand over the Atlantic Ocean. The Olympians watched in awe as a dolphin appeared in the water, hopping in and out of waves.

"Think of what you wish to see and wave your palm where you believe you'll find it. If you've guessed the correct place, you can observe what is happening at that exact moment."

Athena brushed her hand over the same spot, grazing her palm over the dolphin. The dolphin faded from sight and the map stood still. Then, Zeus waved his palm over the drawing of Greece. Instantly, a clear picture of Cronus and Uranus appeared.

"They're on the side of Mount Parnassus!" said Aphrodite.

"Oh no! They're in search of Pythia, the Oracle of Delphi," sighed Hermes.

"Is she there? Well of course *she* isn't there, but what about her heir?" asked Hera.

"I cannot see her. Neither can Cronus and Uranus. By the looks of things, it seems as though the seer has moved on…or worse," said Apollo.

"It looks as though Cronus and Uranus are angry," said Artemis.

The two gods on the map were indeed upset. The being whom they searched for was nowhere to be found.

"Zeus, try searching for the Oracle. It has been centuries since Pythia was at Delphi. By now her heir could be anywhere," said Hephaestus.

Zeus waved his hand over Cronus and Uranus and the two gods faded away. Slowly, he circled his palm over the entirety of Greece.

Nothing.

Zeus began scanning all of Europe. Having no luck, he moved over each continent in turn.

Moments passed and nothing happened. Finally, Zeus reached for the corners of the map. As his arm hovered over North America, something appeared. The gods moved in closer, staring at the miniature figure that had emerged.

"Behold, the heir of Pythia, the Oracle of Delphi!" cheered Zeus.

On the map stood a woman who was indeed related to the Greek prophetess. She stood casually, unaware that a group of ancient gods were studying her every move.

"So she is the one Cronus and Uranus are searching for?" asked Epimetheus.

"Yes," answered Zeus.

"Zeus, we need to keep her safe. They must be seeking her powers, to learn of their fates and how to destroy us," said Poseidon.

"I agree," said Hades. "If they get a hold of the Oracle, I promise that it will lead to our downfall."

"What if we can use *her* to help *us*?" asked Athena.

"What do you mean?"

"In the beginning of the Titanomachy, we asked Pythia how to destroy the Titans. We came to her for help, and she guided us. What if we offered our help to Pythia's heir to protect her from Cronus, and asked for her assistance in return?"

"How would we be able to help her if we cannot get down to Earth?" asked Hermes, intrigued.

"We could send the Oracle a physical power through one of Zeus' lightning bolts. She would then be able to defend herself against the Titans. Able to help defeat Cronus and his army!" said Athena.

"One power wouldn't be enough to fend off twelve gods. She would need her own legion, a set of magical guardians that could protect her," said Poseidon.

"Those magical beings could help her kill Cronus as well, not just defend her," said Hephaestus.

"But how would they dispose of the Titans?" asked Artemis. "Gods are remarkably strong! *We* had incredible difficulty when we tried to kill Cronus. Besides, gods aren't visible to humans. The mortals would never see the Titans."

"On the contrary, the Oracle of Delphi can see any type of mythical being, for she is one herself. As for the other mortals, once we send powers to them, they will no longer be completely human. They will be able to see everything we can see. The Titans will no longer be safe," said Athena.

"That still doesn't explain how they would defeat the Titans," said Apollo.

75

"Well, there are two ways," said Zeus. "The first option would be to kill them. It would take great skill and impeccable planning, for Cronus expects an attack. However, to ask the Oracle to kill the Titans is absurdly impractical, if not impossible. Nevertheless, there is a second, more realistic way to defeat them. May I remind you about Epimetheus' encounter with a certain woman?"

The table of gods drew silent, pondering Zeus' words. Then, it hit them, all at the same time.

"Is it still on Earth?" asked Hades anxiously.

"It's never been touched since we left it," said Zeus.

"How would we get the guardians to find it?" asked Poseidon.

"We guide them to its location. It is crucial that we protect the prophetess at once. The longer she is left exposed, the more vulnerable she is." Zeus waved his hands over the surface of the table. Fourteen golden rods emerged from his palms, sparking erratically.

"Here's the plan," said Zeus. "Each of us will grab a lightning bolt and bless it with an ability. When it is time, we shall release the bolts and send them to Earth in search of targets. As the lightning bolts cross into Earth's atmosphere, they will morph into pure energy. In the form of beams, the energy will strike each human, giving them a power.

"We will send our abilities in the shape of a pentagram. The power of the pentagram will ensure that our beams seek humans who are strong enough to fight. We will strike the Oracle at the apex, ensuring her safety at all costs. The other powers will be distributed to whomever is standing at the other four points." Zeus raised his arms. "My friends, I do believe there is hope. Keep your spirits high. We shall do everything in our power to guarantee that this new generation of gods succeeds. Having our own lives at stake should be incentive enough."

Zeus lifted one of the bolts into his palm. He turned it in his hand and gestured to the gods.

"Come, opportunity awaits. The future of the Olympians, the Oracle and the universe depends on us now."

The Olympians followed Zeus as he exited the room. Together they left the castle and proceeded from Mount Olympus. The gods soared above planet Earth and aligned in five distinct positions, with Zeus stationed in the center. With lightning bolts in hand, they awaited the command.

Zeus gazed at the Olympians, his arm raised. "Now!"

CHAPTER SIX

Struck by Lightning

Melanie

It was the beginning of the sixteen-hundred-meter relay and the gun was about to sound. An official stood at the head of the track, checking the position of the lead runners. Once he finished the inspection, he raised a megaphone to his mouth.

"A two command start, my mark and then the gun."

The runners held still.

"Ladies, set...."

BANG!

The athletes took off.

L.B. began the first leg, making the first turn of the track. Melanie watched her eagerly. The copper highlights of her short brown hair looked like flames as she ran.

"All right, L.B.! You get 'em, girl!" yelled Mika.

L.B. raced for the second curve, riding on the heels of another runner. She passed the girl on the short straightaway, taking third place. Kira waited impatiently next to the start, her hand raised. L.B. rushed to the passing zone and handed off the baton.

Melanie watched as Kira whizzed around the track, catching second place at the halfway mark. A girl in a scarlet uniform ran in front of her; she belonged to the same team as Felicia Turner. With all of her might, Kira flew past the first place runner and took the lead. She leapt into the passing zone as Mika reached for the baton and started to sprint.

Mika nearly flew through the first turn, holding first place. Melanie approached the starting line.

Here we go! thought Melanie. She watched as Mika dashed into the last stretch. One hundred meters remained.

Mika sprinted for the finish. As she ran, a scarlet uniform bolted past her taking the lead. Mika fell to a close second. She pushed her legs with incredible force, rushing toward Melanie.

Felicia pushed past Melanie, holding her hand steadily in the air. Her teammate reached the exchange zone and gave her the baton in a quick snap. A split second later, Mika waved the baton at Melanie. Melanie grabbed it and took off.

Melanie chased after Felicia, who was three meters ahead. Within a few seconds, she closed the gap, hanging on to Felicia's right shoulder.

Stick with her, Melanie thought to herself.

The two rivals sped into the backstretch of the track. Running out of time, Melanie surged forward, attempting to pass her opponent. As she moved, her elbow knocked into Felicia's. Felicia shoved Melanie with her arm. Mel ignored the shove and matched her rival's pace.

Mika, Kira and L.B. were huddled on the sideline.

"Come on, Mel! Everything you've got. You have nothing to lose!" cheered Kira.

"Yeah, Mel! If she shoves you again, smack her in the face!" bellowed Mika.

Kira glared at Mika.

"I mean, beat her in the race!"

"You've got this, bud! She's got nothing on you; show her what you're made of!" shouted L.B.

The three held their breath, hoping for the best.

Melanie and Felicia hit the second curve of the final lap. Only one more straightaway remained.

Suddenly, one of Zeus' lightning bolts came zooming into the earth's atmosphere. The lightning bolt transformed into an energy beam, aiming at the academy's track. It entered into the stadium at full speed and crashed into its target.

"Ah!" Melanie shivered. A sudden jolt swept through her body, pushing into her legs.

"Oh my god!" Mika, Kira, and L.B. gasped in unison.

With incredible ease, Melanie sped past Felicia, taking the lead. Her legs blurred as she moved toward the finish. With two final steps she lunged past the finish line and turned around, breathless. Melanie watched Felicia, her eyes wide. Felicia had fifteen meters left in the race.

Suddenly, Melanie's vision flashed black and

white. The track seemed to be spinning around her. Melanie wobbled forward and fell to the ground, her eyes closed.

"She's unconscious!" yelled Kira.

A group of paramedics rushed onto the track, oxygen tanks clutched in their hands. Mika ran to Melanie's side and held her head, splashing water over her sweat-covered face. With one touch, Melanie fluttered her eyes and lifted her head. She looked up to find Kira, L.B. and the paramedics all gazing at her. Mika kneeled at her side.

"You okay?" Kira asked frantically.

Melanie rolled her eyes.

"Did...did we win?" she stuttered.

"Is that all you've got to say?" laughed Mika. "Of course we won!"

Melanie smiled and grabbed the water bottle, taking a sip. L.B. and Kira helped her to her feet.

"Miss, you may want to come with us. We can take you to the trainer's station and examine your condition, just to be safe," said one of the paramedics.

"Okay."

After aiding Melanie to a trainer's table, Kira and L.B. left to find Toren. Mika stepped away to get her own water bottle.

Left alone, Melanie leaned back and closed her eyes.

"Good race, Taylor," a voice called out.

Melanie looked up. Surprised, she found Felicia standing at the end of the table.

"You too, Turner," said Mel.

"That was one heck of a finish, definitely took me by surprise. Looks like a lot has changed over the course of a year," said Felicia.

"Thanks. It's certainly been awhile."

"It has." Felicia glanced at the ground. "Well, I just wanted to say, nice job. Good luck at Nationals." She turned around.

Melanie fell back on the table.

"Hey, hey, hey! You oughtta be glad it wasn't me you were racing out there! You woulda been face first on that track, tryin to push people outta your way. I'll catch you next time around. You better watch out, Ms. Thang!"

Mika stepped in front of Felicia.

"Is that a threat?" Felicia asked sharply.

"Oh no! That's a promise!"

Felicia slipped past Mika quickly. She left with her head lowered, checking over her shoulder as she moved.

"Let's not send anyone else to the paramedics," chuckled Melanie.

"Oh ha, ha, ha!" mocked Mika. "You watch her next meet. I bet that's the last time she ever tries to mess with any of us on the track."

Melanie grinned. "I'll keep an eye out for that."

"So what happened out there? As much as I hate that Turner girl, she was right. That was one hell of a race! I've never seen someone move so fast!" cheered Mika.

"Honestly, I don't know what came over me. I mean, I knew I was fast, but I wasn't sure if I was gonna win. One second I was tied with Felicia, and the next thing you know, I was crossing the finish, fainting!" Melanie exclaimed.

"Well whatever you did, do it again at Nationals. Lord knows we're going to need it. Heck, if all four of us could pull that off we'd be sure to win the U.S. title!" said Mika.

Coach Toren approached the trainer's station with Kira and L.B. at his side.

"Glad to see you're okay. I bet you want to know your times."

The girls listened anxiously.

"L.B. ran an opening time of fifty-five seconds. Kira pulled a fifty-two-point-three, Mika ran fifty-three-point-nine-five and Melanie finished off with an impressive forty-nine-point-nine."

"Forty-nine-point what?" asked Kira.

"Forty-nine-point-nine," repeated Toren.

"That can't be right," said Melanie.

"Nope, it's definitely right. It would have been fifty-three, but you kicked it in pretty well at the end."

"I knew you had gone faster than ever before!" said Mika. "Forty-nine seconds! What is that, a state record?"

"Don't count on it," said L.B. "The state record is probably closer to forty-eight."

"Well, it's a new record for us! Nationals, here we come!" said Mika.

"Yeah, here we come," repeated Melanie.

Dazed, Melanie leaned back and closed her eyes. Her head was spinning as she attempted to soak in all that had happened.

Alice

At Odyssey Academy's dining hall, the Weddingsworth Cook-Off was heating up. It was nearly two and a half hours into the challenge, and only ten minutes remained.

"Nikki, toss me that tomato!" said Alice, shouting over the noise of a blender.

"You got it, boss!" Nikki threw the tomato over Niroo's head, skimming his hair.

"An inch lower and you woulda knocked me out cold!" yelled Niroo.

"But I didn't! Keep working."

Alice cut up the tomato and added it to her soup. She took a few tastes and sprinkled a dash of ground pepper.

"How's the cake coming?" Alice asked Niroo.

"Looking good, looking good! I'm icing it right now."

"Nikki, what about the tomatoes?"

"We're cutting it close. I just put them in the oven," said Nikki.

"Just now? I thought you had them prepared over an hour ago. We have less than ten minutes!" said Alice.

"I did. But I think they need an extra few minutes to bake. Don't worry, I'll have them ready in no time."

84

"I'm gonna hold you to it."

"Hey! Hey! Lindsey, what are you doing?" Ryan's voice cracked. "You're doing it all wrong. You're going to ruin my creation!"

Ryan ran to his assistant and snatched a cruet of his Caesar dressing out of her hand.

"It's just dressing!" barked Lindsey.

"*It's just dressing!*" mocked Ryan. "No it's not! It's the key ingredient to my salad! You cannot drench everything completely. A little bit is all you need! I guess I was wrong about thinking you had a brain." He set the cruet on the counter and walked back to his station.

Discreetly, Alice tried to catch a glimpse of what Ryan was preparing, but a large gray screen shielded his post.

"Ryan?" asked Chris.

"*What?*"

"When the baked ziti is finished, where do you want it?"

"Oh for God's sake!" screamed Ryan. "How about on a plate! Dear Lord, I truly am surrounded by idiots."

Molly Hibber entered the kitchen.

"Fi-fi-five minutes remain in the competition," she announced.

"Did you catch that, Alice?" asked Nikki.

"Yeah. You almost done over there?"

"Don't worry, I've got everything under control. You just worry about that soup."

WHOOSH!

As Alice turned off the stove, an explosion erupted in the kitchen. Ryan had been taking his pasta out of the oven when the front burner of his stove burst into flames.

"What did you do?" Ryan yelled at Chris.

"Nothing! The stove wasn't even on!" cried Chris, bewildered.

Ryan ran to the island counter and grabbed a fire extinguisher that sat beneath it. He pressed the top handle, taming the flames with a blast of foam.

At the same time, another energy beam made its way onto the academy's campus. The beam whizzed into the dining hall's kitchen, making a clean strike into Alice's back. Alice lurched forward. She grabbed onto the handles of her pot of soup, trying to break her fall without hitting the hot stove. The pot began to tip, ready to spill. Scared, Alice squeezed her eyes shut, pushed off of the pot with her hands, and lurched backwards. A second later she opened her eyes. Surprisingly, the soup was secure in the metal container.

Out of breath, Alice leaned over the stove, her hands clutched to the neighboring counter. Niroo ran to her side and patted her back.

"You okay?" he asked anxiously.

Alice took in a deep breath. "Yeah."

"Take it easy, man. You can't die on us now! We've gotta beat Rivera!" Niroo exclaimed.

Alice cracked a smile. She took another deep breath and stood up. "I think I'm good."

"Are you sure?"

"I'm fine, but that was weird. I felt like I got

pushed from behind and then kicked in the stomach."

"If it's any consolation, Ryan's stove exploded."

"I saw that. Is his food okay?"

Niroo glanced at Ryan's cooking station. The fire was extinguished and the entrée was unharmed. "Looks like he's still in the game."

"I knew it was too good to be true," Alice grinned.

Molly reentered the kitchen. Her voice squeaked.

"Time! Martha Weddingsworth is waiting in the cafeteria. Take a few moments to collect your meals and we will begin the judging promptly."

Niroo looked at Alice. "Ready?"

"Ready."

Both teams began to gather their creations, holding them carefully as they entered the cafeteria. Alice was first through the door. Having recovered from her potential accident, she glided to the judges, her face beaming.

"Hello!" Alice greeted.

"Hello Ms. Payton," said Martha. "Ah, and what is this?"

"Your appetizers for today are stuffed tomatoes. They are thoroughly baked, fresh from the oven and sprinkled with a dash of garlic."

"My, my, it looks wonderful! Thank you, Alice." Martha cut one of the tomatoes and lightly bit it.

Alice took a step back and headed for the kitchen, reaching for the door.

SMACK!

At full force the door rammed into her head. Ryan snuck from behind it.

"Looks like I've hit a bug," he sighed.

Without a second look, Ryan strode past her.

Alice wobbled backwards, reaching out for anything she could grab. After a few seconds, she caught herself and entered the kitchen.

"He just hit me with the door!" she yelled, approaching Nikki and Niroo.

"No way!" roared Nikki.

"When he gets back, I'm gonna smack him and see how he likes it!" said Niroo, reaching for a pan.

"You're not going to touch him," said Alice firmly. "As much as I'd like to see his butt hit the floor, we can't stoop to his level. C'mon, we've got more work to do."

"Here's the next dish, the minestrone soup," said Niroo. He handed Alice a tray with five bowls.

"Hold on!" shouted Nikki. She ran to the door and smashed it open.

"Nikki!" Alice cringed.

"Just making sure!"

Fortunately, the judges hadn't noticed the door crashing into the wall. They were all mesmerized by Ryan.

"All right, Mrs. Weddingsworth, I'll just slip into the kitchen and attend to your next incredible course," said Ryan.

Alice rolled her eyes.

Over the next ten minutes, the judges and taste testers sampled both chefs' entrées. Soon enough, it was time for the big finale. The desserts would finish the contest.

"Niroo, you got the cake?" asked Alice.

"Yes ma'am! It's perfect!"

Alice hugged both of her partners. "Did I ever tell you guys that I love you?"

"You can repay us by paying our college tuition when you win," said Nikki.

"Well, that's *if* I win, and I really don't think that twenty-five grand will cover all three of us. Heck, it won't even cover one year of schooling for me," Alice laughed, taking the cake from Niroo. "Here goes nothing!"

As Alice entered the dining room, Martha squealed.

"Oh! It's an Italian Wedding Cake!"

"Yes, ma'am, it is," said Alice. "A treat for any chocolate lover, perfectly topped with a cream cheese frosting."

Alice laid the cake on the table and took a step back, watching the judges anxiously. Ryan entered the room and walked toward Martha Weddingsworth. In his hands, he held the secret dessert that Alice had been unable to see. Alice's mouth dropped at first sight of the dessert. Ryan grinned at her reaction.

"Is that the Leaning Tower of Pisa?" asked Martha.

"You are correct!" said Ryan. He placed the giant cake on the table. "A beautiful dessert made to your fancy, candy for the eyes and a glorious sculpture of one of Italy's finest structures. It is hand-crafted by yours truly, an identical but miniature version of the original and tilted on an angle, just as its relative. A double fudge Italian Wedding Cake drizzled in authentic Italian chocolate and coated with a fine layer of cream cheese."

"You made this in the allotted time?" asked Martha.

"Yes. I knew coming into the competition that I would create something spectacular, and when Mr. Pear announced that the theme was Italian, well, the Leaning Tower of Pisa was the first thing that came to mind. Do you like it?" asked Ryan, already sensing Martha's answer.

"Why! This is the most brilliant piece of work I have ever encountered! It's a piece of art!" Martha raved. She clapped her hands and took a deep breath, trying to contain her excitement. "Mr. Rivera and Ms. Payton, if you may excuse us momentarily, we have plenty to discuss! I'll see that Ms. Hibber calls you when the time is ready."

As they retreated to the kitchen, Alice studied Ryan cautiously. An unsettling feeling curled in her stomach. Ryan stood in the middle of the room and took a gloat-filled bow.

"Thank you, thank you! I am truly honored to win such a prestigious competition and I would be glad to accept the money along with the everlasting fame," he jeered. "Now tell me, Alice, should I thank you in my acceptance speech, or just push you aside like the bug that you are?"

"Save your breath," Alice growled.

Alice approached Nikki and Niroo.

"Niroo, how long did it take you to make that cake?" she asked.

"About an hour and a half. Why?"

"Because I don't think our friend over there played by the rules. Have you seen his big finale?"

"No. We couldn't see anything he was doing behind that screen," said Nikki.

"Well, it was a giant Italian Wedding Cake made into an identical replica of the Leaning Tower of Pisa," said Alice, shaking her head.

"That no good, dirty rotten…" huffed Nikki, her voice trailing into a low growl.

"How did he cheat? How *could* he cheat?" asked Niroo.

"I have no idea, but he had to have cheated! If it took you an hour and a half just to make a round, normal sized cake, how is Ryan going to carve the entire Leaning Tower of Pisa in just two and a half hours with a cake so big?" Alice questioned.

"You have to be able to prove it to call him guilty," said Niroo.

Molly reentered the kitchen.

"Um…Martha Weddingsworth would like all of you to come into the cafeteria. It's time for the crowning of this year's winner."

The six chefs filed into the cafeteria. Ryan grinned as he approached the judges' table. Alice clenched her fists, hoping for the best.

"My, my!" cheered Martha. "As the competition comes to a close, we have a very important announcement to make. First of all, let me tell you both how much I have enjoyed your meals today. You truly are a pair of talented students. Alice, your stuffed tomatoes were excellent, and

I can honestly say that they had the perfect amount of garlic. Ryan, your mozzarella sticks were to die for. What was the secret spice?"

"I can't say," said Ryan.

"Oh, chef's secret, I understand. However, it was marvelous. Who knew that mozzarella sticks could be so unique? No one's ever prepared them for me before because they can be so plain. But you! You made them extravagant! And, your Caesar salad was fantastic. It had just the right amount of dressing."

Ryan shot a dark glance at Leslie.

"And Alice, the minestrone soup was amazing," said Martha. "Now, the entrees were exceptional. The baked ziti was very unique, Ryan. I notice you used a blend of six different cheeses, quite impressive. Alice, your lasagna was a delight, and I was quite surprised at how beautifully the sauce mixed in with the cheese. Finally, the desserts were outstanding!" Martha's voice became higher in pitch.

"Alice, your traditional Italian Wedding Cake was lovely. I particularly liked the chocolate that you used." Niroo smiled, pretending Martha had spoken directly to him. "But I must say, Ryan stole the show in round four! The Leaning Tower of Pisa? Honestly, it was pure genius! I must tell you, though, the judges and I had to review the camera's tape to see how Ryan created his dessert. Upon review of the footage, they proved that Mr. Rivera did create the cake on his own, with *our* ingredients and without cheating. Of course, we did not suspect any foul play, but for the sanctity of the competition, we had to double check."

Alice scratched her head. *Did Ryan make it on his own?*

"Now," continued Martha, "I must announce the winner of the cook-off. Based on the categories of taste, quality, and originality, the winner of the fifteenth annual Weddingsworth Cook-Off Challenge is...Ryan Rivera!"

The cafeteria echoed with applause as Ryan took a huge bow. Alice clapped, but lowered her head. Martha rushed next to Ryan and handed him an enormous check made out for twenty-five thousand dollars. Ryan snatched the check and clapped in approval.

"Come on guys, we better go clean up," said Alice, heading for the kitchen.

"Hey, you gave it your best shot. Second place isn't so bad," said Niroo.

"Second out of two," said Alice.

"Seriously, though, Niroo and I are only here because you asked us to be. Martha Weddingsworth didn't. Hell, she doesn't even know our names, but she knows yours. That's pretty cool," said Nikki.

Alice grinned. "Thanks for all your help."

Alice, Niroo and Nikki began cleaning their cooking stations. Despite the outcome of the competition, Alice still felt uneasy. Something didn't seem quite right and she trusted her instincts.

Jenn

"Scott, here they come!" Jenn exclaimed.

"Just remember to relax. Don't seem too eager for the judges."

A teenage boy and an older woman walked toward Scott and Jenn's lab station.

"You have the key?" asked Scott.

"It hasn't left my hand," said Jenn.

The judges arrived.

"Good afternoon, Mr. Meyers and Ms. Andrews," said the woman. "I'm Cheryl Wesman, and this is my son, Ruepess Wesman."

Ruepess stuck out his hand. "Nice to meet you! Nice to meet you! Just call me Rue," he smiled, his dimples sinking into his chubby cheeks.

"Good afternoon," said Jenn.

"So what have you brought for us today?" asked Cheryl.

"Mr. Meyers and I have created an incredible vehicle, one that we would hope to see other people using in the near future," said Jenn. "A cross between a jet and an automobile, I give you, our hovercraft. We call it the Air Taxi."

"And what is so special about this hovercraft?"

"Aside from the obvious feature that it can attain stability above the ground, the Air Taxi is one-hundred percent environmentally friendly. We've created a new fuel blend of high-grade alcohol that sustains the vehicle. A titanium machine that can power over two hundred miles per hour," said Scott.

"Why did you choose to make it go so fast?" asked Rue.

94

"Just for the sake of doing it. We experimented to see how far we could take our invention, and because of its aerodynamic shape, the vehicle was able to attain such high speeds. Anyone who pilots this machine must be a very cautious and experienced driver," said Scott.

"May we see a demonstration?" asked Cheryl, her tone indifferent.

Jenn hopped into the driver's seat and placed the key into the ignition. She pulled her aviator goggles over her eyes and turned the vehicle on. The hovercraft hummed, slowly rising off the ground.

"You can hardly hear the engine!" exclaimed Rue.

At that moment, another one of Zeus' lightning bolts came shooting into the earth's atmosphere. The large bolt morphed into an energy beam as it rocketed towards the science hall. Jenn was about to turn off the hovercraft when the beam zipped into the building, striking her in the chest. Instantaneously, the vehicle lost control and began waving through the air.

Jenn sat stunned as the car swung wildly, its switches and gages beginning to spark. The Air Taxi whizzed toward the science hall's ceiling. Cheryl and Rue ran away from the machine.

"Turn it off!" yelled Scott.

Jenn couldn't see. She was blinded by a white light.

"Jenn! Turn it off!" Scott repeated.

After a few moments, the white light disappeared and Jenn's vision restored. Immediately, she flipped a few switches, held onto the steering wheel and tore the key out of the ignition. The car fought back, bucking like a horse. Then, the machine began to falter, calming itself to a halt as if it had been tranquilized.

Jenn unhitched her seat belt and exited the vehicle, her chestnut colored hair in disarray.

"What happened?" asked Cheryl.

"I, I don't know!" Scott exclaimed.

"A malfunction of some type caused an electrical surge that temporarily knocked the gyroscope out of balance," said Jenn. "The gyroscope controls the stability of the hovercraft. Immediately recognizing the gyro imbalance, I was able to adjust the controls and override the malfunction, getting the vehicle back under control. Letting the craft rest for about twelve hours should give the system enough time to recharge and correct the malfunction. The Air Taxi will be ready to go in no time!"

"Wow!" shouted Rue. "That was incredible!"

Jenn nodded. "Thank you."

"*Thank you,* Mr. Meyers and Ms. Andrews. Despite your invention's bad temper, it was an impressive presentation. Well done," said Cheryl.

Jenn and Scott shook hands with Rue and Cheryl. Once the judges had moved on to the next lab station, Scott looked at his girlfriend.

"How did you know that?! That was mind-blowing! That was *beyond* mind-blowing! I had no clue as to what had happened to the Air Taxi, and there you were, absolutely calm and in control. Genius…greater than genius!"

"It just popped into my head. I just, knew it!" Jenn

exclaimed.

"For a hot second I thought we were finished, but now I think we're back in the game!"

Jenn set down her goggles. She studied the Air Taxi, running her hand across its side. The vehicle remained still.

A few hours later, the judges finished examining all of the experiments and inventions. Cheryl Wesman made her way to the podium. She turned on the microphone, a bronze trophy in hand.

"Good afternoon, ladies and gentlemen. After thorough examination of each of your inventions, the judges and I have agreed upon the winners. It is my honor, to announce the third place winner of the science fair. Third place is awarded to Spencer O'Neil, inventor of the Automatic Toothpick."

The crowd applauded as a young man walked onstage. Rue made his way to the podium holding a silver trophy.

"All right, it's my turn," he grinned. "Second place, which coincidentally was my favorite invention of the day, goes to Mr. Scott Meyers and Ms. Jenn Andrews, inventors of the Air Taxi! Despite the mishap with the vehicle, it was profoundly impressive. You definitely caught our attention."

Scott and Jenn hurried onto the stage and accepted the award. Jenn smiled at Scott, holding his hand as they descended the steps.

"Second place, not too shabby," she sighed.

"And with the way the Air Taxi acted, I would have been happy with tenth!" said Scott.

Cheryl Wesman retook the microphone.

"Finally, this year's first place trophy is awarded to Preston Flowers and Greta Rudolph, inventors of the Multilingual Hat! Put on the hat and speak into its built in microphone. Any language you wish to speak will emit through its amplifier. Well done!"

Preston and Greta flew onto the stage as everyone applauded.

"With that, we conclude the science fair. Congratulations to all of our winners, and thank you to everyone who participated. We look forward to next year's competition."

Izzy

"Hurry, Ms. Izzy! They're coming quickly!"

Izzy walked onto the stage and looked out into the audience. From the bright lights, it was difficult to see, but she was able to make out lines of adolescents and children piling into the rows. Izzy walked behind the red curtain. Natalie joined her, both waiting for their instructions.

"Okay ladies, I'll go out and captivate the audience with a few simple tricks, introduce myself and then we'll get started," said Mario. He wore a royal blue robe, a wand in hand.

When every seat had been filled, the house lights were dimmed, and Mario walked onstage.

"Good morning, ladies and gentlemen, children of

all ages! I am Mario the Magnificent!"

The lights above the stage flickered on, illuminating the room in a blue glow. Mario waved his wand and a bouquet of flowers appeared out of thin air. Then he pulled a white rabbit out of his black top hat, presenting it to the crowd. At once, the audience began to *oo* and *ah*. They watched as the magician took a deck of cards out of his back pocket and tapped them twice. The cards expanded to four times their original size, engulfing his hand.

After the opening tricks, Izzy watched from the side as Natalie lay down in a rectangular box. Mario approached Natalie with a pointed saw. He leaned over her body and began slicing away. Once he had cut all the way through, Mario split the box, revealing that the assistant's legs were no longer connected to her torso. The crowd was stunned. Their cheers grew louder as Mario bowed.

Before Izzy knew it, it was time for the grand finale. Natalie wheeled a giant cloth-covered box onstage. Mario rolled his sleeves and stretched out his hands.

"Ladies and gentlemen! It is time for the spectacular grand finale! Watch as I make my lovely assistant, Ms. Izzy Itello, disappear before your very eyes."

The audience buzzed with excitement.

"Ms. Izzy, if you would please step forward."

Izzy waved to the audience.

"Ladies and gentlemen, I give you, the Disappearing Closet."

Mario pulled a blue cover from the portable closet. Izzy stepped inside and waved to the crowd again. Then, Mario shut the door and gave Izzy a few moments to "disappear."

The room was small and black, bad for any claustrophobic. In the back of the closet was a screen. Izzy lifted the screen and then brought it back down when she was secured behind it. It kept her hidden, giving the illusion that she had disappeared.

Three taps sounded on the door, and Mario shouted the magic word.

"*Alakazam!*"

The door to the closet flew open and the room was empty. The auditorium burst into applause.

Izzy began to giggle, her voice overpowered by the audience's cheers. For a few moments, the door was left ajar, until the crowd settled and Mario gained their attention.

"Now I shall bring Ms. Izzy back. She will reappear at this very moment!"

The crowed silenced.

When the door shut, Izzy lifted the screen. Once she was in front of it, she waited for Mario to open the door.

Just then, another lightning bolt flew into the earth's atmosphere. The golden beam aimed at the auditorium and snuck its way into the very box where Izzy was stationed. She felt a sudden jolt shoot through her body.

Instantly, Izzy felt faint. Her knees buckled

beneath her and she fell to the floor.

Another three taps sounded on the door.

Uh-oh, Izzy thought. She was too woozy to stand up.

"Alakazam!"

Mario touched the box and an electric shock stung his hand. He ignored the shock and opened the door.

SMACK!

Mario closed the door.

The audience gasped in confusion. Izzy shook her head, brushing off her wooziness as best as she could. She pushed herself off of the ground, holding onto the walls for support.

I've got this, she thought.

Mario looked nervous. Anxiously, he rubbed his hands together and knocked on the box three more times.

"AL-A-KA-ZAM!" he bellowed, slowly annunciating each syllable.

The door creaked open and Mario peered inside. To his relief, Izzy was smiling back at him. The crowd cheered wildly as Izzy stepped out.

"Thank you!" said Mario. "I would like to thank all of you for coming out today, and I hope you enjoyed yourselves as much as I have."

Mario took a final bow and held Izzy and Natalie's hands.

As the magic show came to a close, the audience members began heading for the exits. Mario turned to his assistants.

"Thank you, ladies! I am so happy with how the show went. Everyone was thrilled! I saw no frowns!" Mario shook the girls' hands.

"No problem. It was a blast!" said Izzy.

"Yes, it was great," said Natalie.

Mario glanced at Izzy. "Ah, Ms. Izzy, I must ask. Did you have difficulty with the screen inside the disappearing closet?"

"The screen wasn't the problem. I fell after I stood in front of it to make my reappearance."

"Really? You were in front of the screen when you fell? When I opened the door I didn't see you at all. I thought you were still hiding. It must be my terrible eyes. They're tricking me more and more every day!"

"Yeah, sorry about that," said Izzy.

"No, no, Ms. Izzy, my apologies. I should have seen you. Are you all right?"

"Oh yeah! I'm fine. I'm just glad I didn't ruin your show."

"You could never ruin my show. You made it spectacular!" Mario raved.

"Thanks, Mario," Izzy grinned.

A few moments later, Natalie and Izzy went to the dressing room to return their costumes. On the way out, Izzy took a final glance into the giant mirror and struck a playful pose. Once finished, she grabbed her bouquet of flowers, leaving the auditorium in search of her favorite TV weatherman.

Colleen

After the halftime show, the marching band made its way back to the sideline. Colleen settled into her seat as the home team tunnel began to fill. The football players ran onto the field, triggering a roar throughout the stadium.

"All right, second half!" said Chandler.

"Let's see if you can predict our first offensive play," said Lewis.

"Are you kidding me? That'll be an easy one."

"Yeah, that's true. They'll get the opening kickoff and then get tackled a few seconds later," said Colleen.

"Then predict the second play," said Lewis.

"Okay, okay. Check this out," said Chandler. "After the Trojans punt to us, Reynolds will pass the ball to the halfback, Tim Nickels. Nickels will run down the left side of the field, dodge the defense, and outrun everybody. I guarantee we'll get the touchdown."

"I bet you twenty bucks that doesn't happen!" grinned Lewis.

"Deal."

Chandler and Lewis shook hands.

Lewis glanced at Colleen. "You want in on this bet too?"

"Nope, I'm good."

The second play began. Reynolds gripped the ball, searching for an open receiver. Tim Nickels dashed to the left side of the field and turned around. Reynolds saw his opportunity and threw the ball in a perfect spiral. Nickels caught it, dodged each of the defenders and crossed the goal line.

Chandler threw his arms into the air as Lewis' jaw fell to the ground.

"That's twenty bucks, mate!"

"What?" Lewis groaned. He reached into his back pocket and pulled out his wallet.

Suddenly, another lightning bolt was released from the universe. The energy beam flew into Odyssey Stadium, aimed at its target. With a burst of power it pierced into Colleen, knocking her backwards. Chandler grabbed her, helping his friend regain her balance.

"She's so thrilled that she's falling over!" Chandler laughed.

At the same moment, in the excitement of scoring, one of the drummers picked up his bass drum and threw it toward the field. Lewis turned around just in time to knock Chandler out of the instrument's way.

"Colleen, watch out!" Lewis shouted.

Colleen watched as the drum flew toward her. Reflexively, she reached out, snatching the drum in midair and securing it in her arms.

Colleen looked in the direction that the drum had fallen.

"Are you crazy?" she shouted at the drummer, her black and auburn hair whipping in the wind.

Terrified, the drummer ducked behind his fellow band mates. Colleen set the drum on the ground.

"Since when are the percussionists above us?!" she barked.

"Dude! That was amazing!" squealed Chandler, picking himself off of the ground. "That was the most exciting thing I've seen all day! Even better than the game!"

"Nice catch!" said Lewis.

"Are you two all right?" asked Colleen.

"Magnificent!" said Chandler. "Those are some mad catching skills you've got there! And nice save, Lewis."

"Thanks," said Lewis. "Don't worry, I wouldn't let a loose drum kill you."

"Good to know, good to know."

"I think I'm gonna go have a word with that idiot," Colleen huffed, pushing past Chandler.

Lewis grabbed her arm.

"Are you sure? By the looks of things, he's long gone. You'll have a better chance of catching him at practice on Monday."

"Lewis is right. Chill out and enjoy the rest of the game. Worry about that fool later. I'll bring my camera so we can film the fight!" said Chandler.

Reluctantly, Colleen retreated to her seat.

"All right," she sighed.

Chandler looked around. "Now who wants to make a bet on the next play?"

* * *

Cronus left the volcano, the steam already beginning to rise. As he walked away, the base of the volcano roared. Cronus looked at the crater. The land was shaking. Suddenly, a vicious burst of lava erupted into the sky. Explosions of red and orange rained on the ground. A swarm of dark clouds rolled out of the crater. Within the clouds, the black creature broke free, roaring as it sped for the portal.

Cronus smirked. The deed was done. It was time to retreat to the mountain.

CHAPTER SEVEN

Celebrate

Colleen was sitting on the couch in her dorm. Her feet were raised on a footstool as she read the *New York Times*. She had the entire suite to herself, except for Melanie, who was in her bedroom getting cleaned up to go out and celebrate the track team's victory. All was silent and calm.

BANG!

Colleen jumped from her seat. She watched as Alice barreled into the room, slamming the door into the wall. Alice threw her backpack onto the kitchen counter and puffed out her cheeks.

"Cook-off didn't go so well?" Colleen asked hesitantly.

"No," said Alice, taking a deep breath. "You know, I can handle losing, I really can. But there is something very, *very* fishy about what that man...what that imbecile did today!"

Colleen patted the cushion beside her. "Come over here, sit down."

Melanie poked her head into the lounge, curious about the commotion.

"So, what happened?" asked Colleen.

"Everything was going smoothly and everyone was working hard. After two and a half hours of cooking, it was time for the judges to taste the meals and then of course, pick the winner. Both Ryan and I came out with our dinners and presented them, course by course. When it was time for the big finale, the desserts, I brought out my Italian Wedding Cake. Ryan had created the same thing, which was fine. The only problem was that Ryan's cake was an identical replica of the Leaning Tower of Pisa!" Alice threw her hands into the air, her eyes bulged. "A two foot tall, hand-crafted copy of the *Leaning Tower of Pisa*! This thing was absolutely perfect, identical in every detail and tilted to the same degree. The judges were amazed and Rivera won because of his creation."

"Is that bad?"

"Well, yes and no. Honestly, it was pretty impressive, but there is no way that *anyone* could have made something so precise and challenging within the time limit. He had to have practiced that before, had to have known what the theme was or had a picture of the building conveniently on hand," said Alice.

"Are you sure he cheated?" asked Colleen.

"Yes! Well, no. But I *really* think that he did. Seriously, who can make the Leaning Tower of Pisa on the spot?"

"And nobody caught him?"

"No. The judges made sure that there was no foul

play. They declared that he won with his integrity intact."

"Maybe he didn't cheat," Colleen said cautiously. "Maybe he *could* do it on the spot."

Alice paused. "Now I know why I had that dream last night. It was a premonition forewarning me of the death of my cooking career!"

"I doubt that your cooking career is over. You may be working at Coney Island until you retire, but you'll still be a chef," smiled Colleen.

Alice laughed, her face softened.

"Hey! Maybe if you're lucky you could work at Denny's!" said Melanie. "They're open twenty-four-seven and have an incredible breakfast menu. I would definitely come and support you."

"Thanks Mel, but I'm more of an IHOP girl," said Alice.

Alice was finally relaxed. She unfolded her arms and leaned on the couch. "Hey, how'd your track meet go?"

"Amazingly!" cheered Melanie. "We made it to Nationals!"

"Congratulations!"

"Thanks. I'm going out with the four-by-four squad to celebrate. You guys are more than welcome to come."

"Oh, I don't know," sighed Colleen. "My feet hurt from all that marching today. I think I'm gonna pass."

"Yeah, and I think I'll just chill out here and watch some Oprah," said Alice.

"Suit yourselves," said Melanie. She pulled her head back into the bedroom, resuming her preparations.

Alice glanced at Colleen. "So where's Jenn?"

"In the astronomy tower with all of her science equipment. There's some type of eclipse tonight that she's ecstatic about."

"And Izzy?"

"With Jayden."

"Of course."

A light knock sounded at the door. Colleen stood up and opened it. She found Lewis and Chandler waiting eagerly in the hallway.

"Howdy!" said Lewis.

"What's up?" asked Colleen.

"Eh, we were in the neighborhood and thought we'd stop by for a quick sec," said Chandler.

"Oh, in the *neighborhood.* Your dorm is on the other side of campus. What's really going on?" Colleen giggled.

"We were actually on our way to that new café, Arcadia something. You wanna come?" asked Lewis.

"Sure! Just wait a second while I grab my purse," said Colleen, rushing to her bedroom.

"Purse? What's with women and their purses? Can't they just hide their money in a sock and take that with them? Honestly, that's why women get mugged. The thieves know exactly where to get the dough because they all keep it in their purse!" Chandler exclaimed.

Melanie approached the guys with a playful grin.

"I think we should buy you a purse for your

birthday," she teased.

"No thank you," Chandler politely declined. "And what are you doing tonight?"

"Why so curious?" asked Melanie.

"Just curious."

"I'm going out with the track team. We won the state race, and we're on our way to Nationals."

"I believe that deserves one heck of a celebration!" said Chandler. "How about you and I go celebrate sometime, one on one? Go watch a football game, share some nachos and a couple cans of Sprite."

Melanie smiled, leaning against the doorway.

"Hmm...I'd really like to, but I'm pretty much busy for the rest of my life," she teased.

"You'll squeeze me in one day. How's next Friday?"

"Busy. I've got to pack to go back home."

"Friday it is!" Chandler cheered.

Colleen entered the hallway, looking at Alice. "Do you want to come?"

"Sure. I thought your feet hurt?" said Alice.

"It's a miracle! They're all better! And I thought you had a date with Oprah," said Colleen.

"Good point. Should I go invite Jenn?"

"If you can pull her away from her lab stuff, sure," said Melanie.

"All right. Just give me a minute or two." Alice left the room.

"At least she's not going to get her purse," said Chandler, relieved.

"You guys can come inside. Relax for a moment," said Colleen, waving Chandler and Lewis into the lounge.

As the guys entered, they could hear another person's voice echoing down the hallway.

"And then I was like, that woulda been *your* face in the dirt had it been me you were trying to knock on the track! Boy, was I mad, cheating like that. But we got her! Well, Mel got her!" said the voice.

"Who is that?" asked Lewis.

Melanie grinned. "My amigos!"

A moment later, three faces filled the entryway.

"Hey, guys!" Melanie gestured them in.

"Hey, Mel," said L.B.

"You ready to go?" asked Kira.

"Yup. But, can we wait for Alice to come back? These guys are all going to Arcadia Café, so I figured we could go with them," said Melanie.

"All right, but that Felicia Turner better not be there," growled Mika, folding her arms.

"Calm down, Tyson. You showed her who's boss earlier," Kira laughed.

"Seriously! She's lucky that she didn't push Melanie onto the ground. It would have been all over," said Mika.

Alice entered the dorm. "Jenn's too busy. She said she'd pass."

"We better get going. I bet that place is gonna be jam packed tonight!" said Melanie.

"I've got your purse," said Colleen, handing Alice her bag.

Chandler rolled his eyes as he walked out of the door. Everyone followed.

* * *

Jayden and Izzy were at Arcadia Café, seated comfortably at a table for two. The lighting was dim and the speakers emitted a soft melody which hummed in the background. Paintings of Greece lined the walls, accompanied by a navy banner hung high, emblazoned with a golden Phoenix.

Izzy gazed into Jayden's eyes.

"It's perfect out tonight," she sighed.

Jayden grinned. "Perfect like you."

"I bet you knew it'd be this nice out, Mr. Weatherman."

"Actually, it wasn't supposed to be. I reported earlier that we'd see a thunderstorm tonight. I guess we got lucky."

"I guess so."

"So, how was the magic show?" asked Jayden.

"Fantastic! The entire audience loved it! My favorite part was getting to disappear," said Izzy. "What about the news? Did they announce the winner of the cook-off?"

"Yeah. Have you spoken with Alice yet?"

"No. Did she win?"

Jayden shook his head. "Ryan did."

Izzy's eyes lowered. "Oh man, I bet she's bummed. I'll have to bake her a cake or something."

Izzy looked at the entrance of the restaurant. To her surprise, in walked her roommates and their friends.

113

"Oh jeez. Look who's here," Izzy giggled.

"There goes the date," said Jayden.

"Maybe if we duck, they won't see us." Izzy crouched toward the floor.

"Or we could hold up our menus and pretend we're still deciding." Jayden raised his menu, covering his face.

"Too late."

Melanie had spotted Izzy and Jayden. The entire group approached their table.

"Hey! Look who it is!" said Chandler.

"Yeah. Imagine that, seeing *us* here," laughed Izzy.

"You mind if we join ya?" asked Colleen.

"Not at all. Pull up a seat," said Jayden.

The guys arranged a group of tables while the girls collected chairs. Chandler tried to sit next to Melanie, but Mika pushed him aside.

"Thank you!" Melanie whispered.

Mika winked.

A waitress came to the expanded group with a pen and pad in hand. She took everyone's order and then left for their drinks.

Lewis peered at Jayden. "So what's new with you, man?"

"Oh, you know; same old, same old. Just working at the news station. How about you?" asked Jayden.

"Eh, not much. Did you catch the game today?"

"Yes, sir! Phoenix, baby! It got close though. The last two minutes had me worried."

"Same here, but Chandler had it all figured out. He made three perfect predictions. Honestly, he had the plays

114

down to every pass and every tackle!" exclaimed Lewis.

"It's not that hard. You just have to know your players well," said Chandler. "Reynolds favors Nickels, and defense always runs toward the guy with the ball. It's what they're there for."

"Right, but you were dead on," said Colleen. "It was uncanny."

At the front of the restaurant, a large crowd piled into the entrance. Everyone at the table looked up and watched as a brown-haired young man swaggered into the room.

"Oh my god," Alice gasped.

Ryan Rivera stood meters away from her table.

"I gotta go!" Alice pushed back her chair and turned around.

"Wait!" Melanie stood in front of her. "Are you seriously going to let that fool ruin your night? You're here with your friends. Relax and enjoy yourself!"

Mika rose from her chair, her fists clenched. "You need someone to take care of him?"

"Mika! Sit down!" barked Kira.

Mika glared at Kira, slowly resuming her seat.

Melanie looked at Alice. "Seriously, chill out. What's the worst he could do?"

Alice sighed. "I'm sure he could think of something."

"If anything happens, you have us." Melanie waved her hand at their group, and everyone nodded in unison.

"All right, I'll stay." Reluctantly, Alice sat down.

"Is that Felicia Turner here?" asked Mika.

"Mika!" shouted L.B. "Felicia Turner is *not* here. Forget about her!"

"I'm just askin!"

The waitress returned to the table and served everyone their beverages. As requested, she brought a bottle of sparkling grape juice.

"Just in time!" said Chandler. He grabbed the bottle and poured everyone a glass.

Kira raised her drink into the air.

"In honor of today's events, I propose a toast!" she announced.

Everyone raised their glasses.

"Thanks to the determination, dedication and talent of Melanie, Mika and L.B., our relay team was able to take first at the Indiana State High School Track Meet. To running!"

"To Kira!" cheered Melanie.

"To football!"

"To the Phoenix!"

"To love!"

"To Ryan Rivera!" bellowed a voice.

Everyone looked up. Ryan wobbled toward them, an empty glass in his hand.

"And of course, to Ms. Alice Payton. Without her mediocre cooking skills, I wouldn't have had the delight of winning the extravagant Weddingsworth Cook-Off," sneered Ryan.

Alice watched Ryan in shock. Her cheeks flushed scarlet.

Chandler stood from his chair. "Get out, Rivera!"

"A friendly bunch," said Ryan, his eyes glazed.

"You've got ten seconds to turn yourself around before I take you out!" said Mika, her teeth bared.

"Just joining the party! Spending time with my dear friends is all." Ryan smirked, clumsily stepping toward the group.

"I'm warning you," growled Mika.

Melanie and Colleen stood in front of Ryan with Lewis right behind them. Alice was sitting at the table, her mind racing. Then, the manager of the restaurant rushed into the dining room.

"What's going on here?" she shrieked.

"Nothing. Ryan was just leaving," said Alice, standing from her seat.

Melanie shot a glance at Alice and then back to Ryan. Ryan's eyes were wide, a big smile stretched across his face.

"Good. I will not tolerate any physical or verbal abuse in this establishment. Either he leaves or you all leave. Make a decision quick before I kick you all out." The manager folded her arms.

Mika clenched both of her fists, itching to take a shot at Rivera. After a moment, Ryan spoke, his voice cracked.

"It attracts scum anyway. If I waste another minute of my life in this so-called *restaurant*, I might catch something."

"I'll walk you to the door, sir." The manager followed Ryan as he stumbled his way to the exit, leaving his glass on Alice's table.

"Man! Just one punch is all I'm asking for!" Mika exclaimed, banging her fist on the table.

"And ruin your chances of going to Nationals? Smart," retorted L.B.

"It'd be worth it."

Melanie glanced at Alice sternly. "You have to stand up to that guy."

"Back off a little. He caught me by surprise," said Alice.

"Come on guys, he's gone. Forget about it, and let's get back to celebrating!" said Colleen.

"Yes!" said Lewis.

"Fun date," laughed Jayden.

Izzy raised her glass for the final toast. "To friends!"

CHAPTER EIGHT

The Pentagram

As the sky darkened and the stars began to glow, Jenn waited eagerly for the lunar eclipse. She stood on top of the astronomy tower underneath the school's million-dollar telescope. Accompanied by her laptop, Jenn awaited the moment that the moon would disappear behind the earth's shadow. When the clock struck ten, she peered into the eyepiece. There was no sign of a shadow. For a while longer she watched the moon, eyes glued to the lens.

This isn't right, she thought.

Twenty minutes had passed and the moon was shining just as brightly as it always did. Jenn glanced at her watch and sighed. She gazed up at the sky only to see a few bright stars glistening back at her. Jenn noticed a couple of clusters huddled together.

One group in particular caught her attention. Five dimly lit stars were aligned in the formation of a pentagram. The points were equally distanced from one another. Jenn approached the telescope and pointed it in the direction of the formation. She magnified the lens to its greatest power and then looked through, gasping at what she saw. What had appeared to be a group of stars had actually been five large spheres.

It can't be.

She examined the figures closely, astounded at her discovery.

* * *

After the dinner at Arcadia Café, the group headed back to their dorms, ready to call it a night. Jayden walked Izzy home, behind Melanie, Colleen and Alice. When they arrived, the two hung outside, stalling their goodbye as the trio walked upstairs.

"Athens Hall, home sweet home," said Melanie, stepping into the lounge.

"So, tonight didn't end up so bad," said Colleen.

"Not at all. The best part was watching Ryan Rivera being escorted from the restaurant," said Alice.

"He's not all that, but he thinks he is," said Melanie.

"It's too bad his ego's got the best of him. Who knows? He might *actually* have the potential to be a decent guy," said Colleen.

"I doubt it!" Alice laughed. "The day that Ryan Rivera does something genuinely nice is the day that the world will explode!"

"Then we have nothing to worry about," said Melanie.

Izzy entered the room, her eyes dreamy. She set her purse on the counter and took a few deep breaths.

"Someone's happy," said Alice.

"Someone's in love," awed Melanie.

"Oh, sorry guys. Did you say something?" Izzy asked airily.

"Nope," giggled Colleen.

"Have a nice time?" asked Melanie, already knowing the answer.

"Absolutely! He's amazing," sighed Izzy. She closed her eyes, lost in thought.

Alice stepped toward the door. "All right, I'm gonna go down to the cafeteria. I'll be back in fifteen minutes."

"Dude! It's ten o'clock. Can't it wait for tomorrow?" asked Melanie.

"It could, but I'd rather go now. I left my chef's hat behind, and I'd like to get it tonight so I don't run into anyone in the morning."

"You should take someone with you," said Colleen.

"I'll go," said Melanie.

"Okay. Hey, Colleen, can you toss me my keys?" asked Alice.

Colleen picked up a golden set resting on the coffee table. "Catch!" She threw them at Alice.

"WHOA!"

The keys flew toward Alice dangerously fast, as if Colleen had shot them from a cannon. Alice threw her hands up, trying to protect her chest from the jagged bullets. A silver ball emitted from her hands and smashed into the keys, deflecting them toward Izzy.

"Move!" bellowed Melanie. She jumped over the coffee table and ran toward Izzy, reaching for the keys.

Melanie had jumped incredibly high and was running so fast that all Alice and Colleen saw was a blur.

"Ah!" Izzy jumped to dodge the keys.

Instead of falling back to the ground, Izzy remained stationed in mid air, her head almost touching the ceiling. Alice's eyes shot wide open.

"Izzy's floating!" yelled Alice.

The keys smashed into the wall, leaving a half dollar-sized hole next to the door. Instantaneously, Melanie collided with the wall and fell to the floor, her head throbbing from impact. Colleen stared at the hole, then gazed at her hands.

"Help! I can't get down!" yelped Izzy, kicking and grabbing at anything she could reach.

"I'll be back!" said Alice.

Alice bolted through a long glass tunnel connecting Athens Hall to the astronomy tower. She ran up a flight of stairs, reached the entrance to the roof, and burst through the door. Jenn flinched as the door banged open.

"Alice!" she gasped.

"You have to come downstairs now!" panted Alice.

"What's wrong?"

"Everything! Izzy's floating, Melanie ran into the wall, my hand made a silver ball and Colleen smashed my keys through the wall!" Alice huffed.

"Wait, what? Slow down, I didn't catch a word you said," said Jenn.

"Come on!" Alice grabbed Jenn's hand and dragged her down the staircase. They returned to the dorm room where they found Colleen and Melanie grabbing at the air. Izzy was nowhere to be found.

"Where's Izzy?" cried Alice.

"I'm right here!" Izzy was heard, but there was no sight of her floating friend.

"Izzy's invisible!" yelled Melanie.

"Invisible *and* flying!" Colleen added nervously.

"What?!" shrieked Jenn.

"You have got to be kidding me!" said Alice.

"I've got her!" said Colleen.

"Ouch!" yelped Izzy. "Loosen your grip!"

"Sorry! I don't know what's wrong with me!"

"I've got her too! What do I have?" asked Melanie.

"You've got my right arm, Colleen has my left leg," answered Izzy.

"Alice, Jenn, grab her other arm and leg," instructed Colleen.

"We can't see her," said Jenn.

"Just grab something!" Melanie barked.

Jenn and Alice rushed toward the invisible body. For a moment Alice's hand waved clumsily in the air until she hit Izzy's foot. Jenn did the same, running into Izzy's right arm.

"You've got me!"

"We gotta bring her down," said Jenn. "On the count of three. One, two…three!"

The four girls slowly pulled Izzy's body to the floor.

123

"I'm down!" Izzy exclaimed.

"We still can't see you!" groaned Alice.

"How do we fix that?" asked Melanie.

"I don't know...think visible thoughts," said Colleen.

"Think visible thoughts?" yelled Melanie.

"Actually, that might work. Do it, Izzy," ordered Jenn.

For a few moments longer, Izzy was still invisible. Then, in the blink of an eye, her tiny figure reappeared.

"I'm back!" Izzy cried.

Jenn was shocked. "What is going on?"

Frantically, the girls told Jenn what happened. When their story finished, Jenn froze, thinking to herself. After a moment she spoke.

"Mel, turn on the TV."

Melanie flicked on the television, which was set to the school news station.

"What's going on?" asked Izzy.

"Watch," said Jenn.

The news anchorman began a new stream of stories.

"In other news tonight, scientists have recorded a first in the history of the earth. The axis on which our planet is tilted is slowly shifting. Scientists estimate that if Earth continues to move in its new direction, we will start to witness severe climate changes within the next few weeks. As a result of the tipping of the earth, the lunar eclipse was not visible from North America. For all you moon lovers out there, be patient. We'll keep you posted on any further developments.

"The earth's new rotation can possibly be explained by a massive earthquake that hit Greece earlier today. Mount Etna in Sicily, which erupted without warning, may also have played a role in the shift. The earthquake measured seven-point-nine on the Richter Scale, destroying many houses and buildings. Fortunately, in both events few were injured, and no fatalities have been recorded." The reporter winked at the camera. "This is Brian Stevens, reporting live from O.A. News, keeping you up to date on world events. Now here's Lisa Lucket, with today's Weddingsworth Cook-Off Challenge."

"Turn it off!" Alice groaned.

Melanie shut off the TV.

"Ugh, it'll be winter in May," sighed Izzy.

"Trust me, that's *not* our biggest problem," said Jenn.

"What's going on?" Colleen asked cautiously.

"I'm not sure, but I have a bad feeling," answered Jenn. She picked up her cell phone and dialed Scott's number.

"Hello?"

"Scott! You have to come over to my dorm immediately. It's urgent," said Jenn.

"What's wrong?"

"It's too much to explain over the phone. Please just get here as fast as you can, and bring the Air Taxi."

"Okay. I'm on my way."

Jenn hung up the phone.

"Does the tipping of the earth's axis have anything to do with what just happened?" asked Alice.

"I don't know. I really don't," said Jenn.

"Then what's happening? The world's in chaos; *we're* in chaos!" exclaimed Melanie.

"Just wait until Scott gets here."

After two minutes, he arrived at the dorm.

"What's up?" asked Scott.

"Have you seen the news tonight?" Jenn questioned.

"Yeah. Why?"

"Did you catch the story about Earth falling off its axis?"

"Yeah. Weird, huh?"

"Definitely. Why would it do that?" asked Jenn.

"I'm sure there are plenty of reasons why, but I'm not aware of one specifically," said Scott.

"What would cause a volcano to erupt without a moment's notice?"

"Not sure."

"A random, severe earthquake in Greece?"

"I don't know, the movement of tectonic plates? Why is this so important? I know it's fascinating, but…" said Scott, his voice trailing into silence.

"This is why," said Jenn. "Alice! Think fast!" Jenn threw the TV remote straight toward Alice. Shocked, Alice threw up her hands in an attempt to guard her face. A silver ball jumped from her palms, blocking the channel changer and knocking it to the ground.

"Whoa!" yelled Scott.

"And that's not the end of it. I won't get her started, but Izzy can float *and* turn invisible. Melanie is supernaturally fast. And you see that hole?" Jenn pointed to the gap in the wall. "Colleen did that."

"Jenn!" Alice gasped. "It's from my dream!"

"What dream?"

"The one I told you about earlier. It's not exact, but the abilities are the same! They're powers!"

"You had a premonition?" asked Scott.

"I hope not," said Alice, "but this is very similar to what happened in my nightmare!"

Jenn stood silent for a moment.

"Scott, you have to see something else." She walked into the hallway and gestured for him to follow. Together, they ascended to the rooftop of the astronomy tower.

Jenn pointed to the sky. "Do you see those dull stars?" She outlined the formation with her finger.

"A pentagram," whispered Scott.

"Yes, but not just any pentagram. Take a look through the telescope."

Scott approached the eyepiece.

"They're not stars!"

"What do they look like?" asked Jenn.

Scott studied each of the figures.

"It can't be," he stuttered. "Planets?"

"Exactly what I thought."

"But how? They're completely off their orbits."

"The earth's off its axis."

"Mount Etna erupted."

"Greece had an earthquake."

"The whole universe has gone mad!" Scott exclaimed.

"And my friends have supernatural powers," said Jenn.

"What's your power?"

"I don't have one."

"Are you sure?"

"Well, it hasn't shown up yet."

Jenn raised her hand and waved it flimsily in the air. Nothing happened.

"So what's going on?" asked Scott.

"That's what I'm trying to discover," said Jenn. "There has to be some sort of connection between all of these events. I can understand one unusual thing happening, maybe two at the same time, but this is an overload of peculiar stuff. Coincidence? Definitely not."

"Well let's see. Which planets are off their orbits?" asked Scott.

"Mercury, Venus, Mars, Jupiter and Neptune."

"What about Saturn and Uranus?"

"They're fine."

"And Pluto?"

"It's not a planet anymore."

"But it still has an orbit." Scott looked into the telescope again. After a few moments, he found the former planet. "Looks all right to me."

"So what do Mercury, Venus, Mars, Jupiter and Neptune have in common with Earth?" asked Jenn.

"They're all planets," answered Scott.

"Obviously. Something deeper, though."

"They're off their orbits. Maybe the earth is too. Maybe we just don't know it yet."

"A change in orbit could lead to a change in the earth's axis," said Jenn.

"Something could have knocked them all off their orbits, a force possibly," said Scott.

"But Saturn and Uranus were untouched," said Jenn. "Whatever force moved Neptune and Jupiter would have had to affect Uranus and Saturn as well."

"True. The planets are in a formation, a pentagram. It's as if they were pulled together on purpose."

"Maybe they were. Where is the earth aligned with these planets?" asked Jenn.

"It looks as if we're right in the center. Earth would be the middle point to the pentagram."

"So the planets are surrounding us," said Jenn.

Scott nodded. "The planets are surrounding us."

* * *

Melanie, Alice, Izzy and Colleen waited anxiously in the dorm room.

"I have to go down to the dining hall now," said Alice.

"How can you go at a time like this? It'd be better if you stayed," Izzy protested.

"No. What's so different about going now or later? I'm leaving, and I'll be back quickly."

"I'm coming too," said Melanie.

"All right, let's go."

CHAPTER NINE

Typhon

Melanie and Alice were walking across campus to the dining hall. Street lamps guided their way through the dark.

"I can't believe we have powers!" Melanie exclaimed.

"Neither can I...I hope that Jenn's figuring this all out," said Alice.

"Me too. What do you think is going on?"

"Honestly, I have no clue. All I know is that last night I had a dream about us having powers, and today...we've got powers."

Melanie pinched Alice's arm.

"Ouch! What was that for?"

"Just checking to see if this was a dream."

Alice cracked a smile.

As Melanie and Alice moved closer to the dining hall, something caught their attention. In the distance, a glowing red and orange light came flickering into view.

"Is that fire?" asked Melanie.

"Looks like it. What's burning?" asked Alice.

Both girls followed the light. The fire settled in one spot, dancing brightly in the night. The flames looked as if they were floating, stationed a foot above the ground. Melanie and Alice approached the blaze. A few yards away, they heard a deep panting noise as if someone was breathing deeply over their shoulders. They turned around only to find the night's darkness behind them.

Melanie gazed into the fire. She reached out her hand and felt beneath the flames, patting her hand on a black scaly surface.

"Alice, there's something dark underneath it."

As she uttered her words the heavy breathing stopped.

Alice froze. "What's that?"

A low rumble broke the silence. Melanie jumped back. Instantly, the ball of fire flinched, moving higher.

"Mel, let's go!" Alice pleaded.

Melanie watched as the flames grew, splitting into countless upward paths. The rumbling grew louder as the fire illuminated a massive figure. Black scales glistened in the flickering light.

Standing before Melanie and Alice was a gigantic beast. The fire revealed its hundred heads, weaving into the sky, and its mammoth tail. Its fangs were razor sharp.

The beast growled, each of its mouths screeching in rage.

"Mel...RUN!" shouted Alice.

Melanie grabbed Alice's hand and the two began to sprint. The beast chased after them, hissing venomously. It whipped a group of its heads toward Alice and snapped at her body. Alice waved her hand at the beast's mouths. A silver ball emitted from her palm, shielding her body and pushing the heads away.

"Alice! You have to go faster!" said Melanie. "You're holding us back!"

"I'm trying! I wasn't privileged with the power of speed!" yelled Alice. "You have to go get help!"

"I'm not leaving you!"

"Mel, you have to! We need it!"

"It's suicide! I can't leave you!"

"Mel, go!" Alice pleaded.

Melanie pulled Alice into her arms. She took a forceful leap to the top of the dining hall and landed firmly on the roof. A brick wall surrounded a series of metal pipes and chimneys, hiding the girls from the creature's sight.

Melanie set Alice upright. "I'll be back. Stay hidden," she whispered.

Melanie jumped off of the building, landing gracefully on the ground. She escaped the sight of the dragon-like creature and sprinted into the dark.

Alice sat motionless behind the brick wall, her heart pounding in her chest. The screeching and roaring of the monster had ceased, and the only noise to be heard was Alice's heavy breathing. She could feel the vibrations of the beast's footsteps thundering on the ground. It shook the dining hall and all of its surroundings.

Suddenly, the vibrations stopped. Alice sat still, her hand cupped to her mouth. For a while, there was complete silence. Feeling secure, Alice slowly stood up. She peered over the brick wall and instantly regretted her action. Directly in front of her was a pair of glowing eyes.

The beast drew its head back, getting ready to strike. Alice screamed, running to the right of the wall. Several of the creature's heads crashed into the brick and followed behind her, fire shooting from its mouths. Frantically Alice ran, dodging the flying debris. With every step, another group of heads crashed through the structure, shattering the blocks and metal. Streams of fire trailed at her ankles.

Alice came closer and closer to the end of the rooftop. As she reached the edge, the beast came around the corner, snapping one of its mouths toward her. Instinctively, Alice created her silver force field, pushing the head away from her body. She turned back to her left but was blocked by the fallen bricks.

As Alice looked over the remaining part of the wall, she saw the beast preparing to make a final blow. Terrified, she took a deep breath and did the only thing she could think to do. Alice leapt off of the rooftop, plunging toward the ground. She shut her eyes and crossed her fingers for any form of luck.

THUD!

Alice opened her eyes. She found herself lying in a cotton seat, soaring above the ground.

"Catch your breath, bud!"

She looked up to find Colleen seated next to Jenn, who was piloting the Air Taxi.

"Where's Melanie?" panted Alice.

"Down below. Don't worry, she's got Izzy with her!" yelled Jenn.

The car flew around the dining hall toward the beast. Alice watched as Melanie ran on the ground and Izzy flew in the air, dodging the creature's snapping jaws and jets of fire.

"What are they doing?!" shrieked Alice.

"Stalling!" said Colleen.

"They'll get killed! We have to do something!"

"I'm working on it," said Jenn. She drove the craft toward Melanie, who was struggling to dodge the monster's claws and heads.

"Alice, shield!" ordered Jenn.

Alice raised her hands and generated another force field. The shield guarded Melanie, causing the creature to stumble on contact.

"Thanks, Alice!" said Melanie, weaving away from the monster.

Above Melanie, Izzy was flying in front of the creature's heads. She was toying with the beast by zooming in close to its jaws and waiting for it to lunge. As the monster snapped its mouth, Izzy flew backwards and blended in with the dark sky. The creature became enraged, thrashing its heads. Izzy took another swing at the beast, this time diving deeper toward its fangs. The black monster whipped one of its heads at her, crashing into her side. Izzy whizzed through the air toward the hovercraft.

"Izzy!" screamed Alice. She prepared to make another force field, but didn't need it. Colleen caught Izzy in her arms.

"What do we do to this thing?" asked Izzy.

"Kill it?" asked Colleen.

"Yes!" said Jenn.

"How?" asked Alice.

"Improvise!" said Colleen.

"We can't do anything to it or we'll get burned," said Izzy.

"Then extinguish the flames," said Jenn.

"With what?"

"Water!"

"There's a hose on the side of the dining hall," said Alice.

"That won't be enough," said Jenn.

"The school water tower," said Colleen.

"We can't break into that!" exclaimed Izzy.

"I can punch through it."

"And how are we going to explain that to the dean?"

"How are we going to explain *this* to the dean? We're fighting an enormous monster, for heaven's sake!" said Alice.

"Find another hose," said Jenn.

"There's a fire hydrant down below," said Colleen.

"Good. Anything we can get our hands on."

"Fire extinguishers!" said Alice. "I know where they are in the cafeteria."

"Here's the plan," said Jenn. "I'll drive us back to the dining hall. Alice, you get the fire extinguishers. Izzy, you take the hose and start spraying the beast's heads.

Colleen, you go to the fire hydrant, and I'll lure the creature toward you. Tear off the top and get this thing. Mel will get another hose, and we'll take it from there."

"Let's do it," said Colleen.

Jenn flew the hovercraft to the dining hall. Alice hopped out and rushed into the cafeteria. Izzy located the hose on the side of the building. She unraveled it quickly and flew toward the beast's largest head.

"Melanie!" called Jenn. "Go grab a hose! Start dousing the monster!"

"You got it, boss!" Melanie ran away from the creature. She returned a few seconds later with a green hose.

As Colleen reached the fire hydrant, Jenn flew the Air Taxi in front of the monster. The creature charged the hovercraft. Jenn maneuvered the car toward Colleen, the monster chasing behind.

"Now!"

Colleen smashed the lid of the fire hydrant and water shot into the air. It crashed into a group of the beast's heads, killing the blaze. Izzy and Melanie used the hoses, extinguishing more of the flames. Jenn flew the hovercraft toward the dining hall and landed near Alice, who was waiting at the entrance with two extinguishers in hand.

"Jump in."

Alice hopped inside and they flew toward the monster. Izzy and Melanie continued to dodge the beast's attacks, killing the flames with water.

"Jenn! This isn't enough. There's too much fire!"

yelled Izzy.

Jenn drove the Air Taxi toward the creature's heads. Alice flipped the nozzle of the fire extinguisher and held it tight, aiming the foam at the flames. Very slowly, some of the fire disappeared. Only three heads had been extinguished.

"Izzy's right," Alice whispered.

The monster whipped its tail toward the hovercraft. Jenn dodged it, evading the fire and tail at once.

"Alice, I'll shoot the extinguishers. Generate a silver ball and push the foam toward the creature. You got that?" asked Jenn.

"Yes."

"Izzy, Mel! Spray the hoses toward us!" Jenn shouted.

The girls followed her command.

Jenn positioned the hovercraft over the creature's body.

"Okay, Alice. Go!"

Alice raised her arms and flicked her hands. The silver ball formed out of her palms, growing larger and larger. Jenn took hold of one of the fire extinguishers and shot foam into the air. She waited until the force field was big enough and then motioned for Alice to let go.

"Now!"

Alice pushed with all of her might, aiming her power toward the dimming beast. The silver ball caught the foam from the extinguisher and the water from the hoses, magnifying in size. Rapidly, the ball reached the body of the creature. It exploded on contact, spreading the elements over the monster's body. The flames quickly died.

"Nice hit!" said Melanie.

"Watch your step!" said Jenn.

With a final screech, the creature crashed to the ground. Its entire body lay still. Every flame was gone.

Colleen gazed at the silent monster. "It's dead!"

Izzy landed next to her and leaned on her shoulder.

"We did it," she whispered.

In a slow, subtle movement, the creature lifted one of its heads from the ground. It kept silent, opened its mouth and snuck behind Colleen and Izzy. The monster drew its head back and shot straight for the two girls.

SMACK!

The Air Taxi rammed into the creature. The head fell to the ground. Without warning, the beast's body puffed into ash. The scales were gone, the heads had vanished, and the fire was extinguished. All that was left were its sandy remains covering the ground.

Jenn brought the hovercraft next to Izzy and Colleen, and Melanie jogged toward them. Everyone was frozen for a moment, unsure of what to say or how to react.

Slowly, Jenn lifted her head, her eyes heavy. "We should get back to the dorm. There's a lot of work to do."

"What was that thing?" asked Alice.

"Typhon."

CHAPTER TEN

M.A.J.I.C.

When the girls entered their dorm room, they found Scott seated at the kitchen table. He was hunched over, peering at a map with his glasses glued to his nose. At the sound of the shutting door he flinched in his chair and sighed.

"You're all right."

"For now," said Jenn.

"So what was it?" asked Scott.

"Typhon."

"Typhon, as in, Gaia's Typhon?"

"Yes," said Jenn. "The actual, living, breathing mythological monster."

"What's a Typhon?" asked Izzy.

"Do you know anything about Greek mythology?" asked Jenn.

"Not much."

"In Greek mythology, it's said that Gaia, the goddess of Earth, had a beast for a child. The beast, known as Typhon, was a monster with one hundred heads who could spit lava from his mouths. At some point in his life, Typhon tried to overthrow Mount Olympus. Zeus, the leader of the gods, threw a lightning bolt at the ravenous creature, keeping Typhon from reaching the mountain. Admitting defeat, the creature went into Mount Etna and is said to produce the lava that spills from its top."

"Mount Etna? The volcano that erupted earlier today?" asked Colleen.

"Yes."

"Wait a minute," Melanie interrupted. "You're saying that some *random* monster from *mythology* just showed up on our campus? Greek mythology is fiction, hence 'myth.'"

"So how do you propose that you became so fast?" said Jenn.

"I don't know."

"How does Izzy know how to fly? What else could that creature have been?"

"I don't know," Melanie repeated. "It's just…how can Greek mythology be real?"

"A myth is something that is either false or unproven. No one has ever proved that gods and goddesses, monsters and different worlds don't exist, which means that there's a possibility that they do. Give me proof that these supernatural beings are fake," Jenn challenged.

"No one's ever seen them."

"You can't see air, but you know it's there. And I don't know about you, but I saw that giant dragon thing outside. It looked pretty real to me."

Melanie was at a loss for words.

"What did you mean when you asked Mel how she became so fast? You think Greek mythology has something to do with our powers?" asked Alice.

"Definitely. Come take a look."

Jenn gestured for her friends to gather around the table. She unraveled a map of the academy's campus and set it next to the map Scott was studying, a map of the universe.

"Tonight as I waited for the eclipse, I noticed something peculiar in the sky. Five glowing figures were positioned in the formation of a pentagram, equidistant from one another."

Izzy glanced at Jenn, confused.

"Pentagram is another word for five pointed star," whispered Colleen.

Melanie shook her head. "Sometimes I wonder how you got into a school for special talents."

"Getting a high IQ score isn't the only special talent a person can have. And you're not exactly Steve Jobs either," Izzy said defensively.

Colleen nudged Mel, keeping her from retorting. All three refocused on Jenn, who hadn't missed a beat.

"I looked into the telescope and discovered that the figures were five of the eight planets, Mercury, Jupiter, Neptune, Venus and Mars," said Jenn. "The way in which they were ordered didn't make much sense, especially since Uranus and Saturn were still in their normal orbits. So Scott and I tried to piece together what these five specific planets have in common."

"We tried explaining a force that could have pulled them together, something so strong that it messed with the entire universe," said Scott, "but there wasn't anything that could have placed Neptune next to Jupiter and leave Uranus untouched. The two planets were too close together, so whatever grabbed one would have taken the other."

"Now, this may seem *out there*, but after seeing that creature, Typhon, this could very well be the answer we've been searching for," said Jenn. "Including Pluto, a former planet, there is something that all of the planets have in common. Each one has another name representing a mythical god or goddess from ancient Greece."

Jenn grabbed the map of the universe where Scott had drawn the pentagram. She took a pen and labeled each of the planets. The upper left point of the pentagram was marked 'Mercury', the top point 'Jupiter', the upper right 'Neptune', the bottom right 'Venus' and the bottom left 'Mars'. To the left of the pentagram was Uranus and to the right was Saturn.

"Now," continued Jenn, "Mercury is the planet of the god Hermes. Jupiter represents Zeus, Neptune identifies Poseidon, Venus is the goddess Aphrodite and Mars belongs to Ares. Uranus represents the god Uranus, and Saturn represents the god Cronus. Finally, Pluto, our outcast, signifies Hades. Now, if you take a look at *our* map, you'll notice something very interesting." Jenn pointed to Odyssey Academy's map and took hold of her pen. "Mel, you were at the track today, right?"

"Yes," Melanie affirmed.

142

Jenn scribbled on the map.

"Alice, you were at the cafeteria?"

"Of course," said Alice.

"Izzy, where were you earlier?"

"At the dorm, the auditorium, Arcadia Café," answered Izzy.

"The auditorium, for the magic show," mumbled Jenn. "And, Colleen, you were at the football stadium?"

"Football stadium, the dorm and Arcadia café," said Colleen.

Jenn laid the map on the table for everyone to see. On the paper were four dots labeled, Melanie, Alice, Izzy and Colleen.

"Alice, can you hand me a ruler and compass from that drawer?" asked Jenn.

Alice handed her the tools. Jenn used the ruler to connect the dots, drawing three perfect lines. She measured the line segments, each one coming out at the same measurement of six inches. Then, she measured the angles, calculating each to be at a perfect one hundred and eight degrees.

"What is it?" asked Izzy.

"This is the beginning of a regular pentagon. There are only four points, but one more will complete the shape," said Jenn. She took the ruler and drew the last two lines, intersecting at the final point.

"A regular pentagon has five equal sides with each angle measuring at one hundred and eight degrees," said Scott.

"And from a perfect pentagon, you can create a perfect *pentagram*," said Jenn.

Jenn connected the dots to form a five-pointed star.

Colleen gazed at the drawing. "We made a pentagram too?"

"Yes," answered Jenn. "Just like the planets."

"But who's on the last point?" asked Alice.

On the star, Melanie's name was positioned at the upper left vertex, Alice's at the apex, Izzy's at the bottom right corner, and Colleen's at the bottom left. The upper right vertex had no label.

"Wouldn't it be Jenn? It's right on top of the science hall," said Melanie.

"Exactly!" said Jenn. "At least it's what we think. During our presentation, the Air Taxi went haywire, and I lost control of it. But as soon as the hovercraft went berserk, I knew what had happened. It was weird. Without examining the machine, I already knew what the malfunction was. It was like knowing the cause of someone's death before an autopsy is performed. And by knowing what happened to the hovercraft, I was able to regain control of the Air Taxi before things got way out of hand."

"It was incredible! She probably saved our chances at placing in the competition," said Scott.

"So Jenn's super smart?" asked Izzy.

"Not to sound cocky, but yes, omniscient." said Jenn. "Now, ladies, this is very important. Did anything unusual happen while you were at each of these locations? It could have been something relatively huge or something

144

quite small."

All four thought in a moment of silence.

"Yes!" said Colleen. "At the football game, one of the percussionists threw his bass drum when we scored a touchdown. It hurtled at Lewis, Chandler and I, but I caught it before I could get out of the way. This drum was huge, but I held it in my arms as if it were light as a feather!"

"Mel, what about you? Did anything happen with speed?" asked Jenn.

Melanie's eyes shot wide open.

"Actually, yeah. I was running in the race with only about one hundred meters to go when all of a sudden I started sprinting insanely fast! I didn't just beat Felicia Turner, I *creamed* her and didn't realize it until I regained consciousness and Mika confirmed our win."

"Consciousness? You passed out?" asked Jenn.

"I collapsed right after the finish line. They kept me at the trainer's station for the rest of the meet."

Jenn turned toward Izzy. "What about you?"

"Um, nothing out of the ordinary. I went to the magic show and helped out with a few tricks." Izzy froze. "There is something! During the disappearing act, I fell right before Mario opened the door to show the audience that he could make me reappear. When Mario opened the box's door, he shut it right away. I thought he shut it because I was on the ground, but after the show he told me that when he looked into the closet, I wasn't there…but I was! I was invisible!"

145

"And Alice, what about you? There's a theme going on here with each of our powers. Did anything happen where you had to block something?" Jenn asked eagerly.

"Block something, block something," Alice mumbled. "I don't know if it counts, but at the cook-off, I felt like I got pushed in the back and kicked in the stomach. I fell forward, grabbed the pot of minestrone soup to break my fall, and when it started to spill I pushed off it so I wouldn't hit the stove. At the angle the pot was at when I pushed off of it, the soup should have spilled, but it didn't. I guess I protected it."

"But what does all of this have to do with the planets and gods?" asked Izzy.

"All right, here comes the missing link. At some point during the day, we were at these five locations at the same time, creating a pentagram." Jenn pointed to the academy's map. "At the same time our pentagram was formed, five of the planets were aligned in the same formation. Scott and I analyzed the planets, and we've discovered that Mercury is directly above the track, Jupiter is above the cafeteria, Neptune hovers over the science hall, Venus is above the auditorium, and Mars hangs over the football stadium. One planet was above each of us, perfectly aligned.

"Now, why this is all so important comes back to the planets' connection to the Greek deities. The five gods that are linked to the planets that overshadowed us all belong to a specific group called the Olympians. Hermes, Zeus, Poseidon, Aphrodite and Ares are Olympians. They

146

were seen as the heroes of all the gods. Supposedly, they keep the universe in order, as opposed to their nemeses, the Titans. There are only two planets that are named after the Titans, the bad guys, and they are Saturn and Uranus. Coincidentally, Saturn and Uranus are directly following their orbits and haven't moved. The only planets that have shifted are the ones belonging to the Olympians.

"So what I'm trying to say is that the Olympians' planets were directly above us today. We were in the formation of a pentagram, one of the most powerful ancient symbols that exists, at the same time that the good gods' planets were aligned in a pentagram, just above us. As you probably know, the gods had specific powers, abilities they used to control the universe. And now, we have supernatural talents that are similar to those of the gods. Guys, as simply as I can put it, the ancient Olympians have given us god-like abilities."

Jenn looked at her friends, wondering what they were thinking.

"Oh I get it, it's a joke!" Izzy laughed.

"Izzy, this isn't a joke," said Jenn.

"It has to be! It's the craziest thing I've ever heard!"

"Izzy, I'm serious!" exclaimed Jenn. "This isn't the time to mess around."

"You're telling me that some make-believe god has just given me a supernatural power?! What's next, a magical genie? I want my three wishes," Izzy teased.

"Izzy!" huffed Jenn.

"I'm with Izzy on this one," said Melanie.

"Guys, the Olympian planets formed a *pentagram*!" said Jenn, flustered.

"Planets move all the time. Just because the five planets that *happen* to represent the Olympian gods swirled around into a badly shaped circle doesn't mean that this has anything to do with Greek mythology," said Izzy.

"That's what I'm trying to tell you! This *didn't* just happen! Only the planets that depict the Olympians moved. The planets of the Titans haven't gone one millimeter off of their track! This wasn't some random thing that just happened. Everything happens for a reason, and I've figured out this phenomenon's purpose! You can fly, for heaven's sake! Explain that!" Jenn challenged.

Izzy stuttered for a moment, her mind was blank.

"See, you don't even have an answer, but I do!"

"What about Pluto?" Colleen interjected. "You said that Pluto represents Hades. Which set of gods does he belong to?"

"The Olympians," said Jenn.

"Then why didn't Pluto move?"

"I'm not positive, but I have a good theory. Hades is more of a neutral god. He's the king of the underworld. He probably doesn't mess with the whole good and evil thing. Plus, the pentagram is one of the most powerful ancient symbols. Add a sixth point, and it's no longer a pentagram."

"What's the significance of the pentagram?" asked Alice.

"To the ancient Greeks, it represents the elements

148

that make up man: air, earth, fire, water and psyche. But it means other things in other religions and cultures."

"Do you think that the Olympians gave us *their* powers?" asked Colleen.

"Partially. I believe that the Olympians sent us powers but not theirs specifically. Although Hermes and Melanie are both incredibly fast, Alice doesn't control thunder and lightning like Zeus does. Poseidon, god of the sea, has water powers whereas I'm just really smart. Our abilities are godlike but unique."

"When I kept the soup from spilling, I didn't see a silver orb," said Alice. "I don't know if there was a protective shield or not because my eyes were closed. Are you sure that's when I got my ability?"

"That could be why you can produce the silver shield," said Jenn. "Melanie was running while she got her power, and now she's supernaturally fast. Izzy was doing a disappearing act when she turned invisible, and I was at a science fair, presenting a high-tech project, when I became omniscient. At the exact moment you pushed off of the pot, you got your powers. Same with Colleen. When she caught the bass drum, that's what triggered her to become incredibly strong. What we were doing at the moment we got our powers determined what we can do now."

"So hypothetically," said Izzy skeptically, "*if* the Olympians sent us powers, why did they?"

"Because of Typhon. They probably saw where he was headed and distributed abilities so that someone could destroy him," said Jenn, pleased that Izzy had stopped protesting.

"Why wouldn't they take care of it themselves?" asked Melanie. "They're the gods; they should know how to handle these situations."

"What if they couldn't?" said Alice. "What if they had to send us powers because they had their hands tied?"

"We got rid of the monster. Why do we still have our powers?"

"Maybe we're not done," said Jenn.

"What about the earthquake and the tipping of the earth's axis?" asked Colleen. "Could those have something to do with all of this?"

"They could and they couldn't. I haven't figured those out yet," said Jenn.

"What about my dream?" Alice asked anxiously. "These powers are from the nightmare I had last night."

"I was thinking a premonition," said Scott.

"A premonition or a warning from the gods. We'll see if you have any more and take it from there," said Jenn.

"I'm still not sure about this," said Izzy. "It just seems so unrealistic."

"Time will tell," said Jenn, "but I encourage you to trust me. Something's up, whether we can accept it or not. We just have to make sure that we're prepared for whatever happens."

Melanie looked at the map, observing the vertices of the star. She made a connection and grinned at her discovery.

"Guys, look!" she exclaimed. "It's magic. Magic with a J."

"What?" asked Alice.

"Our names," said Melanie. She took the pen and circled the first letter in each of the girls' names. "M, A, J, I, C. We're M.A.J.I.C.!"

CHAPTER ELEVEN

Gadgets and Gizmos

During the night, Alice drowsily ventured to her bed and settled in. When she awoke in the late morning, she walked into the kitchen, her eyes drooping. In the dorm, all was quiet. Melanie and Colleen were asleep in their room, but Alice wasn't sure about Izzy or Jenn. Quietly, she peered into their bedroom, finding both beds empty. Alice closed the door and went to the kitchen cupboard. She grabbed a box of cereal and poured herself a bowl.

Ready to relax, Alice hopped onto the couch with all of her weight. Oddly, she didn't land on the cushion but rather on top of a strangely shaped lump that she hadn't seen. As Alice made contact with the lump, she heard a painful yelp.

"Ah! Alice!" a voice shrieked.

Something moved beneath her.

"Izzy?"

"Yes! Get off!"

As she spoke, Izzy became visible, revealing that Alice was seated on her back. Alice jumped off, spilling milk from the cereal bowl onto the carpet.

"Sorry, Iz! You were invisible."

"That's okay. You wouldn't have done that if you could have seen me, I assume," said Izzy.

"Yes, that's correct," Alice giggled. "What are you doing out here invisible?"

"I didn't mean to. I fell asleep on the couch last night, and I guess my powers decided to kick in."

"Jenn will probably know how to keep that from happening. Speaking of Jenn, do you know where she is?"

"That note may help," said Izzy. She pointed to the door where a piece of paper was hanging.

Alice grabbed the note and read it silently.

Hey guys,

Grab something quick to eat and then come down to the science hall. Scott and I will be in our lab, which is room 56A. Don't let Melanie sleep past noon.

- Jenn

P.S. Don't use your powers in front of anyone, even Jayden Kinney.

"She's at the science hall," said Alice. "We have to go there when the other two get up, and she says not to use our powers in front of anyone, including Jayden."

"All right," said Izzy. "Should we wake them up?"

Alice smirked. "I have an air horn."

"Let's do it!"

The girls tiptoed into Alice, Melanie and Colleen's bedroom, rummaging through Alice's dresser in search of her air horn. When they found the device, Izzy grabbed it.

"Just push the button and plug your ears," said Alice.

When Izzy pushed the button a deafening blast shook the room. Startled, Melanie fell out of her bed and crashed to the floor, her dark hair tangled in front of her face. Colleen grabbed her pillow and covered her ears.

"Good morning!" Alice and Izzy smiled. Colleen glared at them both as Melanie scrambled from the floor to her bed.

"It's eleven! Too early," Mel cried.

"Yes, but we've got places to go, people to see," said Alice.

"Places to go, people to see, *after* noon!"

"It's Sunday. I've got nothing planned," said Colleen.

"Now you do!" Izzy chimed. "Get up, get up, get up! Jenn wants us down at the science hall."

"Five more minutes," Melanie argued.

"Science hall?" asked Colleen. "What for?"

"We don't know, but we'll find out when we get there," said Alice.

"Come on!" Izzy pleaded. She hopped on top of Melanie's bed and jumped on the mattress.

"Okay, okay, okay," said Melanie. "I'll be ready in

a few minutes."

Izzy and Alice waited outside of the room. Soon enough, Colleen and Melanie emerged. Together the girls walked through campus and made it to the science hall, which was buzzing with noise. The circular show room where the science fair had been held the day before was almost empty, but the hallways that led to each lab room were overflowing with people. Students with pristine lab coats walked past, holding beakers and clipboards.

"It's a building full of Jenns," said Melanie.

"What was her room number?" asked Colleen.

"Fifty-six-A," answered Alice.

The girls approached lab room 56A and knocked on the door. Jenn scurried to the entrance.

"Hey, guys! Come in."

They piled into the room, staring in amazement. In the lab, Jenn had everything from welding equipment and fireworks to a physical display of the elements and a lead box containing radioactive material. A set of high-tech laptops sat on a transparent desk where Scott was stationed, seated next to an entire wall of glass cupboards. The ceiling was painted in a mural of the universe, showing the sun, planets and constellations within a swirl of black and blue.

"Wow," said Colleen.

"Have you ever been here before?" asked Jenn.

The girls shook their heads.

"Well, this is my lab...I mean, *our* lab. It's pretty self-explanatory. We work with chemicals, experiment, explode things and make new discoveries. I have to say

I'm a little surprised you're here before noon."

"Me too," mumbled Melanie.

Izzy and Alice laughed.

"It's amazing what a single toot of an air horn can do," said Izzy.

"I see," Jenn grinned. "Well, anyway, it's good you came. The sooner the better. Come over here and take a seat."

Jenn led her friends to an island counter in the middle of the room. Each person took a stool and sat down. Scott stood next to Jenn.

"To go along with our powers, Scott and I have made a few inventions that we think will help." Jenn reached under the counter and pressed a green button. A round shelf appeared from the center holding a pair of running shoes.

"My spikes!" said Melanie.

"Yes, but they're not ordinary spikes anymore. Try them on."

Melanie grabbed the blue and gray shoes. The outline of a lightning bolt had been engraved on each side. Once the spikes were on, Melanie began to walk. They felt normal, as if nothing had changed. Then, Melanie began to sprint. The instant she shifted gears from a walk to a run, the metal spikes within the shoes popped out, gripping into the tile floor.

"Whoa! What did you do?" asked Melanie.

"We fixed your shoes so that the moment you begin running, the spikes poke out, giving you the best traction so that you can reach your fastest speeds," said

Scott. "When you're walking, the spikes retract back into the sole."

"These are fantastic!"

"I'm glad you like them." Jenn turned toward Alice. "For *you* we made something else." She pushed a second button, which revealed a shelf containing a pair of leather gloves. The gloves were predominantly gray with a magenta stripe diagonally set above each knuckle. The palm had a pentagram, outlined in silver, and the tips of each finger were cut off, exposing Alice's fingertips.

Alice put on the gloves, breaking in the leather.

"These will give you the best grip on your force field," said Scott. "Just aim and hold."

Alice held up her hands and generated a silver ball. It magnified in size and force.

"I can feel it," said Alice. She played with the force field, mesmerized by its strength.

"And Izzy," continued Jenn, "you get something a little bit bigger."

Another circular shelf popped up from the counter, containing a folded outfit. Izzy picked it up and unraveled the clothes.

"A spandex suit?" she asked, embarrassed.

"Yes, but I promise it'll be helpful," Jenn assured.

The suit was just as long as Izzy was from the neck down, covering every inch of her body but leaving her feet and hands exposed. It was light yellow with a gray stripe on both sides, outlining the perimeter of her body. Next to the stripe on the pants was a small set of white wings, stitched into the fabric on the upper left side.

"This suit is form fitting and aerodynamic so you can fly faster," said Scott. "Plus you won't get it snagged on anything."

"There's a bathroom down the hall, go try it on," said Jenn.

Izzy took the suit and exited the lab.

"Next is Colleen. Yours is the simplest, but don't let the look fool you. You'll find this tool very useful and powerful."

From the counter, two bands of reusable athletic tape rose. They were dark purple with a hint of gray. On the tape were two flames that were to be centered on both of Colleen's palms.

"The flames represent defeating Typhon. The bands will give you support when you punch. Hopefully you'll be able to get the most momentum through these devices," said Scott.

Jenn walked to the back corner of the room and dragged a punching bag toward Colleen. Colleen set herself square in front of the target. She took a powerful swing and hit the bag dead center. It flew backwards, smashing into the wall and leaving a dusty imprint.

"That felt pretty good," said Colleen.

"You can do a lot of damage," said Jenn. "Be careful when you use it, and watch yourself with everyday actions. You don't want to break someone's back while giving them a hug."

"True," Melanie laughed.

A light knock came from outside the hall. A small hand waved back and forth in the window of the door, and

Alice went to greet the visitor. Izzy was in the hallway wearing the yellow and gray spandex suit.

"Does it look totally ridiculous?" asked Izzy.

"Not *totally* ridiculous," giggled Melanie.

"Looks all right to me," said Colleen.

"Is it too tight?" asked Jenn.

"No. It fits just right," said Izzy. "So what do I do with this?"

"Just hop into the air and try to fly. Or become invisible and see what happens," said Scott.

Izzy held her arms up. She took a small hop, trying to float. To her surprise, her flying tactic worked, and Izzy found herself suspended above the ground. Playfully, she flipped through the air. Then, she changed from visible to invisible, sneaking behind her friends and reappearing in front of their faces.

"Someone's having way too much fun with that," said Alice, amused.

Izzy retreated back to the ground.

Colleen looked at Jenn. "How'd you build all of this in one night?"

"With Scott's help, super smarts and lots of coffee."

"Did you make anything for yourself?"

"The Air Taxi is my gadget. I made a few adjustments on it last night. Check this out!" Jenn beckoned her friends to the side of hovercraft. The yellow M.A. logo that had stood for Meyers-Andrews now read M.A.J.I.C.

"Awesome!" said Izzy.

"So what is it all for?" asked Alice.

"The question I've been waiting for," said Jenn. "I've been thinking all night long about the connection between the eruption of Mount Etna, Greece's earthquake, the aligning of the planets and the tipping of the earth's axis. Mount Etna and the planets connect because of mythology, but the other two don't connect in the same way. There are numerous reasons why an earthquake could occur in Greece on the same day that the earth fell off of its axis, and the reasons may go together, but they also may not. So instead of guessing and trying to piece together an explanation based on theory, we're going to go and find out for ourselves."

"You mean go to Greece?" asked Melanie.

"Precisely. We are going to travel to the epicenter of the earthquake and see what evidence we can find. We'll check to see where the tectonic plates are, if buildings fell down, and how powerful the earthquake actually was," said Jenn, her face brimming with excitement. "And just in case we run into another Typhon, we'll have our new devices to help us."

"Another Typhon? You mean there's more of them?" asked Izzy, frightened.

"Not another Typhon, but if he exists, I'm guessing other mythical monsters exist as well."

"True," said Colleen.

"So when do we leave and how are we getting there? I'm pretty sure that's a long plane ride," said Alice.

"Ah, but we're not going by plane," said Jenn. She walked toward the back of the lab. To the left of the Air

Taxi, a large platform led to a drape-covered object. Jenn clutched the fabric and tugged. "Check this out. Our new method of transportation."

The cloth fell to the ground, revealing a metal archway. The archway was tall and wide. It was filled with a cloudy, purple and blue substance that cast a dim glow in the lab. The colors swirled within the arch, spreading in all directions while remaining within its boundaries.

"This, my friends, is our personal Transporter," announced Jenn. "Say goodbye to planes, trains, and automobiles because this will take you any place at any time."

"You...you built this last night?" asked Alice, stunned.

"Of course not. I've been working on this for over a year, preparing it for the science fair."

"But you didn't enter it into the contest," said Colleen.

"That's because it didn't work. But thanks to the intellectual boost I received yesterday, the missing link finally came to me," Jenn beamed.

"How does it work?" asked Melanie.

"Stand on the platform and think of where you want to go. Then, just walk underneath the arch and into the portal."

"So let's say I wanted to go to Mount Everest," said Colleen. "I'd just think of the mountain and walk through?"

"Yes, but I don't recommend going to a place like that. With the drastic difference in air pressure and oxygen levels, you wouldn't last very long."

"Right," Scott affirmed.

"You truly are super smart," Izzy marveled.

Jenn smiled "All right, go back to the dorm or do whatever you have to do, but make sure you're all well rested for tonight. At one A.M., we'll meet back at the lab and travel to Greece."

"We're going tonight?" asked Alice.

"Well, yes and no. It'll still be night here in the States but eight A.M. in Greece."

The girls became very quiet.

Jenn clapped her hands. "Okay, go take the day for yourselves and remember to come back at one."

"I guess we'll see you later then," said Izzy.

"Yeah, we'll see you soon," said Alice, heading for the exit.

The four girls filed into the hallway.

"I can't believe she's serious. I can't believe we're going to Greece tonight!" said Colleen.

"Oh, you know, it's a typical day. Everyone does it," said Melanie.

"And to think that at this time yesterday, the most exciting thing I had planned for the entire week was to perform in the magic show," said Izzy.

"I wonder if we'll actually find anything overseas," said Alice.

"I don't know, but we'll see tonight…or tomorrow morning, rather. You know what I mean," said Colleen, scratching her head.

The girls exited the science hall and went their separate ways. Each person was ready to go through her normal Sunday routine. All were anxiously awaiting the adventure that lay only hours ahead.

CHAPTER TWELVE

The Oracle of Delphi

Later that night, the five roommates ventured toward the science hall. The sky was pitch black and the only lights on campus were the flickering street lamps. Stars were visible, and the pentagram formation could be seen past the clouds.

The girls approached the science hall.

"This doesn't feel right," whispered Izzy. "It feels like we're breaking and entering."

"Izzy, I have keys. We're not breaking in," said Jenn.

"You're still entering! It's half a crime!"

"That's not a crime! If it was, it'd be totally bogus!" Melanie exclaimed. "Imagine asking your mom if you can have the last cookie in the cookie jar, her saying yes, and then later you get in trouble for eating it. Contradictory."

"Bad example! Eating a cookie isn't illegal," Izzy huffed.

"If you feel that bad about it then just turn

invisible," said Alice.

"That's worse! Then I'd really be sneaking in!"

"Calm down," said Jenn. "The cameras will see us; we're not hiding anything. I'm allowed to be here."

"Oh my god...they'll see us on tape and then kick us out of school!" Izzy gasped.

"Can we leave her behind?" Melanie asked.

"No one's staying on campus. Just come on," said Jenn. She unlocked the entrance and gestured her friends inside. With a gentle push from Colleen, Izzy entered the building.

As they moved through the hallway, a fellow student passed them. His eyes met Jenn's.

"Hey, Jenn."

"Hi, Collin."

"A witness!" whispered Izzy.

"See, Izzy," said Jenn, "other students are here too. It's called an all-nighter."

The girls approached Jenn's lab and entered the room. Scott was waiting at the island counter.

"Is Scott coming too?" asked Alice.

"Nope. He's here in case we have any technical difficulties," said Jenn.

"I'll be here if you end up in Australia instead of Greece, or if someone's leg gets left behind," said Scott.

Izzy's eyes bulged. "Wha-what?!"

"It's a joke! He was only kidding," said Jenn.

"Don't mind her. She's been a little jumpy," said Colleen.

Izzy glared at Colleen.

165

"Okay, ladies," said Jenn, "grab your equipment and tie up your hair. Whenever you're ready, we'll get going."

"To Greece!" said Melanie.

"Wait," Alice paused. "Once we're in Greece, how do we get back to Indiana?"

"I have a portable teleportation device." Jenn took a remote control-like object from her pocket and gave it to Alice. Alice pressed the control's center button and pointed it toward open space. Instantly, a wall of purple and blue colors appeared.

"It works the same way as the original. The only differences are that you can take this one anywhere you'd like and once the person holding the remote walks through the portal, it disappears," said Jenn.

"Sounds good to me," said Izzy.

"At least something does," retorted Melanie.

"We should get going," said Jenn. "I can hardly wait!"

"If you have any trouble at all, call me," said Scott. "I don't want anything happening to you guys. Wherever you go, I can be there within seconds."

"We should be fine," Jenn assured him. "All right, Izzy and Mel, if the two of you could stand on the platform, please. Alice and Colleen can take a seat in the Air Taxi."

Alice returned the portable remote and stationed herself securely in the hovercraft. Jenn took a pair of aviator goggles and climbed into the driver's seat.

"Mel and Izzy, hold onto Colleen and Alice's

166

hands. Everyone keep an empty mind and let me direct the machine," Jenn ordered.

The girls concentrated on thinking of nothing, which proved to be easier said than done. Scott gave Jenn a thumbs up, signaling that everything was clear. A moment later the girls were traveling into the swirling substance.

In her mind, Jenn repeated, *earthquake, Delphi, Greece, earthquake, Delphi, Greece.* The ride felt like an elevator, smoothly traveling through space. Alice watched the serene colors circling around her. Soon, a bright flash of white light blinded her, and the next moment the Air Taxi and its passengers hit solid ground.

The vehicle bounced, its engine hissing from contact with the ground. Both Melanie and Izzy landed hard on the cement.

Jenn took off her goggles and exited the hovercraft. "A bit of a bumpy landing. I'll have to practice that."

The girls took a few moments to recover from the landing and then stood up. Colleen studied their surroundings.

"This is Greece?" she asked.

The group was in a small alleyway in between two white apartment buildings.

"It appears to be," Jenn answered, looking past the alley. Within the streets, debris from collapsed buildings littered the sidewalks. "This is the place."

"Where are we exactly?" asked Alice.

"Delphi, Greece."

"Ha!" Izzy smiled. "Delphi, Greece. We're from Delphi, Indiana."

"Yup. Our Delphi was named after Greece's," said Jenn.

"This is where the earthquake hit?" asked Melanie.

"All of the debris is from the tremor. You can see where it extended," said Jenn, pointing to a row of collapsed buildings.

"That's a big earthquake," said Colleen.

Jenn studied the ground. A short distance away, she spotted a rift in the surface of the earth. The rift stretched past the collapsed buildings and extended up the side of a nearby mountain.

"Guys! Do you see that crack?" asked Jenn. "That split was formed by the earthquake. Wherever it leads to is where the quake started. If we follow it, we'll be able to determine what caused the tremor."

"Then let's go," said Colleen.

"Great!" Jenn exclaimed. "I noticed it goes toward Mount Parnassus, the mountain just straight ahead. We'll have to do an upward climb, but that should be no problem for the Air Taxi."

The girls situated themselves in the flying car with Izzy clinging onto the back and Melanie doubling up with Alice. In no time, they traveled up the side of the mountain, following the path of the rift. The higher up they went the colder it became. Jenn looked at the icy ground and pointed for her friends to see.

"We're almost there. The ground's opening wider."

As Jenn finished her sentence, the deepest part of the fissure came into view. The rift trailed from a large cave sitting on a cliff. Jenn flew the Air Taxi to the edge of the cliff and parked on the ledge.

"That's a big drop," said Izzy, inching away from the ledge.

"It's a good thing you can fly," said Melanie.

"Yeah," Izzy said nervously.

"Shh. Listen," Jenn whispered.

She could hear voices from within the cave. The five girls were to the side of the cavern. They were temporarily hidden from any being that was inside.

"And when they come back, we shall know of Typhon's location…the location of the Sibyl," a deep voice growled.

"When we find her, we will kill her," a second voice threatened.

"Are you sure you want to kill her? She can foresee our fate. We will know our future against the Olympians…a warning of what is to come!"

"But she may lie. We cannot trust the Oracle, for last time our trust got us locked in Tartarus. There is no one, no being, we can depend on other than ourselves."

"Then I agree. We shall kill the seer the moment we lay eyes upon her."

Alice looked at Jenn and mouthed the word "Typhon," confused. Jenn's eyes were wide as she listened to the conversation.

"I can hardly wait for the day we take over Mount Olympus!" the second voice bellowed.

"Cronus, we will have our day soon."

"I long to see mighty Zeus pinned with his own lightning bolts, sentenced to an eternity of hell," Cronus jeered.

Izzy drew her hand over her mouth in horror. Her arm had been resting on a boulder, and as she pulled it away, a bottle-sized rock fell from the stone. The rock rolled off the cliff, tumbling to the bottom of the mountain.

Cronus halted. "Uranus, did you hear that?"

"Yes. There is movement outside."

The two gods walked toward the entrance of the cavern. Outside, they found a blonde-haired blue-eyed young woman staring back at them, her knees shaking.

"She can see us!" yelled Cronus.

Uranus waved his arm back and shot a dull icicle at Izzy, hitting her in the stomach. Izzy hurtled backwards.

"Izzy!" Alice screamed. She watched helplessly as her friend plummeted toward the valley, clutching her stomach and gasping for air. Jenn sprinted to the Air Taxi and jumped in with Colleen right behind her. Immediately, the Titans took notice of the other four people.

"They can all see us!" yelled Uranus.

Cronus shot a fireball at Jenn and Colleen. Alice deflected the flames with a force field.

"A shield!" bellowed Uranus.

"Like Hades!" snarled Cronus. "They're not human! They can see us, and she has powers. One of them must be the Oracle!"

"But which one?"

"It doesn't matter. Kill them all!" Cronus ordered.

Jenn started the hovercraft. Colleen pulled Alice into the vehicle and the three took off down the mountain, trying as fast as they could to find and catch Izzy. Melanie took a vigorous leap off of the cliff, using the mountain as a slide as she whisked down the slope. Cronus and Uranus chased after her. One by one, they shot icicles and fireballs at both Melanie and the hovercraft.

In the Air Taxi, Alice kneeled backwards in her seat, holding her hands steady and blocking each object that was fired their way. On the mountain, Melanie moved too quickly for the gods. She dodged their powers by jumping from cliff to cliff.

As Jenn flew the hovercraft, there was no sign of Izzy. Fearing the worst, she pressed harder on the accelerator. With the drastic increase in speed, the Air Taxi rocked violently to the right. Alice clutched onto the side of the aircraft to maintain her balance. At the same time, Uranus launched an icicle. The ice smashed into Alice's right hand before she could produce a shield. Alice screamed, shaking her wrist back and forth to help relieve the sting, but her fingers fell limp, unable to move. With only her left hand, she tried to generate a force field, but the power ball was too weak.

"Alice!" yelled Colleen. "We need a force field!"

"It's not big enough!" hollered Alice. "Without both hands, I can't fend them off! They're too powerful!"

"Come on, Izzy," Jenn muttered as the hovercraft reached closer to the ground. There was still no sign of her.

Cronus and Uranus began to catch up with the Air Taxi. They were moving faster than the hovercraft, and it wouldn't be long before they were within arms length of the girls.

"Jenn!" yelled Melanie. "You have to go!"

With both palms, Cronus created a mammoth fireball. Melanie leapt off one of the cliffs, soaring past Cronus' face in an attempt to divert his attention from the hovercraft. The Titan followed her body, waiting to launch the flames.

SMASH!

A pile of rocks rained down on Cronus' head. The Titan lost his balance, and the fireball missed Melanie. As the rocks fell, Izzy revealed herself above Cronus. She flew toward the Air Taxi as Melanie continued down the slope.

"Jenn! It's Izzy!" said Colleen.

Jenn sighed in relief.

The hovercraft reached the bottom of the valley and now traveled above flat ground. The girls were in a huge field, stretching farther than the horizon. Melanie jumped off of Mount Parnassus and sprinted as fast as she could toward the Air Taxi.

"Uranus! Use my fireballs; your icicles are too weak," said Cronus.

The Titans began throwing fireballs at the five moving targets.

"Izzy! Hurry up! They're gaining on us!" shouted Melanie. She looked back to see how far away Izzy was from the group. Izzy had lost some of her speed and was struggling to keep up.

"You think I don't know that?" Izzy yelled.

"Just come on!"

Izzy began to catch up and made her way above Melanie to the right of the hovercraft.

"Hold on tight!" yelled Jenn, calling to Alice and Colleen.

Alice and Colleen watched from their seats as Cronus and Uranus glided closer toward them. The gods were definitely moving faster than the Air Taxi.

"Alice! Do you think you can set off a force field?" asked Colleen.

Alice flicked her limp wrist and held up her arms.

"I don't know...I can give it a...no! No, I can't! Jenn, fly to the right!" Alice screamed.

"What?"

"To the right! Fly to the right!"

Jenn maneuvered the hovercraft toward Izzy and Melanie. The runner and the flyer followed her lead, hanging close to the vehicle.

"It's the dream! My dream, Jenn!" shouted Alice.

"Um...guys...GUYS!" Melanie hollered. "We gotta go!"

Izzy swooped to her left, dodging Uranus' fireball that whizzed past her ear. The gods were nearing the Air Taxi.

"Jenn, the Transporter!" roared Colleen.

Jenn pulled the Transporter's remote from her pocket while maintaining control of the hovercraft.

"Alice, we need one final force field. You have to do it!" ordered Jenn.

"My hand!" Alice cried.

"Alice, take my hand!" said Colleen. "Maybe we can combine our powers, strength and the shield."

Alice linked arms with Colleen. Together, they aimed their palms in the direction of the gods.

"On three! One, two, three!" Alice commanded. She pushed with all of her might, emitting a silver shield. The glowing orb ballooned to an enormous size, much bigger than anything Alice had ever created before. Colleen held on, the purple tape moving with her palm. The fire that Uranus and Cronus threw at the girls bounced back into their faces. The silver shield kept everything from reaching the hovercraft.

"Melanie and Izzy!" said Jenn. "The second I turn on the Transporter, go directly into it!"

Izzy and Melanie continued to run and fly as they waited for their cue. Jenn pointed the remote in front of them and turned it on, creating the purple and blue wall.

"Go!"

Melanie and Izzy rushed into the substance, disappearing from the field.

"Alice and Colleen, let go!" Jenn instructed.

Colleen and Alice shot the silver ball toward Cronus and Uranus. The shield crashed into the gods and knocked them to the ground. A second later, Jenn steered the hovercraft into the portal with the swirling colors disappearing after them. Cronus and Uranus were left behind, stunned, as the young ladies vanished into thin air.

CHAPTER THIRTEEN

The Great Oak Tree

The girls stumbled onto the floor of the lab.

"Are you all right?" Scott asked, alarmed.

Jenn shook her head, remaining in her seat. Melanie and Izzy were lying on the floor while Alice and Colleen were slumped in the hovercraft. They were all trying to catch their breath.

"What happened?"

Jenn exited the Air Taxi.

"Titans," she whispered.

"What?" Scott asked incredulously.

"The Titans, damn it! We went to find the start of the earthquake, which led us straight to Cronus and Uranus," said Jenn.

"Did they see you?" asked Scott, horrified.

"Yes! They tried to kill us! Obviously they didn't succeed, but they came pretty close!"

"Did they cause the earthquake?"

"Probably, but I'm not certain. They were hidden in a cave on Mount Parnassus. For a while we eavesdropped on their conversation, but we didn't get very far. They mentioned Typhon and said that when 'the others' come back, they'll know the location of the seer. They're looking for the Oracle of Delphi."

"Do they want to see their destinies?" asked Scott.

"They want her dead. They think one of us is the Oracle because we could see the-" Jenn paused. She turned toward the Air Taxi. "Alice, what's your family heritage?"

"You mean like nationality?" asked Alice.

"Yes. What are your parents?"

"Well, my dad is half Irish, half German, and my mother was Greek."

"Are you close with your mom?" asked Jenn.

"No, I never knew her. She ran out on my dad when I was two and she died before I was three."

Scott gazed at Jenn. "What are you getting at?"

"Alice's premonition came to life," answered Jenn.

Scott tilted his head back, seeming to understand.

"Alice, you said that was your dream, when we were getting chased. Did everything happen the exact same way, or was anything different?" asked Jenn.

"A part of it was the same. In the dream Melanie was running, Izzy was flying, and they were both dodging fireballs. We all said the same things, like Mel telling Izzy to hurry up and you telling us to hold on, but the outcome was different. The only other difference was that in the dream the things that were chasing us were more of a blur. They were just dark shadows that could speak," said Alice.

"The outcome was different," Jenn muttered.

176

"That's why she told me to fly to the right, she knew what would happen. We escaped our fate."

The girls gathered around the island counter.

"You're an only child, right?" Jenn questioned.

"Yep," said Alice.

"Was your mom?"

"I think so."

"And your grandmother?"

"I have no idea."

Jenn turned toward Scott. "We have to go back to Greece."

"What?" asked Scott, stunned.

"Not *we* as in you and I. I meant Alice and I."

"You can't be serious! Five minutes ago you came hurtling through the Transporter saying you'd been chased and nearly *killed* by Titans, who by the way are supposed to be rotting in hell, and now you say you're going back?"

"I have to go to Dodona," Jenn said firmly.

"What's in Dodona that's so important?" asked Scott.

"An oak tree. Think about it."

"Honestly, do you have to go now? Right this second? You need to rest. You need to recover from what just happened."

"If we don't leave now, we'll have to wait until tomorrow, and I don't have the patience," Jenn protested.

"This is crazy! You're not thinking clearly!"

"No, this is me tired of guessing what the hell's happening, and now I'm going to get answers. I'm not waiting twenty-four hours and taking the risk that one of my friends, or myself, will end up dead!"

"You could die if you leave! It's an enormous risk!" said Scott.

"At least we know what we're getting into. It would be far worse to fall asleep on campus, naively trusting that we'll be safe. Typhon showed up without warning and so could the Titans. Ignorance is dangerous."

"I can't let you go. I can't let you put yourself in harms way."

"I was meant to die today, but I lived, and I did it without your help. I can do this without you; I don't need your permission," Jenn snapped.

Scott stared at his girlfriend, overwhelmed. He couldn't keep Jenn from doing what she wanted.

Jenn faced Alice.

"I know this may seem crazy, but it's urgent."

"Okay," Alice agreed, unwilling to start an argument that she knew she would lose. "Before we leave, can you take a look at my hand? I think it might be broken."

"Of course." Jenn reached for Alice's wrist, carefully pulling the glove off. Alice cringed as a sharp pain seared through her palm. Her bare skin was horribly bruised.

"Ouch," Izzy mouthed.

"Open and close your hand," said Jenn, studying the injury.

Painfully Alice created a fist. Then, she slowly stretched her fingers.

"It's not broken," said Jenn. "Just bruised. Give it some time; the color will fade, along with the pain. For now, we'll ice and wrap it. That'll help."

Jenn rummaged through one of her cupboards, finding a roll of white athletic tape. She wound the tape around Alice's hand, and carefully replaced the glove.

"Can you still make a force field?" asked Jenn.

Alice held up her left palm. Effortlessly, she created a silver orb.

"Good as new," said Alice.

Jenn gave her a bag of ice. "All right then. Let's get going."

Alice followed Jenn to the Transporter.

"If you're going, you're not going by yourselves," said Colleen.

"Right. We're coming with you," said Melanie.

"You can't keep us here," added Izzy.

"Fine," said Jenn. "Step on the platform."

"What about the Air Taxi?" asked Alice.

"We don't need it."

The five girls stepped before the Transporter, their hands linked together.

"My phone is on," said Scott.

Jenn stared hard into the portal. She led the group into the archway, all the while thinking of their destination.

Soon enough, through the flowing of colors and the blinding light, the girls found themselves in the middle of another field.

"We're not back at Mount Parnassus, are we?" Izzy squeaked.

"No, we're not. This is Dodona," said Jenn.

"And we're here to find an oak tree?" asked Melanie.

"Yup."

"Because...why?"

"Because it's not your typical tree," answered Jenn, beckoning her friends to follow. "There's a myth that Zeus planted a tree that allowed him to communicate directly with humans. While he sat on Mount Olympus, King Zeus could speak to the people that were at the great oak. And *we* are going to go and speak to Zeus himself, as long as the mythical tree physically exists."

"Why not go to Mount Olympus to talk to Zeus?" asked Alice.

"Because I'm not sure what we would find there. With Cronus and Uranus on the loose, there's a chance Mount Olympus may not be under the control of the Olympians."

"You think he'll talk back?" asked Izzy.

"I hope so."

"How do we find it?" asked Colleen.

"It's right there," said Jenn.

The girls looked up. An enormous tree stood in front of them, its green leaves swaying in the breeze.

"Ladies, this is the Oracle of Zeus," said Jenn.

"What's with all of these oracles?" asked Izzy.

"What do you mean?"

"Well, first Cronus and Uranus were talking about

the Oracle of Delphi or something, and now you mentioned the Oracle of Zeus. What are oracles?"

"An oracle is a source of wisdom. It could be a thing, a person or a place. Some share wisdom while others reveal prophecies and fates. The Oracle of Zeus is kind of like a knowledge hotline," said Jenn as she approached the tree, touching the bark.

"Prophecies and fates? As in visions or premonitions?" asked Colleen.

"They can come in those forms, yes."

Jenn plucked a leaf from the tree and paused. As if expected, the wind picked up, blowing the leaves. The trunk began to quiver, and from the center of its core an opening appeared, chipping away the aged bark. A basketball-sized circle had been formed and the girls inched closer to take a look.

A booming voice bellowed from hole. "Who goes there?"

"Jenn Andrews, of Delphi, Indiana."

"Have you come alone?" asked the voice.

"No. I come with Melanie Taylor, Alice Payton, Izzy Itello and Colleen Benton of Delphi."

"What is your purpose?"

"We come asking to speak with Zeus, king of the gods," said Jenn.

"It is I, Zeus. What do you wish to speak about?" he asked, his voice stern.

"We would like answers about our new powers, and we need to know what's happening on Earth."

"Powers, you say? What might they be?"

"Gifts of intelligence, speed, strength, invisibility, flying and deflection," said Jenn.

For a moment the tree was silent. The girls were relieved when Zeus began to speak.

"You are the new generation of Olympians?" he questioned.

"Yes, sir, at least I think so."

"I suspect you are the intelligent one," said Zeus, his voice calming.

"Yes."

"And there are only five of you?"

"Yes."

"There are no others?"

"No, sir. Just us."

"Welcome!" Zeus cheered. "I am happy you have found your way to this oracle, and I am pleased that you are alive. My guess, though, is that you are all confused."

"I'm confused!" said Izzy.

"And who is this?" asked Zeus.

"Izzy Itello, the flyer and invisible woman," said Izzy.

"Ah, the work of Aphrodite, I assume."

"Right," Jenn affirmed. "Representing the planet Venus."

"Correct!" Zeus applauded. "So you have discovered the power of the planets, the power of the pentagram?"

"I believe so," said Jenn. "Each planet portrays a god, either a Titan or Olympian. The Olympians bound together at their planets and-"

"Sent down godly powers to mortals! Exactly!" Zeus finished. "You're breaking the code already!"

"So it's true? Our powers were sent by Greek gods?" asked Melanie.

"We do not just serve the Greeks, but yes, the gods have sent you your powers," said Zeus.

"But what are our powers for?" asked Colleen.

"Was it not obvious?"

"No, sir."

"A couple of reasons. Have you noticed or encountered anything unusual very recently? Perhaps within the last day?"

"Yes!" the girls responded in unison.

"Such as?" asked Zeus.

"We met Typhon. He was bundles of fun," said Melanie.

"And Cronus and Uranus," added Alice.

"An earthquake hit Greece," said Colleen.

"And the earth has been tipped off of its axis of twenty-three-point-four-five degrees," finished Jenn.

"More is happening than I expected," said Zeus. "You mentioned Typhon. Where did you find him?"

"It was more like he found us," said Melanie. "Last night Alice and I were walking on our school's campus when we approached a ball of fire. When we went to check out the flames, we discovered they were a part of Typhon."

"Your school is in the United States, North America?"

"Delphi, Indiana, yes."

"Typhon was searching for someone," said Zeus.

"For who?" asked Izzy.

"I am positive that he was sent by Cronus, looking for the Oracle of Delphi. Is the Oracle present?"

Melanie, Alice, Izzy and Colleen looked at each other, confused by the question.

"Well, no," said Colleen.

"No, the answer is yes," Jenn corrected. "Yes, Zeus, the Oracle is here."

"Does she not know that she is an oracle?" asked Zeus, surprised.

"She doesn't know," Jenn confirmed.

"Who is she?"

"Alice Payton."

"What?!" Alice squeaked.

"Remember when Izzy asked what an oracle was?" asked Jenn. "I said that they were a person, place or a thing that could reveal prophecies and fates. Your nightmare was a prophecy, a vision that forewarned you of how we were all going to die. Unknowingly, you saw the future; you saw our fate."

"Couldn't it just be one of my powers?" asked Alice. "Izzy has two, maybe I have two."

"When did you have this dream? asked Zeus.

"Two nights ago."

"For your vision to be a second power you would not have gained the ability of foresight until yesterday. The premonition came to you because it was to be your fate. Prophecies are hereditary. It is in your blood, which means that you are the heir of Pythia," said Zeus.

"I'm not buying it," said Colleen. "Find another way to prove that she's an oracle."

"All right," said Zeus. "The Olympians and I were able to see the Oracle using a special map. Does Alice not have green eyes and golden curled hair?"

Colleen looked at Alice. There was the golden curly hair tied in a ponytail and her sage eyes, staring back at her.

"Are you *positive*?" Izzy asked suspiciously.

"The map does not lie," said Zeus. "Do you have proof enough that she is the heir of Pythia?"

"I don't know," said Alice. "You said it's in my blood, that I inherited it, but my dad has never had a vision."

"Your mom could have," said Jenn.

"The powers of the Oracle are typically passed through the maternal side," said Zeus.

"That'd be the only thing she ever gave me, besides life," mumbled Alice. "Well thank you, Mom...now I've got mythical beings trying to kill me!"

"I have one more question," said Izzy, approaching the tree. "Who is Pythia?"

"Pythia was the first known Oracle of Delphi. She was a priestess who could foresee the destinies of others," said Zeus.

"So Typhon was searching for Alice because she's an oracle?" asked Colleen.

"Yes, and not because she's just any oracle but because she's the Oracle of Delphi, the most powerful prophetess that exists."

"What the heck did Typhon want with me?" asked Alice.

"It's not necessarily what Typhon wants with you; it is what Cronus wants with you."

"Please enlighten us on the subject," said Jenn. "What are Cronus and Uranus doing on Earth? You locked them in Tartarus. I know about the Titanomachy."

"And this is where you learn the dreadful truth," Zeus sighed. "As you said, Jenn, Cronus was imprisoned in Tartarus, along with the other Titans. The Olympians were told, however, that Uranus had been killed. I am afraid to say that was a lie. Exactly one day ago, he resurfaced from hiding. Uranus broke into Tartarus and released Cronus. Together they released the rest of the Titans and the souls of Tartarus. I must warn you, Cronus and Uranus are not the only gods that you are in danger of encountering. All twelve Titans who fought in the Titanomachy have returned to Earth."

"There are TWELVE of them?! And a bunch of living dead people?" yelled Izzy.

"Yes," said Zeus. "But the spirits are not a threat to you. They are only ghosts. You may not even encounter any."

"But what does Cronus want? Why would he send Typhon to find me?" Alice asked, her voice strained.

"Cronus wants to use your premonitions so he can learn how to defeat the Olympians," said Zeus.

"No," said Jenn. "When we encountered the Titans, Cronus specifically said that he wanted the Oracle dead and that he *didn't* want to see his destiny. He said

186

that they couldn't trust the prophetess and that she would probably lie to them."

"That is not what I had expected," said Zeus. "You see, one reason why you all have active powers, minus Alice's prophecy, is so that you could protect Alice from the Titans. We cannot let them use her powers to take over the universe."

"You mean, we were chosen to obtain powers?" asked Melanie.

"Well, yes and no. When we found the Oracle's…Alice's location, we sent down a lightning bolt containing a power specifically meant to hit her. The other lightning bolts were sent down based on the remaining four points of the pentagram. Whoever was stationed where our lightning bolts were thrown gained a power."

"We were at the right place at the right time," said Jenn.

"Precisely," said Zeus.

"Wait, wait, wait," said Colleen. "Let's back-track for a moment. Zeus, both you and Jenn mentioned the Titanomachy. What's that?"

"The Titanomachy was a war between the Titans and the Olympians. It was a battle of power, who would rule the universe. Ultimately, the Olympians won and the Titans were sent to hell."

"What's the big deal if you both want to rule the universe?" asked Melanie. "You're all gods, does it really matter who's in control of what?"

"Most definitely," said Zeus. "The Olympians want to rule over the universe for the sake of creation, to let not only humans but all of nature thrive. The Titans, however, are literally mind-controlling. They are not interested in growth and peace but rather destruction and war. The Titans merely desire one thing: power. They do not care for creations such as humans. They would rather turn all living beings into their slaves. If the Titans were your rulers, your entire world would be horribly different."

"So what are the other reasons why we have powers? You said there was more than one," asked Colleen.

"There are two reasons why you have powers. As I said, the first is to protect Alice from the Titans, for you to be her guardians. The second reason, however, is to defeat the Titans along with the souls."

"We're supposed to do *what*?!" barked Melanie. "Why can't you take care of it? You're the king of all gods!"

"Indeed, I am king, but I am not invincible. At the end of the Titanomachy, Cronus set a curse upon the planet Earth, eternally blocking the Olympians from its grounds. I cannot set foot upon your planet and neither can the other gods and goddesses who fought against Cronus and his army. We are forever banished unless the curse is broken," Zeus explained.

"But you're on Mount Olympus. That's a real mountain in Greece," said Jenn, perplexed.

"We have founded a new Mount Olympus, one that is much larger and much farther away from Earth."

"Where?"

"On the planet Jupiter. Have you ever wondered

what that big red dot is? It's Mount Olympus. You see, gods and goddesses control much more than just the planet Earth; our range is endless. Originally we were living on Gaia because that is where life is most abundant. Now that we are banished, Jupiter is our home because it is the largest planet and one of the most powerful places in existence."

"Where is Tartarus?"

"Tartarus and the underworld are hidden within the planet Pluto."

"But Pluto's not a planet," said Jenn.

"It may not be to humans, but it is a planet to the gods," said Zeus.

"And Hermes," said Jenn, "he assists passed souls to the underworld. How does he manage to do that if he can't pass into the earth's atmosphere?"

"Thanatos, the god of death, escorts the souls out of Earth where he entrusts them into Hermes' care."

"Go back to the part about our mission," said Alice. "About us having to defeat the Titans."

"Of course. Now that the Titans have made it to Earth, it is your duty to clean up the mess. You will be responsible for preventing the Titans from taking over the universe," said Zeus.

"And you can't do anything about it?" asked Melanie. "So what, you can't come onto Earth, and now that's *our* problem? What do you do on Jupiter everyday? Watch all the meteors float by?"

"Not being on Earth does make our job difficult," said Zeus. "But we work with what we have. I can control the weather to an extent, just as Poseidon continues to manage the seas. Sometimes we lose control of our tasks and things get out of hand. Hurricanes tend to result from Poseidon's limited power, unless he creates them himself. Other things like storms and rains come naturally, as if the world is on autopilot. And although the Olympians are banished from the earth, other gods stroll among Gaia. They are enough to keep things in order, just as they should be."

"So why is the world tipped off of its axis?" asked Izzy. "Don't you control that?"

"Actually, I do not," answered Zeus. "The world was held by the Titan Atlas, and until yesterday he has always held it. But Atlas has escaped from his post, and now, without his support your world is spinning in a new direction."

"How do we go about doing this? How do we defeat the Titans?" asked Colleen.

"There is something hidden on the earth that will help you significantly," said Zeus, his voice becoming thick. "In the Parthenon there stands a statue of the goddess Athena. This statue hides something very powerful, something so important that only the Olympians know its location. Now, out of fear that somehow an outsider is listening in on our conversation, I cannot tell you what is hidden. All I can say is that you need to retrieve what rests in the statue and use it to defeat the Titans."

"Are you speaking of the Athena Parthenos?" asked Jenn.

"Yes," replied Zeus.

"It doesn't exist! It was burned in a fire centuries ago," said Jenn.

"That's what you were meant to believe. Hephaestus created the fire as a decoy. The statue never burned."

"Then how come it hasn't been discovered?"

"Because the statue is not visible to the mortal eye. Had Alice ever visited the Parthenon, she would have seen it as clear as you can see this tree. Today, having your powers, if you go to the Parthenon you will see the Athena Parthenos. Those without a mythical aura cannot see it. They are blinded by their mortality," said Zeus.

"So are we immortal?" asked Izzy.

"No. Nothing is completely immortal, not even the gods. You are still to care for yourselves, for your souls are always in danger."

"You said that you can't tell us what's inside of the statue because someone could potentially be listening in, but you told us its location. Isn't that just as dangerous?" asked Alice.

"It may seem that way, but I promise that there is no threat in revealing the whereabouts of this item. Even if Cronus knew exactly where it was hidden, there is only one way he could actually retrieve it. There is only one way in which anyone can get a glimpse of it."

"And how is that?" asked Melanie.

"You are to go on a quest in search of a key. Actually, in search of three keys. Hidden within the dimensions of the universe lie three very real objects.

191

Your task, your quest, is to retrieve these items and take them to the Parthenon."

"Sounds easy enough," said Colleen.

"It may sound simple, but this is a difficult challenge. You will find your senses of wisdom, strength and patience tremendously useful," said Zeus.

"And how do we know where to find these items?" asked Jenn.

"You shall receive your first clue momentarily. However, a word of advice from someone with experience in fighting the Titans: I suggest that you study their powers. Please, learn from the mistakes of the Olympians. The past is a good reference for the future," said Zeus. "With that being said, it is time for you all to begin the quest. Remember, whatever happens, you must stick together. I am afraid to say that you are in graver danger than I had expected, as are we all. The future of the world and of the universe rests with you. Trust yourselves and follow your instincts. I have faith that you will not let me down."

The wind picked up, rustling the leaves of the oak tree and muffling Zeus' voice. A small green leaf fell from a branch and fluttered toward the ground. It landed in Jenn's hand. Instantly, golden letters began to scribble their way across the leaf's surface.

"It's a clue," said Jenn.

The other four girls moved in to take a look. Jenn read,

"A third leg you need for the key that you seek,
Is tucked away safe at the top of the peak.

192

At the edge of old Khafre you might get to see,
The ancient secret of man and the beast."

"Zeus. Is this what we're looking for?" asked Alice.

Zeus did not answer; the opening in the tree had closed.

"He's gone," said Melanie.

"What do we do now?" asked Izzy.

"We figure out this clue," said Jenn. "Start from the first line."

Colleen took the leaf and examined the words.

"A third leg you need for the key that you seek...."

"What's a third leg going to do for us? We're not seriously going to have someone's chopped-off limb, are we?" asked Izzy.

"I hope not," said Alice. "But I doubt it."

"Reread the first and second line," said Jenn.

"A third leg you need for the key that you seek, is tucked away safe at the top of the peak," repeated Colleen.

"The third leg, or item that we need, is hidden at the top of something."

"That's pretty literal, right from the text, Sherlock," retorted Colleen.

"It's something to work from," countered Jenn. "Think of things with peaks."

"A mountain." said Alice.

"Tall buildings."

"A water tower."

"Trees."

"Pyramids," said Melanie.

"Pyramids," repeated Jenn. "At the edge of old Khafre you might get to see…Khafre was an ancient Egyptian Pharaoh. One of the three major pyramids of Giza is dedicated to him. This clue takes us to Egypt."

"So we'll find one of the keys at the top of a pyramid?" asked Alice.

"No. You've forgotten, there's one more line."

"The ancient secret of man and the beast," read Colleen.

"Do any of you know what's in front of the pyramid of Khafre?" Jenn asked eagerly.

"A desert," said Izzy.

"That too, but there's something else."

The girls stared blankly at Jenn.

"Oh, come on! Didn't any of you take geography or study ancient Egypt?"

"Like five years ago," said Melanie.

"Okay, I'll give you a hint. It's huge, with a man's face and a lion's body," coaxed Jenn.

"The Sphinx!" said Alice.

"Yes!"

"The third leg we're looking for is at the top of the Sphinx?" asked Izzy.

"Yes, or it should be. As long as we've decoded the clue correctly."

"Then what does it mean by third leg?" asked Melanie.

"Ah, within the clue is a riddle," said Jenn. "There's a myth about a man named Oedipus. You may have heard of him. Well, on his journey, Oedipus

194

encountered a Sphinx, which was a creature with a woman's head, a lion's body, a snake's tail and a pair of wings. The particular Sphinx Oedipus met was asking people to answer a riddle: What creature walks on four legs in the morning, two at midday, and three legs in the evening? Oedipus was a clever man and answered the riddle correctly."

"What was the answer?" asked Colleen.

"Man. When people are babies, before they can walk, they crawl, hence the four legs. Throughout the middle of our lives we walk on two legs, and as humans age, many use a cane to assist their movement. The first item we're searching for is a cane, a third leg," said Jenn.

"If that's all we're looking for, I can go to the store and buy a cane. Never mind this traveling thing," said Melanie.

"I don't think it works like that," said Alice. "I bet Zeus jinxed the riddle so that only one specific cane will work as a key," said Alice.

"Right. We have to go directly to the Sphinx ourselves and take it from there," said Jenn.

"When do we go?" asked Colleen.

"Soon, but not today. We have something more important to do."

"What could be more important than finding the keys?" asked Izzy.

"Like Zeus said, we need to study our opponents. We need to find out what went wrong during the Titanomachy so we don't make the same mistakes."

"We're just finding the keys though. We're not actually battling the Titans...are we?" asked Colleen.

"I don't know," said Jenn. "Yes, we're finding the three keys, but we're finding them so we can unlock something. Who knows what that something is and what we'll have to do with it. If Zeus advised us to learn about the Titans, I think we should honor his words."

"So we probably are fighting the Titans," sighed Izzy.

"There's a good possibility. We at least have to be prepared in case the Titans find us. Ignorance in this situation is as life-threatening as a blind man walking alone through a busy street. We can't go blind."

"Where do we go from here?" asked Alice.

"Home. I think we all need sleep," said Jenn.

"Sounds good," sighed Melanie.

"What if the Titans find us on campus? You said it yourself that there's a chance they could show up while we're sleeping," said Izzy.

"We'll go back to the dorm and keep the portable Transporter on hand. That way if anything happens and we need to escape, we can teleport ourselves to wherever we wish," said Jenn.

Izzy sighed in relief.

"Let's head back now." Jenn pulled the remote from her pocket and aimed it away from the oak tree. The wall of blue and purple colors appeared. Jenn thought of their destination, and soon enough, they were back at the lab.

"Gets easier the more we do it," said Alice.

"Welcome back," said Scott. His face brightened at sight of the girls.

"We're all right," said Jenn, avoiding Scott's eyes.

"Did you speak with Zeus?"

"Yes. We were right about the powers and how they're linked to the gods. In a nutshell, mythology is real, the Titans are real, and it's our job to defeat them. Cronus is their leader, who's trying to locate Alice, the heir of the Oracle of Delphi, and we have to protect her for her own sake and the sake of the entire universe. We have to find three keys to unlock a hidden item that will help us against the Titans. We'll start that soon, but first we have to learn about the Titans and their abilities so we know what we're up against," huffed Jenn.

"All in one breath," Melanie said in awe.

"And now, we're going to bed. By the way, what time is it?"

"Four A.M.," answered Scott.

"Dang it. I have class in three hours," said Alice.

"Don't worry about it," said Jenn. "I'll take care of everything. For now, we all have to go to the dorm and rest. Try not to think too much about everything that's happened. You'll lose sleep over it."

"Easier said than done," mumbled Melanie.

The girls headed for the exit with Scott lagging behind.

"That's it?" asked Scott. "All I hear is the synopsis and then it's off to bed?"

197

"We'll talk about this one-on-one tomorrow," said Jenn. "You need to take a break too. I appreciate your concern, but we just need to rest right now."

Jenn walked out of the room, following the other four. Scott turned off the lights and locked the door. As he exited the science hall, he called to Jenn.

"If you need anything, I'll have my phone on."

Jenn nodded quickly and turned around, catching up with her roommates. The walk was long and silent. Not a word was spoken between the exhausted girls. Quietly, they entered their dorm and split off in their own ways.

After a quick shower, Alice entered her bedroom. Colleen was already asleep in her bed, and Melanie was nowhere to be found. Slowly, Alice pulled back the sheets on her mattress and crawled in, laying her head on her pillow.

The door creaked open and Melanie walked into the room. She headed for her own bed and lay down. For a few moments the room was still. The only sound to be heard was Colleen's deep breathing, puffing rhythmically in and out. Alice was nearly asleep when she heard a whispered hiss.

"Pssst. Alice, you awake?"

"Yeah," Alice replied, her voice hushed.

"Are you all right?" whispered Melanie.

"I guess. You?"

"I've been better, but I've been worse."

"How much worse?"

"When my grandfather died," Melanie said softly.

"Were you guys close?" asked Alice.

"Like two coats of paint."

"How'd he…you know, move on?"

"Had a stroke when I was twelve. I was at the middle school regional meet when it happened."

"I'm sorry."

"What about you? You said your mom left you when you were little," asked Melanie.

"Yeah. Skipped out on my dad and I. She left a note saying she was sorry she had to leave, but she had problems she needed to work out with herself. Last I heard about her was that she died by the time I was three," said Alice.

"Was it tough?"

"Was what tough?"

"Growing up without her."

"Um…yeah, at times. My dad was my rock, and he tried to make up for her void. There were days though, like Mother's Day, when I really wished she was there. I was the only girl at school who didn't have a mom to fall back on." Alice sighed. "I don't know how I should feel about her."

"So it was just you and your dad?" asked Melanie.

"Just the two of us. What about you? You just have two older brothers, right?"

"Yep, Brian and Chase. Both are about six-one with jet black hair and blue eyes."

"The guy version of you I bet."

"Minus the height. That's the gene that skipped over me."

"But you're not short. Five-six is pretty good. I'd like to be that tall," said Alice.

"Five-five isn't much of a difference," said Melanie.

"Yeah, right," Alice giggled. "You know, in three years of living together I can't believe we've never asked about each other's past."

"I guess it's because you're getting to know me now...you didn't meet the Melanie before high school."

"Is there a big difference between you now and then?"

"No. Well, not until yesterday."

"That doesn't count. Your powers aren't a part of who you are, it just happened," said Alice.

"Yours are a part of you. You were born an oracle," said Melanie.

"But I never knew it. My first vision was two nights ago."

"Chris Daughtry didn't start singing seriously until he was sixteen or seventeen but it's a part of who he is. Sometimes you don't know everything about yourself."

"He's a singer though," said Alice.

"Different story, same concept."

"Then I guess your powers are a part of who you are."

"How?" asked Melanie.

"You've always been fast, now you're just a teensy bit faster," said Alice.

"A teensy bit," Melanie laughed softly. She paused. "What do you think is in the cards for us?"

"What do you mean?"

"Like our destinies and futures. What do you think the big guy in the sky has planned out?"

"As in God?"

"God, Zeus, Buddha, pure luck…whatever you believe in."

"Um…I don't know, but I hope something good. I hope something great," answered Alice.

"Same here."

There was another pause.

"You think we'll be all right?" asked Alice.

"I think that whatever happens, we'll have been better and we'll have been worse," said Melanie.

"And you know, if you ever need anything, I've got your back."

"Ditto."

Silence filled the room once more and Alice waited to hear from Melanie. After a few minutes, she could hear two sets of soft breathing, with Melanie's breaths countering Colleen's. Alice looked up to find both of her friends fast asleep. Slowly, she lay down and turned on her side. Soon, the only noise in the room was the breathing of three exhausted roommates.

CHAPTER FOURTEEN

Flashback

Alice woke up slowly; her eyelids heavy. Through her bandages, she could feel her battered hand throbbing.

That'll need some ice, she thought.

Carefully, Alice stretched out her arms and rolled her head and neck. She sat up and looked at her roommates' beds. To her left, Colleen was nowhere to be found, but to her right Melanie lay cuddled with her linens. Alice peered at the alarm clock. She was shocked to discover that it was one-thirty in the afternoon.

Eight and a half hours...that's better than a school night.

She could hear her stomach rumbling.

Food.

Alice walked into the lounge. Izzy was lying on the couch dressed in her pajamas, watching TV.

"Hey Iz," Alice yawned.

"Hey Al."

"How's your stomach?"

"Bruised. How about your hand?"

"Haven't changed the bandage yet, but I bet it's not pretty."

"Hey, it could have been a lot worse. Thanks to that dream of yours," said Izzy. "Speaking of which, did you have any last night?"

"No dream," answered Alice, thankful that there hadn't been any other visions of death. "Is Jenn here?"

"Nope. She left before I got up."

"And Colleen?"

"She went to class."

Alice grabbed a carton of milk from the fridge, then took a bag of ice from the freezer.

"Hey Iz. We got any Wheaties?"

"Yeah. Mel keeps 'em in the upper shelf," said Izzy. "What's with the Wheaties? You're more of a cook-your-own-breakfast kind of girl."

"Since we've been doing all this running around I figure it'd be smart to eat the breakfast of champions," Alice grinned.

Izzy laughed. "That makes sense."

There was a light knock at the door. Alice went to the entrance and greeted Jayden, who was holding a box of chocolates.

"Hi. Is Izzy home?" Jayden asked eagerly.

At the sound of Jayden's voice, Izzy sprung from the couch. Alice jumped out of the way as Izzy flung herself into her boyfriend's arms. Jayden dropped the chocolates and spun around.

"Jayden!" Izzy squeaked.

"Izzy!"

"What are you doing here?"

"Well, I haven't heard from you in awhile. I just wanted to come by and make sure you're okay."

"Oh," Izzy hesitated. "Well, I've…been busy."

"So everything's all right? No one I gotta beat up?" Jayden asked jokingly.

"No. I'm okay," Izzy cautioned, unsure of whether or not she should speak about the previous day's adventures.

"Good," said Jayden. "Oh, these are for you. I got your favorite." He bent down and picked up the box of chocolates.

"Thank you!"

While Izzy and Jayden spoke in the hallway, Alice stayed in the lounge to give them privacy. Just as she poured herself a bowl of cereal, the phone rang.

"Hello?"

"Alice, it's Jenn."

"Hey, Jenn. What's up?" asked Alice.

"Is Melanie awake?"

"Nope, why?"

"I need you guys to come down to the lab. Colleen's already here."

"Okay, when?"

"As soon as possible."

"All right, we'll be there in a little bit."

"Oh, and wear something athletic. Make sure to bring your M.A.J.I.C. gear too," Jenn ordered.

"My *what* gear?" asked Alice.

"M.A.J.I.C. gear. You know, your gloves, Izzy's

suit, Mel's spikes."

"Oh, okay. Is that it?"

"Yup."

"All right, see you soon." Alice hung up the phone and walked into the hallway.

"Hey Izzy, Jenn just called. She wants us down at the lab A.S.A.P.," said Alice.

"Okay," Izzy sighed. She gazed at Jayden. "I have to get going, but I'll see you soon."

"Do you want me to escort you to the lab?" asked Jayden.

"No, that's okay."

"All right. Call me soon." Jayden kissed Izzy on the cheek. He gave her a warm hug and walked down the hallway. Izzy sighed and stepped into the lounge. She walked into her roommates' bedroom, where she found Alice poking Melanie.

"Mel...*Mel*...MEL!" Alice repeated. "Izzy, she won't budge. It's like trying to get a rock to dance. You can't do it!"

"I've got an idea," Izzy smirked.

Izzy ran toward Melanie's bed and lunged full force onto the mattress.

"WAKE UP!" she hollered at the top of her lungs, jumping up and down.

Melanie shot straight up, her eyes dazed.

"Good afternoon," Izzy giggled.

"Ugh," Melanie huffed. "Not again."

"Come on, get up. Jenn wants us down at the lab," said Alice.

"So early? Déjà vu!"

"It's two P.M.," said Izzy.

"And Jenn wants us there soon," said Alice.

"Come back later," Melanie protested, turning over on her side.

"Don't make me get the air horn," Izzy threatened.

"All right, I'm up, I'm up." Melanie mumbled.

Within fifteen minutes Melanie was ready and put together. The three girls left the dorm room. Alice wore a ruby t-shirt and black shorts, Melanie had on a blue tank top with gray running shorts and Izzy wore a white sweater and jeans, fully covering her yellow spandex suit.

"You know, with this suit underneath my clothes, it kind of makes me feel like Superman," said Izzy, pulling down her collar so her friends could see.

"Superman, only cooler," said Melanie.

"Looks like someone's more awake," said Alice, glancing at Melanie.

"I'm not a morning person."

"You're not an afternoon person either," teased Izzy.

In no time the girls arrived at the science hall. As they approached room 56A, they could hear a pair of voices in a heated argument.

"We'll be fine!" yelled the first voice.

"You have no idea what you're going up against! Who knows what could happen!" shouted the second.

"We won't be battling anyone, we'll be observing!"

"You could still get hit by something. This is the

Titanomachy! Who knows what happened?!"

Colleen held the door open for her friends. When they entered, they found Scott and Jenn arguing in the center of the room.

"They've been at it since I got here," Colleen winced.

"What are they fighting about?" asked Alice.

"Jenn wants us to watch the Titanomachy, but Scott thinks it's too dangerous."

"Watch the what?!" squealed Izzy.

"I'll let Jenn explain," said Colleen, directing their attention to the fight.

"We'll be invisible! I didn't make the goggles for nothing," growled Jenn.

"And what if you don't see a stray fireball coming toward you? Invisible or not, you're not invincible!" Scott replied, his voice lowered.

"It's not going to happen because I'm not going to let it. I'll keep an eye out for myself. We'll watch out for each other."

"Jenn, I know you'll be careful. It's just, I don't trust-"

"Me?" Jenn interrupted.

Scott sighed. "I don't trust history. I don't trust that Zeus and Cronus will go out of their way to make sure they don't throw any stray powers. I don't trust that the Titans won't find you. But I do trust you and that's what scares me. There are so many things that could happen that would be far out of your control! If the time machine gets destroyed, you're lost in the ancient world forever. If one

207

of our friends gets hit, they'll be lost forever.... Jenn, if you get hit, I'll lose you, and I can't get you back."

"Time machine?" Izzy whispered to Colleen.

"You'll see."

"Scott, we need to do this. This isn't just another science experiment, it's reality. If we don't stop the Titans, then who will? This decision is not up to you," said Jenn.

Scott was at a loss for words.

Jenn turned toward her friends. "I have to show you something."

"Jenn...we're going to see the Titanomachy?" asked Izzy.

"Yes."

Izzy's eyes widened.

Jenn led her roommates to a large rectangular contraption in the corner of the lab. The machine was tall and silver, closed on all four sides like a closet.

"This," said Jenn, pointing to the room, "is our very own time machine."

"How in the world did you create this?" asked Izzy.

"Same as the other gadgets. Lots of wires, metal, time and coffee."

"So you didn't sleep last night?" asked Alice.

"Not a lot."

"So what? You just built a time machine in one night?" Melanie asked incredulously.

"This is a combination of years of studying dimension displacement and getting to see through the eyes of a god. The time machine was my pet project years before the Transporter came along. When I couldn't figure out time travel, I switched to teleportation. Consequently, after receiving my intellectual boost, the pieces came together. I've finally gotten it to work," Jenn grinned.

"Have you used it?" asked Izzy.

Scott raised his head.

"Yeah, twice. First I went back only a few hours. When that worked, I took a trip to ancient Greece."

"This is getting more dangerous by the second, Jenn!" Scott exclaimed. "You used yourself as the guinea pig last night?"

"To bring the time machine back, someone has to be inside directing it. What else was I supposed to do?" Jenn questioned.

"How about not use it at all? What if you hadn't been able to come back from Greece?!"

"What if the time machine erupted right now? What if a tornado swept up the lab and took us to an entirely new land? What if the sun burnt out and all life ceased to exist? Nothing bad happened. Leave it alone, Scott. These are my decisions, not yours."

"Your decisions affect my life too, you know."

"And they affect theirs," said Jenn, pointing to her friends. "If I didn't make the Transporter, we'd all be dead. The time machine will prepare us for the Titans. It's going to help us survive a little bit longer."

Izzy gulped. Scott glared at Jenn.

Jenn turned to her friends. "Back to what I was saying. You know how Zeus said we should learn our enemy's powers and strategies? Well, this is how. Ladies, in just a short while we will witness something that no human being has ever seen. We will watch the actual Titanomachy." Jenn opened the door to the contraption, gesturing her friends inside.

"We're not leaving now, are we?" Alice asked frantically.

"No way. There are a few things we need to go over before we leave. I just wanted to show you how this works."

Jenn stepped into the device and approached a set of switches. As she pressed a blue button, a keyboard and a computer monitor emerged from the silver wall. Jenn typed in a five-letter word and the phrase *access granted* appeared onscreen.

"F.Y.I., the password is magic, but spelled with a j," she announced.

A globe of the earth came onto the screen.

"To operate this device you plug in the location." Jenn typed Paris, France and watched as the virtual map closed in on the city. "Then you decide the time. It can be as vague as a time of day, or you can be specific and put an actual date. Either way, you'll end up at some point in the past."

"Sounds easy enough," said Colleen.

"Yeah, it doesn't take a rocket scientist to make it work," said Jenn.

"It just takes one to make one," said Melanie.

"What are the bars for?" asked Izzy, running her hand over a pair of wooden railings.

"To hold onto. It's a bit of a bumpy ride," said

Jenn. "All right, there's something else we have to discuss. Just exit and go to the island counter."

The girls left the time machine and gathered around the counter. Jenn grabbed a pair of posters and positioned the first on a wooden stand. The poster was a list of the Titans, accompanied with humanlike sketches that attempted to place a face with each god.

"These figures are who we're trying to protect the universe from, the Titans. Just like us, they all have their own individual powers, weaknesses and strengths," said Jenn. "And so we'll know who they are, you're getting a crash course of the gods of the Titanomachy.

"First is Mnemosyne, goddess of memory. Basically, she erases or alters memories." Jenn pointed to a picture of a woman with scrambled black hair. "Next are Hyperion and Thea, god and goddess of light. They are husband and wife and share the same ability of controlling what you can see."

"Oceanus and Tethys are god and goddess of the seas. They have water powers," said Jenn. "Then there's Coeus, Iapetus and Atlas. Coeus is intelligent. It's his ideas and plans that are put into action. Be careful if you try to outsmart him, it's difficult to do. Iapetus is a warrior god, which means that he's quite skilled with weaponry. And Atlas is the god who held the earth on his back. Obviously, he's very strong.

"There's also Crius and Phoebe. I must admit that I don't know what their powers are, so keep an eye out for them. They're just as dangerous as the others. And finally, there's Cronus, the Titans' ringleader. We've seen his fire powers, but he might have other abilities. If you look out for no one else, watch him."

"What about Uranus?" asked Alice.

"Uranus, although he is a Titan, was not present during the final battle of the Titanomachy, so he won't be there. Like Zeus said, by then the Olympians had presumed him dead."

Jenn placed the second poster on the stand.

"Now to the Olympians, the gods on our side. Ares, god of war. Athena, goddess of wisdom. Apollo and Artemis, brother and sister who use bow and arrows. Apollo also has the power of healing. Next is Hades, god of the underworld. I'm unaware of his abilities, so make note to observe him. Hera is Zeus's official wife who can transform into anything she pleases. And Hestia is the goddess of the hearth, but I don't know what she can do.

"Then there's Aphrodite, the goddess of love, and her husband Hephaestus, god of fire. There's also Poseidon, another god of seas. He's the Olympian who carries a trident, so he'll be easy to recognize. Hermes is the messenger god. He carries a golden staff called a caduceus. Also, there are actually two *Titans* who converted to the Olympians' side. Brothers Prometheus and Epimetheus once fought against Zeus, but now fight *with* Zeus. Prometheus is the god of forethought and Epimetheus the god of afterthought.

"Finally, there's Zeus. He can be seen as Mother Nature because of his active powers. He controls rain, wind and lightning. My guess is that he, too, will be easy to point out," Jenn paused. "These, my friends, are the

Olympians."

"Jenn, that's a lot of gods. How are we supposed to remember who's on what side and who has which power?" asked Melanie.

"My guess is that the Titans and the Olympians will be wearing different color tunics. And as we watch the Titanomachy, you'll get to see each of the gods' powers, so you'll remember who has what ability," said Jenn.

"Can we go over the Titans' names again?" asked Izzy.

"Sure. The eleven Titans that we will see are Mnemosyne, Hyperion, Thea, Oceanus, Tethys, Coeus, Iapetus, Atlas, Crius, Phoebe and Cronus," said Jenn.

"Just rolls off the tongue," Melanie retorted.

"And the Olympians are?" asked Izzy.

"Ares, Poseidon, Hades, Apollo, Artemis, Hera, Athena, Hermes, Aphrodite, Hephaestus, Prometheus, Epimetheus, Hestia and Zeus."

"I think I've got it," said Izzy.

"Now, one more thing before we depart." Jenn opened a drawer from behind the counter and retrieved four pairs of blue-rimmed goggles.

"These are not your ordinary specs," said Jenn. "They're made specifically so that invisible things can become visible. When we arrive in the past, Izzy will use her power to make each of us transparent. With these, we'll be able to see each other. Izzy won't need them because of her ability." Jenn glanced at Scott. "We actually have Scott to thank for the device. He's been

213

studying light refraction and was able to come up with a plastic that lets us see the invisible. I inserted the new plastic into regular swim goggles."

Jenn handed each of the girls a pair. "Let's go."

"Let's go as in *now*?" asked Izzy, cringing.

"Of course."

"And the Titanomachy as in *the* Titanomachy?"

"Yes," Jenn confirmed. "Izzy, what's wrong?"

"Oh, I don't know…maybe the fact that we're going to watch the Titans and Olympians fight *might* concern me a little. I doubt this'll be like a boxing match. You know, where there's a nice big ring in-between the fighters and the audience."

"Izzy, I promise we'll be fine," said Jenn.

"And you're sure they won't see us?"

"I promise they won't."

"Do you always keep your promises?"

"Izzy!" Jenn sighed.

"Sorry, I'm just nervous," said Izzy.

"That's understandable, but like I said, I promise we'll be fine. This journey is important. We need to do this."

Izzy nodded. "Okay, let's go then."

"Follow me."

Jenn led her friends back to the time machine. Scott sat in a corner of the laboratory, his arms crossed.

As she opened the door to the machine, Jenn paused. She turned around and approached Scott, her eyes calm. "You know, I'm gonna need you on my side."

"I'm always on your side. I just don't want to see

you get hurt," said Scott.

"You don't have to worry. With Colleen's super strength and Alice's shield, we're covered."

Scott took a deep breath.

"Kiss for luck?" Jenn asked.

Scott hugged Jenn and kissed her lightly. He whispered into her ear, "Just come back safe."

"You've got it." She turned back to the time machine and stepped inside.

Once the girls were situated in the contraption, Jenn approached the keyboard.

"Do you know the exact date of the Titanomachy?" asked Colleen.

"No one does," said Jenn.

"Then how are we getting there?"

"I just need a few key words. This can also work like a search engine."

Jenn typed in the words, *B.C.*, *Olympians vs. Titans*, and *final battle*. She pressed the enter key and the time machine began to shake. A green light that hung over the entrance flickered to red.

"Hold on!"

The time machine zoomed full speed into the dimensions of the universe. Its walls rattled, rocking uncontrollably in all directions. The girls held onto the railings to stay upright.

After a series of tremors, the bumpy ride smoothed to a halt and the red light turned to green.

"Remember," said Jenn, "we can't let anyone or anything become aware of our presence. We are in the past, but at this time the past is the present. Anything we do could potentially change the future and could drastically alter reality."

"No pressure," said Melanie.

"Be serious," Jenn warned. "Izzy, can you make us all invisible?"

"Yep," Izzy touched each of her friends. On contact, the girls disappeared.

"Put on your goggles," said Jenn.

The girls placed the blue specs over their eyes.

"I see you guys!" said Alice.

"I can see me!" cheered Colleen.

"We look like old photographs," said Melanie.

"As long as you keep your goggles on we'll be able to see each other," said Jenn.

"What about the time machine?" asked Colleen.

"What about it?"

"It's still visible. What if someone finds it?"

"Right. Izzy, if you wouldn't mind," said Jenn.

Izzy touched the time machine. Jenn lifted her goggles and looked for the device.

"Can't see it. Now we're ready."

The girls began walking through a thicket of woods, a compass clutched in Jenn's hand. They had landed in a forest that stretched out far. Giant olive and laurel trees soared into the sky, with massive leaves blocking the sunlight.

A low rumble began to sound. Jenn looked up.

"Rain," she whispered.

The canopy trees kept them sheltered.

"It means we're getting close."

Suddenly, they heard a rustling sound. The girls looked for the source of the noise. To their left, hidden behind the trees, was a woman. The woman was tall and elegant. Long black hair flowed down her back and a white toga hung from her shoulder. A dark man followed behind her, their hands intertwined.

The woman pulled the man toward her, lightly pinning herself to the tree. They embraced each other sensually.

Izzy looked toward Jenn and whispered. "Who are they?"

"Just observe."

The girls listened to their conversation.

"Let us not go back," the woman pleaded.

"And where shall we go?" the man asked in return.

"Anywhere. Anywhere but here!"

"Wherever we go they will find us. We shall never be safe!"

"Then it is a price to be paid, but a fair price."

"You value me equal to your life?" questioned the man.

"Yes, if not more," said the woman, stroking his shoulders.

"You should not! I have tried to kill you. How can I mean anything to you?"

"And I have done the same. We are guilty of the same crime! Love is worth the risk of death."

"But is lust worth the same?" asked the man.

"Lust, you say? How can it not be love?" the woman raged. "Here we are, running from Cronus and Zeus. We are two sides fighting one another and yet, we are two sides joining together, rebelling."

"Aphrodite, I do not know."

"Crius, know me. That is all you must know."

"What shall I do?" asked Crius.

"Kill Cronus."

"Then you shall kill Zeus. We can kill them at the same time. Opportunity awaits!"

"I cannot," said Aphrodite. "I do not possess a killing power."

"Have Hephaestus do it."

"He would never betray Zeus."

"Then ask Hestia."

"Hestia is pure of heart. She cannot."

"Then I cannot kill Cronus. How can you demand something so profound and not fulfill my request in return?" asked Crius, confused.

Crius paused. Aphrodite gazed fearfully into his dark eyes, letting go of his arms. Crius pinned her to the tree.

"You lie!" Crius bellowed. "Love? Love! You are but a trick, attempting to blind a man to fulfill your desire. It is *you* who I shall kill! You are beautiful, Aphrodite, but I am smarter than you are fair."

Crius pulled his sword from its sash. Aphrodite held still.

"Enjoy your freedom while it lasts," she hissed.

Aphrodite broke away from Crius' grip. In an

218

instant, her body faded. Jenn removed her goggles and looked directly where Aphrodite was standing. The woman had disappeared from sight but was still physically there.

"She's invisible," whispered Jenn.

Crius, who could not see the beautiful goddess, swung his sword through the air. Aphrodite ran toward the opening of the forest. She was soon out of sight. Unsure of his target's location, Crius charged through the forest. The girls rushed for the opening, keeping their distance.

"Aphrodite and Crius?" asked Colleen.

"Yes," said Jenn.

"She was trying to trick him?" asked Alice.

"It seems so."

"Why?" asked Izzy.

"Like Zeus said, the Titans and Olympians were battling over who would have control of the universe. Whichever side gets killed or locked away loses. So if Cronus or Zeus are taken out of the picture, the other side will have a better chance of gaining total control."

"So she tried to trick Crius into killing Cronus?" asked Izzy.

"Yep."

"That was a sorry attempt," said Melanie.

"You miss every shot you don't take," said Colleen.

"Where are the rest of the gods?" asked Alice.

"Probably outside of the forest," said Jenn.

The girls left the woods. The forest led to a long stretch of sand, ending at the shore of the Mediterranean

Sea. Choppy waves crashed onto the shore as the downpour flooded the ground.

Immediately, they became aware of the battle that lay in front of them. Small battles of gods were scattered over the land. Powers were whipping back and forth at dangerous speeds.

"This is a war movie, but minus the movie!" said Melanie.

"Guys," Jenn beckoned, "even though we're invisible, we could still get hit by something. We need to take cover." She positioned herself behind a large rock.

Her friends followed, peering over the top.

"The Titans are wearing the gray tunics. The Olympians are in white," said Jenn.

"Who's fighting on the water?" asked Alice.

On the waves of the Mediterranean Sea, two gods fought by sending tsunamis at one another.

"That's the Titan Oceanus and the Olympian Poseidon," said Jenn.

"What about them, the gods by the cliff?" asked Colleen.

At the base of a cliff, the two largest gods were fighting with their fists. The larger of the two wore a gray tunic. He picked up the other god and threw him into the cliff.

"Atlas and Ares," said Jenn. "Atlas is in the gray, Ares is dressed in white."

"What about the gods in front of us?" asked Melanie.

"Titans Hyperion and Thea, who control light, and

brother Olympians Prometheus and Epimetheus, the seers."

Each of the four duelists held a sword, and Epimetheus held a shield. The opponents swung at each other, their weapons colliding.

Thea caught a hold of Prometheus and waved her hand over his eyes.

"Epimetheus, she has blinded me!" Prometheus shouted.

"Try for a premonition. See what is to come next!" Epimetheus replied, blocking Hyperion with his sword.

Prometheus placed his hands on his head, searching for a vision. Luckily, the next moment of battle played in his mind.

Prometheus envisioned Thea attacking him with a sword.

As Thea drew her arm back, sword in hand, Prometheus clutched her bicep, holding the weapon over her head. Thea struggled to break free. Prometheus picked up the Titan and threw her at Hyperion, knocking them both to the ground. The forceful blow reversed the blinding power over Prometheus, returning his eyesight.

Prometheus and Epimetheus leaned over their opponents. Neither Titan moved.

"Jenn, what happened?" asked Izzy.

"Thea and Hyperion are cornered. These two Titans have surrendered," said Jenn.

Across the battlefield, the Olympian Hephaestus and the Titan Tethys were dueling. The battle was unequal, favoring water over fire, Titan over Olympian.

Hephaestus shot a ball of fire at Tethys.

"Send another flame my way. I think I'll put it out with water!" Tethys cackled, shooting a stream of water at the blaze.

As the forces collided, the water extinguished the fire, creating a cloud of steam.

"Your cockiness will hurt you," Hephaestus warned. He sent a set of pellet-like fireballs at Tethys. Tethys created a wall of water, easily dousing the pellets.

"Keep it coming. I can do this all night!" she challenged.

The Olympian Hestia watched from afar. Wanting to help her brethren, she ran toward the battle, a stream of electricity glowing in her palm. Hestia released the current and electrocuted Tethys.

Suddenly, Crius stormed into view. He locked eyes onto Hestia. With a sharp wave of his hand he beckoned toward the sky. A black orb hurled from the clouds. Without warning, the orb crashed into Hestia's back, throwing the goddess into a nearby gorge.

As Crius laughed, something pierced his abdomen. The Titan fell to the ground wounded, a sword jutting from his midsection. Aphrodite hovered over him, holding the sword.

"Aphrodite!" Crius choked.

"Your freedom is dying," Aphrodite hissed. She flickered invisible and flew away.

In the gorge, Hestia was unconscious. Hermes had witnessed the attack and scurried to her side, dodging fireballs and orbs that crashed around him. When he reached the fallen goddess, he found her motionless, eyes shut. Her body was smothered in dirt and her beautiful skin was battered.

"Apollo!" Hermes bellowed.

"Hold on!" Apollo yelled.

Apollo was one hundred yards away, battling Iapetus alongside his sister, Artemis. Both were trying to shoot Iapetus with their mighty bows and arrows. With a sword in each hand, Iapetus deflected the whizzing arrows into the ground.

"Apollo!" repeated Hermes. "She's terribly injured!"

Apollo heard Hermes' second cry and looked at Artemis, hesitant to leave his sister.

"Go!" Artemis commanded.

Apollo ran to the gorge. When he reached Hestia, he brushed his hand over her chest.

"Can you heal her?" asked Hermes, his caduceus raised in defense.

"I believe so. Her spirit is weak, but I do not think Crius is strong enough to kill," answered Apollo.

He held onto Hestia's wilted body. Within a few moments, the goddess' eyes opened.

"She'll be fine!" Apollo called out. He gazed at Hestia with relief. "Welcome back."

Away from the gorge, the Olympian Hera and the Titan Mnemosyne were battling. Mnemosyne was attempting to brainwash Hera, shooting streams of black and purple energy at the Olympian. Hera weaved back and forth dodging the dark rays, determined to remain safe.

As Hera moved toward Mnemosyne, she transformed into a large bear. Hera jumped at the Titan, her teeth ready to snap. Mnemosyne shot a stream of power directly at the bear. The purple stream smashed into Hera, throwing her into the ground. The power of the blow changed the Olympian back to her original form. Her long gray hair whipped with the wind, and her womanly body was beaten and bruised.

Hera took a moment to stand on her feet. She peered at Mnemosyne, an expression of uncertainty emblazoned her face.

"Go after Hades," Mnemosyne commanded.

Hera left immediately. She caught sight of her fellow Olympian and stormed after Hades. Hades was battling the Titan Phoebe, an army of souls aiding his fight. The souls were in human form and were faded like ghosts.

Phoebe was shooting meteors at Hades, while Hades deflected them, emitting a blue shield from the palm of his hand. The souls were struggling to reach the Titan. Many were crushed by the galactic rocks.

Hera ran toward Hades.

"Hera!" Hades called, relieved. "I need your help. Please strike Phoebe!"

Hera ignored the request and ran full force into his

side.

On the ground, Hera slashed at her brethren. Desperately, Hades tried to separate their bodies while at the same time search for Phoebe's meteors. He watched as another meteor whizzed toward him.

With all of his strength, Hades threw Hera and quickly rolled to the right. The meteor hit the spot where he had lain.

Hera charged after her brother again. Hades created another blue shield that sent her falling backwards.

"Souls! Hold her down and keep her away from other Olympians!" Hades commanded.

The souls grabbed hold of Hera; the goddess fought back. As she struck the spirits, their bodies shattered into a million pieces.

"Your own kind is trying to kill you! Pathetic!" shouted Phoebe.

Suddenly, the Titan Mnemosyne joined the battle. Mnemosyne shot a black stream of power at Hades. Hades deflected the stream with a force field, ricocheting the stream into Phoebe. Phoebe stumbled backwards with a blank stare.

"An easy fix," Mnemosyne cackled. She aimed her palm at Phoebe and struck her with a purple stream of energy.

Suddenly, a golden stream electrocuted the two Titans. Mnemosyne and Phoebe were temporarily paralyzed. Hestia stood behind them, sparks flying from her palms.

Mnemosyne's paralysis reversed the curse on Hera's memory. Instantly, the Olympian remembered who she was and what side she was fighting on. Hera broke free from the souls. She stood over Mnemosyne and Phoebe, pinning the Titans to the ground.

Farther out, Athena and Coeus were dueling. Both were draped in armor with shields and swords in hand. They circled around each other, mimicking each other's steps.

"For a goddess you are exceptionally bold," said Coeus.

"For a god you are exceptionally weak," Athena responded.

"Then why haven't you claimed a victory yet?"

"Even a fool takes time to beat."

"And what do you define as a fool?"

"Someone fighting on your side, on the side of the Titans," said Athena.

"But we are battling for the same thing! We are different, yet the same. What divides me from you?" asked Coeus.

"Our actions after we claim the victory. Your desire to control the universe is based on your selfishness. Titans want the universe for their own sake, for total control of all living beings. Olympians, however, desire the universe *for* the sake of all living beings. We wish to see life forms produce their own world, their own joys and sorrows, not create their miseries for them."

"Then I am a fool in your eyes, and you are a fool

in mine." Coeus swung his blade at Athena.

Athena jumped, evading the attack of the blade. On her descent to the ground, she took her own weapon and forcefully thrust it at the hilt of Coeus' sword. The Titan watched helplessly as his weapon clanged to the ground. Athena landed on the dirt, holding her blade to Coeus' throat.

"It took time, but the fool is beat."

Coeus held up both of his hands in defeat.

In the center of all the battles stood Cronus and Zeus. The two leaders were surrounded by a circular wall of fire. It acted as their barrier, keeping any other beings from joining their fight. Back and forth they threw their powers, Cronus using fire and Zeus using the wind and rain.

"Back down, Zeus!" bellowed Cronus. "Death would be a cruel price to pay when you can foresee who will win!"

"From what I foresee, it is you who should back down!" said Zeus.

As he spoke, Cronus shot a tornado-shaped blaze at Zeus. Round and round the flames spun, towering high into the sky as black smoke flew from its top. Immediately, Zeus waved his hands down and beckoned the rain to fall harder. The raindrops sped into the twirling inferno and sizzled upon contact, having little effect on the blaze.

The fiery tornado barreled toward Zeus. Zeus created a huge gust of wind, shielding his body from the flames. As the two elements clashed, the flames stalled. The fiery tornado and the shield of wind teetered to and fro between the gods. With a giant heave, Zeus shot a stream of air into the forces. The collision created an eruption of steam and hot air, quickly extinguishing the flames of the ring. A cloud of smoke emitted and Cronus was knocked off of his feet, his vision blinded by the smoke.

Out of the fog, Zeus approached Cronus.

"It is over," said Zeus.

The smoke began to clear, and the entire battlefield became visible. Cronus looked at the result of each fray. He was alarmed to find each of his brethren wounded, pinned to the ground or surrounded by Olympians. Each Titan had surrendered and now remained defenseless.

"It cannot be," whispered Cronus. "It cannot be!"

"It is time to give up," Zeus demanded.

"The battle is lost, but the war is not!" Cronus growled.

Hermes slammed his caduceus onto the ground, sending a small tremor throughout the earth's surface. From the command of the staff, silver chains appeared in the air and wrapped around the Titans' wrists.

"There will come a day you will wish you had lost," Cronus threatened.

"That day shall never come," said Zeus.

"Enklei en tartaro!"

"Se d'apelauno apo choras!"

Zeus and Cronus simultaneously recited an incantation. Their voices ripped through the battlefield. A look of horror consumed Zeus' face, and Cronus sneered triumphantly at his son.

Suddenly, the Titans began to rise from the ground, pulling away from the earth's surface. At the same time, the Olympians and the souls rose, shooting toward the sky. Neither group was leaving by choice; both were under the spell of the two incantations. In nearly the blink of an eye, the Titans, Olympians and souls flew up and out of sight.

What had been the grounds of a vicious battle transformed from chaotic to still. The rain had ceased, and the dark clouds began to disappear.

Melanie, Alice, Jenn, Izzy and Colleen climbed out from behind the giant rock. Izzy touched each of the girls, restoring their visibility. They approached the battlegrounds. In the center where Cronus and Zeus had fought, an outline of a large black circle was singed onto the grass. Dark patches were scattered everywhere, places where fireballs exploded, and pools of water drowned the terrain.

Alice broke the silence. "Is it over?"

"What Zeus and Cronus said finished it off," Jenn confirmed.

"What did they say?" asked Colleen.

"In Greek, Zeus said 'lock in hell', and Cronus said 'banish from the world'."

"So that's the curse Cronus set upon the Olympians?"

"Yes."

"Then why didn't he say that earlier? Why didn't *either* of them cite their incantations earlier? They wouldn't have had to go through this whole conflict," asked Colleen.

"It doesn't work like that. In war there are rules and guidelines. There aren't many, and they're not always enforced, but they do exist," said Jenn. "For humans, we are not bound by any power to abide by rules if we are free. There are consequences for your actions, but there is no invisible force that keeps you from free will. For the gods however, because they are such powerful beings, their rules and guidelines are enforced magically. In order for Zeus to chant the words that will lock Cronus away, Cronus has to be in a position of surrender. One can surrender willingly, like Coeus did, or forcefully. In Cronus' case, it may have been a little of both. *He* would never give in, but since his entire army was defeated, Cronus went down with them."

"But why would Cronus give in? He seems like someone who would fight to the death," said Melanie.

"That's exactly *why* he gave in. Had Cronus continued to fight Zeus, he would have been killed. All of the Titans were guarded by the Olympians, and Zeus had a direct shot at Cronus. Once a god is dead, that's it. If Cronus dies, there's no way he can ever return to rule the universe, but if he lives, there's always a hope that he can reclaim the throne."

"Then why didn't Zeus just kill him? Why didn't any of the gods kill each other?" asked Izzy.

"I'm not certain, but I think it was because of the power factor. To kill a god takes a heck of a lot of energy. After a ten year war, I doubt that any of them had the

230

strength to actually kill their enemies singlehandedly," said Jenn.

"Then what about Crius? He was stabbed with a sword," said Colleen.

"That would be enough to kill a human, but like I said, it takes an incredible amount of power to kill a god. A stab wound wouldn't necessarily do the job. Crius will recover, it'll just take awhile. But he has plenty of time. When he comes back to Earth…in our world, he'll be as good as new."

"And why was Cronus able to set a curse upon the Olympians? He was the one who lost," said Alice.

"Although Cronus was the one in chains, even the losing side can call on a curse at the end of a battle. As long as the curse isn't too extreme for the winning team, it can be enforced. Being banished from the world isn't half as bad as being locked in Tartarus. The Olympians still have plenty of places in the universe where they can travel. The Titans, however, are confined to a stone cold cell," said Jenn.

"And you know this how?" asked Izzy.

"Omniscient, remember?"

"Oh, right."

"That's too bad for the Olympians," said Alice.

"It's just like wars in our lifetime. Although one side ultimately wins, along the way they suffer many losses. Soldiers die, money is lost…there's a downside to every fight," said Jenn. "Trust me, the Olympians could have had it way worse."

"I'm curious, why didn't Zeus use his lightning bolts? I didn't see any," asked Alice.

"He must not have gotten the power to wield lightning bolts until sometime after the Titanomachy," said Jenn.

"Jenn, what was the orb that Crius threw at Hestia?" asked Colleen.

"A star. Phoebe can call meteors into Earth and Crius can summon stars," said Jenn.

For a few moments longer the girls lingered on the battlefield. Soon, they began to walk back to the time machine. When they reached it, Izzy touched the metal, making the device visible. Inside, Jenn pressed a green button that was labeled *home*. The girls held onto the railings and waited for the machine to deliver them back to campus. Their mission was complete and everyone was safe, just as promised.

CHAPTER FIFTEEN

The Riddle

The sky was dark and gray. Heavy clouds rolled with the wind, slowly moving above the mountain. Cronus paced back and forth within the cavern.

Outside, a thundering roar began to sound and the mountain shook fiercely. Cronus glanced at the cave's entrance, watching as Uranus rose onto the cliff. A group of figures stood behind him, their tunics torn and battered.

"Cronus," said Uranus, "all of the Titans are here."

"And the souls?" Cronus hissed.

"Exploring the world they once knew, as promised."

"Good."

"Cronus!" Hyperion cheered. "It is invigorating to be back! To be on Earth!"

"Enjoy it, my brother. You have waited too long for this day," said Cronus, pleased.

"I sense that it has been worth the wait," said Oceanus.

"Indeed. We shall have our vengeance soon," said Cronus. He looked at the Titans sternly. "Did you find him?"

"Yes. Typhon is in North America. However, we did not find his body, but rather his ashes. The beast was killed," said Phoebe.

"By what?" cried Uranus.

"Uranus, you already know by what," Cronus snapped, turning toward Phoebe. "So you have found the Oracle's location?"

"Yes."

"Did you see her?"

"No, only Typhon's remains."

"The location is good enough. Uranus and I have seen the Oracle ourselves. We know that she still exists," said Cronus.

"You have seen the Oracle?" asked Coeus. "But how?"

"The prophetess was on the mountain; she came to us. I must warn you. She was not alone."

A hush fell over the Titans.

"Brethren," said Cronus, "I bring you forth to share news. Not only is the Oracle alive, but she has godlike powers, similar if not identical to Hades'."

"Has Lord of the Underworld shared his ability?" asked Mnemosyne.

"It appears so," said Uranus.

"The Oracle is accompanied by four other beings. Four female humans who also have powers resembling those of the Olympians," said Cronus.

234

"Pythia merely had her sacred visions. How can she have evolved to gain other abilities?" asked Crius.

"I do not believe that the Oracle has evolved on her own," said Cronus. "Zeus and his army are aware of our presence on Earth. It would surprise me if they did nothing to defeat us."

"You think that the seer is working under Zeus' command?" asked Atlas.

Cronus nodded.

"Then we kill her at once!" yelled Iapetus. "We must obliterate the seer *and* her guardians before they destroy us!"

"I agree," said Thea.

"But how shall we kill her?" asked Tethys.

"We know where she rests. We can return to her territory and attack," said Hyperion.

"Go to her territory and do *what*? *Hope* that she doesn't have an army waiting for our arrival?" Coeus asked mockingly. "We must bring them here, where *we* are in control."

"Then who will fetch her?" asked Uranus.

"I will," said Mnemosyne. "I can wipe her memory. She will not know who she is."

"I will assist you," said Iapetus. "I am fair backup."

"Good," said Cronus. "Fetch the Oracle, along with her guardians. Uranus, show them the prophetess. You will return immediately, for we have more to discuss."

"Yes," said Uranus.

Uranus, Mnemosyne and Iapetus exited the cave.

"As for the rest of us," said Cronus, "having ample time on our hands, we shall plan what will become of the Oracle."

The Titans began to laugh, their voices cackling. Soon, they would attain what had been too long denied. Their centuries of confinement would no longer matter.

* * *

When they arrived back to the lab, the girls found Scott pacing back and forth across the room. At first glimpse of the time machine he smiled.

"That took ten seconds," Scott said excitedly.

"Perks of a time machine," said Jenn.

"Did you learn all you hoped to?"

"Yeah."

"And everyone's all right?"

"Yeah."

"Now what?"

"We go back out."

"What?" Scott barked.

"Yeah, what?" asked Colleen.

"We learned all of the Titans' and Olympians' powers. Now we have to go and collect the keys," said Jenn.

"The third leg…or cane rather?" asked Alice.

"Yup."

"You're not going to recuperate first?" Scott asked.

"We'll be fine. We have to go while it's dark in Egypt. Approaching the Sphinx in daylight might look suspicious when all of the tourists see us," said Jenn.

"Just wait until tomorrow," Scott pleaded. "And Izzy can make you invisible. You can go during the day."

"We're going now." Jenn climbed into the Air Taxi and maneuvered it onto the Transporter's platform. Before Scott could say another word, the girls were gone.

They landed in Giza at midnight. The sky was pitch black, only lightened by the stars. Jenn turned on the lights of the Air Taxi. From a distance, she could distinguish the outline of an enormous figure.

"There it is," said Jenn. "The Sphinx."

"It's bigger than I imagined," said Izzy.

"Oh, it'll get bigger. We're pretty far away," said Colleen.

"Let's go to it." Jenn pressed the accelerator.

Melanie and Izzy followed the vehicle, running and flying along its side. When they arrived at the statue's base they looked up, gazing at the stone mammoth.

"Colleen, do you still have the leaf?" asked Jenn.

Colleen pulled the golden lettered leaf from her pocket. Jenn turned on a flashlight, aiming its light onto the words.

"A third leg you need for the key that you seek,
Is tucked away safe at the top of the peak.
At the edge of old Khafre you might get to see,
The ancient secret of man and the beast."

"We've found the beast," said Alice.

"All we need is to go to its top and look for the leg?" asked Melanie.

"That doesn't sound so bad," said Izzy.

"That's what I'm afraid of," said Jenn. "It sounds too easy. There's probably a catch."

"So let's find out," said Colleen.

Jenn prepared the Air Taxi for liftoff. "Melanie, double up with Alice in the back."

Melanie squeezed her way into the hovercraft. Jenn began steering the vehicle toward the top of the statue, with Izzy soaring beside the car.

The girls neared the Sphinx's head. When they floated in front of its mouth, the statue moved. The Sphinx slowly shook its head. Stiffly, its crusted mouth began to open.

"Ah!" Izzy hid behind the hovercraft.

"What's it doing?" asked Alice.

A deep, low voice rang clearly from the Sphinx's throat. "One riddle. One answer. One chance."

"Is this the catch?" Izzy asked nervously.

"Yes!" said Jenn, elated. "Remember when I told you about a man named Oedipus, and how he had to solve a riddle that was given from a sphinx? Well, that's the catch! We have to solve a riddle."

"Do you accept the challenge?" bellowed the Sphinx.

"Yes," said Jenn.

Izzy peeked from behind the hovercraft.

"What is seen from the top and the bottom, is seen half of the time, and is always up above?" the Sphinx asked.

The girls thought silently. After a few moments passed Izzy sprang from behind the hovercraft.

"I know what it is! The sun!" she announced.

Jenn looked shocked, crossing her fingers for luck. The giant statue opened its mouth.

"Incorrect!"

Suddenly, the ground began to shake and the Sphinx began to move. The figure broke free of its stiff mold, shaking its head back and forth. Slowly, the creature arched its back. The once frozen statue shook its entire body, shaking off loose rocks that rested upon it.

The girls were stupefied. Jenn thought back to what the statue had said, replaying its words in her mind.

One riddle. One answer. One chance.

She thought of Oedipus' encounter with another sphinx, reviewing the story's warning.

All those who answered the riddle incorrectly were killed.

"It's going to kill us!" Jenn muttered. She glanced at the monster and watched as it rose to its feet, ready to charge. "IZZY! GO!"

Izzy turned her back on the Sphinx and took off as fast as she could. Jenn did the same, reversing the hovercraft. The Sphinx gave a menacing roar that rattled the ground. It lunged after the flying car.

"Why's it chasing us?!" Alice screamed.

"It wants us dead!" shouted Jenn. "Melanie, hold on!"

Melanie had no seatbelt and was gripping the side of the Air Taxi for dear life. Alice held onto her arm, trying to keep her from bouncing out.

Izzy soared frantically, her heart racing as fast as she flew. She took a sharp turn to her left, hoping to shake the Sphinx from her trail. Jenn followed Izzy's move, sharply turning the hovercraft. The vehicle swerved as if it had hit a bump, jostling the back seats. The force of the jolt flung Melanie into the air. She dangled on the side of the Air Taxi with Alice's grip on her wrist.

"Hold on Mel!" Alice pleaded. She tightened her grip on Melanie's hand.

"I'm coming!" Colleen announced.

She leaned over the side of the hovercraft and reached for Melanie. Instantly the Air Taxi began to plummet, tilting to the left.

"Colleen, no!" yelled Jenn. "There's too much weight on one side! We're going down!"

Colleen moved to the right side of the vehicle, leveling the machine. Melanie started to slip as Alice's grip loosened.

"Alice! Let me go!" Melanie commanded.

"What!? No!" Alice screamed.

"Let go!"

Alice shut her eyes and shook her head. "No!"

"Alice, please! Trust me!" Melanie pleaded.

Alice took a deep breath and stared at Melanie, terrified. With great reluctance, she let go.

"MEL! NO!"

Melanie plunged through the air. As she neared the ground, she positioned herself for impact. With her legs bent and her arms outstretched, she crashed to the sand, landing safely.

240

"She made it!" Alice gasped.

"She's still not out of the woods!" growled Colleen.

Directly behind Melanie was the Sphinx, its massive legs tearing through the desert. Melanie sprinted as fast as she could, but the beast was faster. Impulsively, she ducked to the right of the Sphinx. The statue took no notice and continued running forward. Melanie trotted to a halt, watching as the statue charged toward the Air Taxi.

"Jenn!" cried Alice. "It's not after Mel! It's after *us*!"

Jenn watched the Sphinx from her rearview mirror. The creature continued gaining speed.

"It's getting closer!" yelled Colleen.

"Hold on!" shouted Jenn.

Jenn steered the hovercraft to the right, just as Melanie had done. The statue was unaffected by Jenn's maneuver. It continued forward without pause.

"It wants Izzy!" said Jenn. "Izzy said the answer!"

Melanie caught up to the Air Taxi. "It's gonna kill her! She won't be able to out-fly it!"

"What if she turns invisible?" asked Alice.

"It can't kill her if it can't see her," said Colleen.

"We have to get to Izzy before it's too late." Jenn slammed her foot on the accelerator with Melanie racing alongside.

The Sphinx was getting much closer to Izzy. Izzy struggled to keep ahead, pushing with all of her might. She passed the pyramid of Khafre and now flew above the open desert.

Jenn drove the hovercraft by the top of the pyramid and signaled to Colleen. Colleen cupped her hands to her mouth.

"IZZY! GO INVISIBLE!"

Izzy heard Colleen's cry and turned invisible. The Sphinx, who had been watching the flying girl, couldn't figure out what happened to its target. It scanned the area, searching for her furiously.

Cautiously, Izzy began gliding away from the beast, hoping that it couldn't trace her scent.

"So Izzy answered the riddle incorrectly, and the Sphinx only tried to kill her. Since there are five of us, my guess is that we all have one shot at the riddle," said Jenn, halting the Air Taxi.

"What else could the answer be?" asked Colleen.

"What is seen from the top and the bottom, is seen half of the time, and is always up above?" Alice repeated the riddle. "How in the world did Izzy get *the sun* from that?"

"No, she was on the right track," said Jenn. "Think about it. You can see the sun from the top of the world and at the bottom of the world because the earth is always rotating around it. You can only see it for about half of the day, from dawn to dusk, and it's always above you when you see it, never below."

"But it's not the answer," said Alice.

"Stars do the same thing," said Colleen.

"We still need the cane. The answer's worth a shot," said Jenn.

"What if it's wrong?" asked Alice.

"Let's hope it's not." Jenn brought her hands to her mouth and yelled as loud as she could. "STARS!"

At the sound of Jenn's voice the Sphinx turned in the direction of the hovercraft. Jenn kept the vehicle stationed where it was, waiting for the statue's reaction. The creature walked toward the Air Taxi. It had forgotten about Izzy and now directed its full attention toward Jenn.

"Jenn!" Alice said, panicked.

The Sphinx continued walking toward the hovercraft, its paws pounding into the sand.

"Wait. It didn't answer," said Jenn.

The Sphinx paused and glared at the Air Taxi. It crouched as if ready to pounce. From the root of its throat, the Sphinx roared.

"INCORRECT!"

"JENN!" Alice screamed.

The Sphinx bolted into a sprint. Jenn put the vehicle in reverse and sped backwards. Preoccupied with the statue in front of her, Jenn neglected to look behind the hovercraft.

SMASH!

The Air Taxi crashed into the Pyramid of Khafre and began to skid down its golden slope. Panic-stricken, Jenn punched the hovercraft's brakes.

"The brake is jammed!" Jenn shrieked.

"Drive us off the pyramid!" shouted Colleen.

Jenn attempted to twist the steering wheel. Just like the brake pedal it held firm in one position.

"The steering wheel's jammed too!" Jenn yelled.

"No!" Alice screamed.

243

Melanie ran out of the way of the falling car. Both she and Izzy watched helplessly as it plunged to the desert floor.

Sparks flew as the hovercraft skidded down the side of the pyramid. Jenn, Colleen and Alice screamed as it dove. As they fell, the Sphinx charged closer. Alice looked over the side of the vehicle, staring at the ground. Despite her injury, she raised both of her hands and pushed with all of her might. A large silver force field grew from her palms. Alice directed the shield underneath the Air Taxi.

The craft bounced up and down on the shimmering bubble for what seemed like an eternity. Finally, the hovercraft settled and Alice released her grip on the shield. The machine plunked to the ground, steam shooting under the hood.

Although they had landed, the girls were anything but safe.

The Sphinx was almost on top of them, within fifty yards of the Air Taxi. The statue leaned back for one final lunge.

"NO!" Izzy screamed.

Melanie watched in horror, her stomach dropped.

The Sphinx leapt forward, shooting at Colleen, Alice and Jenn.

Alice raised her hands, emitting another force field. The shield was much smaller than the first and she knew that the Sphinx could break through it. Regardless, she kept her palms raised.

The Sphinx flew through the air, its mouth open

wide. It lowered its head, aiming at the base of the pyramid.

Alice shut her eyes, counting down in her head. She was too afraid to look her killer in the eyes.

Three…two…on-

"THE MOON!"

Alice looked up. Colleen was left breathless, trembling in the back seat. All of her energy had been thrust into those two words.

Suddenly the Sphinx halted. Its massive head froze with its mouth open. Its body crashed into the ground at the base of the pyramid.

Alice's shield quivered, her hands trembling. Colleen was shaking in the back seat and Jenn was stunned, gaping at the immobilized monster. The hovercraft was untouched. The mouth of the Sphinx was within an inch of its hood.

From the Sphinx's mouth, an object rolled off of its tongue. Jenn caught the item, grasping it tightly in both hands. When she realized what it was, she collapsed. In Jenn's hand was an old brown cane. The Sphinx had given them the key. Colleen had answered the riddle correctly.

Slowly, the girls crawled out of the Air Taxi. Melanie ran over to Alice, her face cringed.

"You okay?" she asked.

Alice nodded, speechless.

Everyone was silent. Only the footsteps of the Sphinx could be heard. The giant statue had picked itself up and walked back to its base, assuming its original position on the ground.

After composing herself, Jenn took the portable Transporter and pointed it in front of her friends. With their help, she pushed the hovercraft through the portal. When they entered into the lab, Scott was alarmed by the girls' battered appearance. The smashed hovercraft startled him even more.

"Oh my god! What happened?" he yelped.

"We're fine," said Jenn, irritated.

"What?" asked Colleen, her face creased.

"I said we're fine," Jenn repeated.

"Fine? No we're not!" said Colleen, turning toward Scott. "Your girlfriend almost killed us!"

Jenn froze, anger welling in her chest.

"It's not like that was on purpose!" barked Jenn. "You think I planned that? You think I wanted to get us killed?"

"That's exactly it! You didn't plan it! You didn't have a plan when you yelled '*stars*'! When the Sphinx came after us, you crashed us straight into a pyramid!" bellowed Colleen, towering over Jenn.

"You suggested stars! It was *your* moronic answer!"

"And it was my *moronic* answer that kept you alive!"

"It doesn't matter anyways. We've got the next clue," said Jenn, holding up the cane.

"Oh, well, if we have the next clue *everything's* better!" Colleen mocked. "You don't get it, do you? Nobody cares about that damn stick! I almost died tonight, Jenn. I almost watched my friends die, and it would have been all your fault!"

"I don't need this from you. I get enough crap from Scott!" Jenn growled.

"Maybe if you took a minute to shut up, you'd actually hear what he has to say! Scott has some good points about this whole *protecting the universe* thing. You're not always right, Jenn. You don't know everything!"

"What I do know is that I *don't* need you! Get out of my lab!" Jenn demanded.

Colleen didn't hesitate. She stormed out of the lab, slamming the door on her way out.

"Colleen!" Izzy chased after her.

The room was still as Jenn fumed.

"I've never seen her this upset," said Melanie.

"I've never *seen* her upset," said Alice.

"Yeah, well, who needs her?" grumbled Jenn.

"What are you doing?" asked Scott, his voice lowered.

"Scott, don't get into it," Jenn warned.

"No. Colleen's right! You just kicked her out because you can't admit that everything she said was true. This isn't a game, Jenn. This is your life! These are your friends' lives! If you die, there's no second chance. You're not invincible."

"You know what? I didn't ask for any of this. I didn't ask for powers and abilities, and I sure as hell didn't ask to have the fate of the universe rest in my hands! You're right, this is not a game. But if I'm not out there trying to stop Cronus and the Titans, then who is? If she can't handle it, I don't need her. If you can't handle it, you know where the door is," said Jenn.

Scott didn't move.

Jenn laid the cane on top of the island counter. "Let's decipher the next clue."

Engraved into the cane was a second golden message.

"Who so pulleth has my rights,
And with it a table of knights.
A crown you shall claim if it's destined to be,
Second item of the hidden three," Jenn read, her voice relaxed.

"This one is easy," said Scott. "Camelot has a table of knights; the Round Table. And the first three words...they sound familiar."

"That's because they're on the Sword in the Stone."

"How do you know? No one's ever seen the sword," asked Melanie.

"Good point, we don't know for sure. It's a myth, but if we understand the clue correctly, the myth is true," said Jenn.

"Look at the third line," said Alice. "'A crown you shall claim if it's destined to be.' Pull the sword from the stone and you're declared king, right?"

"Right," said Scott.

"The sword fits with the clues," said Melanie.

"Is there anything else that it could be?" asked Jenn.

"What about Excalibur?" said Alice.

248

"Excalibur was given to King Arthur from the Lady in the Lake, but in some versions Arthur pulled it from the lake," said Scott. "It could be referring to that version of the story."

"But when he gained Excalibur, Arthur was already king," said Jenn. "The clue says that you'll get a crown if you pull the item out of something. It has to be the Sword in the Stone. It's the only sword whose reward is a crown if you pull it free."

"Then go for the Sword in the Stone."

"How do we get to Camelot at the right time?" asked Alice.

"The time machine should be able to find it," said Jenn.

"When do we go?"

"Tomorrow morning. We've been through enough today." Jenn placed the cane under the counter. "Let's push the Air Taxi off of the platform and call it a day."

Together, Alice, Melanie, Jenn and Scott moved the Air Taxi to an open corner. The hovercraft's body was mangled. Dents sunk deep into its frame and lots of paint had chipped away.

"I'll start fixing it tomorrow," said Scott.

"Thanks," said Jenn, her eyes glum. "We better rest up. Let's meet here at ten o'clock."

"I'll be here."

On the way out, Alice turned to Jenn. "What about our classes and our homework? Finals are coming soon and I haven't been to class in two days."

"I told you, don't worry about. I have everything covered," said Jenn.

Without another word Jenn locked the door to the lab, desperately wanting to go home and relax.

* * *

Outside of Odyssey Academy's science hall, Mnemosyne, Iapetus and Uranus watched intently for the Oracle. They were hidden behind two giant trees, shadowed by the night sky. They hadn't been waiting long. They had seen many people come in and out of the entrance, including two young women who had exited furiously. One was small with long blond hair and the second was taller and darker, her eyes fierce. Other than the teenage girls, the surveillance had been quite uneventful.

Finally, a young woman with golden curly hair pushed through the doors, accompanied by two other young women and a young man.

"That's the Oracle!" said Uranus.

"Are they her guardians? There are only three," said Mnemosyne.

"That boy is not her guardian, but the girls are," said Uranus.

"Where are the others?" asked Iapetus.

Uranus reflected on whom they had seen throughout the day. "The humans who exited before them, a few minutes ago"

"That would have been good to know a few minutes ago!" Mnemosyne growled.

"Well excuse me, but I was looking for the Oracle,

not her protectors!"

"Never mind that," said Iapetus. "We will stay until they return. We need all five beings together at the same time."

"Then you wait for morning," said Uranus. "They will not return until the sun has risen."

"Then we will wait," said Mnemosyne.

"Fine. I must return to Mount Parnassus. Cronus is impatient," said Uranus.

Uranus glided away from the watch post, disappearing into the night. Mnemosyne and Iapetus remained hidden, waiting for dawn.

CHAPTER SIXTEEN

Battle of the Knights

The next morning, Melanie, Alice, Jenn and Izzy walked to the lab, ready for their venture to Camelot. When they arrived, Scott was huddled next to the Air Taxi, repairing the damages. To Jenn's dismay, Colleen was nowhere to be found. She hadn't come home to the dorm the evening before. She had spent the night at Lewis and Chandler's.

"Is Colleen coming?" asked Alice.

"I told her ten o'clock," said Izzy.

As if on cue, the door opened and in walked Colleen, her fire tape wrapped around her palms.

"I knew she'd come!" chimed Izzy.

"You're here," said Jenn, somewhat surprised.

"We're still a team," Colleen mumbled.

"We'll catch you up." Jenn pulled the cane from the island counter.

"Who so pulleth has my rights,
And with it a table of knights.
A crown you shall claim if it's destined to be,

Second item of the hidden three."

"We're searching for the Sword in the Stone," said Alice.

"As in, King Arthur's sword?" asked Colleen.

"Well, he uses Excalibur, but yes, Arthur's sword," said Jenn.

"Where do we find it?"

"Camelot. The plan is to go to King Arthur's castle, find the sword and steal it. We'll keep it to find the next clue and open up the Athena Parthenos. When this is all over we'll return the sword precisely where we found it," said Jenn.

Colleen nodded.

"All right, I think we're ready."

The girls stepped inside the time machine. As Jenn turned to close the door, Scott called to her.

"Good luck!"

"We'll be back soon," said Jenn.

Inside the machine Jenn typed in their destination; *King Arthur, Camelot.*

"Here we go!"

The time machine began to quiver. The light above its entrance flickered red, and the door locked. The girls held onto the wooden railings, awaiting their arrival.

Soon, the machine settled and the red light flickered green. Jenn reopened the door and the girls exited.

SMACK!

A loud clang sounded. The girls turned around, searching for the cause of the noise. To their surprise they found a spear jutting out of the time machine's roof.

"What the-?" Alice stuttered.

Melanie could hear something clattering closer and closer toward her. She turned around to see what it was.

"Guys, watch out!"

Without warning, a bronze horse charged in front of the girls. A rider sat on the horse's back, his body shielded in armor.

"Izzy!" Jenn gasped. "Make us all invisible!"

Izzy rushed to each of her friends and tapped them on the shoulder.

"The time machine too!"

With one touch the time machine disappeared from sight.

Alice spun around, observing their destination. The girls were in the middle of a jousting arena, standing between two colossal horses and their riders. Thousands of people looked down at the spectacle from their seats.

"I can't see you guys!" said Alice.

"I can," said Izzy.

"Where are the goggles?" asked Colleen.

Jenn reached in her pockets. She came up empty handed.

"I must have left them at home! They're not here!"

"Then what do we do?" asked Alice.

We have to get out of this stadium," said Jenn. "Head for the exit where the horses enter, the one under the press box!"

"They have a press box?" asked Melanie.

"It looks like a press box! Whatever, just go!"

"What about the time machine?" asked Izzy.

"Colleen, can you move it off to the side? We can't let the jousters destroy it," said Jenn.

"Move it? I can't even see it!" said Colleen.

"I'll lead you to it," said Izzy, grabbing Colleen's invisible hand.

Izzy directed her friend to the time machine with ease. Gripping its sides, Colleen pushed the contraption safely to the corner of the arena.

"I'm done!" said Colleen.

"Let's go! Run!" yelled Jenn, heading for the open gate.

As they ran, Izzy made sure her friends stuck together. After they left the stadium a man stood from the royal box.

"Who are they, and where did they go? I want every knight searching for the intruders! Arrest them and bring them to the chambers!" the man commanded.

The knights rushed out of the stadium.

Melanie, Alice, Jenn, Izzy and Colleen sprinted away from the arena. They stepped onto a cobblestone path and continued to run, steering their way through an old medieval town. After a few turns, they came across an alley.

"Guys in here," said Jenn.

They turned into the passage.

"Izzy, I think we're safe for now. Can you make us visible?" asked Jenn.

"Sure." Izzy touched each of her friends.

All five could see one another.

"I think we're in the right place," Jenn chuckled nervously.

"Why did we end up in the arena?" asked Alice.

"I wasn't specific enough when I told the time machine where to take us. All I wrote was 'King Arthur, Camelot'…and, well, we're in Camelot."

"Was Arthur there?" asked Melanie.

"I'm pretty sure. I bet we ran underneath him when we left," said Jenn.

"So now what do we do?" asked Izzy.

"We go ahead as planned. The castle shouldn't be hard to find. First, we go there and sneak in. We search the entire place until we find the sword."

"And then we peace out and forget this place," said Melanie.

The girls could hear clip-clopping hooves trotting down the cobblestone path.

"Izzy! Make us invisible!" said Colleen.

Izzy reached for Jenn and Alice. Before she could touch either of them, the girls found themselves cornered, silver blades poking at their throats. From both sides of the alley groups of knights surrounded them. All of the knights were draped in shimmering armor.

One knight directed his horse in front of the teens. He flipped back his helmet revealing his black matted hair and fierce dark eyes.

"Who are you and for what have you come?" he asked.

"Who the heck are you?" asked Izzy, pushing away the sword pointing at her throat.

"Izzy!" Jenn whispered harshly.

"I am Sir Mordred, knight of the Round Table. Now, you will state your name and your purpose," Mordred commanded.

Jenn was about to speak, but Izzy cut her off.

"Mr. Mordred, if you wouldn't mind, do ask your knights to lower their weapons. I don't appreciate their hostility."

Alice rolled her eyes and Colleen looked astonished. Melanie bit her tongue to keep from laughing.

"'Tis *Sir* Mordred and the blades stay where they are," said Mordred, his tone bitter. "What is your name?"

"Idona," said Izzy. "Idona Preciate swords being used against my friends *or* myself!"

"Izzy, shut up!" Jenn shrieked.

"Your appreciation is not taken into consideration. Say another word other than your name and I shall have you slain," said Mordred.

Jenn looked at Izzy and shook her head, silently pleading for her not to speak.

Suddenly, a beautiful black stallion pushed its way through the crowd. The knight who rode it positioned himself next to Mordred, his helmet flipped back. Izzy studied his features. He had brown hair and stunning blue eyes, matching her own baby blues.

"There will be no slaying of any kind. What is the issue, Mordred?" asked the knight.

257

"This wicked sorceress will not tell her name," Mordred growled.

"Ah, and what proof do you have that she is a wicked sorceress? Has she told you, or yet, have you seen her wicked ways?"

"You witnessed her grand entrance. What else can she be? Having the *pleasure* to speak with her, I have learned she is nothing but trouble."

"Then you are wicked as well, but you are a knight. Wickedness is not punished by swords. And I'm sure you've met Merlin, a family friend who practices spells. He is but a humble man, not a threat," said the knight.

Mordred grimaced. He steered his horse away from the crowd. The unnamed knight dismounted his horse, standing face to face with Izzy.

"Lower your weapons," he commanded.

The knights obeyed.

Gently, the knight took Izzy's hand. "I am Sir Lancelot. Who my fair lady, are you?"

Izzy nearly fainted. Quickly, she gathered her thoughts and spit out the first thing that came to mind.

"Isabel."

"Isabel?" asked Melanie, looking at Colleen. "Who's Isabel?"

Colleen shrugged.

"Lady Isabel, 'tis a pleasure to meet you." Lancelot bent down and kissed Izzy's hand. "Now, King Arthur wishes to speak with all of you. I am commanded to bring you forth to his castle, where you will meet with him. You will each ride upon the saddle with a fellow knight. Lady Isabel, you will ride with me. Mordred, you will help Lady Isabel to her seat."

The girls followed the knights, mounting onto their horses. Reluctantly, Mordred dismounted his steed and picked up Izzy, placing her on Lancelot's saddle.

Lancelot raised his hand. "Onward!"

As the castle came into view, the girls studied their destination. It was enormous in every way, with towers that seemed to touch the billowing clouds. The bricks were snow white, and a wide moat surrounded its base. After crossing a drawbridge, they arrived.

Upon dismounting, Lancelot approached the girls. "I must warn you, under orders I must assist you to the chambers. However it is only temporary. When King Arthur returns from the jousting tournament you will be called forth to meet him. Follow me."

With Lancelot's lead, the girls quickly found themselves in the fortress dungeon.

"Ladies, if you will." Lancelot opened the door to a prison chamber.

Reluctantly, the girls filed into the dungeon and heard the click of a lock behind them. Lancelot spoke through a small window.

"Do not fret. You will soon be free," he assured before he left.

The prison chamber was big enough to hold all five young women with room to spare. The floor and walls were tiled with brown stones and the dungeon was lit by a pair of candles sitting in metal holders hammered into the rocks. Jenn and Alice approached a wooden bench at the back of the cell. Colleen leaned up against one of the walls and Izzy paced around the room. Melanie sat on the floor, stuck in a corner with one leg outstretched and the other one bent.

"Cheery old place," said Melanie, her voice light.

"Reminds me of home," said Alice.

"At least Mordred's not here," said Izzy.

Jenn glared at her. "Speaking of whom, now is not the best time to cop an attitude."

Izzy smirked. "It's like I told him, I didn't appreciate having those swords pointed at us. Mordred wouldn't have done anything anyways."

"If you had kept provoking him he would have!"

"Oh, relax. I was gonna stop talking."

"And *I'm* the one trying to get us killed," Jenn mumbled.

"Shut up!" barked Colleen.

"And why did you come back?" asked Jenn.

"To make sure nobody gets killed."

"Tell that to Izzy."

"Tell that to yourself," said Colleen.

"Colleen, you know I would never do anything to hurt you guys…not on purpose," said Jenn.

"I know, but I also know that there are things you can't control. There are forces way beyond your power."

"If things are so uncontrollable then why are you here?"

"Because it's better than nothing." Colleen was adamant.

Jenn lowered her head. "For what it's worth, I'm glad you came."

Colleen looked away.

"So Izzy, who's Isabel?" asked Melanie, forcing a new topic.

"Me. It's my first name," said Izzy.

Melanie's eyes widened. "Your real name is *Isabel?*"

"*Yeah.*"

"I thought it was Izzy! How come we never knew that? We've known you for three years!"

"Izzy's a nickname, and you never asked."

"Well, Mel, you know my name's really Alicia, right?" asked Alice, her face composed.

"Seriously?" Melanie's jaw dropped.

"Just kidding!" Alice grinned.

"If I ever change my name, I'm not telling you guys. You'll have to figure it out for yourselves," said Melanie, folding her arms.

"Okay," Izzy and Alice laughed together.

The girls ceased talking. For what seemed like an eternity, they waited to be summoned upstairs. Bored, Colleen approached the door and peeked out of the window. She watched as another knight walked down the hallway toward their cell. He quickly opened the prison door.

"King Arthur wishes to see you," the knight called.

The girls followed him upstairs. They passed through a hall lined with suits of armor all the way to a pair of giant wooden doors. The knight pulled on the metal handles, opening the doors with ease.

When they entered, the girls were astonished with the room. There in its center was the famous Round Table. Tarnished and old, it was by far the largest table they had ever seen, stretching throughout the entire hall. Over one hundred knights were seated at it, mystified by the five ladies that stood before them.

King Arthur sat at the head of the table, a gold crown encrusted with rubies upon his head. A golden beard hung from his chin, accenting his reddish locks.

To Arthur's left sat Lancelot and across the table was Mordred, who almost looked content.

As the girls lined up in front of the king, the knights grew silent.

"Name yourselves," demanded Arthur.

"Melanie Taylor."

"Alice Payton."

"Jennifer Andrews."

"Isabel Itello."

"Colleen Benton."

"Where have you come from?" asked Arthur.

The girls hesitated, waiting for someone to answer. Finally, Jenn began to speak.

"From another kingdom, in the future."

Arthur looked up, intrigued. "From the future, say you?"

"Yes. I have built a time machine, and we have arrived from many years ahead of your time," said Jenn.

"Are you sorceresses?"

"No, but we do have powers."

The other four girls looked concerned. They were unsure of how King Arthur would react to Jenn's honesty.

"What is your purpose here?" asked Arthur.

"We are in search of the Sword in the Stone," said Jenn.

A huff came from the table of knights.

"The Sword in the Stone? Of what use is it to you?" asked Arthur, his eyebrows raised.

"It is a key that we need to unlock something...." Jenn hesitated.

"And what must you unlock?"

"Well...we're not sure."

"She lies!" yelled Mordred, standing up. "She does not know what the key opens? Ha! They want the sword for themselves. Wicked sorceresses, I tell you!"

"Silence!" commanded Arthur. "You will not speak until spoken to."

Mordred lowered into his seat, enraged.

"Is it true that you do not know what you are unlocking?" asked Arthur.

"Yes," said Jenn. "Your Majesty, in my time there is a great evil afoot. This evil is so powerful that it may destroy our world. With the sword we will be able to unlock something. Something that...God...told us would destroy the malevolence."

The knights began to whisper to one another. Murmurs of "God!" hissed from the table. The other four girls were deeply perplexed, but tried to keep their confusion from showing.

"God spoke to you? Are you prophets?" asked Arthur, moving to the edge of his seat.

"Yes."

What? Alice thought.

"King Arthur, I tell you they are liars! They are not women of God! If they were, then why would they plan to steal the sword?" bellowed Mordred, pushing his chair back.

"You planned to steal the sword?" asked Arthur, irate.

"Umm...well...steal is such a vague word," Jenn stuttered.

"See! They lie!" said Mordred.

"We never said we would steal the sword," said Alice. "Sir Mordred has jumped to preposterous conclusions."

"Then why else would you turn yourselves invisible? If you do not plan to go through with a shameful act, then why must you hide as if you are to be shamed?" asked Mordred.

"*You* travel hundreds of years into the past, end up in a stadium full of people who are already dead in your lifetime and see if *you* hide!" shouted Melanie.

"Silence!" roared King Arthur.

The room fell silent.

"As rude as Mordred is, I confess that I cannot help but think that what he says is true. There will be no thieves in my kingdom. Lock the prophets in the chambers. We shall hear no more of their wickedness."

"What!" bellowed Izzy.

264

"You can't!" shouted Colleen.

"King Arthur!" interrupted Lancelot, standing from his seat. "I have yet to see wickedness from any of the ladies and I beg that you listen to sources other than Mordred. If the prophets are speaking the truth, then do give them the chance to prove their worthiness. Have Sir Galahad, the pure of heart, detect if they are liars."

Arthur sat quietly for a moment, contemplating Lancelot's words.

"Fine. But if Galahad senses a single ounce of deceit, the prophets are banished to their cell. Sir Galahad, please be the judge of our visitors."

Next to Lancelot, a young knight rose and walked toward the girls. He had a coarse bronze beard, and warm navy blue eyes.

"Shall I question them all?" asked Galahad.

"One is sufficient. Take your pick," said King Arthur.

Galahad walked down the row of the girls, observing each individual. He turned back around and approached Alice, holding out his hand. Alice clutched it tight.

"What is your name?" asked Galahad.

"Alice Payton."

Galahad turned to the knights and smiled. "She told the truth!"

The rest of the table laughed.

Galahad turned back to Alice. "Are you from the future?"

The distant future, Alice thought to herself.

"Yes," she answered aloud.

"Have you come in search of the Sword in the Stone?"

Yup, we're looking.

"Yes."

"Do you need it to protect your future's time?"

Cronus plus Titans equals total domination.

"Yes."

"Will it be returned to Camelot?"

Eventually...

"Eventually," said Alice, concerned by her answer.

"One more," said Galahad. "Have you spoken with a god?"

Alice thought about the question for a moment, afraid to answer. She reviewed it in her mind meticulously.

He said a god...not God! We spoke with Zeus!

"Yes!" Alice answered, grinning as she spoke.

Galahad faced Arthur, his face content. "She is as pure and truthful as I."

Jenn gave her a thumbs up, delighted with the results.

"Then we shall leave the chambers empty and hand the Sword in the Stone in the prophets' care," said Arthur.

"Your Majesty, you cannot!" yelled Mordred. "If they are to handle your precious sword, then they must prove that they will keep it safe. I say we duel the prophets!"

"Fine," said Arthur. "Five knights shall battle the five prophets. One on one you must duel in the jousting arena. Prophets may use their powers, seeing as my knights are so talented with their blades. Each contender will carry a sword and a shield, and they shall all wear armor. Instead of fighting to the death or until there is bloodshed, the duel will end at the drop of a sword. Whoever is left holding their weapon is the winner."

"I will fight Lady Isabel, your Majesty," said Mordred.

Izzy gasped.

"No, your Majesty! I would like her for myself," said Lancelot.

"Sir Lancelot will duel Lady Isabel," said Arthur.

Izzy let out a sigh of relief.

"Sir Galahad will face Lady Alice, Sir Gawain will fight Lady Jennifer, Sir Kay shall battle Lady Melanie and Sir Mordred will duel Lady Colleen. Now, escort our guests to the arena. Have them dressed in suits of armor and prepared for battle. The duels will begin in one hour," said King Arthur.

The five 'prophets' were escorted out of the room and taken through the castle. They remounted the horses and were ushered to the arena. Inside, each girl was fitted for a suit of armor. It took a few rounds of trial and error, but soon all of the girls had their own metal suit, their own sword and their own shield.

Before they left for the field, Jenn spoke to her friends.

"Quick pep talk! We almost have the sword. All that's standing in our way are the five knights and their weapons. Just smack their blades from their hands and keep yours safe off the ground. Oh, and use your powers! That's a huge advantage," she said matter of fact.

"Yeah guys, we've got this," said Alice.

"Down with Mordred!" cheered Izzy.

"Down with the swords!" said Melanie.

"Let's get 'em," said Colleen.

Together they climbed the stairs to the royal box. The knights were already there.

King Arthur addressed the combatants. "To be granted the rights of the Sword in the Stone, the prophets must each defeat their opponents in battle. If a single duel is lost, the prophets shall return home empty-handed. However, if they leave the arena victorious, the Sword in the Stone shall be theirs for the taking. At the sound of the horn the duel may begin. Lady Melanie and Sir Kay is our first match."

Melanie took a deep breath and left the royal box, walking toward the arena. As she entered the field, Melanie could see and hear thousands of people cheering. She hadn't noticed that the stands were full. Melanie shook her head, trying to concentrate so she could hear the call of the horn.

Sir Kay and Melanie walked to the center of the field. From the royal box a musician began to play a few notes on his horn, signifying the start of the duel. Melanie's heart skipped a beat as she watched the knight begin to advance. Sir Kay took the first swing, ramming his sword into hers. Melanie held onto the handle and moved with the swipe, guiding it to the ground.

"Come on Mel!" Izzy shouted from the stands.

"Run!" yelled Alice.

Their voices blended with the cheers of the crowd.

After taking turns back and forth, bashing each other's blades and shields, Melanie decided to give her power a chance at the duel. She stepped away from Sir Kay's body and started to run.

Melanie moved so quickly that he could not see her figure. All he saw was a blurred motion that was too fast for his eyes to follow. Melanie ran as fast as she could in a small circle, rotating around Sir Kay's body. He spun wildly, trying to keep up with the blur and swinging at it clumsily. After an ample amount of spins, the poor knight started to wobble and slowed down to catch his balance. Seeing the first chance to attack, Melanie took her sword and cut it as powerfully as she could, smashing it into Kay's. Barely able to stand, the woozy knight loosened his grip and released his sword.

The crowd gasped as Sir Kay's weapon fell to the ground. The girls yelled as loud as they could. Melanie slowed down to a halt and waited for the knight to realize what had happened. When he finally caught his balance, Sir Kay looked down and saw his sword resting on the field. Angered, he grabbed his weapon and stormed out of the arena.

King Arthur called to the duelists.

"Lady Isabel and Sir Lancelot are up next."

Izzy grabbed her sword and Alice gave her a high five. She walked down to the field, passing Melanie on the way.

"Go get 'em, tiger!" Mel cheered.

Izzy grinned and approached the gate. Lancelot was waiting for her.

"Are you ready, Lady Isabel?" he asked.

"The question is, are *you* ready, Sir Lancelot?" retorted Izzy.

"As ready as one can be."

Izzy and Lancelot walked onto the field and approached the center of the arena. Soon, the horn sounded. The battle began.

From the start, Izzy used her powers. Every time Lancelot would reach for her sword, Izzy would blink invisible, ducking away from his weapon. It almost became a game for her. She would pop up behind Lancelot or directly in front of him, displaying her advantage. Growing weary of the unfair game of keep away, Lancelot flipped back his helmet so that Izzy could see his face.

"Useful ability you have," Lancelot laughed, continuing to fight.

Izzy waved back her mask. "It comes in handy!"

"Have you always been able to do that?"

"It's a new talent."

"And how does one come by such a skill?"

"Pure luck."

"Do you come by luck often?"

"About as much as anyone else. Although, I have to thank you," said Izzy. "You've brought me great luck. You've helped me twice and I've known you for less than a day."

"And how have I helped you?" asked Lancelot.

"For starters, you arrived at the right moment when

Mordred threatened me."

"You are an outspoken lady, which is a quality I admire."

"It works against me sometimes," said Izzy.

"Nonetheless you speak your mind as you wish. You are quite bold and would make a good knight," said Lancelot. "What was the second way in which I helped you?"

"This is it," said Izzy. "I'm dueling you instead of Mordred!"

"Your life is precious, I could not let him take that away."

"Thank you."

"And now, if I may help you once more, Lady Isabel," said Lancelot, his eyes sincere.

"I can't ask for anything else," said Izzy. "You've done enough already."

"And yet there is more I can do. Turn invisible and then reappear right before my face. Strike my sword and watch as you step closer to the Sword in the Stone," said Lancelot.

Izzy blinked invisible and approached Lancelot as close as she could. In one motion she became visible and swiped at his sword. Lancelot acted surprised as his blade fell to the ground. The sword settled onto the floor as a roar erupted from the crowd. Melanie, Alice, Jenn and Colleen screamed in delight and danced around, unable to control their excitement. Izzy looked at Lancelot, mouthing the words *thank you*. Lancelot bowed and escorted her off the field, carrying her sword and shield.

King Arthur called the two opposing sides back to his seat.

"Lady Jennifer and Sir Gawain, 'tis your turn."

The two duelists stepped onto the field. Almost immediately the horn sounded and the battle began.

Jenn used her shield quite a bit. Her style was more defensive, blocking each of Gawain's shots while keeping her sword gripped in her hand. For twenty minutes the battle dragged on, continuing in the same pattern. Gawain slashed with his sword as Jenn held up her shield. Occasionally Jenn would throw in a swipe or two. The suspense had died in the crowd and the only people who seemed anxious about the fight were the four other girls. They continued to watch with as much focus as they had when it started.

While battling, Jenn began to notice something strange about Gawain. In the beginning of the duel his movements seemed perfect and exact, but as the fight crawled on, Gawain's stability began to diminish. The knight would stumble or his sword would slip from his grip. His swings weren't as powerful as they had been and his reflexes were lagging.

Gawain...Gawain...what is it? Jenn thought to herself. Something bothered her about the way he stumbled. Then it dawned on her. Something she had learned in elementary school played in her mind.

Sir Gawain of the Round Table was cursed. Every day, Gawain's strength would peak at noon and then severely decline, leading to the end of the day when it would crash. If Jenn's suspicions were correct, Gawain would continue to fight worse and worse with each passing minute.

Jenn glanced up at the sky. The sun was past its high point, slightly sinking to the west.

It's past noon, she thought.

She turned to Gawain and grinned.

"I see your curse is in affect."

"How…how do you know about that?" asked Gawain, dumbfounded.

"I'm a prophet, what can I say?" Jenn smirked.

She put down her shield and began fighting with her sword. As Jenn's confidence skyrocketed, Gawain's plunged. With a crisp thrust Jenn struck her blade into the knight's shield, knocking it out of his hand. With another blow she targeted his sword, tearing it from his grasp. As the sword fell to the ground the stadium burst into applause. Gawain exited the field, his chin tucked into his chest the entire way out. Jenn followed behind him, thrilled as King Arthur announced the next pair.

"Lady Alice and Sir Galahad, you may approach the field."

"Good luck, bud!" Melanie called.

Alice made her way down the stairs, stepping onto the field where Galahad was stationed. Without a moment to spare, the horn sounded and the duel began.

Alice found the defensive part of the battle to be easy. She hadn't brought her shield into the fight, using her silver force field instead. As Galahad swiped his sword, Alice deflected the weapon. In turn, the knight met Alice's advances with his own sword.

After a great time of dueling, Sir Galahad pushed back his helmet.

"I know your secret," he whispered.

Alice pushed back her helmet.

"What?"

"Your secret," said Galahad. "I know you're not a prophet. None of you are, but I commend you. Your quest is noble and your heart is brave."

"You knew when you asked me the questions. You lied for us?" asked Alice.

"I am pure of heart, I cannot lie."

"You fixed the questions so that my answers would be truthful, didn't you?"

As Alice's sword clashed with Galahad's, the knight's weapon fell out of his hand. The swipe had been no more powerful than anything Alice had done before, and yet, Galahad's blade fumbled to the dirt. He approached her and whispered.

"Good luck with your quest."

Galahad bowed to his opponent. They left the field, the roar of the crowd echoing throughout the stadium. Alice approached Colleen in the royal box.

"Well done!" said Colleen.

"Thanks. Try not to embarrass Mordred too badly," said Alice.

"I'll try."

King Arthur beckoned Colleen to his side. "Finally, for our last duel, Lady Colleen versus Sir Mordred."

Melanie gripped her shoulder. "All right, this is it!

It's up to you, bud!"

Colleen took a deep breath and descended the stairs. She stepped onto the field with Mordred directly opposite her. All the way to the center the knight taunted her.

"Do not blink, you might miss watching your sword slip to the ground. I assure you, this will be very fast," Mordred snickered.

Colleen ignored Mordred. The two duelists stood ready on the field, crouched low. For the last time, the horn sounded. Colleen and Mordred swung at the same time. Their swords collided.

CLANG!

"AH!" the crowd gasped into silence.

Mordred and Colleen stood still in the center of the field. One of them held their sword, while the other's was limp on the ground.

Colleen looked at Mordred and pulled back her helmet. "You were right, that was fast."

With one hit Colleen had overpowered Mordred, sending his weapon tumbling to the ground.

Mordred stared at his blade, his jaw dropped. "How...how....how did you....how did...how...?"

The four other girls were cheering out of control.

"Woohoo!" yelled Izzy.

"Yeah Colleen!" shouted Jenn.

"That's my roommate! That's my roommate!" Alice hollered.

"Okay Colleen! I see you!" said Melanie.

Colleen tossed her sword in the air, flipping it round and round. On its way down, she caught the hilt, holding the weapon firmly in her hand. On her way off of the field, she passed by Mordred and gave him a pat on the back.

"Maybe next time."

Mordred didn't respond. He was too busy staring at his sword. "How did…how…how did you…?"

When Colleen made it to the top of the staircase, Izzy jumped into her arms. Their armor clanked oddly together.

"You did it!" Izzy squealed.

"*We* did it!" said Colleen.

Countless hugs and high fives were exchanged between the five girls. They had conquered the knights of the Round Table. All that was left to do was collect the Sword in the Stone.

King Arthur stood from his throne and called the stadium to attention. He beckoned the girls and the knights to gather around him.

"Today is a day that no man, woman or child in Camelot will ever forget. Five strangers appeared in our kingdom, in search of the Sword in the Stone. On their quest they were faced with challenges that put their honesty, courage and strength to the test. And now they stand before me, five champions, five women who are victorious. It is an honor and a privilege to award these heroes with the Sword in the Stone. May they always be strong and may they protect their kingdom and time."

Lancelot handed Arthur the sword, and the king

pulled it gently out of its case. He studied the weapon, flipping it back and forth.

"Before I place the sword in the care of the prophets, I would like to honor them. Prophets, please kneel before me."

The girls lined in front of King Arthur, with one knee settled on the ground and the other propped up. Arthur placed the sword on Melanie's left shoulder. He then moved it over her head to her right shoulder, tapping both with the metal blade.

"Since in this world only men can be knights, I dub ye, Lady Melanie, the quick." Arthur moved to Izzy, repeating the action down the line. "Lady Isabel, the spirited. Lady Jennifer, the wise. Lady Alice, the pure, and Lady Colleen, the strong."

King Arthur faced the crowd.

"Ladies and Gentlemen, I give you the five newest and loyal friends of the Round Table!"

The audience applauded, the entire stadium rumbled with noise. The knights clapped for their fellow brethren, removing their helmets out of respect. The only person who wasn't clapping was Mordred, who still stood on the battlefield mumbling in disbelief.

King Arthur gave Jenn the Sword in the Stone. "Keep this safe, but more importantly, keep yourselves safe. Good luck on your quest. I have faith in you. You are always welcome in Camelot." He placed his hand on Jenn's shoulder. "Now you must go. The future awaits you."

The girls turned toward the stairs and began to walk down, on their way to the invisible time machine. As Izzy began her descent, she heard Lancelot calling her name.

"Lady Isabel! Lady Isabel!"

Izzy turned around. Lancelot approached her and took her hand.

"Lady Isabel, I have something to give you." From his hand, Lancelot presented a scarlet silk cloth. He placed it into Izzy's palm and gazed into her eyes. "It isn't much, but take it as a token of remembrance. Always know that if you need protection, I am a friend to whom you can forever turn."

"How can I ever repay you? You have done so much for me," said Izzy.

"You have paid me more than I have helped you. I consider myself very lucky to have made your acquaintance."

"Do you come by luck often?" asked Izzy.

"About as much as anyone else, but today has been an exceptionally lucky day," Lancelot smiled. "Now you must go, Lady Isabel. Your friends are waiting."

Izzy leaned up to Lancelot and kissed him on the cheek.

Lancelot bowed his head and whispered. "Hurry."

Izzy turned around, pulling her hand away from Lancelot's. As she walked down the stairs she turned back for the last time. Lancelot watched her as she exited the stands, joining her roommates.

"Let's go home," said Jenn.

278

As the girls crossed the field for the last time, the crowd cheered. Izzy made the time machine visible and the girls turned around before they entered. They waved to King Arthur and Lancelot, who waved in return from the royal box. The girls watched Mordred, who was still in the field mumbling.

"Bye, Mordred!" said Izzy.

The dumbfounded knight was too preoccupied to hear Izzy's farewell.

The girls stepped into the time machine. Jenn reached for the green button when Melanie started to speak.

"So, Jenn...prophets?"

Jenn smiled, handing Melanie the sword.

"Maybe I embellished a little...or a lot."

"Eh, make a white lie and help save the universe, or tell the truth and get locked in prison," said Colleen, holding out her hands like a balancing scale. "I choose option A."

"Me too," giggled Izzy.

"I'm glad you guys approve," said Jenn. She turned to Colleen, her eyes nervous. "So...Col, are we cool?"

"Are we cool?" Colleen repeated. "Jenn, we're better than cool!" She hugged her friend close.

Jenn let out a sigh. Comforted, she reached for the green button marked *home* and pressed it. The time machine began to rattle.

"Two down, one to go!" cheered Alice, gazing at the sword.

The girls were on their way home, ready to decipher the third and final clue.

CHAPTER SEVENTEEN

The Hidden Village

"One day, one chance to find where I live,
But if someone leaves, it'll stop the trick.
I'm used all the time to catch what can't walk,
You must hurry to get me before time is up,"

Colleen read, setting the sword on the island counter.

"You're knights!" said Scott.

"We're Ladies of the Court of King Arthur Pendragon!" cheered Izzy.

"That's a heck of an honor. You must have made quite an impression on King Arthur."

"Yeah, just back talk one of his best knights and beat them at their own game, and you could be a Lady too," Melanie retorted.

"Guys, back to the clue," said Jenn.

"Oh, right," said Izzy. "Hey, does it have that 'who so pulleth' message on the other side?"

Izzy grabbed the sword and flipped it over.

"Izzy focus," Jenn scolded. "Why are you so distracted?"

Alice smirked. "She only gets like this when Jayden's around."

"Or Lancelot!" said Melanie.

"What? I do not," said Izzy.

"You *so* do!"

"Do *not*!"

"Do too!"

"Do no-"

"Melanie! Izzy! Hush!" hollered Jenn. "You sound like five year olds! No, never mind. Five year olds are less obnoxious!"

Melanie and Izzy shut their mouths.

"Thank you," Jenn huffed.

"I don't understand this clue," said Colleen.

"Same here. Let's take it line by line," said Alice. "One day, one chance to find where I live."

"So we have one day to find the key. Literal, but true," said Colleen.

"But if someone leaves, it'll stop the trick," Alice paused, scratching her head. "If you leave something, some trick will stop? I'm just rearranging the words, this isn't helping."

"No, keep going," said Jenn.

"I'm used all the time to catch what can't walk."

"It's a trap of some kind, like a net or a cage," said Colleen.

"You must hurry to get me before time is up."

"We have a time limit."

"Does this sound familiar at all?" asked Alice, doubtful.

"Actually, it does. Wait a sec." Jenn approached a tall bookshelf and searched through its rows. After a few moments she found what she was looking for and brought back a green encyclopedia.

"Encyclo One-O-One?" asked Melanie.

"Yep," said Jenn, flipping through the guide. After a moment she came to a halt. "Ah ha!"

"What?" asked Izzy.

"Brigadoon!"

"Brig-a-who?"

"Brigadoon!"

The girls stood still, confused.

"What's Brigadoon?" asked Alice.

"It might be our next destination," said Jenn. She ran her finger over the entry. "Straight from the book, 'Brigadoon - once every century a small fishing village appears somewhere in the countryside of Scotland. The village appears for one day, only to disappear twenty-four hours later. Any person who finds the hidden town may enter, but if any of the residents leave, Brigadoon loses its charm, breaking its enchanted spell. Its inhabitants would be eternally unhidden, and the village would remain where it was found.'"

"It's a lost city, like Atlantis?" asked Colleen.

"Kind of," said Jenn. "They're similar, but Brigadoon isn't necessarily lost. According to the legend it can be found quite easily, but only if you know its location and the day it will reappear."

"So why do you think the clue leads us there?" asked Alice.

"Well, it says here Brigadoon comes around for one day every hundred years. Typically, humans only live within a hundred years, which would give us one chance to find Brigadoon."

"Not unless you're my Great Aunt Tillie," said Izzy. "She lived to be one hundred and two."

"Like I said, typically you would only have one opportunity. And like the clue said, you have 'one day, one chance to find where I live'. Secondly, if the residents of Brigadoon leave on the day that it unveils itself, then its spell is broken and the village will stay put wherever it landed, forever. Referring back to the clue, 'but if someone leaves, it'll stop the trick'. The trick is the spell that keeps the village returning once every century. Exit the village and you stop the trick.

"My third reason comes from the last line, which says that you have a time limit. Brigadoon only sticks around for twenty-four hours before it disappears, hence 'you must hurry to get me before time is up'. Finally, Brigadoon is a fishing village. The clue stated that whatever we're looking for is constantly used, catching something that can't walk."

"Fish can't walk!" said Izzy.

"Way to go, Einstein," Melanie laughed.

"Oh, be quiet," sighed Izzy. "It's the connection, that fish can't walk. In a fishing village, what do they catch? Fish. What's something that can't walk? Fish."

"Precisely," said Jenn, closing the book. "Which means that the third key must be a fishing pole."

"Then I guess we're off to Brigadoon," said Alice.

284

"But how do we find it?" asked Colleen. "We don't have one hundred years to search for it."

"The time machine will locate it," said Jenn.

"When do we go?" asked Melanie.

"If you're ready, now," said Jenn. "Just take off your armor. Brigadoon's residents might find it alarming."

"Good point," said Alice.

The girls stepped out of the armor that they had received at Camelot, leaning the suits up against a wall. They took a few moments to prepare themselves, readjusting the gadgets and gizmos that Jenn and Scott had created and quickly devouring a few snacks. When all five girls were set, they approached the time machine.

"I'm not sure how long we'll be gone. Don't freak out if we're not back right away. If we aren't home before tomorrow…you'll have to find a way to track us down," said Jenn, calling to Scott.

"Will do," said Scott, his heart heavy with concern.

Jenn closed the time machine and stepped inside. She booted up the computer and typed in their destination, *Brigadoon*. Immediately, the box began to shiver and the red light glowed. The girls were on their way.

The time traveling ride was exceptionally long. The box shook relentlessly.

"What's the hold up?" asked Izzy, clinging onto the railing.

"I don't know," said Jenn.

"Are you sure the machine be able to locate Brigadoon?" asked Colleen. "It's not supposed to be easy."

"I'm telling you, the time machine can do this."

THUNK!

The machine crashed onto the ground.

"Whoa!" Alice yelped as her body lurched forward.

A few clicks and clanks sounded from the time machine's interior. The computer monitor flashed the word *overload*.

"No, no, no!" Jenn groaned, her fingers dancing on the keyboard. "Dang it!"

"What's it mean, *overload*?" Melanie asked, unsettled.

"Colleen was right. Brigadoon was too difficult to find," Jenn murmured. "I have to fix the device. You guys should step outside. This may take awhile."

"How long is awhile?" asked Alice.

"A few hours, possibly more."

"A few hours!" squeaked Izzy. "Why so long? You're super smart."

"Yeah, but I didn't take crashing into consideration. I didn't bring any tools with me. Plus, I have to get inside the machine and figure out what went wrong."

"Let's see where we landed," said Colleen.

Outside, dark green grass stretched into the distance with thick hills rolling in every direction. A dim sea reached outwards, set below a gray sky. Grass led straight to the bank of the water, where waves lapped onto the shore.

"Wow," Alice sighed.

"This beats Indiana," said Melanie.

"What if this *is* Indiana?" asked Izzy.

"Then we went *way* back into the past," said Colleen. "There's not a building in sight."

Izzy found a large rock and sat down, staring at the sea. The others stretched out on the grass.

Hours passed, and the time machine hadn't been fixed. Jenn worked diligently as the others became restless. The sun began sinking toward the horizon, signifying late afternoon.

"We've been out here for days!" Izzy groaned, falling onto the ground.

"It's been four hours, Izzy," said Colleen.

"You kept track?"

"I put on my watch when we returned from Camelot. After sitting in that dungeon for God knows how long, I though it be best to keep the time close by."

"Good idea," said Alice.

"Well, I'm going to walk around and explore this place. If I sit for another minute, I'll explode!" said Izzy.

"I'm coming too," said Melanie.

Together, Izzy and Melanie left the temporary campsite, eager for any type of amusement. They followed the shoreline at the base of a hill. After they had walked about a mile, the sea turned into a wide river, winding to the left. The girls followed the river.

Melanie halted as they rounded the hill. "Hey, look!"

Izzy peered forward. Raised over the river was a long wooden bridge, its planks shabby and aged.

"Let's cross it," said Izzy, stepping forward.

"Wait!" Melanie cautioned.

Izzy halted.

"Look at it."

In front of the bridge's entryway, something moved. In the shape of an arch, a clear substance flowed back and forth, winding loosely in circles. Intrigued, Melanie gazed into the fluid. Through it, she could see a man on a rowing boat traveling on the river. In the background was an assembly of small stone houses sloppily clayed together.

Melanie looked away from the clear substance, peering around the bridge. The man and his boat vanished, and the village disappeared. All that lay on the opposite bank was grass.

Confused, Melanie gazed back into the fluid, viewing both the man rowing his boat and the miniature buildings.

"Izzy, I think it's Brigadoon."

Izzy peeked through the substance and then peered around the bridge. She too saw what Melanie had; the man and the village only appeared when she looked through the fluid.

"We better tell Jenn!" said Izzy.

The girls took off with Izzy soaring through the air and Melanie sprinting on the ground.

At the campsite, Alice and Colleen were laying on the grass, enjoying the peace and serenity of their pit stop. Jenn was with the time machine, her head under the device's hood. Excitedly, she pulled away from the hood.

"Done!"

Alice and Colleen sat up.

"It's fixed?" asked Colleen.

"Yes ma'am!" Jenn smiled, wiping her greasy hands on her lab coat. "Now we can go find Brigadoon. Where are Izzy and Mel?"

From the base of the hill, Izzy and Melanie came hurtling into sight.

"Jenn! Alice! Colleen!" yelled Izzy.

"We found Brigadoon! We found Brigadoon!" shouted Melanie.

The girls slowed down when they reached the time machine.

"What'd you say?" asked Jenn, alert.

"We think we found Brigadoon!" Melanie exclaimed.

"Brigadoon! Where?"

"Follow us."

Izzy and Melanie guided their friends to the bridge. They positioned Jenn so that she could gaze into the flowing substance. Through the translucent archway, Jenn observed the buildings and the boatman. Anxiously, she peered around the bridge, only to see the empty bank.

"If that's not Brigadoon, then I don't know what is!" said Jenn, amazed.

Izzy winked at Mel.

"So this is it? What we're looking for?" asked Alice, excited.

"It has to be. We asked the time machine to take us to Brigadoon and we found this place, a mile away. It got us as close as it could before it crashed," said Jenn.

"You're saying that Brigadoon's been here the whole time we've been chilling by the sea?" asked Colleen.

"Looks like it."

"How long do you think it's been here? Do you think we're close to the time limit?" asked Izzy.

"I don't know," said Jenn. "There's no way to tell. Since the time machine broke before it brought us near Brigadoon, then we may not have the entire twenty-four hour limit. We could try resetting the machine to find Brigadoon at the moment it appeared."

"But what if it breaks again?" asked Colleen. "This could be our only chance to locate the village."

"We need a fishing pole," said Melanie. "If we go now, we'll just have to be quick."

"Okay, but if something doesn't seem right we leave as fast as possible," said Jenn. "Izzy, you go first."

Izzy cringed. "What? You do it."

"You're the one who found the portal. Go for it!" Jenn encouraged.

"I think Mel should go first," Izzy protested.

"It's all you, home girl," said Melanie, giving her a light shove.

Izzy gulped. She approached the portal apprehensively, shutting her eyes as she stuck her hand into the clear substance. A moment later she slowly opened her eyes.

"I'm okay!" she exclaimed.

Once everyone was across the bridge, the girls took a second to observe the village. The sky was gray and the breeze was cool. The village was filled with ponds and lakes, and the river wove throughout the town. Small stone and brick buildings were scattered about, a few huddled together and a few alone. In the center of the village was what appeared to be its main street. Fifteen little buildings were standing in two straight rows.

Although Brigadoon was small, its villagers were busy. On the docks that jutted into the lakes, men were fishing everywhere. Two women waded in a nearby stream, washing their clothes and their husbands' gear. A few boats were seen floating on the ponds, waiting to bring in a fresh catch, and a couple of boys were running together, chasing a frog that was frantically hopping away.

The girls began walking through the marsh toward the town. None of the residents seemed alarmed by their presence.

"Where do we get the fishing rod from?" asked Izzy.

"We could ask one of the fishermen for a pole," said Alice.

"Or we could buy one," said Melanie.

"We don't have any money," said Colleen.

"I like Alice's idea. We'll just ask to borrow someone's extra pole," said Jenn.

"How about that guy? He's got tons of 'em," said Izzy. She pointed to a burly man standing alone on a dock.

"Let's give it a shot," said Alice.

"Hold on. I think only one of us should go and ask. If we send all five it might look a little suspicious," said Jenn.

"I'll go," said Izzy.

"Okay. Just ask him if you can borrow one of his poles."

Izzy approached the man on the dock. He wore a large straw hat and black boots that were drenched in mud. Politely, Izzy tapped his shoulder.

"What do you want?" the fisherman grumbled.

"Excuse me, sir. Do you mind if I borrow one of your fishing poles?"

"Take it."

She grabbed one of the rods and retreated to her friends.

"That was easy," Izzy smiled.

"We have the third key!" said Alice.

"Let's go back to Indiana and get ready for the Parthenon," said Jenn.

The girls started walking toward the bridge. As they got closer, one of the villagers stepped in front of them.

"Where are you going?" the villager demanded.

"Over the bridge," said Colleen.

"You can't leave!"

"What?"

"Keep walking," Jenn instructed.

The girls continued toward the portal

The villager turned toward a group of fishermen. "Oi! They're tryin to leave!"

Immediately the fishermen looked up. As they realized that the visitors were trying to leave, the men began chasing after the girls.

"Uh oh!" Izzy squealed.

"Run for the portal!" yelled Jenn.

The girls took off. A group of seven men stepped in front of the bridge.

"Uh...Jenn, look!" said Melanie.

Jenn froze. She realized that they wouldn't be able to pass without force and she was afraid to lose the fishing pole, their number one priority.

"Izzy, throw the fishing pole into the portal!" commanded Jenn.

Izzy swung back her arm, ready to hurl the rod when something grabbed her. Izzy looked back and saw a man gripping her wrist, the pole raised above her head.

"Help!" Izzy screamed.

Colleen stepped up to the fisherman, positioned to punch. The fisherman held out a small, sharp knife and pointed it at Izzy's throat. Colleen froze. Izzy whimpered at the sight of the blade, standing absolutely still. The blade's tip pricked her throat, drawing a few drops of blood.

"You cannot leave," he growled.

Izzy recognized the gruff voice. Her aggressor was the man who had given her the fishing pole.

"Let her go!" shouted Alice.

A group of men encircled the girls.

"Lock 'em up until the portal closes. Release them after dusk," the fisherman ordered. He grabbed the rod out of Izzy's hand and lowered his knife.

"Not again," groaned Colleen.

The fishermen took the girls to the village prison. Unlike the dungeon in Camelot, their new chamber wasn't completely enclosed. The left and back walls were made of inescapable gray brick, and the front and right walls were sealed with iron bars. There were no lamps or candles and no bench to sit on. The only light that trickled into the room came from a pair of small slit windows, barred with metal.

A man locked the prison door, and the villagers left the building.

Izzy looked out of the door, her hands gripped to its bars. "You could have at least given us a bench!"

"They're friendly," Melanie sighed.

"Jenn, I thought that only the residents couldn't leave Brigadoon, so that the spell doesn't break. Does it work for visitors too?" asked Alice.

"I guess so. Why else would we be locked in here?" said Jenn, her voice drained.

"Well, I don't know about you guys, but I'm getting out," said Colleen, stepping to the door.

"What are you doing?"

"They only want us in here until dusk, which means that's probably when the portal will close. The sun's creeping its way toward the west, and I refuse to live in this dump for the rest of my life. I'm getting us out," said Colleen. "Back up, Izzy."

294

Izzy let go of the bars, and walked to the back of the cell. Colleen positioned herself in front of the entrance, lifted her right leg and kicked with all of her might. Instantly, the ironclad door broke off its hinges, flying across the hallway. The door crashed into the brick wall.

"Nicely done!" said Alice.

The girls stepped into the hallway.

"Peace out!" Melanie smiled as they moved down the corridor.

From around the corner, one of the villagers came running down the hallway. The clang of the door had drawn his attention.

"What are you doing?" he yelled.

"Go!" commanded Jenn.

The girls ran down the back of the hallway, away from the villager. They reached the corridor's end and turned right. Luckily, there was a back entrance, but they hesitated to leave.

"We have to get rid of this guy! He'll tell everyone we're escaping!" said Jenn.

"I have an idea!" said Izzy. "Alice, Melanie, come with me!"

With Izzy's touch, all three girls turned invisible. Together, they retreated down the hallway, passing the villager who was running in the opposite direction. Izzy stopped at another cell that still had its door. With a nudge, she pushed Melanie inside.

"Grab the keys when he comes back. Alice, when I say *now*, you'll know what to do."

Before the man turned the corner, Izzy made herself visible.

"Hey you! Over here!" she called.

The man swung around, not having seen Colleen or Jenn who were just around the bend. At first sight of Izzy he chased after her. Izzy was a step away from the chamber's door. The villager got closer, and as he moved in front of the cell's entrance, Izzy shouted.

"Now!"

From across the cell door, a silver force field crashed into the man; Alice stood invisibly with her palm held up. As the villager flew through the cell, keys fell out of his pocket. Melanie picked them up from the ground. She came out of the chamber, shut the door and fumbled the keys in her hand.

As Melanie tried each of the keys, the man stood up and charged at the entrance. Alice created another force field, forcing him back into the wall. When Melanie found the right key, she locked the door as quick as she could. She, Izzy and Alice stormed down the hallway, meeting up with Colleen and Jenn.

"He's not our problem anymore," said Izzy, turning her friends visible.

"Good," said Jenn.

Colleen opened the back door leading outside.

"Now what?"

They observed an unavoidable collection of villagers who were in between the prison and the bridge.

"We have to go," said Colleen, pointing to the sun. "It's almost setting, we don't have much time."

"But all of those people! They'll see us! We'll never get out!" said Alice.

"We could go invisible," said Melanie.

"I didn't bring the goggles! We won't be able to see each other," said Jenn.

"We go through this every time! I can see *us all*!" said Izzy, irritated.

"Every time as in twice," Melanie laughed.

"Option A, we run out visible, able to see one another and most likely get caught again," Colleen reasoned, "or option B, we go invisible and dash for the exit. Izzy will make sure we're together and we leave without anyone noticing."

"I choose option B!" said Alice.

"Option B," said Jenn, nodding to Izzy.

Izzy touched each of the girls. Everyone flickered invisible.

"All right, go around that pond and then sprint to the bridge," said Jenn. "Go!"

The girls took off, sprinting through the village in a desperate race against time.

As they passed a few fishermen, Alice squeaked. "Wait! The fishing pole, the fishing pole! The fisherman took it away from Izzy, we still need a third key!"

"I'll get one!" said Izzy. "Stay put."

Izzy flew to a fishermen-filled dock. She crept behind a scrawny man and leaned over his shoulder. At the right moment, she yanked the fishing rod out of his hands, instantly turning it invisible.

Izzy retreated to the group. "Got it! Keep going!"

The girls raced to the portal. As they reached the riverbank, the planks of the bridge began to break off, falling one by one into the water.

"Ah! What's going on?" yelped Izzy.

"The portal, it's gonna close! The sun's almost set!" said Colleen.

"We have to get across, now!" said Jenn.

"I can't jump that far!" said Alice. "The bridge is breaking too fast."

"Izzy! Turn us visible!" said Melanie.

Izzy tapped each of her friends. Their sudden visibility caught the villagers' attention.

"Guys! We have company!" yelled Alice.

The fishermen began running toward the bridge.

"What if they're right about the portal closing?" asked Colleen. "If one person passes through then Brigadoon will be stuck here forever and we can walk out any time."

"But what if they're wrong?" Jenn asked in return. "The clue said if the residents leave then the spell will break, but we're not residents, at least not yet. We can't risk it. We need to get everyone across now!"

"I can leap across the river and I can carry someone with me," said Melanie.

"And I can take someone across, flying, but only one," said Izzy.

"You guys go!" said Alice.

"We're not leaving you behind!" Melanie snapped.

"I trusted you at the Sphinx, now it's your turn to trust me," Alice demanded.

298

Melanie grabbed Colleen. "Izzy, you take Jenn."

Izzy held onto Jenn and took off flying through the air. They whizzed through the portal and landed on the opposite bank.

"It's still closing!" yelled Jenn.

The bridge continued to break, its planks slipping one after another.

"Izzy, try flying back to us. Then you can take Alice!" called Colleen.

Izzy launched herself into the air, aiming for the swirling fluid. As her head touched the substance, her entire body flew backwards.

"It won't let me through!" yelled Izzy.

Melanie looked at Alice, hesitating to leave.

"Mel go!" Alice demanded.

Reluctant, Melanie took a few steps back to get a running start with Colleen latched to her side. She sprinted toward the river and jumped at the edge of the bank. Easily, she hurled through the portal, landing in between Izzy and Jenn. They all turned around and called to Alice.

"Come on!"

Alice turned around, watching the fishermen closing in. Quickly, she created a force field and aimed it underneath herself. She jumped toward the river, pointing the silver ball on an angle.

"Alice!" Izzy screamed.

Although Alice had jumped toward the water, she never touched it. Instead, she bounced upward, hovering up and down, up and down. She had used her force field like a trampoline, putting her shield underneath herself to block her body from the river. With every bounce she sprang forward.

Little by little, Alice made her way across the river. She took a final spring and bounced onto the bank, just as the bridge's last plank fell to the water. With the final plank, the entire portal closed. The fishermen disappeared along with Brigadoon.

Alice lay on the grass with her arms sprawled out, panting. Melanie crouched down next to her, grinning from ear to ear.

"That was awesome!" said Melanie.

"For a second, I scared myself!" Alice sighed.

Melanie helped her up.

"You all right?" asked Colleen.

"Peachy."

Jenn looked at Izzy, in search of the fishing pole. Izzy's hands were empty.

"Izzy! Where's the third key?" Jenn shrieked.

"It's right here," said Izzy, holding up her hand. She looked down, her eyes opened wide. "Oh."

Jenn's heart sank.

"You lost the fishing rod?"

"Relax, it's only invisible."

The fishing pole appeared in Izzy's hand. She held it out and gave it to Jenn.

"Thank God!" said Jenn, her heart pounding.

"No, my name's Izzy, not God," she teased.

Jenn rolled her eyes but let out a smile. Her chest was beginning to settle.

"You were right about the portal," said Colleen,

glancing at Jenn. "We didn't break Brigadoon's spell by leaving."

Jenn shrugged. "It was more of a guess."

"The fishermen locked us up for nothing?" screeched Izzy. "They wasted all of our precious time, keeping us from leaving when it wouldn't have mattered to them." She crossed her arms in disgust.

Melanie laughed. "We're safe now."

"Safe," muttered Alice.

"Jenn, look!" Izzy gasped, pointing to the fishing rod.

Jenn gazed down at the pole. On the rod's handle, golden letters began carving themselves into a new message.

Alice looked at the phenomenon and sighed. "Not another clue!"

"It's not," said Jenn. She lifted the pole so that all of her friends could see. Engraved on the fishing rod were the words, *Athena Parthenos*. "It's our next destination, to go to the Parthenon."

"This is it, isn't it?" said Alice.

"Yeah. Whatever's in that statue is what we've been working for," said Jenn. "Now all we have to do is go get it."

"Are we going back to the lab first?" asked Izzy.

"Yes. We have to get the cane and the sword."

"Let's get going," said Colleen.

The girls began walking to the time machine. Soon, they were inside of the device and on their way to the lab. The final key was in Jenn's hand.

* * *

On the academy's campus, Scott was striding along the sidewalk. He was returning to the lab from a local auto shop, where he had purchased the final pieces needed in order to fix the Air Taxi.

Thud, thud, thud.

On his way, he could hear distant footsteps following behind him.

Thud, thud, thud.

The footsteps were heavy but swift. Something big and quick shadowed his steps. A few times Scott turned around, but each time there was no one behind him.

Jumping quickly from tree to tree, Iapetus followed Scott. He had recognized the human as the young man who had accompanied the Oracle out of the science hall the night before. The Titan thought that perhaps the seer's friend would lead him to the Oracle and her guardians. Iapetus had seen the Oracle earlier in the day, however, the Oracle had not been with all of her guardians at the same time. Three had accompanied her, but the fourth had come on her own. Iapetus needed the five beings together. He needed to know he had the five correct humans, for if he did not, treacherous things could happen. Not only would Cronus be furious, but the guardians would know who captured the seer. It was a conflict Iapetus hoped to avoid. With patience he would find the Oracle and her guardians. No need for unnecessary confrontations.

When Iapetus came back to Mnemosyne near the entrance of the science hall, he whispered into her ear.

"We shall follow him inside."

Mnemosyne nodded. "We will let him settle in for a moment and then enter. We will catch him off guard."

From a distance the Titans stalked Scott, watching his every move.

Walking toward Scott from the opposite direction was Ryan Rivera. The prodigious chef was mumbling to himself, staring at the ground and kicking away stones that stood in his path.

WHOOSH!

As Ryan and Scott passed each other, Ryan's backpack burst into flames. Ryan threw his bag off his back and yelled. Scott ran to his side, took off his lab coat and hit the flames.

"What do you have in there, a bomb?" shouted Scott.

"Nothing but papers!" screeched Ryan.

Once the flames had subsided Ryan picked himself up, along with his bag. The cloth was completely burned, leaving a gaping hole in its front. He glanced at Scott, his face indifferent.

"Thank you."

Ryan continued forward, clutching his charred bag and muttering with each step. Scott too continued toward his destination. He moved swiftly, anxious to see if the girls were home yet. He could no longer hear the thudding footsteps, but with each stride he looked over his shoulder, just in case.

CHAPTER EIGHTEEN

Secret of the Statue

As Scott walked into lab room 56A, the girls arrived in the time machine.

"Good timing," said Scott.

"How long was that?" asked Jenn.

"About six hours."

"We came back in real time, not what I wanted," Jenn sighed. "The machine broke while we were out there. Looks like I still have to work on fixing it."

"Breaking is what I was afraid of," said Scott.

Jenn changed the subject. "We got the key!"

"When do you leave?"

"Right now."

"Wait, I-"

"Don't Scott. We're *not* resting before we go. We're leaving now."

"I was just coming to give you a kiss," said Scott. He approached Jenn and pecked her on the lips. "Good luck."

Jenn kissed him back. "Thanks. We're going to the

Parthenon to open the Athena Parthenos. We'll come back before we do anything else."

"You should do it quickly," said Scott. "I think there's a chance you're being followed. On the way back to the lab I could hear footsteps as I walked. Every time I turned around I didn't see anything."

"Was it a Titan?" Izzy asked fearfully.

"Mortals can't see gods," said Jenn. "It probably was."

"We can't leave him here! What if they attack?" asked Colleen.

"It's not me they want," said Scott. "It's you. *If* they know who I am, they wouldn't come after me. The only reason they would come to the lab would be to find you guys, but they don't know you're here. They never saw you."

"That doesn't mean they won't come to the lab," said Colleen.

"We don't even know if it was a Titan."

"But you said that you thought it was!"

"With everything that's going on, I could be paranoid. I could have imagined it," said Scott. "Look, enough arguing. You need to finish Zeus' task."

"You're giving us the directions for a change," said Jenn.

"I believe in you," said Scott.

Jenn grinned. "We better go."

"I'll be finishing the hovercraft."

Jenn turned toward her friends. "Mel, grab the sword. Izzy, take the cane."

With all three keys, the girls stepped onto the Transporter's platform. Internally, Jenn chanted their destination and they all walked through.

In the lab, Scott gathered his tools and began working on the Air Taxi again. He had the vehicle set up in the center of the room and was kneeling by its side, tinkering away.

BANG!

Something crashed into the lab's door. Immediately, Scott looked up. As he approached the door, Mnemosyne and Iapetus charged into the lab, knocking him off his feet. At first sight of the Titans, Scott was petrified. He lay on the floor, his hands gripping the tile.

Iapetus tore through the room, breaking through the glass cupboards. In a swift motion, Mnemosyne approached Scott and leaned over his body.

"Where are they?" she demanded.

"Whe-where are who?" Scott stuttered.

"Do *not* play games with us, fool!" Iapetus threatened, joining Mnemosyne's side.

"Where is the Oracle and where are her guardians?" Mnemosyne growled.

"I don't know what you're talking about," Scott lied, his voice unwavering.

Mnemosyne bent down and slapped Scott hard across the face. His cheek flashed bright red as droplets of blood appeared on his face, caused by the Titan's sharp nails.

"You have one more chance. *Where* is the Oracle?"

"I don't know!"

Iapetus grabbed Scott by the collar and dangled him in the air. He swung Scott backwards, gaining momentum to throw his body forward.

"Wait!" yelled Mnemosyne.

Iapetus froze.

"He can still be of use. Let me search his memory. I'm sure we can find some answers there."

Mnemosyne placed her right hand on Scott's forehead. The goddess closed her eyes. Her hand was glued to his head, freezing the skin that she touched.

Scott began to feel dizzy. Without warning his head drooped to his chest.

Mnemosyne replayed the last few minutes that Scott had spent with Alice and the guardians. She could see and hear all that had taken place. Mnemosyne watched as Scott spoke to a brown haired young woman wearing a lab coat.

"Wait," said Scott, "I-"

"Don't, Scott. We're not resting before we go. We're leaving now," the young woman interrupted.

"I was just coming to give you a kiss. Good luck."

"Thanks. We're going to the Parthenon to open the Athena Parthenos..."

"The Parthenon, Iapetus!" Mnemosyne bellowed, pulling her hand away from Scott's forehead and cutting off the memory.

"The Parthenon," Iapetus repeated. "What do they want there?"

"One of the guardians said they were going to open the Athena Parthenos!"

"We must tell Cronus immediately! Come, Mnemosyne! They must be caught before they leave."

Iapetus threw Scott to the floor. A moment later, the Titans rushed out of the lab.

Woozy and in pain, Scott stumbled to his feet and pulled out his cell phone. He began dialing Jenn's number, his hands trembling. The phone rang four times and the answering machine sounded. Jenn's voice came through the speaker but it was merely a recording.

Scott began to panic. He had to try and save them. Jenn had not answered and was unaware of the dangers that chased after her. Unsure of when the Titans would arrive at the Parthenon, Scott devised an emergency plan. He mounted the platform of the Transporter, his mind ringing, *inside the Parthenon, inside the Parthenon, inside the Parthenon.* Scott walked through the portal and disappeared from the lab.

* * *

Soon, after the swirling of colors and the absurdly bright light, the girls made it to Greece, one hundred yards from the Parthenon. They landed behind a wall of marble and crouched down.

"All right, here's the plan," said Jenn. "First we become invisible, then we enter the Parthenon and find the Athena Parthenos. Next, we put the three keys into place and unlock the statue. We take whatever it gives us and then we go back to the lab."

"Do you have the goggles?" asked Colleen.

Jenn smiled. "I couldn't forget a third time." She pulled four pairs of specs from her lab coat. "Just put 'em on and we'll get going. Izzy, if you'd do the honors."

"I'd be glad to," said Izzy, turning everyone invisible.

"Follow me," said Jenn.

The girls walked toward the enormous temple. Thick columns surrounded the building's perimeter, supporting a perfectly carved triangular ceiling. Statues were chiseled into the temple's frame, all created by human hand.

Step by step, the girls climbed into the temple. Sculptures covered the walls, and the floor was glossy and smooth.

Izzy spun around, looking at the ceiling. "Check out the architecture!"

"Pretty cool, huh?" asked Jenn.

"What's with the ceiling?" asked Alice.

"What do you mean?"

"Well, *there's a ceiling*. I read that the Parthenon's roof was destroyed years ago. Why is it here?"

"Notice that the entire temple looks as if it were brand new. All of this isn't real. Well, not that it isn't real, it's just that we're basically the only people who can see it," said Jenn.

"Huh?" Colleen huffed.

"Do you remember when Zeus said that we'd be able to see the Athena Parthenos, and why?" asked Jenn. "He said that because we have a piece of the gods within us, we'd see the statue. The same goes for the temple. We see the Parthenon as it was originally. Initially, the ceiling existed and so did the Athena Parthenos. All of the initial sculptures and figures exist to us."

The girls quickly made it to the second room of the Parthenon, stopping once they realized where they were. Standing across from them at the back of the room was the Athena Parthenos. The statue was of a tall woman, made of marble and gold. Athena wore a long draping tunic and a shining golden helmet. Beneath her left hand was a shield, a serpent stuck to its side. Her right palm held a small woman with wings.

In front of the statue was a rectangular pool, stretching far enough that Athena's reflection gazed back at herself.

"That's pretty big," said Izzy.

"It's a masterpiece," said Colleen.

"It's *here*!" exclaimed Jenn.

"Someone's happy," said Melanie.

"It's just that everyone else believes that the statue was destroyed hundreds of years ago, and here we are, staring at it!"

"Should we unlock the secret item now?" asked Alice.

"Yes."

With excitement, Jenn led the girls toward the statue, walking alongside the pool. When they reached the Athena Parthenos, they stepped in front of it, standing on a short strip of tile that separated the figure from the water.

The base of the statue was pearly white. A golden sculpture was chiseled on its front, depicting some type of story. On the base's top rested three holes, equally spaced in a straight line. Each indent was a unique shape: a small oval, a large slit and a thin circle.

"These are the keyholes," said Jenn. "Izzy, you're on the left with the cane. Melanie, you're in the middle with the sword, and I'm to the right with the fishing rod."

The girls positioned themselves in front of the locks.

"Go ahead," said Jenn.

Izzy took the cane and fit it carefully into the oval-shaped opening. The key locked into the base of the statue with a click. Melanie lifted the Sword in the Stone, sliding the blade into the marble. Finally, Jenn took the handle of the fishing pole and placed it in the circular opening.

With all three keys placed into their locks, the ground began to shake. Slowly, a huge crack formed from the base of the statue, cutting to the right of the sword. After a few moments, the statue halted and the ground stood still.

The base had cut in two, separating the fishing rod from the sword and the cane. Between the two halves was a golden pedestal that held a small rectangular box. Alice approached it. The box was dark brown with a charred appearance, a metal latch hitched to its front. On top, two symbols were engraved. To the left was a lightning bolt and to the right was a set of flames. The left side of the container was engraved with a pair of bow and arrows, a trident, and a miniature shield. On the right, the moon and the sun were carved, along with two raindrops and a sword.

Carefully, Alice picked up the box. On the container's bare front, golden letters began to appear from left to right. The new message read, *Release at the Omphalos, the Oracle of Delphi.*

"What is it?" Alice asked.

Jenn studied the item and gasped. "It's Pandora's box! The statue's secret is Pandora's box!"

"Explain," Izzy demanded.

"A long time ago, Zeus created a woman named Pandora as a present for Epimetheus," said Jenn. "The gods gave Pandora a box, and warned her not to open it. Out of natural curiosity, she flipped back the lid to see what was inside. The contents of the box were horrible. Within an instant of being opened, all of the world's terrors such as disease, torment and hatred were released. By the time Pandora shut the lid, all of the world's evils had escaped. Only one thing remained in the container."

"What was left?" asked Melanie.

"Hope."

Silence fell upon the girls. Alice sensed that the revelation was overwhelmingly profound. She closed her eyes, contemplating the box's deep meaning.

Izzy broke the silence.

"Hope? *Hope?* We went through all of that trouble to find a box of *hope*? We almost got killed by the *Sphinx!* Got locked into prison not only *once* but *twice!* Dueled knights from *Camelot*, almost got stabbed by the knights *and* almost got trapped in some hidden village for the rest of our lives! All for a box of *hope?*"

Alice laughed. Clearly her sense had been wrong.

"Relax," said Jenn. "There's more to it than hope, there has to be. If Zeus and the Olympians hid Pandora's box so that it would be *nearly* impossible to find, then there's something more powerful within the box."

Izzy took a few deep breaths to calm herself down.

"Why would the gods give Pandora a box full of such terrible things?" asked Colleen.

"Although Zeus said Pandora was a present for Epimetheus, she was really intended as a punishment for humans. Zeus did not want people to have fire. The god Prometheus gave the human race fire, and when Zeus found out, he was livid. As punishment for the betrayal, he let loose anything that would harm people," said Jenn.

"And we're fighting *for* Zeus?" growled Melanie. "After hearing that I think I'd like to be on Cronus' side. Sounds like Zeus deserves a friendly beat down."

"Mel, relax," said Jenn. "Do you know how many thousands of years ago that was? Let it go. Zeus is on our side now."

"I still think he deserves a beat down," said Melanie.

"We have to take the box to the Omphalos, which is the Oracle of Delphi?" Alice asked quickly.

"Yes."

"What's the Omphalos?" asked Colleen.

"Omphalos is the Greek word for *center of the world*."

"We have to go to the earth's core!" Izzy said incredulously.

Jenn giggled. "No, we're not going there. To the ancient Greeks the Omphalos was a place on the earth's surface. They believed that they had found the actual center of the world."

"So where is the supposed Omphalos?" asked Colleen.

"In Delphi, Greece. It's the site of the Oracle of Delphi, which is inside of Apollo's Temple."

"What's so special about the Oracle of Delphi? Why can't we release it here?"

"There could be a couple of reasons. Like I said, in Greek mythology the Oracle of Delphi was considered the center of the earth. It's supposedly the most powerful point on our planet, so whatever Pandora's box will do, the Oracle of Delphi might give it some extra strength. Or perhaps the box will only react at the oracle. These are just guesses."

Jenn looked from the box to the Athena Parthenos and gasped. She smacked her hand to her forehead. "I can't believe I missed it! The Athena Parthenos was our biggest clue to what we've been searching for! The sculpture on its base shows the creation of Pandora."

Alice gazed at the statue. There on its foundation was the sculpted story of Pandora carved in gold.

Sensing Jenn's frustration, Colleen tried to calm her feelings. "That's okay, we already have the box."

Suddenly, a voice yelled from the distance.

"Jenn? Jenn?! Jenn, where are you?!"

"Who's that?" asked Alice.

The girls turned around.

"It sounds like Scott," said Melanie.

"It *is* Scott!" said Izzy, pointing to the figure of a young man wandering through the temple.

Scott was walking in the front room of the Parthenon. He looked around frantically, his head moving left and right.

"He can't see us because we're invisible," said Jenn.

From behind Scott, two beings appeared. One was black with bulging muscles and the other was white, slimmer yet toned.

"It's Crius and Iapetus!" said Colleen.

Jenn's eyes widened as she recognized the Titans. "Scott! Scott, move!"

Iapetus and Crius charged forward.

"There he is!" yelled Iapetus. "He knows the Oracle!"

Scott turned around. He watched as Crius and Iapetus ran toward him. Desperately, Scott began to run.

"They must be here!" said Crius.

"Kill him!" ordered Iapetus.

Crius drew back his hand, beckoning a star from the universe. From the blue sky, a bright white orb came shooting at the Parthenon. Jenn saw the orb and screamed out to Scott, but to no avail. Scott saw the ball of energy too late. It raced toward him, perfectly set on its target. Scott closed his eyes, bracing for impact.

"NO!" cried Jenn, running toward him.

The star entered the Parthenon.

"SCOTT!"

BOOM!

Something ran into Scott's body, knocking him fiercely to the left. Scott opened his eyes as he crashed to the floor. He watched as the star blasted into a pillar. It had missed him entirely. He lay on the floor with something clutched to his body.

Invisible, Melanie held onto Scott. She had run into him with all of her might.

"You missed!" Iapetus roared.

"He did not move on his own!" yelled Crius. "The guardians and the Oracle are here!"

"Fire away!"

Crius drew back both of his hands, calling forth more stars. Melanie stood up, bringing Scott with her.

"Scott, it's Mel. Hold on tight!"

As they moved, another star came flying into the Parthenon.

"Watch out!" shouted Izzy.

Melanie dodged the star as it shattered another column. Izzy flew toward her friends and tapped Scott, making him invisible.

Enraged, Iapetus and Crius ran toward the Athena Parthenos. Melanie, Scott and Izzy rejoined their friends. Tears set in Jenn's eyes, but she quickly wiped them away. There was no time to cry. Another star was hurtling toward the back of the temple.

"We have to run!" said Jenn. "Colleen, take the keys!"

Colleen reached for the fishing pole, sword and cane, pulling each one from the Athena Parthenos. She ran away from the statue just as the star hit its base.

"Do you see that?" asked Iapetus. "It's floating in the air!"

"It's Pandora's box!" said Crius. "One of them has it!"

"Izzy!" Alice yelped. "The box! It's not invisible! They can see it!"

Izzy swooped toward Pandora's box and tapped it repeatedly, trying in vain to make the item invisible.

"It didn't work!" cried Izzy.

"The box can't be affected by magic!" said Jenn. "It can't be favored by one side of good or evil. It's indifferent and must therefore let each side have an equal opportunity of using it."

"The Olympians hid it. How could they do that?" asked Colleen.

"Because they weren't going to use it against the Titans, and the Titans weren't going to use it against the Olympians. The box was locked away so that neither side could mess with the other."

"Watch out!" yelled Alice. She put up her force field and deflected a star away from Colleen.

"Thanks!" Colleen exclaimed.

"No problem," said Alice.

"Jenn, the Transporter!" said Scott. Still unable to see any of the girls, his eyes followed the box, which he concluded Alice held when he saw a silver shield emerge beside it.

"Right!" said Jenn. She pulled the portable device from her pocket and pointed it in front of the group. "Everyone in!"

The teenagers rushed into the portal. As it shut, a star whizzed toward it. The star crashed into the wall, blowing a hole next to the Athena Parthenos.

"Damn!" Iapetus cursed. "They got away!"

"All is not lost," said Crius. "They have Pandora's box, and they intend to open it. There is only one place it can be released."

"The Omphalos," Iapetus snickered.

"We shall go back to Cronus."

Crius and Iapetus left the temple.

When Scott and the girls landed back in the lab, Jenn hugged her boyfriend fiercely. Izzy made her rounds and tapped everyone, making them all visible. Finally, Scott could see Jenn, and he held her close in his arms.

"What were you doing?" Jenn scolded, holding him tighter.

Scott cracked a sheepish smile. "I was trying to warn you that the Titans were coming. They got here about the same time you left!"

Jenn looked up from Scott's shoulder, gazing at the room. Glass was scattered across the floor, and all the cupboards were smashed apart.

"What happened here?" asked Colleen.

"Iapetus and Mnemosyne. They barged in demanding to know where you were," said Scott.

"You could see them?" asked Jenn, shocked.

"Yes! They were furious. I didn't know what to

318

do!"

"Did you tell them where to find us?" asked Alice.

"No. Mnemosyne looked into my memories. She listened to Jenn say that you were all going to the Parthenon. I could see the memory with her, and she cut it off before she heard that you'd be right back."

"We're lucky. It could have been worse," said Melanie.

"But you could see them!" Jenn exclaimed.

"Yes, I could see them," said Scott.

"You shouldn't have been able to. You're a mortal and mortals can't see mythical beings, especially not gods!"

"Mythical or not they were very real and very visible."

Jenn paused. After a moment she gazed at Scott, her eyes firm. "We have to go to the Oracle of Delphi and open Pandora's box. We have to reach the Omphalos."

"They know that you have it, they'll be there waiting for you!" said Scott.

"We still have to go. This is it! This is what we've been working for! We can't stop now."

"I know, I know," Scott said softly, holding Jenn's hand. "I'm just scared for you. I don't want to lose you."

"Me either," said Jenn. She nestled her head into Scott's shoulder.

Izzy turned around and headed for the door.

"Where are you going, Iz?" asked Alice.

"I'm going to see Jayden."

"Izzy, we're about to leave," said Jenn.

"I need to see him. I need to say…goodbye," Izzy's voice was soft. She had struggled to say the last word.

"All right. You guys can go too. See anyone you need, but be back quickly," said Jenn.

"I'll be back," said Colleen.

"Alice? Melanie? You guys going?" asked Jenn.

"No," said Alice. "I don't know who I'd see."

"I don't say goodbye," said Melanie.

Izzy and Colleen exited the science hall. Outside, the sun had set hours before but the sky was still oddly light.

Izzy headed to the campus' news station, hoping that Jayden had stayed late at work. She paced anxiously outside of the building; her stomach dropped every few moments.

Finally, Jayden appeared through a set of large glass windows. Izzy watched as he exited the elevator with his black briefcase in hand. He walked closer to the exit and as soon as he caught sight of Izzy, he sprinted through the door.

"Izzy!"

Jayden dropped his briefcase and buried Izzy in his arms.

"What are you doing here?" asked Jayden.

Izzy took a moment to answer. She fought as hard as she could to keep from crying and secretly wiped a tear away from her eye.

"We need to talk," she sighed.

Jayden pulled away from Izzy's body, holding onto

her shoulders so he could see her face. Her eyes were blurry and her face seemed troubled.

"What is it? What's wrong?" he asked anxiously.

Izzy looked into Jayden's eyes and struggled to speak.

"I have to go."

"Go where?"

"I...can't really say. I just have to go," Izzy squeaked, looking away from him.

"Izzy, I don't understand. What do you mean you have to go?"

"I mean that..." Izzy paused, her voice cracking. "I mean that I have to go and I don't know if I'll be back." She lifted her head and looked at Jayden, who still seemed very confused. "I came to say goodbye."

Izzy's mouth began to tremble and a stream of tears flowed down her cheeks. Quickly, the blue sky darkened to a thick gray: black clouds rolling into view. Jayden stared at Izzy and shook his head.

"But where are you going? I'll come with you. I'd go anywhere with you!"

"No, Jayden," Izzy sobbed. "I have to say goodbye."

"But Izzy!"

"Jayden, please!"

Faster and faster tears rolled down Izzy's cheeks. Raindrops began to fall, dripping onto her face. Jayden looked at Izzy as she turned away. After a moment she turned back and held Jayden's hand, gazing into his eyes.

"I'm sorry."

Izzy let go of Jayden's hand and turned around, walking in the direction from which she came. The rain poured harder and faster. Jayden was left standing in solitude, his body becoming drenched. He was numb and frozen. He watched Izzy until she disappeared into the storm, the only thing that separated him from her.

Izzy sped through the campus, sobbing all the way back to the science hall. When she made it to the entrance, Colleen was waiting for her. Colleen took notice of Izzy's puffy eyes and patted her on the back.

"You okay?"

Izzy nodded. She was too upset to speak. Together, they walked back to the lab.

When they entered, Jenn spoke. "Before we go, I have a few weapons I'd like to show you." She approached the walls where the suits of armor hung. "If the Titans are there, we'll definitely be using these." Jenn pulled the five swords from the suits. "Five on twelve isn't a fair match up, and the odds are against us. If we can just open Pandora's box at the oracle, then hopefully we can defeat the Titans."

Jenn moved to the island counter and pressed a small blue button. Two shelves began to rise from the counter, each containing an item. From the right shelf, Jenn grabbed a slim, gray board. She laid it on the ground and stepped on. The device began to hover above the ground.

"This device is like a mini Air Taxi. Think of it as a type of snowboard. I'll be using it, if need be. You guys all have active powers that you can use in defense, so this'll act as mine. Finally, we have these." Jenn reached toward the left shelf and picked up a black bag. She reached inside and grabbed a baseball-sized sphere. The ball was almost transparent, having silver and golden rings swinging in an orbit. Copper-colored dots were fixed on opposite sides, glowing and fading in rhythm.

"These are electroballs. Just throw them at your target, and on contact they'll give that person a nasty shock. There's plenty inside the bag, and anyone can use them."

Melanie looked at Jenn, her eyes glum. "We're really doing it, aren't we? We're going to fight the Titans."

Jenn looked back painfully, but kept a sense of optimism. "It's not a guarantee, but we all saw how Crius and Iapetus went after us at the Parthenon. Scott encountered Mnemosyne too, right here in the lab. They know we have Pandora's box, and they know what it can do. Cronus won't go down without a fight."

Melanie, Alice, Izzy and Colleen looked miserable.

"Guys, this mission, this battle, is bigger than any of us. You heard Zeus at the oak tree. You heard him say how important it is to keep the Titans from gaining control. We were destined to have these powers, and now we have to use them. If we're not fighting against the Titans, then no one is. This is up to us," said Jenn.

Alice looked at her friends. "I'm sorry, everyone. I never wanted to bring you into a situation like this."

"Alice, don't apologize," said Colleen. "You didn't choose your fate, none of us did. Like Jenn said, it was meant to be."

"We're ready for this," said Jenn. "We've seen the Titanomachy and we know our opponents' weaknesses. Ladies, we have each other."

"I'm sick of waiting," said Izzy. "It's now or never and I want to be done with getting chased. I want to be done with the Titans."

"Let's do it," said Melanie.

The girls, who had minutes before looked so disheartened, now looked fierce. They approached the Transporter and waited for Jenn. Alice and Colleen joined her in the Air Taxi, and Melanie and Izzy stood by their side. Scott was behind the platform, watching the girls.

"Be safe," he warned as tears formed in his eyes.

Jenn turned back. She put on her aviator goggles and picked their destination, *The Omphalos*.

CHAPTER NINETEEN

Round Two

The girls were high above the ground, standing on a plateau of Mount Parnassus. In front of them, a hundred yards away, was the shrine of the Omphalos. The shrine was a large stone circular platform resting flat on the ground. A small marble circle was etched in its middle. Three steps led to the platform's surface, and at the top of the stairs were rigid blocks, equally spaced apart from one another. Four tall columns holding a massive block of stone lined one side of the shrine.

Beyond the shrine was open land, extending on the plateau. Trees graced the slope of the mountain, trailing both upwards and downwards. To the left of the Omphalos, a hundred yards away, was a cliff layered in dead grass and dirt.

Jenn pointed to the circular platform. "That's not it."

"What?" asked Alice.

"That's not Apollo's Temple, which means this is *not* the Oracle of Delphi. We're in the wrong place."

325

"What did you use as our destination when we walked through the Transporter?" asked Colleen.

"The Omphalos."

"Then this has to be it. You thought of the Omphalos and it brought us here."

"But we're at the Tholos. Well, what's left of it," said Jenn.

"What's the Tholos?" asked Izzy.

"It's a temple in the center of the sanctuary of Athena Pronaia. *Our* destination, Apollo's Temple, is a couple hundred yards northeast."

"Maybe the Transporter got confused. It can make a mistake, right?" asked Alice.

"Now is *not* the best time to make a mistake," huffed Melanie. "Bringing us to a bunch of ruins at a time like this!"

"Ruins?" muttered Jenn. She took a moment to think. "This is it. We're in the right place."

"Are you sure?" Izzy asked skeptically.

"Not positive, but pretty confident."

Jenn gazed at the shrine.

"You want to clue us in?" asked Colleen.

"Of course," said Jenn. "I thought this was the Tholos because it looks like it. However, what Melanie said reminded me of something. Today the actual Tholos, just like the Parthenon, remains in ruins. When the temple was built it was an entire building, not just the four columns that you see before you. And the Tholos, just like the Parthenon, is a mythical structure, which means that no matter how badly damaged the temple actually is, *we* are able to see it in its perfect condition. If we were at the Tholos we would see a perfectly constructed building with twenty columns on its platform. Instead, we are seeing a smooth stone base with four ancient columns. The small rectangular blocks are not ruins, but rather structures that were placed on the shrine intentionally.

"Also, if this was the Tholos, there would be ruins of other temples to its left and right. But here, only grass leads to the platform. And the sanctuary of Athena Pronaia is located at the base of Mount Parnassus, but as you can tell, we're not at the bottom of a mountain. We're halfway to the top!" Jenn's voice raised with excitement. "Finally, if you look at the four columns on the shrine, you can make out what's sculpted onto their faces even from a distance."

Carved in the pillar to the far left was a large sun, its rays wriggling in the same wavy direction. The next column contained a thin leaf, appearing to be from a laurel tree. The third pillar showed a perfect star, and carved on the fourth was a blank sphere.

"The Tholos doesn't have any of these sculptures on its pillars," Jenn smiled. "Colleen, you're correct. I directed the Transporter to the Omphalos and it brought us here. Wherever we are, we're at the Omphalos, the center of the world. And that, my friends, is where we have to open Pandora's box." She pointed to the shrine.

"But where are the Titans?" asked Alice.

The area was silent. The hovercraft was the only thing that stirred, quietly whirring. The girls were by themselves, or so it seemed.

"I don't know," said Jenn.

"Should we turn invisible?" asked Izzy.

"I don't think so. If anyone's around they'll still be able to see Pandora's box. There's no way to hide it." Jenn jumped out of the Air Taxi. "Let's go to the shrine."

Jenn reached into one of the hovercraft's compartments and pulled out the bag filled with electroballs as a precautionary measure. With Colleen holding Pandora's box, the girls walked toward the shrine.

Suddenly, the sky turned black. The sun had disappeared, blinding the girls without a moment's notice. Instinctively, they huddled together, their backs facing one another in a tight circle. From somewhere in the darkness came a man's taunting voice, jeering with laughter. Louder and fiercer the laughter grew, soon accompanied by a set of voices cackling in the same fanatic tone.

Alice gripped Melanie and Izzy's hands, stuck in between the two. She beckoned for everyone to do the same.

"Hold on!"

The girls held each other's hands. Colleen kept Pandora's box safe, tucked between her palm and Melanie's.

The ominous voice began to settle down. His taunting snickers turned into words.

"Thought it'd be that easy, didn't you?" hissed the voice. "Casually glide to the Omphalos and open the box, taking control of the Titans. That is what you planned, correct?"

The girls were unresponsive.

328

"My apologies, but I cannot let you do that. If you *did* open Pandora's box, then the Titans would be sucked into its walls, unable to escape. If that happened, well, there's no way I can control the universe from inside that container, now is there?"

The body to the voice approached Alice, whispering his question coldly into her ear.

Instantly Alice raised her palm, locked with Izzy's, and emitted a force field. The figure stumbled backwards.

"Feisty aren't we?" he chuckled. "I should have expected that. But soon it will not matter. Your energy will have been a wasted effort."

The voice slightly droned away, as if the mouth from which it came had turned around.

"Titans, grab the box and secure the Oracle, I want her for myself! Dispose of the rest!"

Alice called to her friends. "Hold up your hands and direct your palms to whatever comes your way!"

Colleen nudged Melanie, Pandora's box clutched in their hands.

"Hold on tight," she warned.

Melanie's hand tensed.

The mocking shrills grew louder. Countless bodies inched toward the girls.

"Think you're invincible, eh?" one voice hollered, approaching Izzy.

Izzy held up her hand and directed it at the figure. From her palm a silver orb emerged, ramming into the body and knocking it away.

"Your power!" Izzy exclaimed, squeezing Alice's hand.

"Just keep our hands linked together. Nobody let go!" Alice demanded, deflecting another body away from hers.

A Titan approached Jenn. Jenn created a force field and the god disappeared, flailing backwards into the dark.

Time and time again, the Titans approached the guardians, attempting to break their hand-linked chain. In response, the girls kept their palms pointed out, all producing force fields that were generated from Alice. Simultaneously, they emitted a glowing shield, its enormity surrounding them all. The Titans were forced backward, unable to pass the silver armor.

Slowly, the massive shield simmered to an ember, deflating until it disappeared. The girls hesitated, trying to sense the next attack.

Silence.

There was no movement of any kind. All that the girls could hear was each other's heavy breathing.

"Are they gone?" whispered Izzy.

"No," said Jenn, her eyes alert. "They're still here."

The hissing voice returned. "Your defense mechanism is quite amusing. However, game time is over."

Something crashed in between the girls' backs. Something, or rather someone, was behind them, having entered their group by jumping in from above, dodging the silver shields. Before the girls had the chance to react to the intruder, the being grabbed Alice, sweeping her out of the group. As Alice's hands slipped from Melanie's and Izzy's, the glowing shields disappeared.

"Alice! No!" cried Melanie. She reached for Alice but her friend was gone.

The four remaining girls could hear the Titans closing in on them once more, cackling victoriously.

"What do we do?!" shrieked Izzy.

Jenn opened the bag that she had taken from the Air Taxi. She reached into it and pulled out one of the electroballs.

"Fight back!"

As one of the Titans approached her, Jenn threw an electroball. The electroball collided with the Titan and exploded, erupting like a set of fireworks. Instantly, the blackened sky illuminated and everything became visible. Relieved, the girls now saw the dangers that prowled toward them.

Most of the Titans stormed after the girls, circling them predatorily. Three gods were missing: Mnemosyne, Uranus and Cronus.

Jenn looked to see whom she had hit with the electroball. She found Hyperion quivering in front of her on the ground. Thea was kneeled at his side, trying to help him up.

Closer and closer the Titans moved in on the girls. Their eyes flashed with rage.

Colleen pushed Pandora's box into Melanie's hand. "Take it and go!"

Crius and Phoebe were approaching Melanie, both extending their hands toward the sky. Melanie took a step back and leapt as far and as high as she could. She launched her body above the gods' heads, soaring past them and landing safely on her feet.

Melanie began to sprint away across the side of the mountain, keeping Pandora's box tucked in her arm. Crius and Phoebe chased after her. The gods trailed distantly behind as meteors and stars began falling from the sky, pounding toward the runner.

As Melanie leapt, Izzy flickered invisible and jumped into flight. Colleen and Jenn followed Izzy's lead, running toward the hovercraft. They could not see their pint-sized friend but felt secure that her invisibility kept her safe.

As Colleen and Jenn ran, the remaining Titans followed after them. With the black bag still in hand, Jenn took out a group of electroballs and handed a few to Colleen. One by one, they threw the electroballs at the Titans, hitting each target and knocking the gods to the ground.

Colleen threw an energy ball straight into Coeus' chest. The god froze in place and shuddered.

"I like these. When did you make them?" asked Colleen.

"The morning we went to Camelot. I thought they might come in handy," said Jenn, her breaths short.

"Oh, they came in handy."

Colleen and Jenn made it to the Air Taxi safely. Jenn reached into the vehicle. As she grabbed one of the swords, something touched her wrist. Jenn held up an electroball, ready to throw.

"Hold fire!"

Izzy appeared above the vehicle, her hand on top of Jenn's.

"Sorry Iz," said Jenn.

"You're fine," Izzy sighed. "You take it."

Jenn took the sword and clutched another, handing them both to Colleen. "Use these."

Colleen took the swords and spun around, watching for the Titans. The effects of the electroballs had begun to wear off. The gods resumed their hunt.

"Jenn, hurry, they're on the move," said Colleen.

"Are Cronus and Uranus around?" asked Jenn, now reaching for her hover board. She placed the board on the ground and stepped on.

"No."

"What about Alice?"

"She's M.I.A."

"We have to find her!" cried Izzy.

"Where's Pandora's box?" asked Jenn.

"With Melanie," said Colleen.

Jenn looked to the right. She could see Melanie running from Crius and Phoebe. Horrified, she watched clusters of meteors crashing into the ground, making an imprint as they trailed her friend.

"Jenn, we have to go!" yelled Colleen.

Izzy grabbed a sword, flickered invisible and took off, soaring through the air with her blade in hand. Jenn gave the hover board a good push with her foot, and the machine began to zoom above the ground. Colleen held both swords in her hands, ready to strike.

Almost instantly Iapetus approached Colleen, swiping his sword at her torso. Colleen swung her blade, blocking Iapetus' thrust. Her brawny figure challenged the Titan's massive size. Iapetus lunged at Colleen, knocking her toward the shrine of the Omphalos. Colleen held her balance and struck back. Sparks flew as their swords clashed.

Little by little, Colleen and Iapetus fought their way alongside the Omphalos, circling the shrine and passing it. Directly behind them was the cliff. Their blades countered one another, clashing swiftly back and forth.

At the same time, Jenn approached Tethys and Oceanus. The Titans shot two bursts of water at the guardian. The streams hit the hover board, knocking Jenn off balance. Quickly, Jenn regained control and threw back two electroballs. Oceanus dodged the electroball but Tethys was hit in the waist. She clutched her abdomen as she fell to the ground.

Hyperion and Thea approached Jenn from behind. Thea extended her arm, grabbing for Jenn's leg.

WHOOSH!

Thea was flung backwards and smashed into the ground. A metal blade poked through her chest.

"What?" she gasped.

Hyperion swiped his hand, aiming in the direction from which the sword had come. His hand collided with something in the air, pushing it backwards. Instantly, Izzy appeared, her tiny body whipping through the air.

"Look!" said Atlas, catching sight of Izzy.

"Get her!" said Coeus.

Izzy tumbled through the air. After a few seconds she caught herself, settling parallel above the ground. As she looked up, she noticed Coeus and Atlas running toward her. Instantly she flickered invisible.

Izzy's disappearance enraged the two Titans. Relentless, they swiped wildly in the air, hoping to hit the guardian. To their frustration, Izzy was long gone, now traveling toward Melanie.

Melanie was running uphill, retreating back to the plateau. She had sped down the mountain in hopes of turning back toward the shrine. Phoebe and Crius propelled stars and meteors toward her, missing as she weaved in and out.

Charging uphill, Melanie's legs began to tense. She pushed through the pain and kept up her speed. When she made it to the plateau, she began sprinting toward the shrine. Izzy flashed visible just above her.

"Izzy! Take the box!" said Melanie.

Izzy grabbed the container. "Keep it up, Mel!" she encouraged, flying away as a star crashed into the ground.

Izzy kept her eyes peeled, in search of Alice. Her body was visible, along with Pandora's box.

Coeus caught sight of the guardian. "There she is!"

"Get her! She has Pandora's box!" bellowed Atlas.

As Coeus took off, Izzy spotted him and started to fly. She flickered invisible, hoping it would be enough to shake Coeus and Atlas off of her trail. Izzy sped through the air toward Colleen.

Colleen and Iapetus stepped closer toward the cliff. They threw nonstop, overpowering blows at one another, the clanking of metal ringing loudly. Colleen swiped both of her swords at Iapetus', using all of her might. Just as she had done to Mordred's, she knocked the Titan's blade from his hand. The guardian watched as the weapon crashed to the ground. Colleen pointed both of her swords at Iapetus.

"You gonna surrender?" Colleen asked, her voice firm.

Suddenly, the mountain began shaking violently. Iapetus and Colleen looked toward the cliff, alarmed. From its edge, legions of shadowy figures began to appear. The figures were faded and dark, their bodies nearly transparent. They swarmed by the dozens onto the plateau.

Colleen gasped. She had seen beings like them before and knew what they were. "Souls!"

Iapetus laughed at the souls' grand entrance. He retrieved his sword and backed away from Colleen.

"I shall leave you alone, for they will determine your fate!" He scurried off, eager to watch the battle.

The massive horde of souls charged at the guardian. Colleen took a deep breath and held up her swords. Seeing no way out, she charged forward, meeting the spirits head on.

Behind Colleen, the plateau extended to the wall of Mount Parnassus where the mountain climbed to the sky. Stationed at the wall was a towering stone cage. The cage came down on three sides, nearly forming a room. A large gap faced the upward slope of the mountain, creating the only ground exit.

Within the stone cavern, Alice was pinned to the back wall. She was guarded by a giant python that stretched longer than she was tall. The snake slithered back and forth, its eyes following the seer. Its tongue flicked in and out as its body heaved in waves. Alice kept away from the serpent, her hands raised. A silver orb spewed from her palm.

Although the snake was frightening, it wasn't the only beast from which Alice shielded herself. Mnemosyne reached at Alice with black and purple streams of energy, attempting to brainwash the Oracle. Alice deflected Mnemosyne's powers, using her shield relentlessly.

From outside of the three-walled jail, Cronus watched the other battles that were taking place. He became restless and turned toward Mnemosyne.

"You still have not caught her?"

"No!" snapped Mnemosyne. "She uses her power all too well!"

Uranus watched her struggle.

"She is but one mortal, and you are a goddess! This should be an easy task!" Uranus growled.

"Then you attack her!" Mnemosyne stepped away from the cavern.

Uranus glared at Alice and raised his hand. He waved his palm forward, propelling a set of icicles toward her. Again, Alice emitted a force field and blocked the shards. The ice shot back at Uranus' chest. The Titan ducked, dodging his own projectiles.

"Fine," he snarled, backing away.

Cronus grew impatient. He began walking toward the Omphalos and called to Mnemosyne.

"When you've caught her bring her to me. We'll be waiting at the shrine."

Mnemosyne glowered at Alice. "Surrender your power!" she demanded.

Alice clung to the wall, still creating her trusty shields. Her eyes were glued to Mnemosyne, but she kept watch for the python. The force field held strong, warmly glowing silver.

All the while Alice had been pinned to the cage, she hadn't caught sight of any of her friends. She knew nothing of the war that was taking place just outside of her prison. Concerned, she tried to reassure herself.

I hope they're okay. Izzy should be fine; she can go invisible so they can't see her. Melanie's too fast for any of the Titans. Colleen could knock any of them out and Jenn's…well, Jenn. She has her gadgets and her brain. But what if something went wrong. What if they're de-. Alice shook her head, refusing to finish her thought. *They're fine. They have to be…they* have *to be.*

Alice stopped herself. Until she heard otherwise, she would assume they were all alive and fighting. She held onto the thought that they were all okay, fighting to keep herself alive at the same time.

CHAPTER TWENTY

The Missed Missing Link

Chandler and Lewis were in their dorm room, awaiting the arrival of a pizza deliveryman. Seated on a blue plaid couch, they were watching a taping of the day's Yankees and Tigers' game. The Yankees were up to bat and Justin Verlander stepped onto the pitcher's mound. Derek Jeter was positioned next to home plate, a wooden bat secured in his hands.

"Five bucks says Jeter hits a double," said Chandler.

"You're on!" said Lewis. He pulled out his wallet.

On the mound, Verlander went into his windup and fired a fastball right down the middle of the plate.

"Steeee-rike one!" the empire cried as Jeter held still.

"What was that?" said Lewis. "That was the perfect pitch!"

"Give the man a second," Chandler said calmly. "Jeter knows what he's doing. It wasn't his pitch."

"You better get that five dollars ready!" laughed Lewis. He tucked his wallet back into his pocket.

Chandler focused on the television screen and smirked.

Verlander looked in for the catcher's signal. Focused, he went into his windup and fired another laser in the same location as the last.

CRACK!

Jeter tore into the ball with a vicious swing and hit a line drive between the left and centerfielders. By the time the centerfielder was able to get the ball back to the infield, Jeter was standing at second base.

"Five dollars, sir!" said Chandler.

Lewis' mouth dropped.

"Dang!" he mumbled, pulling a crisp bill from his wallet. "How do you do that every time?"

Chandler smirked. "It helps if you've seen the game before."

"You cheater!"

"Relax, I'm using it as the deliveryman's tip."

"Five bucks, why so much?"

"It's not my money!" Chandler snorted.

Lewis rolled his eyes.

There was a knock at the door. The fresh smell of pizza seeped into the room.

"Just in time!" Chandler sprang up from the couch and opened the door. "Hello!"

The deliveryman handed him a large pepperoni pizza. In return, Chandler paid the bill and five-dollar tip.

"Thanks a lot!" the deliveryman cheered.

"Anytime!" Chandler grinned and shut the door.

He opened the pizza box, grabbed a cheesy slice and raised it to his mouth.

Lewis peered out of the window, watching the rain as it poured from the sky. A roar of thunder shook the building.

"That's one heck of a storm," he noted.

"Get used to it, it's called Mother Nature," retorted Chandler, stuffing the slice into his mouth. "Want a piece?"

Lewis grabbed a slice.

"What was with Colleen earlier?" asked Lewis. "She was acting kind of strange. Just a few things she said seemed weird."

"She *was* unusually anxious," said Chandler, wiping away a trail of sauce from his cheek. "Women."

"Seriously, though. She kept saying goodbye, like it'd be the last time she'd see us."

Chandler froze. His face flushed pale and his eyes grew wide.

"Chandler, you okay? Chandler?"

Without warning, Lewis, the dorm room and the pizza fell out of Chandler's sight. A new set of images flooded his vision.

Colleen was lying on a cliff, surrounded by a mob of shadows. Her eyes were shut as blood trickled down her forehead. The shadows kicked and punched at her, screaming the entire time. One of the figures grabbed a sword from Colleen's hand. He stood over her body and

*laughed, holding the blade to her chest. Then the weapon
fell, piercing its victim.*

Chandler lost the vision. He returned to reality,
only to find Lewis pulling at his shirt and calling his name.

"Chandler! Chandler, snap out of it!"

Chandler shook his head and blinked his eyes. His
body had broken into a cold sweat and the pizza box now
lay on the floor, having been dropped sometime during the
premonition.

"Colleen!" Chandler exclaimed.

"Dude, what? What happened?" Lewis asked
nervously.

"Colleen, it's Colleen! I saw her! She was getting
attacked!" Chandler's voice was frantic.

"What are you talking about?"

"I saw Colleen! She was hurt! They killed her!"

"Who killed her? Wait? A *vision*?"

"Where did she go? Where was she going when
she left here?"

"I think Scott and Jenn's lab."

"We have to go there. Come on!" Chandler dashed
out of the dorm and sprinted down the hall.

Lewis chased after him. They trailed out into the
rain, rushing to the lab as fast as they could.

* * *

Sitting at the island counter and tapping his feet,
Scott was awaiting the girls' return. Every few minutes he
peered at his watch, counting how long they had been
gone. There was no way of knowing what was happening
halfway around the world and his heart continued to sink

as the clock ticked by and the girls still hadn't returned.

Scott began pacing around the room. Glass was shattered everywhere, but he walked through it, oblivious to the shards.

A light knock sounded at the door. Scott flinched at the noise but calmed himself, realizing that no Titans would be politely knocking on his door. He went to open it and was greeted by a dripping wet Jayden.

"You're drenched!" Scott exclaimed.

"Oh, yeah," Jayden sighed, taking little notice of his soaked clothes.

"What's up?" asked Scott. He pulled up a stool for his friend to sit on.

"It's Izzy. Have you seen her around, by chance?" Jayden asked gloomily.

Scott hesitated, not sure of what to say.

"I've seen her around."

"Recently?"

"Sure."

"Did she seem okay to you?" asked Jayden.

"I've seen her better. How come?"

"She came to see me at the news station and kept saying that she had to go. She told me goodbye and then left without an explanation. I don't know what she meant or where she went. I'm really confused." Jayden paused. "And this weather! I swear I'm controlling it."

"What are you talking about?" asked Scott.

"The weather, it's as if it's following my moods. When I'm happy, the sky is perfectly blue and the sun's out, but when I'm upset, the rain comes instantly."

BANG! BANG! BANG! Someone pounded fiercely on the door, making Scott jump. Chandler and Lewis stumbled into the room, both panic-stricken.

"Scott!" panted Chandler. "Where's Colleen?"

"Umm…," Scott stuttered, once again unsure of what to say. "She's, well…she's out."

"Where? It's an emergency!"

"Why, what's wrong?"

"I just saw her getting killed! I need to see her!"

"He had a vision," said Lewis.

"Like a premonition?" asked Scott, alert.

"I don't know!" Chandler wailed.

"And while we're on the subject of unusual stuff," said Lewis. "I have to tell you, something strange has been going on with me lately."

"Wait, what?" asked Scott, his mind racing.

"Watch." Lewis lifted his hand and directed it at a piece of glass on the ground. The glass began to rise, slowly floating toward Lewis' palm. "See?"

"How the hell did you do that?" barked Jayden.

"It just started happening!"

Then, just as Chandler had frozen, Scott became immobilized. His face was blank and he was lost in thought, watching a vision that overpowered the present moment.

Scott and the girls had returned from the Parthenon. They were all standing in the lab, discussing why the room was in such disarray.

"Iapetus and Mnemosyne. They barged in demanding to know where you were," said Scott.

344

"You could see them?" asked Jenn.

"Yes! They were fierce and angry. I didn't know what to do!"

"Did you tell them where to find us?" asked Alice.

"No. Mnemosyne looked into my memories. She listened to Jenn say you were going to the Parthenon. I could see the memory with her, and she cut it off before she heard that you'd be right back," Scott explained.

"We're lucky. It could have been worse," said Melanie.

"But you could see them!" said Jenn.

"Yes, I could see them."

"You shouldn't have been able to. You're a mortal and mortals can't see mythical beings, especially not gods!"

The memory ended, forming into a new one.

Jayden was sitting at the island counter, talking to Scott.

"And this weather! I swear I'm controlling it." Jayden exclaimed.

"What are you talking about?" asked Scott.

"The weather, it's as if it's following my moods. When I'm happy, the sky is perfectly blue and the sun's out, but when I'm upset, the rain comes instantly."

The second vision ended and carried into a third, most recent vision.

Chandler and Lewis crashed into the lab.

"Scott! Where's Colleen?" asked Chandler.

"Umm...She's, well...she's out," said Scott.

"Where? It's an emergency!"

"Why, what's wrong?"

"I just saw her getting killed! I need to see her!"

"He had a vision," said Lewis.

"Like a premonition?" asked Scott.

"I don't know!" said Chandler.

"And while we're on the subject of unusual stuff," said Lewis. "I have to tell you, something strange has been going on with me lately."

"Wait, what?" asked Scott.

"Watch." Lewis lifted his hand and directed it at a piece of glass on the ground. The glass began to rise, slowly floating toward Lewis' palm. "See?"

As quick as the visions came, they ended, bringing Scott back to reality. Chandler, Lewis and Jayden were all staring at him.

"What did you see?" asked Lewis, recognizing Scott's expression as the same one Chandler had at their dorm room.

Scott rushed through a few of the unbroken cupboards. He took a poster board and a rolled up map, and brought them to the counter.

The map Scott had grabbed was the same one that Jenn had unraveled when she was trying to figure out why the girls had powers. It was a map of the academy's campus, complete with all of the locations on campus and the hand drawn pentagram. The five points of the star were each labeled with one of the girls' names, etched at the places where they had all been at the time their powers were distributed.

Scott placed the poster board on a wooden stand.

On it was a list of Olympians and Titans. Each god's power was listed next to their name.

"Gentlemen, what do you know about mythology?" Scott questioned.

"Not much," said Jayden.

"Same," said Lewis.

Scott looked from the board, to the map, to his friends. He thought of the three visions that had just played in his mind. A few key lines stuck out the most. Silently, he debated with himself.

Jenn said I shouldn't have been able to see the Titans because I'm a mortal. Since I saw them, that means I must be mythical. And Jayden! He said the weather follows his moods...Zeus controls the weather. Chandler had a vision of Colleen dying, just as Prometheus can see into the future. Lewis is telekinetic...but which god is that? And me! I just had visions of the past, like Epimetheus' afterthoughts!

Scott pulled a pen from his lab coat. "Where were you all during the football game last week?" he asked.

"The one between the Phoenix and the Trojans?" asked Chandler. "Lewis and I were at the stadium with the marching band."

"I was at the news station just about all day," said Jayden.

"And I was here at the science hall," Scott mumbled.

He began to scribble onto the map, marking each of the guys' names at their locations during the game. Lewis and Chandler's accompanied Colleen's at the

347

football stadium, and Scott's was next to Jenn's at the science hall. Jayden's was in the middle of the map at the news station.

"That's nine powers but fourteen gods. Who are the rest?" asked Scott.

Suddenly, another shocking sensation fell over him. Scott lost sight of the room around him and another set of visions flashed into his view. This time, only two memories presented themselves and the first was broken up, blurred as if he was only meant to see bits and pieces of it.

Scott was at the girls' dorm, and Jenn was asking them where they had been during the day they had obtained their powers.

"Mel, you were at the track today, right?" asked Jenn.

"Yes."

"Alice, you were at the cafeteria?"

"Of course."

"Izzy, where were you earlier?"

"...the auditorium...,"

"The auditorium, for the magic show..."

"Did anything unusual happen while you were at each of these locations? It could have been something relatively huge or something quite small..."

"Actually, yeah. I was running in the race with only about one hundred meters to go when all of a sudden I started sprinting insanely fast! I didn't just beat Felicia Turner, I creamed her and didn't realize it until I regained consciousness and Mika confirmed our win," said

Melanie.

The vision flashed and the next one appeared.

Scott was walking toward the science hall. Ryan Rivera was walking toward him. As Scott and Ryan were about to pass each other, Ryan's backpack burst into flames. Scott ran to his aid, trying to extinguish the blaze.

"What do you have in there, a bomb?!"

"Nothing but papers!"

The vision ended and Scott returned to the present moment.

Ryan Rivera's backpack exploded and all he had were papers in his bag. Hephaestus is the god of fire. Scott studied the map. *And Ryan was at the cafeteria with Alice when she got her powers!* He wrote down Ryan's name next to Alice's. *Ten people, ten powers, fourteen gods...four more. What about Izzy? She was at the auditorium for the magic show. Who could have picked up a power?*

Scott spoke to Jayden. "What's the name of that magician Izzy did the magic show with?"

"You mean Mario?"

It could be Mario, thought Scott. *There's no proof, and it's a long shot, but it's worth the chance.* He scribbled Mario's name next to Izzy's. *Which leaves three more people. Melanie was at the track and there were plenty of people there. She mentioned Felicia Turner...who's not here on campus anymore. But her relay teammates! Mika, Kira and L.B.! It's another long shot, but there are three of them and only three powers left!* Scott wrote Kira, L.B. and Mika next to Melanie's name at the track.

"Fourteen gods, fourteen powers, fourteen mortals." Scott looked up from the map and found Lewis, Jayden and Chandler gaping at him. "Guys, I need to ask a favor, and you can't ask questions. You've got to trust me on this."

"Anything," said Lewis.

"I need Lewis and Chandler to go find Mika, Kira and L.B. Bring them back here immediately and tell them Melanie needs their help. Do you know where they live?"

"Absolutely, it's not far from here," said Chandler.

"Jayden, go find Mario. Get him here as quickly as humanly possible. I have someone else I have to find. We'll all meet at the lab right away."

"Okay," said Jayden.

"I promise I'll explain everything when we return. All I can say is that we're about to go on a rescue mission," said Scott.

The four teenagers darted out of the lab. Three of the four young men didn't know what was happening, but Scott had everything figured out. He had discovered the missing link.

CHAPTER TWENTY-ONE

In Fate's Hands

The war between the Titans and the guardians was growing fierce. Alice was pinned to the wall of her stone prison, Colleen was fighting the souls of Tartarus, Jenn was battling Oceanus and Tethys, Melanie was running away from Phoebe and Crius, and Izzy was keeping Pandora's box away from Atlas and Coeus. As the war dragged on, Cronus became content with its course, predicting the Oracle and her guardians' demise. He and Uranus watched the battle from the center of the Omphalos. Quickly, a storm rolled over the mountain and rain began to fall.

Izzy had Pandora's box secured in her hands and was inching away from Coeus and Atlas. She swerved around the edge of the plateau. The two Titans followed her every move, unwilling to lose sight of the floating box and the invisible guardian who they knew carried it.

351

As Izzy flew, she approached a large stone structure with three walls. Izzy recognized Mnemosyne patrolling in front of the structure. As she passed by, Izzy looked into the stone cavern. Startled, she watched as Alice deflected the Titan's power with a force field.

"Alice!" she yelled.

"Izzy!" Alice called as Pandora's box flew by.

Izzy flew forward but looked over her shoulder. She took note of how close Coeus and Atlas were to her, and how close she was to Alice. Before she had the chance to see where she was headed, Izzy crashed into something rigid. On contact her body became visible. Izzy backed away and looked up to see what she had hit.

Cronus.

The leader of the Titans turned slowly around. His lips curled into a satisfied grin as he spotted Izzy, her tiny body shaking. To Cronus' left stood Uranus. With one swipe of his hand, Uranus knocked Pandora's box out of Izzy's hold. Panicked, Izzy contemplated flying away, but Coeus and Atlas were directly behind her and Uranus and Cronus were blocking her path. There was no way out.

"All for nothing. What a shame!" Cronus hissed.

Cronus created an enormous fireball as Uranus formed a set of icicles in his palm. Both gods bent back their arms, ready to launch their weapons.

Izzy's heart skipped a beat. She watched, motionless, as Cronus and Uranus released their powers. Terrified, she covered her eyes.

BOOM!

A thunderous blow shook the entire mountain.

Alice felt the rumble, Melanie stumbled at the quake, Jenn was unharmed by the tremor, and Colleen felt it the worst, struggling inches away from the cliff.

Slowly, Izzy peeked from behind her fingers. Astounded, she witnessed something that she had never imagined could happen. Cronus and Uranus were violently trembling. Two exploding currents of electricity shot through the Titans. Behind Izzy, Atlas and Coeus had been thrown into the side of the mountain.

Izzy looked to her left and gasped.

"Jayden! Mario!"

"Izzy! Out of the way!" yelled Jayden. He stood next to Mario, his hands raised.

Mario was controlling the golden stream that entangled Cronus and Uranus. His face was cringing and his muscles bulging.

Jayden stepped back and waved at the air. Heavy clouds began to swarm toward him, funneling into a tornado. Jayden beckoned the cyclone in the direction of Cronus and Uranus. The funnel cloud barreled into the Titans, sweeping them backwards. Cronus and Uranus crashed near Coeus and Atlas. They stood up immediately, fireballs and icicles ready in hand.

"You have to go!" commanded Jayden, waving Izzy out of the way.

Izzy left to find Pandora's box.

Jenn was fighting against Oceanus and Tethys. The hover board had proven to be a good idea, as she was able to dodge the Titans' powers. She still had the black bag with her, but was running out of electroballs.

Oceanus created a wave from his palm. He collected the swell and threw it toward Jenn. Jenn maneuvered the hover board above the current, riding it like a surfer. On her descent, she took two electroballs and threw them at Tethys and Oceanus. The Titans easily dodged them. Jenn reached back into the bag, grabbing for another weapon. Her hand fumbled clumsily with the air until she realized that there were none left.

Tethys shot a line of water pellets, directed straight for the guardian. Jenn braced for impact, unconsciously holding both of her hands in front of her face. A wave of water burst from Jenn's palm, knocking the pellets away from her body.

Jenn gazed at her hands in shock.

Did I do that?

With Jenn off guard, Oceanus sent a piercing stream of water at the hover board. The stream crashed into the board, knocking Jenn off of her device. The guardian whipped through the air and slammed into the ground.

As Jenn clambered to her feet she heard a familiar whirring sound. She turned to her left and watched as the Air Taxi flew toward her. Scott was in the driver's seat and Chandler sat in the back, dressed in one of the girls' suits of armor.

"Need a ride?" asked Scott.

Ecstatic, Jenn hopped into the vehicle and strapped herself in. Scott hit the accelerator and they took off.

Since the battle had begun, Melanie had been sprinting nonstop. By now, she was becoming exhausted. Her legs were heavy, and her knees ached from running up and down the mountain. Despite her fatigue, she continued to run, keeping Crius and Phoebe occupied.

Unfortunately, the longer Melanie ran the slower she became. Little by little, Phoebe and Crius inched toward her. The Titans used their abilities relentlessly, sending their ammunition straight for the runner.

As Melanie rounded the mountain, turning back toward the Omphalos, Phoebe sent a meteor directly in front of her body. As the meteor crashed, Melanie skidded face first into the ground. She scrambled to her feet, barely dodging the blow of a star.

"Are you sure you want to keep running? You know how this will end!" Phoebe cackled.

"No. We want her to run for as long as she can. When we beat her, victory will be so much sweeter!" Crius mocked, directing another orb at the guardian.

Melanie watched as the star plunged toward her. With a heavy push she surged forward. The star missed.

From the side of the mountain another figure appeared, sprinting to Melanie's left. Unnerved, Melanie glanced to see who it was. Fifty yards away, an ivory young woman was running at her pace. The young woman had her wavy brown hair tied in a ponytail and wore a blue tank top with silver shorts. She wore blue and gray running spikes with a lightning bolt adorned on their sides.

Her face was covered in dirt, along with her legs and clothes. It all looked too familiar.

Melanie did a double take. The person was more than familiar. Next to Melanie was her exact duplicate.

Crius and Phoebe noticed the matching girls.

"There are two of her!" Crius bellowed.

"Which is the guardian?" shrieked Phoebe.

"I do not know! Is it in her power to duplicate?"

"It cannot be! For she would have done it earlier!"

"Never mind, we shall dispose of them both," Crius declared.

Phoebe drew another set of meteors into the earth's atmosphere. Crius did the same, directing a pair of gray stars at the identical teenagers.

Both Melanie and her double dodged the projectiles.

"Who are you?" Melanie yelled to her replica.

"Mel, trust me!" answered the duplicate.

Crius hurled a star directly in front of Melanie's duplicate. The young woman was knocked off her feet. Instantly, the duplicate morphed into her original form. Melanie looked back, horrified.

"Kira!"

Melanie rushed back to her friend, avoiding a downpour of meteors. As she reached Kira's side, Crius extended his arm toward the sky.

"At last, we come to the end!" Crius bellowed. Both he and Phoebe called for ammunition.

Melanie helped Kira to her feet and the two began to run. The girls turned their heads to locate the stars and meteors, watching as the objects plunged from the sky. Fear pulsed through Melanie's veins. In front of her, only one hundred yards away, was the Omphalos. Her heart sank as she realized that she and Kira might not make it to the shrine.

Seconds passed and nothing happened. Melanie turned around. She watched as the stars and meteors fell on the downslope of Mount Parnassus. The bombs were too far away to have shaken the ground beneath her feet. Melanie glimpsed back at Phoebe and Crius. The Titans had fallen behind and were positioned to the right, glaring at something.

"Oh hell no!" shouted a voice.

Melanie shot a glance to the right. Mika was facing Crius and Phoebe, alongside L.B. They both held gigantic bows in their hands, shooting arrows at the two gods. Phoebe and Crius changed their attention to Mika and L.B.

"Bring it!" Mika challenged.

On the cliff, Colleen was struggling against the souls. They had surrounded her on all sides. Using her swords, she swiped at their bodies, killing all the spirits who encountered her blade. Despite her success, there were more foes than Colleen could keep pace with. The souls continued to drown her within their mob, debilitating her with every blow.

One of the souls reached for Colleen's swords. The silver handles slid out of her hands and she watched as her weapons fell to the ground. With her blades out of reach,

Colleen adapted. One by one she struck the souls with her fists, erasing their clouded silhouettes.

A group of souls joined together and rammed into Colleen. Colleen was forced to the ground. Her head crashed into a rock, knocking her out. She was motionless, blood streaming down her face.

Eagerly, a man's soul towered over Colleen. He held one of her swords over her body, the blade pointing at her chest. The rest of the spirits watched in anticipation, cheering for the assault. The soul lifted the blade and thrust it towards Colleen.

WHOOSH!

As the blade's tip brushed Colleen's skin, the sword flew out of the soul's hand. The spirits looked up, incensed. Then, just like the sword, they were swept up from the ground and thrown backwards. Lewis stood with his arms up, forcing the spirits away from Colleen. With another swipe of his hand, Lewis sent the souls down the slope of the mountain. When the coast was clear, he ran over to his friend and shook her body.

"Colleen! Colleen!" yelled Lewis.

Colleen stirred, her eyes fluttering.

"You all right?" Lewis asked, holding her hand.

At first sight of Lewis, Colleen gasped.

"Yeah."

Colleen eyes widened as she regained consciousness.

"WATCH OUT!"

Iapetus charged at Colleen and Lewis, his sword pointed out.

Reflexively, Lewis waved his hand, directing his palm behind his body. Instantly, Iapetus fell backward.

Lewis helped Colleen up.

Iapetus rose from the ground, his sword locked in his hand. He marched toward the guardians, his voice humming with arrogance.

"What a shame. Your hero arrived before the souls finished you off! I was looking forward to it."

The teenagers ignored him. Colleen noticed one of her swords lying on the ground. She bent down to retrieve it and tightly held the silver handle. She stepped toward Iapetus, the blade pointed out.

From behind Iapetus, Atlas came running into the battle. Atlas held a sword in his hand and charged at Colleen. Colleen stood firm and threatened him with her own sword. The Titan ran toward the guardian and swung. The metal clashed and the two fought, blocking each other's swipes.

Iapetus threw his blade at Lewis, but his swordsmanship was no match for Lewis' telekinetic powers. Lewis blew Iapetus' body back, keeping him trapped on the ground. Lewis turned toward Atlas and pushed with his palm; Atlas didn't move.

Facing Atlas, Colleen pulled her arm back, preparing to swipe at the Titan. Atlas dropped his sword and punched Colleen in the head, viciously knocking her to the edge of the cliff.

Lewis looked back at his friend, terrified. Atlas was stomping toward her, ready to finish her off. As Atlas reached for Colleen, she rolled to her left, her sword tucked parallel with her body. Relieved, Lewis looked away, assured that Colleen could hold her own.

As soon as he turned, something pierced into Lewis' stomach. Lewis froze, his hands gripped at his abdomen. He looked down to find a silver blade lodged in his body. His knees collapsed. Lewis stumbled to the ground.

Colleen watched as Lewis fell to the dirt. She saw Iapetus' sword sticking from his back.

"LEWIS! NO!"

Colleen dropped her sword and grabbed Atlas, flipping the Titan off the cliff. She charged at Iapetus, who had turned his back on Lewis. As soon as she was within reach, Colleen grabbed Iapetus and swung his body backwards. The Titan was taken by surprise and struggled to fight. Colleen whipped Iapetus onto the edge of the cliff, his neck and head hanging over the ledge.

Colleen towered over the Titan.

"Kill your pet, did I?" Iapetus hissed.

Colleen was beyond any level of anger that she had ever felt before. She crouched over the Titan and pulled back her arm, swinging with all of her might. With a destructive force, her fist rammed into the god's jaw, his head jerked from the impact. Over and over Colleen struck Iapetus, putting all of her energy into each blow.

From a distance, Kira watched the commotion. She saw Lewis huddled on the ground and began running toward him. When Kira arrived, Lewis was still breathing, but his breaths were shallow and quick. His eyes welled with fear.

"Hold on," Kira whispered.

She stroked Lewis' head and held his hand. Then she turned toward Mika.

"MIKA! MIKA, HURRY!"

Mika heard her name called. With one look at Lewis she sprinted toward him.

Izzy was scanning the ground for Pandora's box. She had seen the general direction in which Uranus had tossed the container, but hadn't yet found it. Distantly, she could see something dark poking up from the ground. Izzy recognized its weathered look and quickly flew to the object. Indeed, it was Pandora's box. The guardian swept it into her arms.

Suddenly, something grabbed Izzy's leg. The entire world went black. She struggled to break free from whatever trapped her leg, all the while unable to see.

Hyperion was latched onto Izzy's calf. Melanie watched as the Titan held Izzy hostage. Melanie lowered her head and charged at Hyperion. Before the god knew what hit him, he was knocked off his feet.

As Hyperion collided with the earth, Izzy's vision returned.

"Mel! Take the box! I'm going to help Jayden!" said Izzy.

Melanie ran toward the flying woman, catching Pandora's box as Izzy flickered invisible. With the box in her hands, Melanie rushed toward the Omphalos.

"MELANIE! WATCH OUT!" a voice screamed.

Before she reached the shrine, Melanie turned around. Her eyes widened as a black star whizzed toward her.

BOOM!

The star hit the ground.

Something had crashed into Melanie, knocking her away from the orb. She looked down to see what had saved her, and found a suit of armor clutched to her body. Melanie flipped back the suit's helmet to find Chandler grinning at her.

"Now can we go on a date?" asked Chandler, his cheeks bright red.

Melanie cracked a smile, but gazed at her empty hands.

"The box!" she exclaimed.

To her relief, Pandora's box was next to her, nestled on the ground.

In the stone cavern, Alice was still guarded by Mnemosyne and the python. Mnemosyne had become excruciatingly frustrated, ready to give up on her prey as Alice continued to deflect her powers. Irritated beyond measure, Mnemosyne shot a final stream of energy toward Alice. Alice kept her palms raised, the silver shield protecting her.

WHOOSH!

A sudden orange and red flash shot from beyond the cavern. Crackling flames crashed into both Mnemosyne and the python. Almost instantly the serpent was incinerated. Mnemosyne screamed, trying to extinguish the blaze by running through the wind. She left Alice to herself, momentarily unconcerned with the seer.

Alice remained against the prison's wall. Mnemosyne had given her a free opportunity to escape, but Alice refused the offer. She was too afraid that Cronus had staged the inferno, attempting to lure the Oracle from her trap. Playing it safe, Alice hung to the stone, her hands ready to act.

From the side of the dungeon, a tall young man walked into the cavern. Alice looked at him in disbelief.

"Ryan Rivera?"

"Come on!" Ryan called.

Alice followed him out of the cavern.

"Was that you?" she asked quickly.

"There's no time for questions," Ryan snapped.

Alice and Ryan ran closer to the Omphalos. Melanie and Chandler were near its base, fighting Hyperion.

Hyperion stood between Melanie and the Omphalos. He punched Chandler in the stomach, easily knocking him out of the way. Melanie tried to out-maneuver Hyperion, juking left and right, but the Titan was too quick. He blocked her path with each movement.

"Go to the Omphalos' center," Ryan instructed Alice.

Alice dashed up the steps of the Omphalos, ducking past the columns. She stood in the center ring.

Ryan approached Hyperion from behind. He shot a burst of flames at the Titan, enveloping his body. Hyperion roared and turned toward Ryan.

"Go Mel!" yelled Chandler. "Take the box to the shrine!"

Another star fell from the sky. The white orb rushed toward Melanie.

"Alice, catch!" shouted Melanie. She threw Pandora's box at the center of the Omphalos. Alice caught it with both hands.

Cronus glanced past Jayden and stared at the shrine. Alice stood in the center with Pandora's box. Frantically, Cronus blew an enormous fireball at Jayden, pushing the weatherman backwards. As quickly as he could, he directed a stream of flames toward Alice. The blaze screamed toward the Oracle. Alice watched the fire, her hand ready.

BANG!

Water crashed into the flames. Alice stood with her palm raised, but had no need to create a force field. Jenn stood on the Air Taxi with her palms held up. A powerful stream of water shot from her hands, challenging the inferno.

"Alice, the star!" Melanie yelled.

The star that had targeted Melanie was now aiming for Alice.

"Open the box!" yelled Chandler.

The star shot straight for Alice.

"ALICE!" Ryan screamed.

Without a moment to spare Alice flipped the latch on Pandora's box and lifted the lid. Instantly, a rushing gust of wind blew out in all directions, coming from the center of the Omphalos. The star disappeared, destroyed by the wind. Cronus' flames were extinguished at once. The wind engulfed the Titans, pulling them toward Alice and the box one by one.

Hyperion was the first to go, his body swirling into the container. Oceanus and Tethys were next, paired together and struggling to break free. Thea followed, Izzy's sword removed from her chest. Crius and Phoebe were next, kicking and screaming the entire way in. Atlas' body rose from the bottom of the mountain, along with all of the souls who had fallen off the edge. Iapetus was carried away from Colleen's tight grip. Mnemosyne flowed into the box and Coeus was sucked in after her, unable to escape. Uranus fell from Mario's hold, the electrocuting stream following his body. Every Titan was in the container, except for one.

Cronus' body raised above the ground, moving toward Pandora's box.

"NO!" Cronus cried. *"Eme pempe pros ton tartaron!"*

There was a blinding white light. For a split second no one could see. Then, as quickly as the white appeared, it vanished. Pandora's box was closed with its latch secured. The magnificent wind had died and the mountain was still.

Alice stood in the center of the Omphalos, Pandora's box still clutched in her hands. Everything was silent. Then, Colleen's voice could be heard sobbing from the cliff.

"Lewis! Lewis! Stick with me bud, stick with me!"
she begged, huddled next to Lewis as Kira coddled his
head.

Tears were streaming from Colleen's eyes as she
held onto her friend. Lewis' body was convulsing. Sweat
streaked down his face.

"I'm...I'm...sss...sorry," he stuttered, barely
choking out the words.

His eyes flitted tiredly, nearly closing.

"Mika!" Kira called again.

"I'm here!" said Mika, rushing over to Lewis. She
crouched in front of him and grabbed for the handle of the
sword that was lodged in his stomach. "I have to pull it
out."

"Just do it!"

Mika jerked the sword. As the blade released,
Lewis' eyes closed.

"Lewis! Hold on!" Colleen shrieked.

Mika placed both of her hands over Lewis' wound.
The wound closed and started to disappear. Colleen
watched, bewildered. Lewis' eyes opened, and he picked
up his head, gasping for air. His hold tightened on Colleen
and Kira's hands as he fought to catch his breath.

Mika backed away. "He's okay."

In disbelief, Colleen ran her hand over Lewis'
stomach, feeling his smooth, puncture free skin. The blood
that had spilled from his abdomen had vanished and the
stab wound was gone. As she came to believe what she
had witnessed, Colleen swept Lewis into her arms.

"Oh, Lewis, Lewis!" Colleen sobbed, more tears

trailing down her cheeks.

Lewis pulled back from Colleen; a single tear trickled down his face.

"I'm so sorry," he whispered.

Colleen almost laughed, her tone grateful but nervous.

"Don't be! Don't be for one second!"

They hugged each other for a few more moments until Kira and Mika helped them onto their feet. Together they moved toward the shrine, Colleen at Lewis' side the entire way there.

Jayden was walking toward the shrine. Out of nowhere, something flew into his arms. Izzy flickered visible and held on to his chest as tight as she could.

"Jayden!"

"Izzy!"

Izzy sobbed, her eyes blurry with tears.

"I didn't want to say goodbye, I never did! I just didn't know if I would ever see you again!" she cried.

"Izzy, calm down," Jayden hushed, pressing his finger to her lips. "You're okay. I'm okay."

Izzy pulled away and looked at Jayden, who smiled at her sweetly. She leaned in and brushed her soft lips against his, kissing him passionately. Instantly, the rain ceased and the sun shone brightly. Jayden and Izzy held onto each other, complete once again.

Melanie stood near the shrine. She leaned over and reached out her hand, helping Chandler to his feet. The armor-covered teen wore a wide grin, brimming from ear to ear.

"You haven't answered my question," Chandler smirked.

"What's your question?" asked Melanie.

"Now can we go on a date? I did save your life."

Melanie giggled. "How's Friday?"

"Score!"

At the center of the Omphalos, Alice was still clutching Pandora's box, almost afraid to let it go. When she looked up, Jenn and Scott were walking toward her.

"You did it!" Jenn smiled, hugging Alice.

"*We* did it," Alice corrected. "But what's going on?"

"We'll explain in a little bit," said Scott, "once we get to the lab."

"And did I see what I thought I saw you do?" Alice asked Jenn, exhilarated.

Jenn grinned. "Wait until we get to the lab."

Alice hugged them both. Then she turned around, stepping away from the Omphalos.

Ryan was watching Melanie reunite with Mika, L.B. and Kira when someone tapped his shoulder. He turned around and found Alice.

"I, uh…want to thank you," she stuttered, finding it weird that she was thanking Ryan Rivera. "I really appreciate what you did."

"No problem. I couldn't ruin the fate of the universe, could I?" Ryan replied, half smiling.

Alice studied Ryan. The tone in which he spoke was solemn and sincere. His dark eyes had seemed to lighten and his pale skin had more color than the last time she had seen him. And although his face looked indifferent, Alice could detect a hint of joy in his eyes and voice. Almost naturally, she leaned forward and kissed him on the cheek. Ryan was stunned. Stunned herself, Alice turned away, walking toward Melanie. She shook her head, finding it almost unbelievable what Ryan had done and what she had just given him for doing it.

"So much for today being the day the world explodes!" Melanie giggled.

"What?" asked Alice.

Melanie smirked. "You said that the day Ryan did something nice, the world would explode. We're still standing."

"It was a good theory. It almost happened," Alice sighed, both relieved and shocked.

Standing on the shrine, Jenn called for everyone's attention.

"Guys, let's go back to the lab. We have a lot to discuss." She turned on the portable Transporter and pointed at an open space.

Soon, everyone but Jenn and Alice had walked through the portal. Alice turned around, taking one last gaze at the landscape. It was a place of peace and destruction, simply contradictory. With a final glimpse she turned back around, walking into the portal with Pandora's box. Jenn followed, deserting the battlefield.

CHAPTER TWENTY-TWO

Explanations

As Jenn stumbled into the lab, the portal of the Transporter disappeared. Everyone was in the room surrounding the island counter. Physically speaking, the group looked devastated. The teens were covered in mud, and battered with gashes and bruises.

Scott and Jenn stood in front of their friends, seeming very excited. Jenn opened her mouth to speak, but Melanie interrupted.

"What happened?!"

"We just beat the Titans!" Izzy cheered.

"I understand *that*. I'm talking about how we did it," Melanie corrected. "One second, there's five of us getting defeated, and the next, all these guys show up saving us!"

"They seemed to have known what they were doing," said Alice, looking at Scott.

"I'm just glad that we're all alive," Colleen sighed, wrapping her arms around Lewis.

"What happened?!" Melanie persisted.

"Okay, okay, calm down," said Jenn, "I'll let Scott explain."

Scott faced the group. "So as you all know," he said, directing his speech to the girls. "You each have powers, including Jenn. You know that your abilities were sent by the Olympians in order to defend Alice and defeat the Titans. When we figured all of this out, there was an important piece of information that we had missed." He paused. "You weren't the only mortals that were given powers."

The girls looked surprised. However, their feelings of astonishment quickly dissolved. After the events that had just occurred, they knew that what Scott said was true. They just didn't know why.

Scott presented the poster board of all of the gods' names and their powers.

"If you include Prometheus and Epimetheus, there are fourteen Olympians. When you obtained your powers, we believed that only five powers were sent, because there were only five planets lined in formation. What we didn't realize was that it wasn't the number of planets that was significant; it was the connection between the planets and the gods. Each of the fourteen Olympians positioned themselves on the five Olympic planets, Mercury, Venus, Mars, Neptune and Jupiter. From there, they sent us their powers."

Scott pulled out the map with the guardians' names written by the points of the pentagram.

"After you left for Delphi, Chandler showed up here saying he had seen Colleen getting killed. When he

371

told me about his vision, all I could think of was that Prometheus could see into the future. Then Lewis showed me that he was telekinetic, and Jayden had mentioned that the weather follows his moods. Sometime during it all, I had my own vision. A set of memories or afterthoughts consumed my mind and I started seeing things that were filling in the gaps.

"The day you all gained powers, I was at the science hall with Jenn, one of the points of the pentagram. Chandler and Lewis were at the stadium, another point with Colleen. Jayden, however, was at the news station, which isn't a point on the star. His location was in the center of the pentagram, meaning that a god sent their power to the center of the star. Jayden has the ability to control the weather…just like Zeus.

"So with Jayden, Lewis, Chandler and myself, there were now nine mortals the gods had given powers to. I figured there had to be five more. One of the visions I had showed Ryan Rivera. I realized that he and Alice had been at the same place at the time Alice obtained her deflection abilities: the cafeteria at the cook-off, another point of the pentagram.

"At each of the points there was a pattern, that more than one person had received powers at each location. The only two that didn't follow the pattern were the track and the auditorium. I tried to think of anyone who could have been near Izzy and Melanie. Mario was at the magic show, so I picked him as one of the guardians. Only three left. My last guess was that the final three mortals were Mika, Kira and L.B.," said Scott. "My guess was correct."

"After the race!" said Melanie, looking at Mika. "When I passed out, I woke up when you touched my shoulder! You healed me."

"A healing touch is one of Apollo's abilities," Jenn confirmed. "He's also a skilled archer."

"You didn't shoot a bow and arrow at States, did you?" Colleen asked, confused.

"No way!" said Mika.

"Then how come she can use the bow? I thought our powers were determined by what we were doing at the time we were hit by the lightning bolts," said Colleen.

"Because that's not how it works," answered Jenn. "To an extent it makes sense. Melanie was running in the race when she became super fast, but how do we explain Izzy's ability to fly? How do we explain Kira's power to transform into anything she wants to? There's another reason for it. Each of the powers we have are shared by the god who gave them to us.

"Which means Ryan's fire powers came from Hephaestus. Mika and L.B. can use bow and arrows like Apollo and Artemis. Hera can transform into any living thing and so can Kira. Hermes and Melanie are incredibly fast, while Colleen and Ares are incredibly strong. Izzy and Aphrodite can fly and turn invisible and Mario and Hestia have the power of electricity. Alice and Hades can distribute orb-like shields, and Jayden and Zeus control the weather. Scott has afterthoughts like Epimetheus, and Chandler has premonitions like Prometheus. I have Poseidon's power," said Jenn.

"What about Lewis?" asked L.B.

"There's only one Olympian left and that's Athena," said Scott.

"I'm a girl?!" asked Lewis.

"I knew it!" laughed Chandler.

Lewis glared at him.

"A goddess sent you your powers, that's all it means," said Jenn.

"When we watched the Titanomachy, Athena never made anything levitate. She didn't seem telekinetic," said Alice.

"It's like the whole Zeus and his lightning bolts thing," said Jenn. "She may not have gotten that power until after the Titanomachy was over."

"What about you and Poseidon?" asked Colleen. "He's the god of seas, and you don't have any water powers."

"No, she does!" Alice exclaimed. "I saw her use them! She doused Cronus' fire!"

"I thought you were omniscient!" said Izzy.

"I think she *thinks* she's omniscient," teased Scott.

Jenn nudged him playfully. "It's a combination of both. Poseidon gave me an intellectual boost, but the real gift was to be able to fight with water."

Jenn lifted her left hand and directed it at the wall. From her palm, a stream of water came shooting out.

"How come we just found out?" asked Melanie.

"Because I've never had to use it. When I tested to see if I had an active power I didn't give it a real shot because I didn't believe that I had one."

374

"Do you think I can turn into the Hulk and we just don't know it yet?" asked Izzy, flexing her muscles.

Jenn laughed. "That one I doubt"

"Wouldn't you know that you had a power if Poseidon gave you an intellectual boost?" asked Colleen.

"There's a flaw," said Jenn. "I don't know everything."

"So when Melanie obtained her speed ability, it was a coincidence that she was running?" asked Alice.

"Strictly coincidence," said Jenn.

"I'm curious," said Melanie, turning toward Kira, L.B. and Mika, "when did you discover you had powers?"

"Psh, don't ask," said Mika.

"We can tell her," said Kira. "It was the day after the track meet. We discovered my powers first, then Mika's and L.B.'s. The incident hinted at their shooting abilities."

"Mika freaked!" giggled L.B.

"Oh *ha, ha.* I'm warning you, don't say it," Mika growled.

"Anyway, like Kira said it was the day after the track meet," said L.B. "I had woken up and was fixing my hair with the curling iron. Mika was sleeping in Kira's bed, which was weird, but I didn't think much of it. Kira wasn't in the dorm room, so I figured she was out. Then the door opened and in walked Mika."

"L.B.!" Mika shouted.

L.B. laughed. "Boy was I confused! There was a Mika in the bed and a Mika at the door. And then the Mika in the bed woke up. She stepped onto the floor and when the real Mika, the Mika in the doorway, noticed her, she threw her keys at the duplicate. Instinctively, I threw my curling iron at the keys so that it wouldn't hit whoever was in the bed. Unfortunately though, both the keys and the curling iron hit the Mika in the bed on the shoulder. When she got hit, she transformed into Kira. We rushed over to Kira to apologize and when Mika touched the red bump on her shoulder, it disappeared." L.B. paused. "Sorry if that was confusing. There were too many Mika's!"

"One is enough," said Kira.

"P.S., you've gotta be pretty thick to throw a curling iron at someone," Mika barked.

"Shut it," growled L.B.

"How did you guys get the bow and arrows?" asked Mel.

Mika's face flexed from irate to eager. "Those just showed up on our doorstep."

"There was a note attached. It had two letters, A and A," said Kira.

"Apollo and Artemis," murmured Jenn.

"It was sent from the gods?" asked Alice. "Zeus thought that there were only five of us."

"But who else would have sent them?" asked Colleen.

Alice shrugged.

"Did you know how to use them right away?" asked Scott, intrigued.

"Pretty much," said Mika. "It seemed natural to shoot the arrows."

"We didn't use them much," said L.B. "Just a few

times to see what we could do, but when Chandler and Lewis came to get us tonight we brought them with us. They said Melanie needed our help, and we thought they might be useful."

"Kira, why'd you transform into Mika? You were asleep?" asked Melanie.

"Must have been a nightmare," said Kira.

To everyone's surprise, Mika slipped out a giggle.

"What about you, Mario?" asked Izzy, focusing on the magician. "How did you discover your powers?"

"Well, Ms. Izzy, I was practicing for another magic show when the power went out. I raised my hands in frustration because I couldn't see. Then from my palms there came a bolt of miniature lightning. It struck the light fixtures and then I could see!" said Mario.

"I'm glad you have powers. I appreciate you coming to rescue us, all of you," said Izzy.

"For you Ms. Izzy, I would do anything," Mario assured.

"What *I'm* curious about," said Colleen, "is what happened when we left for Delphi. You said you had some afterthoughts and Chandler had a premonition, but what happened after that?"

"You pretty much know the rest," said Scott. "When I had the puzzle pieced together, Chandler and Lewis went to get the track girls, Jayden found Mario and I got Ryan. We came back to the lab and I gave them the short version of the story. When we arrived at Delphi, these guys were informed of what the Titans were trying to do, what *you* were trying to do and the severity of the situation."

"You agreed to come help us? To come save us after hearing that?" asked Colleen, stunned.

"You needed us," said Ryan.

It was the first thing that Rivera had said since they had returned to the lab.

Alice's mind was spinning. This was *not* the Ryan she had come to know and detest. The Ryan *she* knew was arrogant and smug. He would rather walk across a field of broken glass barefoot than offer his help. The Ryan Alice knew would never have dreamed of helping her out, but here he stood having saved both her life and her friends' lives. The idea was unfathomable, the thought outrageous, and knowing that it was true was the most incomprehensible part of it all. But at the same time, she was impressed with his sudden change of heart. For without it, well…she may not be here.

Alice looked down at her hands and realized that she was still holding Pandora's box.

"Hey Jenn, what do we do with this?" she asked.

"I think it's time we paid another visit to a certain tree, if you know what I mean," said Jenn.

"Good idea," said Scott. "You're all more than welcome to join us."

"Where are we going?" asked Izzy.

"You'll see," said Jenn. She approached the Transporter, gesturing Alice through the portal.

"Wait!" Melanie froze. "I just realized something. We're not M.A.J.I.C. anymore."

"What?" asked Colleen.

378

"You know, our names, M.A.J.I.C. Now we're *MAJICKLM...RS...M...J...CL,*" her voice trailed into silence.

"No we're still M.A.J.I.C.," said Izzy. "That will never change."

Given Jenn's okay to go, Alice passed into the portal. Jenn passed next to her, thinking of their destination.

They arrived in a green field, a place that Alice recognized instantly. A row of mountains were off in the distance and a large, sturdy oak tree stood just ahead.

"This is the Oracle of Zeus," Jenn announced. "Basically you come here to speak with the king of the gods himself."

She plucked a small sage leaf from one of the tree's branches and waited. Quickly the wind picked up. The bark from the trunk began splitting until a deep hole opened up. The wind died down as a deep voice bellowed from within.

"Who goes there?" the voice demanded.

Alice recognized it as Zeus'.

"Jenn Andrews."

"Oh, Jenn!" Zeus' voice lightened. "Welcome back!"

"Hey, Zeus!" said Izzy.

"Hello, Izzy. Are the others here as well? Alice, Colleen and Melanie?"

"You're good at remembering our names," said Melanie.

379

"I think I ought to know the names of the people I give powers to."

"Then you're going to learn a few more," said Jenn.

"What do you mean?" asked Zeus.

"You know how you thought there were only five of us?"

"Yes."

"Turns out there are actually fourteen!"

"Fourteen?" repeated Zeus. "That makes more sense. I thought seven was an incredibly low number. My Olympians have better aim than I give credit. Who are these mortals? Are they present?"

"Yes," said Jenn. "They are-"

"Scott Meyers."

"Chandler Comet."

"Lewis Quinn."

"Mika Mitchell."

"Kira Calloway."

"L.B. Francois."

"Mario Montazzio."

"Jayden Kinney."

"And," Jenn searched for Ryan, "there's one more, but he's not present."

Alice spun around, witnessing for herself what Jenn had said. A feeling of disappointment welled in her chest when she discovered Ryan was absent.

"He opted not to come," said Scott.

"And who is he?" asked Zeus.

"Ryan Rivera. Hephaestus' target," said Jenn.

"Wait, wait, wait!" said Melanie, her hands raised in the air. "Let's rewind for a minute. Zeus, you said that seven was an incredibly low number. You only knew there were five of us."

"You are correct. When I spoke with you last time, I assumed there were five powers that had each hit a human. However, after our conversation, I spoke with Artemis and Apollo. They asked if I knew who their powers had been distributed to, and I said that no abilities of archery or healing had been received. But with the perfect aim that they have, they assured me there had to be two more guardians. We then knew that there were at least seven of you. There were two that you didn't know about," said Zeus.

"Why didn't you tell us afterwards?" asked Colleen, flustered.

"Because Prometheus had a vision that you encountered each other. On your own, you found one another."

"We ran into each other because we *already* knew each other. None of us knew that the others had powers!" said Melanie.

"I wasn't gonna tell anyone about our abilities," said Mika.

"Where did the bow and arrows come from?" asked L.B.

"Those were gifts from Artemis and Apollo," said Zeus.

"But how did they get to them?" asked Jenn. "The Olympians can't come onto Earth."

"Rigon, my servant, delivered them. Aside from that, how did your quest go? You have started, haven't you?"

"Started? We've finished!" chimed Izzy.

"Finished?!" The branches on the tree began to shake. "How did it end? You did find Pandora's box, didn't you?"

"Don't worry," said Alice, "I have Pandora's box. It contains the Titans."

"This is fantastic news! The best news I have ever heard!" Zeus exclaimed. "I cannot wait to inform the Olympians!"

"However, I do have a question," said Jenn.

"Ask away!"

"When we opened the lid to Pandora's box and Cronus was getting sucked in, he yelled something. I couldn't hear the first part but he said something about Tartarus. We witnessed the curse that he set upon the Olympians during the Titanomachy and it sounded like another curse. I'm worried about it."

"At the end of a battle even the losing side has the chance to make a final command or curse, which is what happened in the Titanomachy. However, I do not believe it is something to fret over. Whatever Cronus said involving Tartarus, it must not have worked. If he called for a curse to condemn you to the underworld or banish you from the earth, he cannot do it. The winning side cannot be locked in prison and because you are not entirely gods you cannot be banned from the world, for where else would you live? One must be a complete god to live on Mount Olympus, or

382

a perished soul of high importance. In that aspect, you are untouchable," said Zeus.

"You're sure we're safe?" asked Jenn.

"I am positive."

Jenn hugged Scott.

"What about our powers?" asked Izzy. "Do we keep them?"

A soft laugh came through the tree.

"Of course. You have earned them," said Zeus.

"What do we do with Pandora's box?" asked Alice.

"The box is to stay on Mount Olympus. I will send Rigon to fetch it."

Suddenly, something came hurtling out of the sky. A miniature man, or what looked like a man, floated to the ground. The tiny man had small dark eyes and golden hair that almost looked like fur. He wore a small toga, and weathered sandals. When he landed, he approached Alice.

"Rigon, I assume?" she asked, reluctant to give him the box.

"Yes," the creature answered.

"That was fast!" said Izzy.

"Gods and mythical beings are typically fast," said Zeus.

"I know the Titans can travel long distances quickly," said Scott. "It took them minutes to go from Indiana to the Parthenon."

"Gods are exceptionally fast beings," said Zeus. "However, they are not fast enough to travel from one continent to another in mere minutes. The way that the Titans were able to retreat to Greece from the United

States is because there are hidden portals scattered throughout the earth. They simply stepped through a gateway near the academy and wound up in Greece. Gods can also store momentum. If they run down a hill or through something that gives them speed, they can channel that speed for longer distances."

"Where are the portals?" asked Jenn.

"In many places, all tucked away so that mortals cannot find them. For instance, there is one glimmering within Niagara Falls, and one sheltered in the Grand Canyon. The Great Wall of China was built over another, as was the Omphalos."

"There's a portal at the Omphalos?" asked Alice.

"Right beneath its stone platform," answered Zeus.

"Where do they all lead to?" asked Izzy.

"Each leads to a different place. If you stepped into Niagara Falls, you would find Atlantis. The one beneath the Great Wall of China would take you to Shangri-La."

"What about the Omphalos?"

"The Omphalos connects to Mount Olympus."

"Mount Olympus the mountain, or Mount Olympus on Jupiter?" asked Jenn.

"Mount Olympus on Jupiter," said Zeus.

"The Omphalos has been around longer than the Olympians have lived on Jupiter. How can the portal lead to another planet if Mount Olympus was originally on an actual mountain on Earth?" Jenn asked.

"Because the portal follows the king of all gods. When Cronus set the curse on the Olympians, the portal redirected its path to Jupiter, because that's where my new home was located."

"Would we be able to come to Mount Olympus through the Omphalos?" asked Melanie.

"No," Zeus answered, his voice grave. "Because of the Olympians' eternal banishment from Earth, the entry from Mount Olympus to Earth and vice versa has been sealed. No one can exit and no one can enter, unless the curse is broken."

"Hypothetically speaking, however," said Colleen, "*if* the portal were still working, would we be able to go to Mount Olympus? Just to visit?"

Zeus paused. "That I do not know. A regular human would not be able to, for they could not breathe on Jupiter because of its atmosphere. However, you each possess a piece of the gods within you, which may make it a possibility to visit Mount Olympus."

"How do you break a curse?" asked Jenn.

"To break a curse, you must be at the site where the curse was created. The incantation must be reversed and both sides, the victim and their foe, must be present. However, if either the victims or foes are not present, there must be a piece of the participants at the site," said Zeus.

"And when is the end of a battle determined?"

"When one side surrenders, they are locked away, or in your case, something causes them to lose the battle. For instance, in your battle, the moment Pandora's box was opened, the Titans had been defeated, causing the end of the war."

"What about the Omphalos?"

"What about it?"

"I thought that the Omphalos was within Apollo's Temple, in the Oracle's chamber. However, we found it someplace else. I'm not even sure where we were," said Jenn.

"You were in Delphi and you were near Apollo's Temple, but much higher up on Mount Parnassus. The location of the Omphalos is misunderstood. You see, the ancient Greeks were led to believe that the center of the world was only at Apollo's Temple, where the priestess Pythia foretold her famous prophecies. However, the Omphalos is not one location, but rather two. The site that you found is where the prophetess Hiyatha, Pythia's sister, foretold her own prophecies. There she informed all deities and mythological beings of their fates and destinies. The two shrines were kept separate from one another, one being the center of the world of all humanity, and the other the center of the world of all mythical beings, and both being the Oracle of Delphi," said Zeus.

"There were two Oracles of Delphi?" asked Alice, astonished.

"Yes. Both the humans and shrines were sister oracles."

"If there were two oracles, does that mean that there could be another heir of the priestess? Hiyatha's heir?" asked Jenn.

"I am afraid not," said Zeus. "Hiyatha never mothered a child. She died before she bore one."

"How did she die?" asked Colleen.

"Cronus killed her. During the Titanomachy he came to Hiyatha, seeking the help of her visions. Hiyatha

386

told him of a foolproof plan that would defeat the
Olympians. However, Hiyatha had deceived Cronus,
telling him things he must do to overthrow the Olympians,
when in actuality she was plotting against him, working in
favor of the Olympians. Unfortunately, Cronus discovered
that the priestess had betrayed him. As a price for her lies,
he murdered her. Still thirsting for a victory, Cronus
sought Pythia's help, believing that the threat of losing her
life would influence the priestess to truthfully reveal how
the Titans could win the war. However, Pythia did the
same as her sister: she lied to Cronus, having him fulfill
tasks and strategies that harmed him instead of helped
him."

"Did he kill Pythia as well?" asked Melanie.

"He never got the chance. By the time Cronus
discovered that he had been defied a second time, he was
on his way to Tartarus."

"But why are there two Oracles of Delphi? Two
Omphalos shrines?" asked Jenn.

"There are two reasons. First, the Omphalos
shrines both cover something important. They both lie
over a portal. Their locations are placed specifically to
cover two particular gateways, one being the road to
Mount Olympus and the other to Elysium. Second, it is
best to keep mythological beings and humans apart from
one another. Although they live among each other
peacefully now, humans, who are blind and defenseless to
mythical beings, could get attacked. It would be
unfortunate for a mortal to die by a stray fireball."

"In other words, to get killed by Cronus," said Melanie.

"And the other Titans," said Zeus. "At the time that the shrines were built, mortals were in danger. The Titans did not care for human lives and killed freely."

"So why did the portals of Mount Olympus and Elysium have to be covered?" asked Izzy.

"To manage the beings who passed in and out of the sacred lands. Living mortals were not allowed to enter Elysium and passed souls were not allowed to re-enter Earth. There had to be some form of a barrier keeping people from passing through. However, gods and goddesses were not as limited. Most deities could pass to Mount Olympus and Elysium as they wished."

"Zeus, why didn't you use any of your lightning bolts during the Titanomachy?" asked Alice.

"Because I did not have the power to create lightning bolts at that time. My lightning bolts are a special privilege, they are granted only to the king of all gods. Until Cronus was defeated, I was not king. His surrender triggered my claim to the throne. Had Cronus defeated me, he would have gotten the bolts."

"Oh." Preoccupied with the conversation, Alice had forgotten she was still holding Pandora's box. She handed Rigon the sacred container, making sure its lid was shut. Rigon jumped up toward the sky and soared into the stratosphere. The group watched him until he disappeared.

"I guess we're done," said Scott.

"Any more questions?" asked Zeus.

"Just one," said Jenn.

"Go on."

"At both the Omphalos and the Parthenon, Crius destroyed parts of the shrines with his powers. Will the temples remain damaged?"

"Yes," said Zeus. "When a temple is ruined by a mythical being, the damage remains. However, if it is rebuilt or fixed by another mythical being, then of course it will remain mended. Any further questions?"

"That was it," Jenn answered.

"I must thank you all," said Zeus, "for without you, the universe may not have been saved. You are very strong humans, and I am honored to have had the chance to speak with you. Remember to use your powers wisely and to step into the world fighting for what is right. You cannot understand how grateful I am. If you ever need anything, please do return. Once an Olympian, always an Olympian, no matter human or god."

The wind swept up, blowing into the tree. Zeus' voice droned away as the hole closed. Soon, the wind became still and nothing moved. There were no sounds, no crashes, no yelling, no monsters, nothing but the quiet field of Greece.

"Music to my ears," said Izzy, cupping her hand to her ear.

"I agree," said Colleen.

"I guess we're done," said Jenn, staring blankly at the group.

"Back to the lab?" asked Scott, tugging at the Transporter's remote.

"Back to the lab," Jenn confirmed. She held up the control and directed it in the field. "After you."

The guardians began entering the portal.

"We're going on a date, we're going on a date!" Chandler sang, his arm around Melanie's shoulder.

"Did any of that faze you?" she asked, blown away. "You just helped lock away the Titans, saved my life, risked your own life, spoke to Zeus, learned you have powers, discovered mythology is anything *but* a myth and you're *singing* about a *date?*"

"Nope! 'Cause we're going on a date!" Chandler smiled.

Melanie rolled her eyes but couldn't help but laugh. Together, she and Chandler stepped into the portal.

As Izzy and Jayden were about to pass through, Izzy stopped and turned to Jenn. "By the way, I'm glad that we were searching for Pandora's box. It contained some pretty impressive hope!"

"I'm glad you approve," said Jenn.

Izzy grinned, squeezing Jayden's hand. They stepped into the Transporter with Jenn following behind.

CHAPTER TWENTY-THREE

Final Friday

Melanie, Alice, Jenn, Izzy and Colleen were at their dorm, diligently packing away their belongings for the summer. It was their final Friday on campus, and they were to be moved out by Monday. The girls were circled in the living room stuffing their suitcases.

Melanie approached the kitchen cupboard and pulled out an unopened box of Wheaties.

"Taking the Wheaties with you?" asked Izzy.

"Of course! They're vital," said Melanie, squeezing the box into her suitcase. "Without them, how else would I have aced my exams?"

"Aced your exams? You didn't even take them," said Colleen.

Melanie smirked. "*I* didn't, but someone who looked like me did."

"You cheated?"

"Ask Jenn."

Colleen glanced at Jenn. "Wait, what? You took her exam?"

"And Alice's and Izzy's too, along with their assignments," said Jenn.

"How come?"

"Since we were so busy with the Titans and everything, they missed out on the last week of class. Or three days rather, but those were three important days! I couldn't have let them take the exam and risk the chance of flunking. Passing the eleventh grade is a good reward for saving the universe."

"How come I wasn't in on this? You could have taken mine too!"

"You still went to class. You didn't need my help," said Jenn.

"And the teachers didn't notice that you were taking the test instead of them?" asked Colleen.

"Kira helped me out a little."

"I love her power." Melanie grinned, tucking her spikes delicately into their box.

Alice glanced at the running shoes. "Mel, why aren't you going to Nationals? Didn't your team leave?"

"Yeah they're long gone," said Melanie.

"Why didn't you go?"

"I stayed behind because I don't want to race. It wouldn't be fair if we won and I ran. I'm too fast. Plus, I wanted to watch Lewis graduate, and I owe Chandler a date."

"Lewis is a senior?" Izzy asked, taken aback.

"*Really?* For three years you didn't know what

392

class he was in?" Melanie retorted.

"I just assumed he was a junior. He's rooming with Chandler, who's a *junior*," Izzy defended.

Melanie and Izzy glared at one another for a moment, but then burst into laughter.

"Mel, did your team find a replacement?" asked Alice.

"Oh yeah, one of the freshmen, Dominique Dromeda. Kira and L.B. were cool with her, but Mika had to get used to the idea for a while. You know how she is," Melanie chuckled.

"Mel, Lewis is graduating, but it's not like you won't see him again. Going to Nationals could potentially be a once and a lifetime opportunity," said Jenn.

"I know, but it's also the last night I'll ever have Colleen as a roommate."

Izzy looked up, shocked. "Where's Colleen going?"

"She qualified for the senior year honors program, and all honors students live in Ithaca Hall," said Jenn.

"Why would you want to live in Ithaca Hall?" Izzy questioned. "They're famous for studying on Friday nights and going to bed at nine!"

"Relax, I'm not gonna live there. At least, not officially," said Colleen. "Technically I'll be a registered resident of Ithaca Hall, but I'll still live in the dorm with you guys."

"The administration isn't gonna let you do that," said Alice.

393

"They don't have to know I'm here," said Colleen. "I'd rather stick with my friends."

"I'm down with that," said Alice.

"Mel, I think you should have gone," said Jenn. "Colleen will be back, and I'm sure Lewis will be around."

"You just wanna go out with Chandler," said Izzy. "You like him!"

Melanie blushed. "Only as a friend. He saved my life, I think I owe him something."

"Keep telling yourself that," Izzy mumbled.

There was a knock at the door. Melanie dashed to the entrance and pulled it open. In front of her was Chandler, who was smiling radiantly. Immediately Melanie noticed his dressy ensemble. His bright orange hair was gelled upright, and he wore a crisp blue shirt with a black tie and khaki pants.

"These are for you," Chandler smiled, handing her a bouquet of pink and yellow flowers.

Melanie dug her nose into a golden rose.

"You're very sweet," she grinned.

Chandler's cheeks flashed crimson. "Should we get going? I was thinking Arcadia Café, if that's all right with you."

"Sure!"

Melanie set the flowers on the counter. She then left with Chandler, their arms intertwined.

"Don't stay out too late!" called Alice.

"Yup, she likes him," said Izzy.

From the hallway, a familiar face peered into the

room. Lewis stood in the entrance, looking quite satisfied.

"Looks sharp, doesn't he?" he asked.

"Chandler? Yeah. I've never seen him out of a t-shirt and jeans," said Colleen.

"It took a little work, but I got him fixed up pretty good," said Lewis.

"Lewis, where are you going to college next year?" asked Jenn.

"I'm not," he answered. "I'm taking an internship with the Delphi Symphony Orchestra. That's only for a year, though. I'll figure the college thing out after that."

"Where are you gonna live?" asked Alice.

"In my dorm with Chandler, of course!"

Colleen winked. "Great minds think alike."

"If you need any help sneaking in, just come see me," said Izzy.

"Will do."

There was another knock at the door. This time Alice went to the entrance. Surprisingly, she found Ryan Rivera standing with his hands tucked into his pockets.

"What are you doing here?" Alice asked.

"Can I speak with you for a moment?" he asked calmly.

"Sure."

She stepped into the hallway and closed the door. When Alice turned around, Ryan tried to give her something.

"These are yours."

Alice took the objects and looked them over. One was a plane ticket for Paris, France, and the other was a check written for thirty thousand dollars.

"What's this?!"

"It's the winnings from the cook-off. You earned them," said Ryan.

Alice gazed at the check, shaking her head.

"I can't accept these. You won, they're yours." She pushed back the ticket and the check.

"No, they're *yours*," Ryan persisted.

"I don't understand."

Ryan gazed into Alice's eyes, his face sullen.

"I...I didn't win fairly."

"What?" Alice questioned.

Ryan took a deep breath. "I cheated. I knew what the cook-off's category was before you did. You found out when we were both supposed to, but I knew a day in advance. The night before the competition, I ran into Molly Hibber. I had recognized her as Martha Weddingsworth's assistant from previous cook-offs, and I took advantage of her. I pretended that I was attracted to her and flirted my way into convincing her to tell me the category. When I found out it was Italian, I practiced creating the Italian Wedding Cake, the Leaning Tower of Pisa."

Alice was in shock. She had always believed that he had cheated, but had never been able to prove it. She had merely trusted her gut instinct. A rush of anger welled in her chest. Ryan had lied his way to win and no one knew but she and he.

"I can't take these," Alice refused, trying once again to hand him the ticket and check.

"Alice, please," Ryan begged. "I know this doesn't make it right, but it's the best I can do. You deserved to win. If I hadn't known the category, I never would have won. You're the better chef, you always have been. So please, take the money and the ticket. I told Martha everything, and she's expecting your call soon. She wants you to do the photo shoot for her magazine."

Alice's mind froze as she soaked in what Ryan had said. She knew that it had taken a lot of courage for him to admit what he had done, and going to the next level of telling Martha Weddingsworth was beyond her expectations. *All* of this was beyond her expectations. It felt uncanny.

"I still can't take this," she refused. "The winning prize was only twenty five grand, this is thirty."

"Honestly, I don't need it. My college tuition has been paid off since the moment my mother knew she was pregnant."

Alice shook her head. "Ryan, I-"

"Please. Just take it."

Alice pulled back her hand.

"The ticket is for July second. Leonardo Dumont wants to celebrate America's Independence Day...which is weird because he'll be in France, but whatever."

Ryan turned around, his eyes glum. He began walking down the hallway toward the staircase.

"Wait!" Alice called.

Ryan turned around.

"Why didn't you go with us when we went through the Transporter?"

"I felt too guilty to be around you. I had deceived you."

"But you saved my life," said Alice.

"I still felt guilty." Ryan motioned to turn around again.

"Ryan."

Ryan and Alice's eyes met.

"Thank you," said Alice. It was the only thing that she could muster to say. Her mind was spinning too fast for anything else.

Ryan cracked a smile. Smoothly, he began walking toward the staircase. Alice hung outside of her room until Ryan's footsteps disappeared. Mystified, she reentered her room.

"What'd Rivera want?" asked Izzy, disgusted.

"He gave me the winnings to the cook-off."

"What? Why?"

"He said that he cheated," said Alice.

"You were right?" asked Colleen, surprised.

"Yeah." Still in shock, Alice set the check and the ticket on the counter.

"Something's going on with that guy," said Jenn.

"Tell me about it," sighed Alice. She resumed her seat by her suitcase, attempting to pack. Her mind was preoccupied, focused on Ryan.

Izzy pulled out a scarlet cloth. It was the token that Lancelot had given her in Camelot.

"Jenn, you're keeping the Sword in the Stone in

the lab over the summer, right?" asked Izzy.

"Yes, alongside of the cane and the fishing pole."

"How come?"

"The knights know that we're going to return it eventually. So we don't have to give it back just yet. It's a nice temporary souvenir. Plus, it'll give us something to do next year, to go back to Camelot," said Jenn.

From the entrance another pair of visitors appeared over the threshold. Jayden and Scott stepped into the room, both looked excited.

"Hey guys!" greeted Lewis.

"Howdy, howdy!" said Scott.

"Hey!" said Jayden, approaching Izzy. "Do you like today's weather?"

"It's perfect!" Izzy exclaimed, glancing out of the window to see a bright, clear blue sky.

"I thought we were supposed to be experiencing severe climate changes, because of the earth's tipped axis. Isn't it supposed to be fall?" asked Colleen.

"Late summer," said Jayden. "I was feeling more of a sunny, mid eighties kind of day. But if you'd like, I can give you fall."

"That's okay, I'm good."

"So what brings you guys here?" asked Jenn.

"We were thinking about going to Arcadia Café to celebrate Lewis' graduation," said Scott.

"But graduation's tomorrow," said Lewis.

"Lew, Lew, Lew," said Jayden, his words smooth. "Why wait for tomorrow when you can celebrate tonight *and* tomorrow?"

"Chandler and Mel are there," said Izzy, winking at Jayden.

"Oh, payback time!" Jayden cheered.

"I'm game!" said Alice.

"Me too. It beats packing," said Colleen.

"Arcadia Café it is," said Lewis, heading for the hallway.

The rest of the group followed, with Izzy connected to Jayden's hip. As they approached the stairs, Jenn spoke.

"You know what the best thing is that we can celebrate?" she asked.

"The invention of chocolate?" asked Lewis.

"The discovery of Alaska?" asked Izzy.

"What? Well, no, even better..." Jenn paused. "Knowing that we're completely, one hundred percent Titan free!"

"You can say that again," said Izzy, holding Jayden closer.

Jayden glanced at Izzy and kissed her on the forehead.

"We're completely, one hundred percent Titan free," he repeated.

Jayden swept Izzy into his arms. Izzy delicately kissed him on the lips.

"You're my hero," she whispered.

Jayden grinned. "And you're mine."

The group exited the dorm. Comforted, they continued forward, ready to celebrate life in peace.

CHAPTER TWENTY-FOUR

Pluto's Fugitive

Out into the universe on the planet Pluto, the underworld's ferry escorted a passenger. The craft moved across the silent water and swiftly landed at the dock. Furious, the passenger exited. He rushed onto the frozen ground, his steps echoing in the dark.

Walking onto the stone platform, the fugitive found the portals; one to Elysium, the other a route to Mount Olympus. The portals were barricaded shut, keeping any passengers from coming in or going out. The fugitive attacked the golden entry, blasting a fireball at its shield. The power dissipated on contact, having no effect on the entry.

Distraught, the fugitive screamed. His yell was earsplitting, echoing through the underworld's tunnels. Hopeless, he fell to the ground, all the while howling in the dark. He gripped at the stone and clawed at the ground, digging into the floor. Nothing soothed his anger; nothing calmed his rage. Nothing relieved his fury and here he was, lost. Lost to his thoughts and his pity. Lost to his malevolence and frustration. Lost to his pain and his hope. Lost…but not dead. Lost…but not captive. Lost…all alone.

There is someone…there is something…, he thought.

Slowly, the fugitive pulled himself from the ground. He raised his hands into the air and shouted once more. The once defeated cries transformed into a victorious roar. The fugitive knew what he should do. Cronus knew the fight was not over.

APPENDIX OF GODS

TITANS

Atlas – God of strength. Upholds the planet Earth.

Coeus – God of intellect.

Crius – God of constellations. Has the ability to control stars.

Cronus – Leader of the Titans. Controls fire.

Hyperion – God of light.

Iapetus – God of mortality. Highly skilled with weaponry.

Mnemosyne – Goddess of memory.

Oceanus – God of water.

Phoebe – A goddess of the moon. Controls meteors.

Tethys – Oceanus' wife. Goddess of water.

Thea – Hyperion's wife. Goddess of light.

Uranus – Father of Cronus. Manipulates ice.

OLYMPIANS

Aphrodite – Goddess of love. Has the ability to fly and turn invisible.

Apollo – God of the sun, music and healing. Uses a bow and arrow.

Ares – God of war. Has super strength.

Artemis – Twin sister of Apollo. Also uses a bow and arrow.

Athena – Goddess of wisdom and war. Telekinetic.

Epimetheus* - God of afterthought.

Hades – God of the underworld. Produces a blue force field.

Hephaestus – God of fire. Creates weaponry for battle.

Hera – Zeus' wife, queen of the gods. Has the ability to transform into other living things.

Hermes – The messenger. Has super speed and assists souls to the underworld.

Hestia – Goddess of the hearth. Wields the power of electricity.

Poseidon – God of the seas. Carries a trident.

Prometheus* – God of forethought.

Zeus – King of the gods. Controls lightning, the wind and rain.

*Prometheus and Epimetheus are Titans who joined the Olympians in war.